COLD INSIDE

J.W. TAPPER

Also by J.W. Tapper

The Truth About Kate Hayes

Part One: Kissing The Scorpion

Part Two: Playing The Ace
Part Three: Painting The Dragon

Blood:Lust

Book One: Midnight Cocktail

Book Two: Cheating Sunrise

ISBN: 9781549918254

ACKNOWLEDGMENTS

Thanks to my test readers – Ben, Conny, Helen, and Paul – for invaluable assistance with this book.

CHAPTER 1

The lights in the *Golden Hart* all went out at the same time, quarter past ten, on the night of Friday the fifteenth of November, 1985. The jukebox died too, not with a slow fade but with a jarring halt that was as startling as a gunshot. The pub hadn't been quiet, never quiet on a Friday night, but for precisely three seconds after the lights went out the whole place was hushed, as if a lever had been thrown that killed every conversation, the same way something had killed all the lights and the jukebox.

Then a male voice swore in the dark, someone else thumb-flicked a Zippo, and the silent, hulking man who had been sitting alone at the table next to Dan and Rick stood up, let out a howl of despair, and locked his hands around Dan's throat. The hands were strong, calloused and hard, but in the initial moments before surprise and shock had turned to fear and panic, Dan felt the big hands trembling.

Dan grabbed the man's wrists, tried to shout to Rick but Rick had been knocked backwards when the big man had come at Dan, and he had gone down hard with his toppling chair. Dan couldn't tell what had happened after that. Too dark, even with the lighter flame circling like a dazed firefly no more than a couple of yards away from him.

"*It's a set,*" Dan heard the man say, or something that sounded like that. "*It's a set.*" The man's voice was breaking, an adult voice with the anguish of a crying child lost in a supermarket.

"Get off me," Dan tried to say, but his own voice had gone. The darkness was beginning to feel like a tunnel, freezing and inevitable, closing out the flickering light and the sounds around him. There was a dull, unnatural buzzing in his ears, an electric tingling in his fingers and his hair. He sucked in vain at the heavy, smoke-filled air, his stomach painfully dry-heaving with the effort, hands clenching uselessly, and through the numbing waves of panic he couldn't believe how quickly everything was ending.

And then the lights came back on.

The jukebox stuttered back to life, taking several seconds to get the record up to speed, a relentlessly repetitive bassline and harsh percussion behind overproduced operatic vocals. It sounded far louder to Dan than it had before. He didn't like the song, didn't want it to be the last one he ever heard.

Dan felt the hands go away from his throat, felt his legs buckle at the knees as he staggered forward, almost incapable of supporting his own weight. He exhaled hard, despite telling himself he should be breathing in, not out, stopped himself falling, and turned around to either punch the bastard's lights out, or…

"Easy," said the man who hadn't been there before. He said it as if he were calming a startled horse. He was holding the larger man's left arm tight to his side. Dan couldn't see the big guy's right arm, must have been twisted around behind him, between his own body and the newcomer's. The other man was smaller than the guy who had been choking Dan, smaller but he looked stronger, more capable. *Looks handy*, was what Dan thought.

The big guy's eyes were closed, not just closed but squeezed tight, his mouth working mechanically as if he were trying to blow out the flame of an inextinguishable candle. The man holding him was talking softly, constantly.

"Easy. I've got you. The lights are back on. You can open your eyes."

Dan could feel himself shouting at the man who was holding the big guy. Felt it, but couldn't hear it. His voice was gone, nothing but a painful, hoarse rasping that was more in his ears than his throat.

Rick was getting himself up off the floor, looking at Dan like he was trying to reconcile what he must have been hearing in the dark with what he was now seeing.

"Happened?" Rick said. "Danny?"

Dan only heard fragments of what his friend was saying. He was listening to the other two men, thinking he knew as little about what had just happened as Rick did.

"*It's a set.*"

But that wasn't what the big guy was saying. Dan couldn't work it out. The way the guy was saying it gave it a weight that those words simply didn't convey.

"No," said the man who was still holding the big guy's arms. "Not now. It's over now. Easy. I'll take you out of here. I'll take you home."

"You okay, mate?" Rick asked.

Dan nodded but he wasn't looking at Rick. There was something wrong with the big guy, the sort of thing that made you want to take a step or two back, to stay away from him. Even with the other man holding him, Dan felt that he was too close. He no longer wanted to retaliate. He just wanted to get a drink, to feel cold, straw-golden liquid easing the rasping pain in his throat, to sit quietly for a while. He really did not want any more confrontations.

"Yeah," he said, his first audible word since the lights

died, reaching out to his side, pressing his palm flat against Rick's chest. "Leave it."

Dan watched the big guy being led away towards the door. The other man was still holding his arm but Dan couldn't tell whether it was assistance or restraint. When the two men passed in front of the bar the smaller man leaned across, said no more than a handful of words to the barman, then the two men walked to the door and left. Dan closed his eyes, shook his head, and opened them again. He felt himself tuning back into complete consciousness, and he could just about remember what the big guy had looked like. But the other man's face was gone from his memory, as if he had no outstanding features at all.

"Dan?"

Rick sounded concerned, also sounded willing to wade in and do something valiant but regrettable, the way he sometimes did after a few pints.

Dan shook his head. "I'm okay." He knew his voice didn't sound okay. "I just want a beer."

"You sure? You just letting them walk out?"

"Just want a beer. I'll get this round in."

"Up to you, mate."

Dan took his time making his way to the bar. Moving slowly made it seem like his legs were less wobbly than they felt. He didn't need Rick to see that he was badly shaken up. He pulled his thin black wallet out of the back pocket of his jeans, looked at his hands, the joints and knuckles and nails, and he thought about flesh and bones, and mortality.

The barman was wiping something off the hammered copper surface of the bar with a plain navy flannel. He didn't look like he was pondering his mortality, but then he hadn't been having the life strangled out of him a few minutes earlier.

He nodded at Dan. "What can I get you?"

"Two pints of *Boddies*."

The barman held a fresh, straight-sided pint glass under

the Boddingtons tap and eased the bright yellow handle forward.

"What happened to the power?" Dan asked.

"Trip went."

"Why?"

The barman shrugged his shoulders as he watched the liquid filling the glass.

"Those two guys," Dan said.

The barman pulled the handle again, slowly, finishing off the pint, giving it a decent half-inch head of cream-coloured froth. "What about them?"

"The big one, the bigger one, what's wrong with him?"

"Wrong?"

"When the lights went out, he grabbed me around the neck."

The barman nodded as he filled the second pint glass. "You enquiring in an official capacity?"

"Official? No, just wondering why someone might react like that when the lights went out."

"Nothing wrong with him," the barman said. He placed the second full pint glass on the bar next to the first one. The depth of the froth on top of both beers was identical, impossible to say which one had the better head on it.

"Well, I think the bruises on my throat are going to disagree with you in the morning."

"Nothing wrong with him, but something did happen to him."

"What do you mean?"

"What do you think his friend told me, just before they left?"

"I have no idea."

"He said, 'If he asks, tell him.'"

"Tell me what?"

"You heard what he was saying, didn't you?"

"Who?"

"The big lad, the one who grabbed you, the one who

wouldn't open his eyes even when the lights were back on."

"He was saying the same thing, over and over. Sounded like *it's a set.*"

"No, that's not what it was."

"What then? I'm asking, so do what his friend said. Tell me."

"He was on the Sheffield. When the Argies blew it up."

"Shit." Dan reached up and touched his throat.

"Twenty dead," said the barman, wiping at something on the bar. "More than another twenty injured."

"I'm sorry," Dan said, but he wasn't talking to the barman.

"Not your fault, was it?"

Dan shook his head. "I know what he was saying."

"Aye, I reckon you do. That'll be one fifty-four for the beers."

Dan picked the glasses up, one in each hand. He carried them back to where Rick was waiting, the two straw-golden pints with their indistinguishably perfect heads of creamy froth.

It's a set.

But when you knew where the guy had been, when you remembered what had happened, the syllables came together differently and you could never hear them any other way.

He was on the Sheffield. When the Argies blew it up.

Exocet.

CHAPTER 2

Tom had always called the place Gaspari's, and he doubted anyone else called it anything different, but the name on the sign above the entrance said *Caffe Bar Gaspari.* Italian, of course, so *Caffe* meant coffee, *Bar* meant café, but who really cared anyway, because you couldn't get a coffee anywhere else in the whole damn city that tasted half as good as the stuff they served at Gaspari's.

He was sitting in his corner, slouched sideways against the wall, lank black hair hanging over his left eye like a careless paint lick, half watching the attract mode on the battered *Galaga* table-top while he waited for the slim blonde waitress to come over.

She was clearing a table on the other side of the café, stacking the plates first, then balancing the mugs on top before scooping the whole lot up and whisking it all away through the wooden saloon doors to the kitchen.

Half eleven Saturday morning, cold drizzle misting the café windows. Nothing on top of the *Galaga* machine apart from a few scratches, some ciggy burns and a fresh pressed-foil ashtray next to his long-cold, empty coffee mug.

Tom took out a 10p coin and fed it into the *Galaga*

machine. He whistled along with the intro tune for a few seconds, watching the kitchen doors until the first wave of enemies began to fly onto the screen.

She came out of the kitchen exactly three minutes later. Three minutes in his head, based on how many screens of alien space bugs he had cleared, and three minutes according to the LCD watch on his left wrist. Black leather strap, deliberately two holes too loose because that's how he liked to wear it. Made him feel relaxed.

"Taking my lunch early," she said.

"That chair's free."

Sharon hooked the chair out from the opposite side of the *Galaga* machine with her foot, size four in scuffed, black, flat-soled waitress shoes. She sat down, crossed her legs and opened her pink handbag.

"You going to want another coffee before I go out?"

"Yeah."

Sharon reached into her bag, took out the roller, papers, and the old *Sucrets* throat lozenge tin where she kept her tobacco. She rolled two identical cigarettes quicker than Tom could clear the seventh screen of aliens. She held the first one lightly against her lips, inhaling almost imperceptibly as she lit it with a disposable purple plastic lighter. She balanced the lit cigarette on the side of the pressed-foil ashtray and then she lit the second one, drawing harder on that one than the first before tipping her head back to blow a thin stream of smoke up towards the ceiling.

Without looking away from the screen, Tom said, "Thanks." Sharon's brand was Old Holborn. He couldn't taste or smell it without immediately thinking of her.

"Doing much later?" she asked.

"No."

Sharon looked down at the game screen. When she blew the second stream of smoke out, it sounded like a sigh.

"Rob's taking me to see *Prizzi's Honour* tonight."

Tom tapped the fire button a little harder, twice.

"Jealous?" Sharon asked.

"Of course." Another jab at the button, but with less venom. Easier to be flip anyway, to mock himself. "You know how much I cried when he chose you over me."

Sharon ignored it, had heard it all before. "You could come with us."

Tom picked up the lit cigarette, took a quick draw on it and put it back on the ashtray before the next wave of aliens appeared.

"No, I can't."

"Why not? Rob won't mind."

"It's a comedy."

"You don't like comedies?"

"They're never funny."

"Not if you watch them with that attitude."

Tom took his hands off the game controls, looked away from the screen at Sharon. He picked up the cigarette but didn't take another pull on it, just held it down low so the smoke drifted up past his face.

Sharon had her hair tied up in a tight bunch. Tom knew she only ever wore it that way when she was waitressing. Catering hygiene rules or something. It was so much better when it was loose and straight, or in a ponytail halfway down her back, or the way it looked when she wore a beret, with the fringe curved over her eyebrows. Blonde hair. Not a big, fake perm like in *Dynasty*, but naturally full and lustrous. She made the waitress outfit look special, despite it being two shades of beige stained with random milk and coffee splatters. Right then, she wasn't saying anything, wasn't doing much at all apart from smoking and just being there. It was more than enough, as always.

"Ever wonder why I never asked you out?" he said.

"Of course. All the time. I hardly think of anything else." She was smiling at him while she spoke, shaking her head, the smile one of weary sympathy.

The *Galaga* machine gave an agitated bleep as his first ship was destroyed. He didn't look at the screen.

"Did you see *Fix It* last Saturday?"

"No." She shuddered, wrinkled her nose. "I think he's a bit creepy."

"There was a kid on there from our old school."

"From John Blair?"

"Yeah."

"What was he on there for?"

"Wanted to take a penalty against Tony Norman at Boothferry Park."

"I suppose they jumped at it now they're in the second division."

Tom tapped ash into the tray. "You suddenly a Tigers fan?"

"Rob is."

Tom nodded. *Of course.*

"School," he said. "Seems ages since we left, doesn't it?"

"Eight years ago for me."

"Yeah. Seventy-seven."

"But not for the brainy kids who stayed on. Like you."

"What else was I going to do?"

Sharon blew smoke towards the window. "Get a job?"

"I've got one. Well, I will have one eventually."

"It'll be more inheriting the company than working for it, though."

"As soon as I've inherited it, I'll give you a job."

Sharon laughed, gave him a deadpan wink. "Sure, as your secretary, so you can sit behind your big desk and stare at my tits all day."

Tom glanced at the taut front of her stained beige waitress blouse and quickly looked away.

"Whatever job you want."

"Maybe I'll drive one of your HGVs. I think I'd have to, wouldn't I? Biggest haulage company in the North, isn't it?"

"Second. In the North East." He could hear it in his

own voice. The reluctance to talk about his father's firm, his own silver spoon, meal-ticket, handout, and whatever else everyone probably called it behind his back.

Sharon raised her cigarette and held it a couple of inches from her lips. "You never talk about it. Your big inheritance."

"Not much to say."

Sharon mimicked his attempt to feign indifference. "Not much to say." She was taking the piss, obviously, but he didn't mind; she could stub her cigarette out in his eye and he wouldn't mind. Her legs alone were enough to give her a free pass for everything from piss-taking to actual bodily harm.

When she had her roll-up down to an inch she stubbed it out in the ashtray. Three presses and a twist, always with her left hand, same every time. He liked watching her do that, had even memorised her stubbing-out technique.

She fetched him a coffee before she left on her lunch break, put it down on a fresh Gaspari's place-mat on one side of the *Galaga* table-top.

"Cold out there," Tom said. He watched as she pulled the belt of her fake suede coat tight around her slim waist.

"See you later, Tom."

"I'll probably be gone by the time you get back."

"Next Saturday, then."

"Yeah. You can tell me all about *Prizzi's Honour.*"

"You don't like comedies."

She said it without smiling. And then she was out of the door and gone, into the cold.

CHAPTER 3

The irony of driving home from the price-conscious *Presto* supermarket in Bill's Jag was not lost on Deb Mason. She was using the Jaguar that Saturday because Bill had taken her Fiesta runabout to get the timing checked, or the cam belt, or something else mechanically arcane. They hadn't had a conversation about why he should be the one to take her car to the garage, and they never would. Just one of those things. And, all told, she kind of liked driving the Jag despite the impractical size and the incongruity of taking it to do the supermarket shopping.

She took far more care when she turned off the road onto their gated driveway than she would have done in her own car. One of the reasons she loved her Fiesta, it was small and easy to park, or to manoeuvre between a pair of large red-brick gateposts. Gateposts that seemed even closer together when you were driving your husband's racing green Jaguar, less than six months old with not a single scratch anywhere on its pristine bodywork.

Just before five p.m., and it had already been dark enough for her to have had the Jag's headlights on all the way back from *Presto*. It had taken her a minute of anxious button pressing and lever flicking in the supermarket car park before she figured out how to get the lights on, dipped and not full-beam. She had been truly relieved when the drizzle had stopped an hour before she had left the house and she hadn't been obliged to waste even more time working out how to turn on the wipers.

Deb braked to a halt, several safe yards from the closed doors of the double garage. She turned off the engine and took out the key. It was the spare, which normally hung from its own hook on the hallway wall beneath the framed Dali print, the one with the melting clocks. Deb hadn't even bothered trying to clip the Jag's spare key onto her own key ring. It seemed a waste of time and effort, because she was unlikely to be driving Bill's car alone again for a long time, if ever.

She got out of the Jag, slid her handbag strap over her shoulder and nudged the driver's side door with her hip. She smiled at the solid, reassuringly expensive sound as the door closed. Deb unlocked the boot and eased it all the way open. There were three full shopping bags inside. She took the first one out, walked along the gravel path around the house to the front door and rummaged in her handbag for her own key ring. She opened the door and put the shopping and her handbag down on the polished hardwood floor inside.

On her way to fetch the other carrier bags from the boot, Deb heard the phone start ringing in the house. She rushed to the boot, grabbed the bags and turned back towards the house. The boot was still open.

"I'll be just one minute," Deb said, looking from her two full hands to the wide open boot of the Jag.

She hurried along the path, dumped the shopping on the hallway floor, pushed the front door closed behind her, kicked off her shoes and ran into the lounge to answer the phone.

***

"You go, love. I'll finish up here."

"Thanks, Angie," Sharon said.

The older woman smiled at her. "You have a great evening. I'll see you on Monday."

"I will. You too."

Sharon went into the customer toilet and stood in front of the mirror. There were no customers in Gaspari's at ten past five, nothing left to do but tidy up and clean everything that could be cleaned. Lucky if you got home before half six. Angie was pretty much a life-saver. It meant Sharon would owe her the same favour, probably in the very near future, but Sharon didn't mind. You helped each other out, that's what you did. Part of the waitress code.

She took clean clothes out of a large carrier bag and arranged them on the wide shelf next to the sink before slipping out of her waitress uniform. She folded the beige blouse and skirt into a neat parcel that would fit in the empty carrier bag, then looked at her reflection in the mirror, huffing out a resigned sigh as she unclipped her hair and teased it loose. After a whole day fetching and carrying in Gaspari's, how was her hair not going to look a total disaster?

She swapped the underwear she had been in all day for a fresh black bra and matching thong. No precise plans exactly, but it was always best to wear the decent stuff on a cinema date, just in case you happened to end up parked somewhere nice and quiet and neither of you could wait until you got back to Rob's flat. Before she did anything else, Sharon gave herself a liberal all-over spray with deodorant. A shower would have been nicer, but Gaspari's customer toilets didn't quite stretch to that level of opulence.

She took off her flat-soled waitress shoes and put them in the bag, followed by her balled-up underwear and the folded waitress uniform. She had a pair of black ankle boots to change into, decent ones from *Peter Lord*, but they were going to have to wait until she had her jeans on. The tiled toilet floor was cold under her feet. From the small pile of fresh clothes, she picked up a pair of faded Wranglers. Very faded, very tight. She pulled them on, whistling while she did the funky side-to-side shuffle dance to get them up over her bum. The knees were so faded they were almost white. Sharon breathed in, fastened the stud and drew the zip all the way up. Hard work but worth it. They felt great and she knew just how great they looked. Rob loved them. He certainly loved trying to get her out of them.

At last she was able to put on her ankle socks and boots, and get her bare feet off the cold tiles. She pulled a vest top on over her bra, followed by a tight pink jumper over the vest. She spent several minutes brushing her hair until it was as straight as she could get it, before using a stretchy black band to tie it back in a loose ponytail. The brush went back in her handbag, and the handbag sat on top of everything in the carrier bag. Much easier to carry one bag than two. Finally she put on her fake suede coat and pulled the belt tight.

"That'll do," Sharon said, wrinkling her nose at her reflection.

She hoisted the full carrier bag and headed for the front door of the café.

"Bye, Angie," she called as she passed the kitchen. "Thanks again."

Sharon opened the café door and stepped out into the cold. Ten minutes to walk to the Wimpy in King Edward Street if she took a couple of shortcuts. Rob had said to meet there between half five and six, get something to eat before heading to the ABC to watch *Prizzi's* at seven.

A hundred yards from Gaspari's she turned right and headed down a single-lane, one-way backstreet. The narrow pavement was wet and there was mist hanging in the air, dimming the glow from the unevenly spaced streetlights. The street was one of the oldest in the city, and Sharon thought the lights must be equally ancient. They were shorter than the ones on the busier streets, topped with quaint, feeble lanterns.

The rhythmic click-clacking of her boot heels was loud and percussive in the empty street. She heard a car approaching slowly from behind her, saw her shadow appear ahead of her on the pavement, long and thin and inhuman, pivoting gradually anticlockwise as the car drew closer. She watched her shadow grow vertical against the dark windows of a butcher shop on her left. Then the car was past her, its rear lights haloes of red that briefly turned the wet pavement ahead of her to shining, bloody slabs.

***

"I've got to go, I really have to."

Deb cradled the phone against her ear, stealing a guilty glance at her wristwatch. It hadn't been just one minute. It hadn't even been just ten. But it had been over a week since she had spoken to Jan and they had a lot of catching up to do.

"I know," she said. "I'll find out what we're doing next weekend and give you a call so we can meet up. Yes, I promise. I know, but I really have to go."

Five minutes later she finally got Jan to say goodbye and she put the phone down, sighing heavily.

"At least it isn't raining," Deb said, pulling her shoes on, closing her eyes as she thought of Bill's Jag, out there on the drive with the boot wide open.

Wide open, with the key still in the lock.

Deb strode quickly along the gravel path, atoning for the quarter of an hour she had spent on the phone by scowling at herself as she hurried around the side of the house towards the drive.

The inside of the Jag's boot wasn't going to be wet, was it? There was a light mist in the air but didn't the boot have to be warm for condensation to form, or was that only if there were closed windows? It would be fine anyway, because she could wipe down the bare metal if it was damp. It wasn't as if Bill was going to come home and examine the boot for moisture.

She would check the boot quickly, close it, lock the car, go straight back in the house and put the kettle on.

Have a nice cup of tea.

Deb turned the corner and stopped.

With no cars parked on it, the drive looked much longer and wider than usual.

***

Sharon had looked back once.

Two more cars had driven past her since the first one, both travelling slowly in the thickening mist. Mist that was starting to feel more like a proper fog, turning the air damp and the world darker.

The most recent car to drive down the street had been behind her for more than half a minute, maybe a little over fifty feet back, but there had been plenty of time for it to reach her and drive past. Hard to tell exactly how far away it was in the mist, and she didn't want to keep looking back because it had been there for too long now. It was probably someone who wasn't familiar with the street and didn't want to clip the kerb or hit a pothole in the dark. No need to antagonise the driver by looking back again, passing judgement on his driving skills. The one time that she had looked back, she had only seen dipped headlights and the low, looming silhouette of a car that seemed glossy black in the narrow, dimly lit street, but could have been any dark colour at all.

She approached the diffused glow of another streetlamp

and walked through it, glancing at her faint reflection in the window of a closed shop. Ten paces further on, maybe five paces from the next streetlamp, Sharon's shadow lengthened in front of her as the car behind her finally picked up a bit of speed and drew closer.

Four paces to the next streetlamp. She was looking forward to seeing Rob at Wimpy but she was more eager to eat something, hadn't had anything since her early lunch break almost six hours ago. Silly, really, to let yourself go hungry when you worked in a café.

Two paces away. She stepped into the hazy corona a yard and a half out from the metal base of the streetlamp. She heard the sound of the car's engine rise as the driver accelerated.

Less than a single stride from the streetlamp, Sharon heard the sharp squeal of rubber as the car's front tyre hit the kerb right behind her. Her head turned automatically towards the sound, just in time to see the headlights jerk upwards as the car lurched onto the pavement, but not in time to be able to hurl herself out of its path.

The car's front bumper hit both of her legs a couple of inches below her knees. She would have been thrown up and backwards, right over the bonnet of the car, but she had been too close to the base of the streetlamp and her left thigh was rammed into it, crushed between it and the sharp leading edge of the bonnet above the narrow radiator grille. At the same time her right ankle twisted and broke as it snagged against part of the car low down, the sound of snapping bones drowned out by the explosive noise of the impact.

Sharon folded hard at the waist, her instinctive scream of shock cut off as her face slammed down onto the top of the car's bonnet. Her front teeth punctured her lip, two of them breaking against the unforgiving metal surface. The car's four-inch chrome bonnet mascot tore through her coat and gouged the side of her hip, and her left arm was flung around across her body with enough force that her shoulder dislocated. The bag that she had been carrying was torn from her hand and thrown into the air, landing more than ten feet away, upside down in the middle of the pavement.

She was still conscious when the car reversed off the pavement back onto the road. Conscious as she slid backwards off the bonnet, her upper body mostly on the pavement and her twisted, broken legs hanging over the edge of the kerb into the road. Still conscious when the car drove slowly forward, left front tyre screeching and grinding against the kerb, headlights jerking up again, but not quite as far as they had when the car had driven onto the pavement.

The car reversed again, backed up and stopped in the darker area between two streetlamps. The door opened and the driver got out. He was dressed entirely in black. Coat, trousers, boots, gloves. Balaclava. Nothing glossy or reflective. The boots had been scuffed all over to remove any trace of a shine.

Sharon was shivering, lost in shock, watching the driver of the car as he walked towards her, but not thinking about him. Not even thinking about the awful pain. All she knew was the overwhelming terror that she would never see Rob again, never be able to tell him that she wanted more than anything to see him one last time.

The driver crouched down next to Sharon. He lifted her limp left hand and held the tip of her index finger in the blood that was leaking from her mouth and pooling on the pavement. He looked back at the front of the car, then he pressed Sharon's finger against the top of the kerbstone and drew a short diagonal line down, then up, then down, then up again. He dipped her finger back in the blood, left a space after the first letter he had written and wrote a second letter next to it. More diagonal lines. Up, down, up, down. He dipped the finger in the blood one more time, drew something else next to the second letter. Two circles, joined, one above the other.

Sharon's head moved when the driver dropped her arm. She looked up at the blank black mask of the balaclava, into a pair of dark, disinterested eyes. The last thought she had, as the black gloves moved to her throat, was that she would never know why.

CHAPTER 4

Deb looked at the empty drive, the space in front of the double garage, the open gates and the dark road beyond.

She shook her head, and for the briefest moment she wondered whether she had forgotten parking the Jag in the garage. She almost went to the garage to check, but stopped herself before taking the first step in that direction.

"Don't be stupid."

She winced at how loud her voice had sounded. Out there in the dark, alone.

Deb ran back to the front door, slamming it behind her as she hurried to the lounge. She thought she could hear the phone ringing again but it was just the memory of Jan's call, haunting her with guilt. She knew she had to pick the phone up, make the call that would save Bill's car.

She dialled the number, jabbing her finger three times against the button with the nine on it, already speaking before the operator had picked up.

"The car's been stolen. It's gone. It was on the drive."

"This is the emergency service. Do you require fire, police or ambulance?"

"Police, police of course. Our car—"

"Madam, this is the emergency service. Is the theft of

the vehicle currently in progress?"

"It's been stolen. It's gone. Five minutes ago. My husband's Jaguar."

"Is there an emergency there? Do you need to take someone to hospital urgently?"

"Hospital? I don't… It's his car, it's been stolen."

"Madam, I'm sorry, but I'm going to have to ask that you contact your local police station to report a stolen vehicle."

"What? But the car has been stolen within the last ten minutes, from our drive right outside the house."

"Can you give me the first line of your address and your post code, please. I will give you the number of your nearest police station."

Deb exhaled heavily. The phone handset was shaking against her ear and her vision was blurring with tears.

"I haven't got a pen. Let me get a pen."

"Try to stay calm. If you could tell me your address…"

"Twelve Ash Crescent, Kingston upon Hull."

"Ash? Alpha, Sierra, Hotel?"

"Yes. Ash Crescent."

"Number twelve. Do you know the post code."

Deb said she did, and she told the operator what it was.

"Thank you, Madam. Your nearest station is located on Marlborough Road. Do you have a pen and paper?"

"Yes."

The operator gave Deb the phone number of the police station.

"How soon will they be able to do something?"

"As soon as you call them and give them all the details that they need."

"I'll call them now."

"Thank you, Madam. Try to remain calm."

Deb pressed the handset against the cradle, ending the call. She picked it straight back up again and dialled the number she had written down. While she waited for the call to be answered she took a deep breath and tried to think of all the things that she would be asked.

"Humberside police," said a female voice. "Which department or extension do you require."

"My husband's car has been stolen."

"Is the theft in progress?"

"No, the car has gone. Ten, fifteen minutes ago. It was taken from our drive outside the house."

"One moment, please. I'm going to transfer you to the incident desk."

Deb listened to infuriatingly pleasant hold music for almost a minute before someone else spoke to her.

"Incident desk, Sergeant Harper speaking. May I please have your full name, address and the number you're calling from."

Deb sighed with relief. She gave the details as clearly and as patiently as she could.

"How can I help you, Mrs Mason?" Sergeant Harper asked.

"My husband's car has been stolen off our drive. I was in the house for about ten minutes and when I went back out, it was gone."

"When did this happen?"

Deb shrugged. She felt as though she had been on the phone for hours. "Fifteen, twenty minutes ago."

"Did you witness the theft?"

"No, I was in the house."

"Is it possible that your husband took the car?"

"No, he's not here. He took my car to the garage." She gasped, turning her wrist to look at her watch. "He should be back any minute."

"Does anyone else live at that address?"

"Only my son, but he has been out all day. I don't know when he will be home."

"Okay, Mrs Mason, I'll need to take down some details about the vehicle. Do you know the make, model and registration?"

"Yes, yes I do. It's a Jaguar XJS. The registration is WM triple eight."

"Whisky Mike, eight, eight, eight. Is that correct?"

"Yes."

"And the model is XJS. X-ray, Juliet, Sierra?"

"Yes, yes it is." Deb nodded, willing the policeman to hurry up, to send out an all-points bulletin or whatever they did to actually get things moving.

"Do you have the vehicle identification number?"

"What is that?"

"It will be on the vehicle's registration document."

"I don't know where that is. My husband would know, but he isn't here. I already told you that."

"What colour is the vehicle?"

"Green. I think it's called racing green."

There was a brief pause. Deb assumed the sergeant was writing it all down or possibly typing, although she couldn't hear the sound of a keyboard or typewriter.

"Do you have a pen and paper? I'm going to give you the crime reference number which you will need if you make an insurance claim. You can also use it to claim a vehicle tax refund if the vehicle is written off or not recovered."

"What?" Deb shook her head. "But the car was just taken. It can't be that far away. Can't you start trying to find it?"

"The registration and description will be added to our register of stolen vehicles. The DVLC will be notified if the vehicle is found. Your insurance company will be able to assist you if you proceed with a claim."

"Are you going to send someone here to investigate? The car isn't even six months old."

"I'm sorry, Mrs Mason. Nationally, there are approximately a quarter of a million reported vehicle thefts every year, with almost as many reports of unsuccessful thefts. Unless the theft of a vehicle is linked to a serious crime, the theft is not investigated."

"That's ridiculous." Deb shook her head. The Jag couldn't just be gone, like that, with nobody willing to try to find it.

"As I said, the vehicle details have been added to the register. You will be contacted if the vehicle is found."

Deb was still shaking her head.

Behind her, the lounge window briefly flared as it was lit up by the headlights of a car pulling onto the drive.

Deb spun around, crying out with relief as the brightly lit window went dark once again.

"Bill's back," she said into the phone. "My husband is home."

"That's good news, Mrs Mason. If there isn't anything else…"

"I have to go. Thank you. Goodbye."

Deb dropped the handset into the cradle, realising for the first time since she had come back into the house that she hadn't taken her shoes off. The surge of relief that she felt, knowing that Bill was home, and that he would take charge and deal with this utter nightmare, was too much to cope with. She rushed to the door, wiping her eyes with her coat sleeve, desperately needing to see him, to feel his arms around her. She knew he would be cross, knew that she had let him down, but she didn't care. She just wanted to close her eyes and crush herself against him.

Deb pulled open the front door and stepped out. Into the cold.

The gravel crunched under her feet as she approached the corner of the house. She had a strange thought, a brief moment of confusion as she wondered how much it had cost to have her car repaired. And then she thought of Bill's big expensive Jaguar, taken away from her by some stranger, to somewhere she might never know.

She turned the corner, but stopped before she set foot

on the drive.

No Bill. No repaired Fiesta.

The car on the drive was big and dark and she could hear the reassuringly expensive ticking of the engine as it cooled. The driver's side door was wide open, the empty interior lit by the courtesy light. The key was still in the ignition, the fob swinging gently back and forth like a tiny pendulum beneath it.

Deb Mason didn't say a word, didn't make a sound until she realised that the wet, smudged hand prints that she could see on the side of the driver's beige leather seat were fresh bloodstains.

And then she screamed.

CHAPTER 5

Dan pulled up close to the kerb and wound the window down. There was a jam-sandwich Ford Granada parked across the junction to the narrow one-way street on the right, effectively blocking it. The two uniforms from the patrol car were standing in front of it, redirecting any traffic and waiting for CID to arrive. The uniform on the left raised his hand when Dan showed them his warrant card through the open window.

"DS Blacksmith," Dan said. His voice sounded normal. He caught himself listening to how it sounded and his left hand moved to his throat. There had been no bruising, no lasting damage.

"Two seconds, Sarge," said one of the uniforms. He climbed into the patrol car and backed it up far enough to give Dan room to drive his unmarked BMW onto the side street.

Rick stretched his legs into the passenger footwell and shook his head. "Don't need this at half six on a Saturday night."

Dan didn't reply. He could already see the ambulance and the glare of the portable crime scene lamps reflecting off the wet ground and the windows of nearby shops. He parked the BMW fifty feet behind the ambulance. There were two paramedics and a uniform standing in the road next to a lumpy black plastic sheet that was half on the road and half on the pavement. One of the paramedics was a woman, the other para and the uniform were male.

Dan and Rick got out of the car and walked towards the illuminated crime scene.

The uniform was a sergeant. He nodded as Dan and Rick approached. "Sergeant Ramsey."

"DS Blacksmith and DC Price," Dan said.

Ramsey said, "We've got a young woman, dead at the scene. Looks like a hit-and-run. It was called in anonymously from a public telephone at about twenty to six. The paramedics confirmed that the victim had been dead for some time. No attempt was made to resuscitate. I put a call through to CID because I didn't think it looked as straightforward as a simple hit-and-run."

"Thank you, sergeant," Dan said. "Let's get this sheet off her, Rick."

Dan and Rick took a corner each and folded the plastic sheet all the way back. Neither of them touched the body.

"Hit-and-run?" Rick said, shaking his head. "How many times?"

"Okay," Dan said. "Nobody touched anything apart from to confirm she was dead, right?"

"That's right," said Ramsey. "There's a carrier bag over there that we assume is hers but we haven't touched it."

Dan looked in the direction Ramsey was pointing. He saw the bag on the pavement but he didn't immediately go over to it. He crouched and looked closely at the ruined face of the dead woman, her broken legs, her bloody left hand, and the awkward way her left arm was twisted across her body, then he looked at the two letters and the number that had been written in blood on the edge of the kerb.

"First impressions, Rick?"

"Car hit her, ran her over. Driver backed up because he was jammed against the streetlamp, which is probably why she has multiple injuries. She managed to write whatever that is using her own blood before she died. WM and either an eight or a B. What is that, someone's initials?"

Dan walked over to the carrier bag. He righted it and looked inside before taking out two items of beige clothing and a pink handbag. He opened the handbag and rummaged through the contents. Old receipts, all the makings for a whole lot of roll-ups, a hairbrush, and a black purse. Inside the purse, Dan found a driving licence.

"Sharon Hall," he said. "Twenty-four. Local girl according to the address on the driving licence." He picked up one of the pieces of beige clothing and read the words that were embroidered across the breast pocket. The blouse was stained in several places with what appeared to be coffee. "Looks like she was walking home from work, or at least walking somewhere from work, assuming these are her clothes."

"Where did she work?" Rick asked.

"A place called *Caffe Bar Gaspari*. Do you know where that is? I'm guessing it isn't far away."

"It's not. We drove past the street it's on just before we turned into this one."

Dan walked back to where Sergeant Ramsey was standing. "Sergeant, I need you to keep everything here exactly as it is until the pathologist and forensics have been all over it. I want absolute confirmation of cause of death."

"What's up?" Rick asked. "It's a hit-and-run, right? A messy one, but still…"

"Two things," Dan said. "Nobody writes that well when they are in shock, or they've got a dislocated shoulder. And nobody writes anything at all after they're dead."

Rick shook his head. "I didn't spot the shoulder."

"I know."

"Maybe she wrote it with her right hand."

"No blood on the right hand."

"Why do you think she was dead before she had a chance to write it?"

"Because the broken legs, broken teeth and the dislocation wouldn't have killed her. So something else did."

"Maybe she had heart failure."

"Maybe. Let's go see if there's anyone working late at Gaspari's."

Dan reversed the BMW all the way back along the one-way street, which was safe to do because the roadblock at the junction was preventing any oncoming traffic. He followed Rick's directions and parked outside Gaspari's. The door was locked but there was light coming from the back of the café, probably from the kitchen.

Dan rapped on the glass of the door with his knuckles. He had to repeat it a couple of times before he saw someone moving towards the door. It was a woman who looked to be in her mid thirties. She pointed at the sign that was hanging on the door and mouthed the word CLOSED at Dan and Rick.

Dan took out his warrant card, held it against the glass above the CLOSED sign and mouthed the word POLICE at the woman.

She came up to the door, unlocked it and opened it.

"Whatever happened, I didn't do it," she said. She was smiling as she spoke, the mischievous grin of one who has had a long day at work, soon to be over, and is absolutely confident that she has nothing at all to be worried about where police matters are concerned.

"I'm Detective Sergeant Dan Blacksmith. This is DC Rick Price. I'm sorry, but you might want to hear what I have to tell you before you say anything else. Can we come in, please, Miss…?"

"Bowes. Angie Bowes. It's Mrs, not Miss, but that doesn't matter."

"You might want to sit down, Mrs Bowes."

"Why? I don't understand. What's happened?"

"Can you confirm that a woman called Sharon Hall works here?"

"Sharon? Yes, of course, but—" Angie's eyes went wide. "Has something happened to her?"

"Are you related to Sharon Hall, or did you just work with her?"

"Related? No." Angie took a step backwards and sat heavily onto one of the wooden café chairs. "What has happened? Is she okay?"

Dan sat on the chair opposite Angie. Rick waited near the café door.

"There was an accident earlier, a hit-and-run involving Sharon. She was seriously injured and died at the scene."

Angie pressed both her hands over her mouth, shaking her head, her eyes filling with tears.

"I'm very sorry," Dan said.

"No," Angie said. "I was only talking to her two hours ago, not even two hours."

"Rick, go in the kitchen and make Mrs Bowes a cup of tea."

"Sharon," Angie said. "That poor girl."

Dan took out a notepad and a biro. "I'd like to ask you a few questions, Angie. You don't have to answer them now, but it might help us if you could."

"I can't believe it. She was so happy, so full of life."

"Do you remember what time she left here today?"

"Today? Five. No, a little later because she got changed before she left. Because she was going out… Oh no, her boyfriend."

"Boyfriend? Was she on her way to meet him?"

"Yes. Oh no, this is just terrible. He will be waiting for her, and… and she is never going to arrive."

"Do you know where Sharon was going to meet her boyfriend?"

Angie closed her eyes, shaking her head. She opened her eyes. "Wimpy. She said she was meeting him there before they went to the cinema. Oh no, I can't believe this is happening."

Dan looked at his watch. Twenty to seven.

"Do you know her boyfriend's name?"

"Rob," Angie nodded. "Rob Musgrave."

"Robert or Robin, or something else?"

Angie sniffed, dabbing at her eyes with a napkin from the table. "I'm not sure. She only ever called him Rob."

"You're doing really well, Angie. I'm sorry to have to put you through this."

"They've been together for almost a year. I can't imagine what this is going to do to him."

"Can you give me a description of Rob Musgrave?"

"I've never seen him, and Sharon never said what he looked like, just that he was really gorgeous."

"He's never been in the café?"

"Not when I've been working, no."

"What about his age? Do you know how old he is?"

"Two years older than Sharon. Twenty-six."

"Do you know where the Wimpy is that she was going to?"

Rick came out of the kitchen carrying a cup of tea on a saucer. He said, "If she was walking there from here, it's got to be the one on King Edward."

Dan checked his watch again. "Have you got a phone here, Angie?"

"Yes. Not a pay-phone. It's in the kitchen, on the wall at the back."

"Can I use it, please?"

"Of course."

"Rick, stay with Mrs Bowes. I'm going to make a quick call."

Dan went into the kitchen and found the phone. He dialled 192 for Directory Enquiries.

"Which town, please?" asked the operator.

"Kingston upon Hull."

"Which name or business?"

"The Wimpy restaurant on King Edward Street."

"Wimpy, King Edward Street. One moment, please."

The operator told Dan the number and asked if he would like to be connected directly.

"Please, if you could."

After a few seconds he heard the call connect. A little over ten seconds later it was answered.

"Wimpy, Brian speaking. How can I help you?"

"Brian, this is Detective Sergeant Blacksmith from Humberside police. From where you're standing, can you see the customers in the restaurant?"

"Yes, most of them."

"Can you see a single man, mid to late twenties, at a table on his own?"

"A man on his own?"

"Yes. He might have been there for some time, waiting for someone."

"I'll have a look."

Dan waited. He hadn't had time to fully consider what he would do if Rob Musgrave was still in the restaurant.

"Hello?"

"Did you see him, Brian?"

"There's someone who sounds like what you were describing. He's had three coffees so far. Cheryl said he's been here since five."

"How confident are you that Cheryl is right about the time he's been there?"

"Well, the way she was smiling when she was telling me, I think she's been drooling over him ever since he came in here."

Sharon never said what he looked like. Just that he was really gorgeous.

"Okay, Brian. Listen carefully, I want you to go and ask

him if his name is Rob Musgrave. If it is, tell him there's a phone call for him, and bring him to the phone. On no account tell him that there is a police officer on the other end of the line."

"Rob Musgrave?"

"Yes."

"Okay."

Dan listened. He could tell that Brian was still on the line. "What is it, Brian? Do you understand what I asked you to do?"

"Yeah. Is he dangerous?"

Dan tossed a coin in his head. Would someone who had just run down their own girlfriend be chain-drinking coffees in the Wimpy where he had planned to meet her?

"No, Brian. He isn't dangerous."

Dan waited again. He could hear the distant clatter and chatter of the restaurant. He knew he should have taken the BMW and driven to the Wimpy instead of making the phone call, but he didn't know how patient Rob Musgrave was, didn't even know for sure if he really was still in the restaurant.

"Hello?" Different voice. Not Brian. Deeper. Curious but confident, possibly anticipating some kind of wind-up.

"Rob Musgrave?"

"Yeah. Who's that?"

"Rob, this is Detective Sergeant Dan Blacksmith from Humberside police. I'd like you to stay where you are and I'll be there as soon as I can. I need to talk to you."

"Talk to me now."

"I would prefer to speak to you face to face. This isn't something I want to talk about on the phone."

"Why not? What is this about?" There was a pause, possibly while he put his girlfriend's absence together with an inexplicable call from the police. "Has something happened?"

"Like I said, Rob, I would prefer to talk to you face to

face."

"You'd better tell me right now."

"I'm sorry," Dan said. "It's about an accident involving Sharon Hall."

"Tell me," Rob said. His voice was strained, the words forced out through clenched teeth.

"Sharon was killed in a hit-and-run accident earlier this evening. I'm very sorry. I would never choose to pass on information like this over the phone. I wasn't even sure you would still be at the restaurant."

There was a dull click on the line, then nothing. The phone had been hung up at the other end. If it was picked up again the line would still be open, but Dan suspected it wouldn't be picked up again, at least not by Rob Musgrave.

Rick looked up as Dan came running out of the kitchen. "What is it?"

"I have to go to that Wimpy. I want you to stay here and look after Mrs Bowes.

"What happened?"

"He hung up on me."

"Was he there?" Angie asked. "Did you speak to Rob?"

"Yes, I did. My mistake." Dan stopped at the door, looked back at Angie. "Was Sharon left-handed?"

"Yes, she was. Is that important?"

"Maybe. Thanks again for all your help, Angie. Sorry I had to put you through all of that."

CHAPTER 6

Dan radioed for the quickest route to King Edward Street as soon as he was back behind the wheel of the BMW.

After she had told him how to get there, the female constable on the radio said, "Still learning your way around our wonderful city, Detective?"

"Feels that way, Paula. Certainly feels that way."

"But we are much friendlier here, aren't we?"

Dan still had the image of Sharon Hall's lifeless, broken face front-and-centre in his mind. "Sometimes."

He arrived at the Wimpy less than five minutes later. The city centre roads were as busy as he had expected so he pulled the BMW over on the double yellows right outside the restaurant, rather than wasting time trying to find a legitimate parking space. The BMW had nothing visible to identify it as a police vehicle. It wasn't even clean, because Dan Blacksmith believed a car with a month-old film of grime looked even less like a cop's car. He doubted he would be in the Wimpy restaurant long enough to pick up a parking ticket. If he did get one, it would go in the same bin as all the others.

As soon as Dan walked into the restaurant he could tell

that something wasn't quite right. Almost every table was occupied and almost every head was down, or conspicuously turned away from the one table where a young man was sitting alone.

Dan made his way through the restaurant to the four-seat table with the single occupant. He looked over at the counter area and spotted a tall, lanky member of staff standing to one side. The man was holding his hand over the right side of his face. His visible eye was fixed on the man Dan was about to speak to.

"Rob Musgrave?" Dan said.

The young man looked up. He had honey-blonde hair in a short, spiked-pompadour style, three days' worth of dark designer stubble, and cornflower blue eyes that probably looked utterly mesmerising on any day when their owner's girlfriend hadn't been pronounced dead at the scene.

"I'm DS Blacksmith. We spoke earlier."

"Is Sharon dead?"

Dan pulled out the chair diagonally opposite Rob Musgrave and sat down. He rubbed the side of his neck with his thumb. No bruising. No lasting damage. Still felt sore when he swallowed.

"Yes, she is. I apologise for breaking the news over the phone. I shouldn't have done that."

"Doesn't matter."

Dan looked over at the man who was still covering half his face with his hand. He guessed the man was probably Brian.

"Did you hit him?"

"Yeah."

"You reacted while you were in shock. You don't remember exactly what happened."

"He was the nearest one."

"I'll sort it out. Can I get you a coffee or a tea? I need to ask you some questions if you're willing to answer them now, just to help confirm a few details."

Rob shrugged, swallowed hard and blinked the tears away.

"I'll get you a coffee," Dan said.

Dan went over to the counter. He stood in front of the injured man. The badge on the man's red Wimpy shirt had the name Brian on it.

"Evening, Brian. I'm DS Blacksmith. We spoke earlier. Would you like to tell me what happened?"

"I brought him to the phone, like you asked. I didn't listen to what he was saying, but I saw him hang up. Then he just stood there, with his head against the wall. He stayed like that for ages, so I went over and tapped him on the shoulder, really light, just to ask if he was okay."

"I see."

Brian took his hand away from his face. His right eye was already half closed, the cheek swollen and red beneath it. "He turned round and hit me, for no reason."

"It's my fault, Brian. I gave him some extremely bad news over the phone."

"What news?"

"That isn't something I can discuss. Suffice to say, he wasn't thinking straight and we can't hold him responsible for his actions."

"What does that mean?"

"It means you're going to have a shiner in the morning, but nothing worse than you might get in any Sunday league football match. It also means that my official recommendation is that you don't report this incident or attempt to bring it to any kind of personal conclusion."

Brian nodded. "I suppose so."

"Good man. Now, can you tell me where Cheryl is?"

"That's Cheryl over there," Brian said, pointing at a petite brunette who was serving a male customer at the far end of the counter.

"Thanks, Brian. You might want to put a bag of frozen peas on that cheek. Bring the swelling down."

"Yeah. Okay."

Dan waited behind Cheryl's customer until the man had paid for his order and walked away towards a table where a middle-aged woman and two teenage boys were sitting.

"Hi," Cheryl said. "How can I help you?" Her eyes were bright with excitement.

"Hello, Cheryl. I'm DS Dan Blacksmith, Humberside police."

"I know. Brian told me you were probably coming here. Are you supposed to show me your ID?"

Dan took out his warrant card and held it out so that Cheryl could read it.

She leaned across the counter to take a closer look. "Wow. Cool."

"Could I have two coffees, please?"

"Coffees?" Cheryl looked disappointed. "Of course. Black or white?"

"One of each will be fine."

Cheryl made two coffees and put them on a tray in front of Dan. The cups and saucers were white, with the word Wimpy in chunky red lettering across the side of each cup. She left both coffees black and placed a small jug of milk on the tray.

"Can I ask you a couple of questions, Cheryl?"

"Sure," she said, the gleam of excitement returning to her eyes.

"The fair-haired man over there at my table, can you tell me what time he first came into the restaurant today?"

"You mean the cool looking guy who hit Brian?"

"Do you know what time he came in?"

"Five o'clock."

"Can you be certain of that?"

Cheryl nodded in the direction of a large white clock on the wall to the left of the counter. "It was five o'clock when I served him his first coffee."

Dan glanced at his watch. The clock in the restaurant

was a couple of minutes fast.

"He was definitely in here at five o'clock this afternoon, according to that clock?"

"Definitely."

"Did he leave the restaurant at any time between then and now?"

"No."

"Are you absolutely sure of that?"

"I think he went to the gents once, probably all that coffee."

"How long was he gone?"

"Two, maybe three minutes."

Dan looked at the two coffees on the tray. "Have you ever seen him in here before?"

"Couple of times," Cheryl said. She frowned, as if the memory wasn't exactly one of her favourites.

"Was he with someone else or alone?"

Cheryl shrugged. "Just some blonde airhead."

"Do you remember the last time they were in here together?"

"Couple of weeks ago, maybe."

"And did they seem happy together?"

"Yeah." Cheryl rolled her eyes. "Totally."

"Thanks for your time. You've been very helpful."

Dan paid for the coffees and carried the tray back to the table where Rob Musgrave was still sitting in exactly the same position.

"He won't be reporting the assault," Dan said.

Rob stared at him. "Like I'd care."

"When did you last see Sharon Hall?"

Rob flinched at the sound of her name. He blinked, rubbing at his eyes with the sleeve of his black leather jacket. "Yesterday evening."

"Did she seem any different than usual to you?"

"Different? No."

"Did she mention anyone she had argued with recently,

or who might have been following her, or hanging around her place of work?"

"No." Rob reached out to pick up one of the cups of coffee. He nudged it with his hand and hot liquid spilled out onto the tray. He picked up the cup and drank some of the coffee, oblivious to the dark liquid that dripped from the cup onto his jeans. "I thought you said it was an accident."

"It was, but with a hit-and-run we need to make certain checks."

"You don't know who did it."

"No, we don't."

Rob put the cup down in the puddle of coffee. "I want to see her."

"That won't be possible at the moment."

"Why not?"

"The accident is being actively investigated. Next of kin have to be informed, and the body will need to be formally identified."

"The body?"

"I'm sorry."

"Where did it happen?"

"On a street not far from Gaspari's."

"Which street?"

"It's closed at the moment. You won't be able—"

"I don't want to go there. I just want to know where she died."

"Old Park Lane. We think she was taking the shortest route to get here."

Rob shook his head, then his eyes narrowed. "Hang on, that street is straight. It's a thirty speed limit, pavement all the way. How did she get hit by a car walking along there?"

"We think the car struck her while she was on the pavement."

"And they just drove away after?"

"We believe so."

"Some pissed-up asshole," Rob said. He wiped at his eyes again. "Just left her there."

"Someone phoned it in," Dan said. He watched Rob Musgrave's eyes. "It could have been the driver. It's possible he left the scene of the accident to find a phone."

"How are you going to find him?"

"We'll do everything we can." Dan drank some black coffee. He had tasted worse. "Is your full name Robert?"

"Robson."

"Can I have your address and home phone number, your work phone number if you have one?"

"Why?"

"I may need to get in touch with you again."

Dan wrote on his notepad while Rob gave him his address and home phone number.

"No work number? What do you do?"

"Carpenter."

Dan looked at the address. He didn't recognise the street name. "How far away do you live from here?"

"Few miles."

"How did you get here?"

"Bus."

"Do you have a car?"

"Yeah."

"But you didn't use it this evening?"

"Thought we might have gone for a drink after the film. Would have got a taxi home."

Dan looked over at the counter. Cheryl was serving a young couple. "Do you know any local taxi phone numbers?"

"I've got a couple of cards in my wallet."

"Could I see them?"

Rob took his wallet out of his inside jacket pocket, flipped it open and pulled out a couple of taxi company business cards. They were dog-eared, crumpled at the corners.

Dan took one and looked at it. "I'm going to call you a taxi, make sure you get home. I'll get them to charge the fare to Humberside police."

"You don't have to."

"I'd take you myself, but there are a few things I need to deal with."

Dan went to the phone on the wall, the one Rob Musgrave had been using when he had been told that his girlfriend was dead. He dialled the taxi company number, told the girl who answered that he needed a taxi to take one person from the Wimpy on King Edward Street to the address Rob Musgrave had given him. He gave her the details to allow her to charge the fare to the Humberside police force.

Dan hung up and looked at the taxi company card again. The company was called A to Z Taxis. There was a logo at the top of the card that looked like a car registration plate with A2Z written on it.

Dan picked up the handset again and dialled the number of the phone he had used in Gaspari's.

"Hello, Gaspari's," said a nervous female voice.

"Angie, it's Dan Blacksmith. Is Rick still there?"

"I'll fetch him." There was a slight pause. "Did you see Rob?"

"Yes I did."

"How was he?"

"As well as could be expected."

"Oh no. I'll fetch Rick for you now."

Dan looked across at the table where Rob Musgrave was still sitting. Based on what he knew, and what he had seen, Dan thought there was less than a one in ten thousand chance that Musgrave had been responsible for the death of Sharon Hall. From a purely practical perspective, it was virtually impossible for him to have been in the Wimpy from five o'clock if he had been driving the car that had hit his girlfriend.

Rick's voice on the phone said, "Danny?"

Dan turned away, facing the wall. *Danny* was an off-duty name, but he would let it slide. Rick had made a commendable attempt at hiding how shaken up he had been by the dead woman, but he was still relatively young, still quite green when it came to pulling plastic sheets off corpses.

"I'm on my way back. Get WM8 traced as part of a vehicle reg."

"What about Musgrave? Is he in the frame?"

"Extremely unlikely."

"Poor bastard, then."

"Yeah. I'll be back as soon as I can."

Dan went back to Rob's table but he didn't sit down.

"I called a taxi to take you home."

Rob didn't look up, just kept staring at the top of the table. "Thanks."

"Sharon was left-handed, wasn't she?"

"Yeah."

Dan took a business card out of his own wallet. He handed it to Rob with the taxi card. "If you think of anything that might help, anything at all, or you remember something else from this evening or earlier in the day, call the station number on my card."

Rob looked up, took the two cards without enthusiasm. "Okay."

"I have to go. I'm very sorry about Sharon, Rob. We'll do everything we can."

CHAPTER 7

"You're not going to believe this."

Rick had been standing on the pavement outside Gaspari's when Dan drove up and parked outside. He yanked open the passenger side door and jumped into the car.

"How's Angie?" Dan asked. "Did you leave her on her own?"

"She's okay. She said she had a few more things to tidy up and then she's going home. Her car is that black Capri parked over there."

"What am I not going to believe?"

"The car reg. There are hardly any cars in the North East with registrations that start with WM. Only one that has WM8 at the start."

"One car, and it's the one that was involved in that hit-and-run? Do you know what the odds are?"

"Wait, it gets better. The registration is WM *triple eight.*" Rick nodded, mouth slightly open, waiting for Dan to get it.

"Am I supposed to know why that's significant?"

"Triple-Eight Haulage. Biggest haulage company in the North East, or one of them. Owned by William Mason."

"WM. Triple-Eight. This sounds a bit too good to be true."

"It gets even better."

"How the hell can it get better?"

"The car is a six-month-old Jaguar XJS. It was reported stolen earlier this evening by Mason's wife."

"Stolen? That doesn't really make it any better."

"And then about half an hour later it was reported to have been returned, with damage to the front bumper and bonnet. And blood on the side of the driver's seat."

"Stolen and returned? Are you serious?"

Rick nodded. "I've got William Mason's address right here."

Dan put the BMW in gear. "Where do I go?"

With Rick giving directions, it took Dan just over twelve minutes to reach the wide, tree-lined road where the Masons lived.

"Nice area," Dan said, slowing down so that they could read the house number plaques on gates and fence-posts.

"Might move here one day," Rick said. "If I ever win the pools." He pointed out of the window. "Next house on the left. That's it."

"Under fifteen minutes. Probably would have taken longer between five o'clock and half past."

"Still feasible, though."

"Definitely."

Dan parked the BMW against the kerb to the right of the Masons' gated drive. The gates were open. Dan and Rick got out of the car and walked onto the drive. There were two cars parked side by side in front of a large double garage, both facing forward towards the closed garage doors. One was a red Ford Fiesta, the other was a racing green Jaguar XJS with a number plate that bore the registration WM 888.

Rick frowned. "There's something very weird about this."

"Come on," Dan said. "Let's talk to them before we look at the car."

They followed a gravel path around to the front door. Dan lifted the metal door knocker and rapped three times. After no more than five seconds they heard a security chain being pulled back and then the door was opened by a tall, slender, dark-haired woman who appeared to be in her mid forties.

"Hello?"

Dan already had his warrant card in his hand. "Mrs Mason? I'm Detective Sergeant Blacksmith from Humberside CID. This is Detective Constable Price."

"Oh, is this about the car?" She half smiled, as if it was a relief to see police officers on her doorstep.

"Is your husband at home, Mrs Mason?"

"Yes he is."

"Could we possibly come in for a few minutes? We'd like to talk to you and your husband about the car theft that you reported, and other events this evening."

"Of course." Deb Mason stepped back to allow them inside. "Did you come from the Marlborough Road police station?"

"No, we're from Campbell Road. Marlborough is a small station, no CID officers are based there."

"I wasn't expecting the police to come here. I was told you didn't do anything about car thefts unless they were related to serious crimes."

Dan stepped into the hall, took one look at the immaculate hardwood floor and removed his shoes. "Where did you hear that?"

"The sergeant who took my call at Marlborough Road station told me. Something about a quarter of a million car thefts a year."

Dan turned to glance at Rick. He raised his eyebrows and shook his head before turning back to Deb Mason. "Generally true in the majority of cases. There just isn't the manpower to investigate that volume."

Deb looked from Dan to Rick, back to Dan. "But you're both here now."

Dan nodded, waiting for Rick to remove his shoes. "Is Mr Mason through there?"

"In the lounge, yes."

They followed Deb Mason along the hall into the large, L-shaped lounge. The walls were tastefully decorated in a pale pastel shade of yellow, with corn-coloured carpet and a comfortable looking three-piece leather suite. William Mason was sitting in the armchair that formed part of the suite, thumbing through a quarter-inch pile of documents that he was balancing on his knees. When he saw Dan and Rick he shuffled the documents together before standing up and first offering Dan his hand, then Rick, as they introduced themselves.

"Bill Mason," he said. He held up the paperwork in his left hand. "Insurance claim. Total bloody farce."

Dan nodded, taking in the room with a casual glance. William Mason looked older than his wife, possibly by as much as ten or fifteen years. He was tall, solidly built, dark hair going to grey at his temples. He seemed to be frustrated with the insurance claim paperwork. Dan was surprised the man had left his wife to answer the door, considering how nervous she had looked when she had opened it.

"I'd like to ask you a few questions," Dan said. "We could call back tomorrow but it will help with our investigation if we do it now."

"Take a seat," Bill Mason said. "Please."

Deb Mason sat on the sofa nearest her husband. Dan and Rick both took out notepads and pens and sat together on the three-seat sofa opposite the Masons.

"We know that a Jaguar XJS with the registration WM triple-eight was reported stolen from this address at approximately five-twenty this evening, and later reported as having been returned. Could you tell us what happened?"

"Shall I?" Deb Mason asked her husband.

"Well, you know what happened. I wasn't here."

Deb Mason nodded, agreeing with her husband. "I was using Bill's car today because he had taken mine to the garage."

"To get the timing fixed," Bill said. "Fords. Fix or repair daily."

"Your car?" Dan said to Deb Mason. "The Fiesta on the drive?"

"Yes, that's it."

"Was the repair booked in advance or did you take the car to the garage hoping to get a slot?"

"I booked it in the week," Bill said.

"What time did you leave the house today, to go to the garage?"

Bill looked at his watch. "After lunch, probably half one."

"And what time did you get home this evening?"

Bill looked at his watch again. "After six."

"How long after six?"

"Ten, fifteen minutes. The Jag was back by then."

Dan nodded, checking back and forth in his notepad. "How long does it take to get to the garage from here?"

"Twenty minutes in traffic."

"What time did you leave the garage?"

"Around five. I stopped off at the office to catch up on some paperwork." Bill looked at the insurance forms on the arm of his chair. "Can't get enough of it."

Dan looked at the forms. "When did you get the insurance claim forms? The car was damaged less than three hours ago."

"The insurance company sent a couple of forms with the policy documentation when I first took out the policy."

"I see," Dan said. "Which office did you go to at five o'clock?"

"Triple-Eight's main office. It's near the railway station."

"The office is open on Saturdays?"

"Twenty-four hours a day, seven days a week. A haulage company never sleeps."

Dan looked up from his notepad, keeping his voice neutral. As if the next question wasn't really that significant. "Anyone else in the office while you were there?"

"Couple of drivers checked in. Barry Tate was on shift covering the phone."

"Did you speak to any of them?"

"Yes, I spoke to Barry." Bill Mason leaned forward slightly in his chair. "Has this actually got anything to do with my car being stolen?"

Dan asked the next question calmly, no inflection, watching for any kind of reaction from Bill or his wife. "Do you know a woman called Sharon Hall?"

"Hall?" Bill said. He didn't look at his wife, but she did look at him. "Do you mean Howell? We've got a Sharon Howell in the York office."

"How about a man called Rob Musgrave?"

Bill shook his head slowly. "No, I don't recognise that name."

"Who are these people?" Deb Mason asked. She sounded utterly baffled by the direction the questions had taken.

Dan wrote the words *Sharon Howell* in his notepad, followed by a question mark. He looked at what he had written, shook his head and struck out the two words with a single line from his pen. He said, "Sharon Hall was the victim of a hit-and-run earlier this evening, during the period when your Jag was reported stolen. The first two letters and the first number of the car's registration were written on the kerb at the scene of the incident. They were written with the victim's blood."

Deb Mason reached out and put her hand on the back

of her husband's wrist.

"The damage to the bonnet and bumper," Bill said, nodding. His eyes narrowed with concern. "Is she seriously injured?"

"Sharon Hall died at the scene."

Deb Mason gasped, her fingers tightening around her husband's wrist. "That's terrible."

Dan sat forward on the sofa. "The car is going to have to be examined by a forensic investigator. Have either of you touched it since it was returned to your drive?"

"I closed the driver's side door," Bill said. "It had been left open."

"Mrs Mason?"

"No. No, I haven't been near it since it came back."

"Hang on," Bill said. "Neither of us are suspects, are we?"

"From the evidence we have gathered so far, it seems that Mrs Mason was at this address, speaking on the phone to the incident desk at Marlborough Road station, more or less at the time the incident took place."

"I was in the office until gone five-thirty," Bill said. "Probably closer to quarter to six."

"And you were driving your wife's Fiesta," Dan said.

"Yes, I was."

Dan looked down at his notepad, then back at Bill and Deb Mason. "Who else lives here?"

Deb Mason looked at her husband. He said nothing.

"Our son, Tom." Deb said. "Thomas."

"Is he at home now?"

"No, he went into town this morning. He will be back later."

"Working?" Dan asked.

Bill Mason huffed out a sigh. His wife scowled at him.

"Tom doesn't have a job," Deb said. "He will be taking over running Triple-Eight when Bill retires."

Bill Mason shook his head. "Not that he shows the

slightest interest…"

Dan tapped his pen lightly on his notepad. "Thomas has been out all day?"

"Since about ten this morning," Deb said.

"And when do you expect him home?"

Deb smiled hopefully at her husband. "Any time. He doesn't really have a schedule on the weekend."

"Or any other day of the week," Bill said.

Rick cleared his throat. "Mrs Mason, how old is Thomas?"

"He's twenty-four."

Bill sniffed disparagingly. "Acts like he's still fourteen. About time he grew up and took some interest in the family business, took some responsibility."

Rick saw Dan write the number 24 in his notepad. He underlined it and drew a circle around it.

"How has Tom been lately?" Dan asked Deb Mason. "Has he mentioned any problems, any girlfriend trouble, maybe arguments?"

Bill Mason choked back a cynical laugh. "Girlfriend? He's too busy listening to god-awful music that I wouldn't even call music, and watching sick films."

"Oh, Bill. That isn't true. He has his band." She looked at Dan, nodding encouragingly. "Tom plays the guitar. He's really quite good."

Dan wrote in his notepad, read what he had written and looked up.

"What do you mean by sick films?"

"You know," Bill said. "What they call video nasties. No story. All sex, violence and bad language."

Dan exchanged a glance with Rick. He asked the Masons, "Does Tom have a driving licence?"

"Yes," Deb said. "But he doesn't drive very much."

"Does he have his own car?"

"He uses mine when he needs it," Deb said. "Usually only when he has to take his music equipment to band practice."

"Does he ever drive the Jaguar?"

Bill Mason coughed loudly, sitting back heavily in his armchair. "You've got to be bloody joking."

"You don't allow him to drive it?" Dan asked.

"No, and he's never asked. It's like he's embarrassed about it, like he'd prefer it if we weren't able to afford a car like that."

"I see." Dan made a few more brief notes.

"It wasn't Tom," Deb said. "Tom didn't take the Jag."

"Did you see anyone outside before the car was taken?"

"No. But Tom wasn't here then. He was in town."

"Do you know that for certain?"

"He wasn't here when I got home," Deb said. "The house was locked. He definitely wasn't here."

Dan looked around the room, considering his options. "Unless you have any objections, I'd like to call the station and get them to send one of our forensic investigators over to examine the Jag. The sooner it's done, the sooner you can use the car again."

"Are they likely to damage the car?" Bill asked.

"Unlikely," Dan said. "Surface examination should be all. No need to remove the carpets or dismantle the engine."

"I should hope not."

"Can I use your phone, save me going back to my car to radio in?"

"Of course," Deb said. "It's right there."

Dan called the station to request the immediate attendance of a Scenes of Crime Officer from the Forensic Investigation Unit. He gave them the Masons' address, listened while they told him the SOCO would be there in half an hour, then he hung up.

"Half an hour," he said to Rick. "Let's go and have a look at the Jag while we wait, see what we can see."

Bill Mason stood up. "There's a light on the front of the

garage. I'll come out and turn it on for you."

Outside, Dan and Rick stood near the Jag while Bill Mason opened the garage door, went inside and turned on the light.

"Much better," Rick said, as the two cars on the drive were lit up by the powerful lamp.

Dan didn't reply. He wasn't looking at the cars. He was staring down the drive towards the open gates at the tall, dark figure standing motionless between the gateposts.

CHAPTER 8

Dan walked towards the figure, pulling out his warrant card and holding it in front of him.

"Humberside police. Remain where you are."

The dark figure raised its hands like the victim of a hold-up in a cowboy movie.

"My old man finally called the cops on me, did he?"

Dan stopped walking. "Thomas Mason?"

"Afraid so."

"You can put your hands down."

Dan looked at Tom Mason. Physically, he clearly took after his mother. He was tall and slender, with black hair hanging in a thick loop that partially covered the left side of his face. He was wearing a long, dark coat, open over a monochrome T-shirt despite the cold. Dan could see most of the white design on the front of the black T-shirt. It was a grinning skull wearing a knotted bandana above the stencilled words *Never There.* The air around Tom Mason was heavy with the sweet, pungent scent of rolling tobacco that had been generously mixed with the dried leaves of a cannabis plant.

"My band," Tom Mason said, glancing down at his T-shirt. "Gothic rock."

"I'm Detective Sergeant Blacksmith from Humberside CID. I need to ask you some questions."

Tom looked past Dan towards the garage where his father was standing next to another man.

"I know what this is about."

"Do you?"

"I don't smoke in the house. Neither of my parents have got anything to do with it."

"If you could walk over to the cars, Tom, and stand in the light."

Tom shrugged his slim shoulders inside the heavy coat. Dan followed him back up the drive to where Bill Mason was standing next to Rick.

"Your mother's been worried sick," Bill said. "The police are here because my car was stolen."

Tom looked at the Jag.

Dan said, "Don't touch it." Tom took a step away from the Jag. "Tom, can you tell me where you were today between four and six?"

"In town."

"Where, specifically?"

"Couple of record shops. Bailey's Guitars. Relaxed a bit by the lake in the park. After that I walked to the bus station and caught the bus back here. The stop is about a quarter of a mile down the road. I've just walked from there."

"Were you with anyone else?"

"Not really. Are you including people in shops?"

"Would they remember you?"

"Chad in Bailey's would."

"What time were you in there?"

Tom exhaled heavily. "I don't remember exactly. Between half four and half five, probably."

Dan glanced at Rick before he asked Tom, "How well do you know Sharon Hall?"

"Not as well as I'd like to."

Bill Mason took a step forward. "Christ, Tom!"

Dan held up his hand. "Mr Mason, please stay where you are and please don't interrupt."

"I know her fairly well," Tom said. He frowned at his father. "I was talking to her this morning."

Dan looked at the Jag, at Bill Mason, then directly at Tom. "Did you take the Jaguar today?"

"What? No."

"What time were you with Sharon Hall?"

"About eleven, maybe half eleven. In the café where she works. I was in there having a coffee."

"Which café is that?" Dan asked.

"Gaspari's. Do you know it? *Caffe Bar Gaspari.* It's on Hobbs Road."

"What time did you leave the café?"

"About twelve."

"Was that the last time you saw Sharon Hall?"

"Yeah. She had already left on her lunch break."

"Did you see her again today?"

"No." Tom looked from Dan to Rick, back to Dan. "What's this about?"

"Do you know Robson Musgrave?"

"He's our bass player." Tom waited a second, pulled his coat lapels apart and glanced down at his T-shirt. "In the band."

"Have you spoken to him today?"

"No. He was taking Sharon to the cinema tonight. I'll see him tomorrow at band practice."

Rick let out a long sigh.

Dan shook his head. "Tom, I'm afraid I've got some bad news."

***

Dan was sitting opposite Tom Mason at a solid oak

four-seat table in the Masons' large, harshly lit kitchen. Rick was in the lounge with Tom's parents. Tom hadn't touched the mug of tea on the table in front of him, and the subtle aroma of the tea was doing nothing to mask the odour of marijuana on Tom's breath and clothes. Dan was ignoring the smell of the weed.

"When you were talking to Sharon today, did she mention anything about being followed, or threatened? Did she seem any different from usual?"

Tom shook his head slowly from side to side as he considered the question. "Nothing, no. She was the same as usual."

"I know this is hard, but can you remember exactly what you talked about, what she said to you?"

Tom let out a long, slow breath. He hadn't cried when Dan had told him that Sharon Hall was dead, but he had sagged inside his heavy coat, his blithe attitude to Dan's questions deposed by a newfound melancholy that had nothing in common with the recreational brooding of a gothic rock fan. He had listened silently as Dan told him about the hit-and-run, and about how he had already spoken to Rob Musgrave.

"We didn't talk about much. She told me she was taking her lunch break early, asked me if I wanted another coffee before she went."

"Did she say why she was taking an early lunch break?"

"No. Sometimes it's just to fit in with what the other people who work there are doing."

"I see. Was that all you talked about?"

"She asked me what I was doing later." Tom looked at Dan's notepad, the pen poised over it. "She wasn't asking me out or anything. I told her I wasn't doing much and she said did I want to go to the cinema with her and Rob."

"And what did you say?"

Tom looked at his hands, flat on the table in front of him. "I said I didn't want to go. I told her it was because the film they were going to see was a comedy and I don't like comedies."

"Was that the real reason you didn't want to go?"

"That and not wanting to be a gooseberry."

"Did you talk about anything else?"

"Nothing much. I told her I'd seen a kid on *Fix It* last week who was from our old school."

Dan looked up from his notepad. "You went to the same school as Sharon Hall?"

"Yeah. That's how I know her. We were in the same class all the way through secondary school."

"Which school was it?"

"John Blair Comprehensive."

Dan wrote the school name in his notepad. "What years were you there?"

"Seventy-two to seventy-seven. That's when Sharon left. I stayed on for the sixth form."

"So you left in seventy-nine?"

"Yeah."

Dan Nodded as he wrote, his brow furrowing with a new thought. "Is that how you met Robson Musgrave, through Sharon Hall?"

"Sort of. He went to John Blair too, but he was a couple of years older than me and Sharon. He was already in the band, and Sharon knew I played the guitar. Their guitarist left and she got Rob to ask me to go and try out at one of their practice sessions."

Dan tapped his pen on his notepad. "Why did their original guitarist leave the band?"

"His folks moved to London and he went with them."

"So he didn't leave with any ill will towards the other band members?"

"No."

"Who else is in this band with you and Rob Musgrave?"

"They didn't kill Sharon."

Dan sat back, met Tom Mason's gaze. "Someone did."

"And you think whoever did, did it with my dad's Jag."

"There's a forensic investigator on the way here to examine the car. They should be here in about fifteen minutes."

"Why do you think it's the Jag that was involved? Did someone see it?"

"There was evidence at the scene that led us to identify the Jag as the vehicle that was likely to have been involved."

"What, like part of the bumper or something?"

Dan paused, waited for a few seconds. "Was Sharon Hall right-handed or left-handed?"

Tom answered immediately, didn't need to think about it. "Left."

"Everyone I have asked that question has given me the same answer."

"Who have you asked?"

"You, Rob Musgrave, and a woman who works at Gaspari's café."

"Is it important?"

"I think it might be."

"Why?"

"I'd prefer not to discuss it at the moment."

Tom nodded, stared at the mug of tea but didn't pick it up. "She did say one other thing to me. She said she'd see me next Saturday." He looked up at Dan. "You're going to catch them, aren't you?"

"We're going to do everything we can."

CHAPTER 9

Dan watched the SOCO lifting fingerprints from the Jag's driver-side door handle. The forensic investigator was a woman called Patricia Davies, a stocky forty-something redhead with whom Dan had previously worked several complex crime scenes.

"Hardly ever going to get a clean print from a door handle," Patricia said. "Do you know why that is?"

"Frequent use," Dan said. Pat Davies was very good, but you had to put up with twenty questions every time.

"Frequent use," Pat said, like she was assessing his answer on an exam sheet. She straightened up and turned to where Bill Mason was standing a couple of yards away. "Got the key?"

Bill handed it to her. Pat held it up as if it was an exhibit in court. "Might have managed a usable print off this, if it had been left in situ."

"I didn't think," Bill said. "Just wanted to lock the car up and go inside."

Dan didn't meet Bill Mason's eyes. He could hear the same tone of apologetic resignation in the man's voice that he had heard many times before. It wasn't indicative of guilt, just of a subconscious admission that mistakes had been made. Pat had a knack of bringing out that tone.

It would have been useful for Rick Price to have watched the SOCO at work, but Dan had decided to leave Rick inside with Deb Mason and Tom.

Pat Davies inserted the key into the Jag's driver-side door lock. "I'm going to unlock the door and open it." She pointed at Bill Mason. "Before we do anything else, I would like you to stand no closer than I am standing and look inside the car when I have opened the door. I want you to tell me if you can see anything in there that is not as it should be, or not as you remember it. Anything at all."

"Do you mean apart from the blood on the side of the driver's seat?"

"Was it there before?"

"No."

"Then please mention it. Don't assume I know anything about the previous condition of the car, Mr Mason."

She opened the door and stood to one side so that Bill Mason could come closer to look inside. After a few seconds he nodded excitedly, pointing at something. "That can of Coke. That isn't mine, and Deb doesn't drink the stuff."

Dan waited, pen poised over his notepad, while Pat Davies looked inside.

"Centre storage unit is open," Pat Davies said. "An open Coca Cola can is visible inside it."

"Does Tom drink Coke?" Dan asked.

"Probably," said Bill Mason. "But I can't see how he would have put that in there. He has never been in the Jag. Like I said, he acts like he wishes we didn't own it."

"Drink can as a source of fingerprints," Pat said to Dan. "Better than a car door handle?"

"Much better. High probability of the can only being handled by a single person, also moderate to high probability of a full thumb print and two or more full or partial finger prints."

"The presence of the can also raises an obvious question, of course," Pat said.

Dan nodded. It had already occurred to him. "Why would a car thief leave a can of Coke in a car they returned?"

"Glad I'm only providing forensic evidence and not trying to crack this case. Although the presence of the Coke can may make that job a lot easier."

Dan breathed out slowly, watching the cloud of condensation rise through the cold evening air in the wide beam of light from the garage lamp.

"I think I'm going to leave you to it, Pat."

"This isn't cold," Pat said. "In eighty-two I had to spend a whole day in a frozen ditch with a week-old corpse, and it never got above minus twelve. Now, that was cold."

"Can you print the Masons for me when you've finished out here?"

"Already on my to-do list. Why wouldn't it be?"

"Why do you need our fingerprints?" Bill Mason asked Pat.

"Elimination, Mr Mason. Your latent prints are probably all over the gear stick, steering wheel, rear-view mirror and everywhere else inside the car. If we don't take your prints, how will we know which ones belong to someone else?"

"Assuming Mr Mason's prints are not already on record," Dan said.

"They're not."

"Don't sound so appalled, Mr Mason," Pat said. "Detective Blacksmith is not suggesting that you have a criminal record. There are other reasons that your prints could already be on file. You could have been in one of the armed forces, for example."

"Come back inside, Mr Mason," Dan said. "DC Price and I will be heading back to the station soon."

"I'll be another hour here at the very least," Pat said.

"I'll drop the results off to you tomorrow, unless you can wait until Monday."

"Tomorrow would be better, if you possibly could."

"Have a good evening. What's left of it, anyway."

"You too. Thanks again, Pat."

***

Dan and Rick stood together on the kerb next to the unmarked BMW. The area where the Masons lived was quiet, hardly any cars passing them along the tree-lined road.

Dan shoved his hands deep in his pockets. "We either talk to the neighbours now, or we come back and do it tomorrow."

Rick looked at his watch. "Half eight. Probably worth trying them now, while anything they might have seen is fresh in their minds."

"That's what I was thinking."

"Shall we do the neighbours on either side of the Masons, and the three nearest houses on the opposite side of the road?"

"Sounds good. If they didn't see anything, it's unlikely anyone further along the road did."

"I'll go to the one on the left, then," Rick said.

"Ask them if they know Sharon Hall or Rob Musgrave, as well as asking if they saw anyone hanging around here earlier."

"They're not going to know them, though, are they?"

"The way this case is going, I'm not betting against anything."

Rick set off towards the gated driveway of the house on the far side of the Masons'. Dan walked along the pavement until he reached the open gate of the house on the right. There was a streetlamp to one side of the gate. The lamp flickered occasionally, causing Dan's shadow to fade in and out of existence on the wet tarmac ahead of him as he walked up the drive.

He went to the front door and pressed the large bronze doorbell button, hearing a faint double chime sounding inside the house. He counted the seconds, purely from habit, and reached six before the door opened.

The man who was standing in the gap of the partially opened door was past middle-age, with receding hair that was predominantly grey. He was wearing a purple cardigan and a pair of cow-pat coloured corduroy trousers. He looked to one side of Dan, checking to see whether Dan was alone.

"Help you?" he said, his tone that of a man who had very little intention or desire to help anyone.

Dan showed the man his warrant card. "DS Blacksmith, Humberside CID. I'm investigating the theft of a car from your neighbour's house and I'd like to ask you a few quick questions. Shouldn't take more than a minute or two of your time."

The man leaned out of the door, craning his neck as he peered down the drive towards the flickering streetlamp. "Bill Mason? Did they steal his new Jag?"

"Did you see anything suspicious earlier this evening? Anything at all? One or more strangers hanging around the area, or maybe you heard the car leaving?"

"No, can't say I did. What time did it happen?"

"Between five and half past as far as we can tell. Were you at home at that time."

"Yes, I was."

"Anyone else here at that time?"

"My wife. Neither of us have been outside this afternoon."

"Could I take your names please, just so I have a record of who I've spoken to?"

"Frank Nolan. My wife's name is Pauline."

"Thanks, Mr Nolan. I'm going to leave you this card,

with my contact details on it and a phone number where you can reach me or leave a message. If you remember anything, or if something occurs to you, please don't hesitate to get in touch."

Frank Nolan took the business card that Dan handed him.

"One last thing," Dan said. "Do you know Sharon Hall or Robson Musgrave?"

Nolan slowly shook his head, his eyes narrowing as he thought about the names. "No, no I'm sure I've never heard of either of them."

"Thank you for your time, Mr Nolan. Have a good evening."

Dan went back to the car and waited for a few minutes until Rick returned from the other neighbouring house.

"Nothing," Rick said as he shuddered, rubbing his hands together. "Colder than a witch's tit."

"They hadn't seen anything?"

"No, and they didn't recognise the names, but it still took them all night to tell me."

Dan smiled. "Some people don't like to talk to the police. And others like it a little too much."

"You're telling me."

"Nothing for me either, but at least I got a bloke who wasn't overly talkative."

Rick looked across the road at the houses on the other side. "Want me to take the one on the right?"

"I'll take the one on the left. Whoever finishes first can have the one in the middle."

"Good luck." Rick shivered again and hurried across the road.

Dan crossed the road to the house on the right, walked up the path to the front door and knocked three times with the heavy horseshoe-shaped door knocker. He could see through the rectangular frosted panes in the door that there was a light on in the hall, but he couldn't see any other lights on in the house. He held his breath and listened. No music playing, no Saturday night television gameshow applause or canned sitcom laughter. He knocked again but he was already getting the distinct impression that the house was empty.

He gave it another minute before walking back down the path to the pavement. No sign of Rick. He had probably landed himself with another chatty friend of local law enforcement.

Dan walked up to the front door of the house that was directly opposite the entrance to the Masons' driveway. There were lights on behind the curtains of one of the downstairs rooms, and Dan could hear the sound of the television as he stood on the doorstep. Faced with the choice of doorbell or teardrop-shaped metal knocker, Dan chose the bell and heard four excessively cheerful chimes from the hallway.

He had only counted to three when the door was opened wide by a statuesque brunette wearing a tight purple tracksuit. The jacket of the tracksuit was only half zipped up. She looked to be in her mid to late thirties. She also looked to be an advocate of Saturday night domestic drinking. Dan tried not to look too closely but it was fairly obvious that she wasn't wearing anything at all underneath the tracksuit.

"Bit late to be selling double-glazing," the woman said with a lazy smile.

"Good evening," Dan said. "I'm Detective Sergeant Blacksmith from Humberside CID. I'd like to ask you a few quick questions. Shouldn't take more than a minute or two of your time."

"Bloody hell." She fumbled for the zip on the front of her tracksuit jacket and pulled it up far enough to prevent anything falling out and interrupting the conversation. Even from where Dan was standing, he could clearly smell the tequila on her breath.

"Could I take your name, please, just so I have a record of who I have spoken to?"

"Of course you can, darling. My name is Hazel Beck. Do you need my phone number?" She leaned against the door jamb and tilted her head to one side. "Or are you going to take me in for questioning?"

Dan glanced over his shoulder. No sign of Rick. "That won't be necessary, Mrs Beck. Were you at home between four o'clock and six o'clock this evening?"

"There's nobody in next door," Hazel Beck said, pointing in the direction of the dark house Dan had just come from. "Away all weekend." She winked at Dan. "Second honeymoon."

"I see. And were you at home this afternoon?"

"All afternoon, since about one."

"Did you look out of the window towards the Masons' house at any time?"

Hazel flapped her hand at Dan. "I'm not a nosey neighbour, Detective. I've been hard at it all afternoon." She giggled, covering her mouth with her hand. "The housework, I mean."

"You didn't see a car arrive or leave between five and six?"

"Saw their Jag. Right posh car that is. Puts my six-year-old Merc in the shade, it does."

"You saw the Jaguar. Was it arriving or leaving?"

"I saw it because it came shooting out of the drive backwards, really fast. Lucky there wasn't a car coming along the road."

Dan started to take down what Hazel Beck was saying. "Okay, Mrs Beck. I'd like you to think very carefully about this. What time did you see the Jaguar leaving?"

"Five past five."

"You're absolutely certain of that?"

"Maybe ten past."

"Did you check the time, look at a wall clock maybe?"

"No, I was doing the ironing in the front room with the telly on. I was watching *Brookside* and it hadn't got as far as the first advert. Hadn't been on long at all."

"Could it have been earlier than five past five?"

"No, I don't think so."

"Mrs Beck, this is very helpful. Now, could you see who was driving the Jaguar?"

Hazel Beck sighed, shaking her head. "Come inside."

"Mrs Beck?"

"I want you to stand where I was standing, so you can see the view I had out of the window. Then you'll understand why I couldn't see who was driving the Jag."

"No need for that. I'll take your word for it that your view wasn't ideal."

"I could see enough to know it was their Jag. Couldn't see who was in it. Could have been the entire A-Team for all I know."

"Thank you, Mrs Beck. I'll just note that you couldn't see who was in the car." Dan looked over his shoulder. Still no sign of Rick. "Did you see which direction the Jag went, after it had reversed into the road?"

"Left. That way. Down the hill towards town."

"Thank you." Dan smiled at Hazel Beck. "Have you seen anyone hanging around here recently, maybe outside the Masons' house?"

"Not really. Nobody who looked up to no good anyway."

"Anyone at all?"

"Just the usual people walking their dogs or going to the phone box down the road. This is a quiet area, not many hooligans around here."

"Was anyone else in the house today, between four and six?"

"I should bloody hope not." Hazel Beck laughed, pressing her hand against her chest. "Or if there was, I wouldn't want my husband to find out."

"Is your husband at home now?"

"Ron? No, he's away all weekend with work."

"I see. What does your husband do, Mrs Beck?"

"Hospitality. Takes rich people away on fancy breaks to help them decide to spend their money on less interesting things."

"When do you expect him home?"

"Tomorrow, some time."

"Well, I think we're done. You've been very helpful, Mrs Beck, and I appreciate you giving your time to answer the questions."

"My pleasure, darling."

"One last thing," Dan said. "Do you know a young woman named Sharon Hall?"

Hazel Beck did exactly what Frank Nolan had done, narrowed her eyes and slowly shook her head as she thought about the name. "No, can't say I do."

"Okay." Dan was about to give up. It was as unlikely to be productive as pretty much any question he had ever asked. "And do you know the name Robson Musgrave?"

Hazel Beck didn't narrow her eyes or shake her head. Her eyes briefly went very wide and she started to nod, grinning before she spoke.

"Oh yes," she said. "I certainly know that name."

CHAPTER 10

Rick turned the BMW's heater control up to maximum as Dan pulled away from the kerb.

"Won't do much until the engine warms up," Dan said.

"I know. It's the thought that counts."

The car was travelling down the gentle incline between regularly spaced trees and less frequent streetlamps as Dan drove away from the road where Hazel Beck lived opposite the Masons' house.

"As coincidences go," Rick said, "that's one of the wildest."

"Not really a coincidence, though. And it happened more than six months ago."

"Come on. Her sister had a walk-in wardrobe fitted by Rob Musgrave."

"Musgrave is a carpenter. Tom Mason told Hazel Beck about him because she mentioned her sister was trying to find a decent carpenter."

"Did she say why she was talking to Tom Mason?"

"They've been neighbours for years. Tom Mason has a lot of spare time on his hands, and Mrs Beck, well, I would go as far as to say that Mrs Beck isn't averse to the occasional friendly chat with members of the opposite sex."

"Just a coincidence, then?"

"For now, I think so."

"So how come Bill Mason and his wife didn't know the name Rob Musgrave?"

"Did Bill Mason strike you as someone who takes a great deal of interest in his son's friends and band mates?"

"I suppose not."

"I doubt Tom Mason has sat down and had any kind of heart to heart with his folks for years."

"So who took the Jag? And why did they bring it back?"

Dan shrugged. "We're not going to be able to get much further without the pathologist's report and the forensics from the Jag and the crime scene."

"What time are we starting on this tomorrow?"

"Not too early. Get plenty of sleep. We're going to need clear heads for this one."

"What about this evening?"

"When we get back to the station, you can go straight home. All I'm going to do is check if there's any information back from the crime scene yet. I won't be sticking around much later, not a lot more we can achieve tonight."

"I'm not going to argue with that."

Dan pulled up at a crossroads, waiting for the traffic lights to change.

"I keep thinking about Sharon Hall being left-handed."

Rick held his hands in the weak lukewarm air coming out of the dashboard vents. "Why do you think it's important?"

"I don't think she wrote the car reg on the kerb. She was seriously injured, and she died at the scene. The writing on the kerb was clear, consistent, not the way it would look if someone close to death had written it."

"Who else could have written it? It was written in her blood, and her left hand was covered in the stuff."

"But she didn't pull herself off the road back onto the pavement, and her left arm was dislocated at the shoulder."

"You think someone else wrote the car reg, using her finger dipped in her own blood?"

The traffic lights changed to green and Dan drove across the junction.

"I think whoever was driving the car wrote it."

"But why would they do that?"

"Same reason they took the car back to the Masons' house."

Rick nodded slowly, his eyes brightening. "They wanted us to find the car."

"That's the only possible explanation. They gave us half the registration, but they knew that was enough. And they wrote it with Sharon Hall's left hand."

Rick slapped his palm against the dashboard. "Because they knew she was left-handed."

"So what does that tell us?"

"They knew her. Knew her well enough to know she was left-handed."

"Possibly. Or they watched her for long enough to learn she was left-handed."

"Tom Mason knew she was left-handed."

"So did Angie Bowes and Rob Musgrave. And they all confirmed it without a second thought."

"You think they wouldn't have admitted to knowing she was left-handed if they had been responsible for killing her and writing the car reg on the kerb?"

"It's unlikely, isn't it?"

Rick looked out of the window as they drove along a wide, well-lit street. "What if it isn't about Sharon Hall? What if someone is trying to fit up Bill Mason?"

"I've been trying to make that work ever since we spoke to him."

"And…?"

"I can't."

"You believe him about being twenty minutes away in his wife's Fiesta when Sharon Hall was killed?"

"I'm going to check out his alibi, but I can't see how he could have been driving around in the Fiesta at the same time as stealing his own Jag. And why would he write his own car reg at the scene?"

"Okay. It wasn't Bill Mason. But I still fancy his son for it."

"You think he might have had an emotional motive for killing Sharon Hall?"

"He liked her. She was involved with someone else."

"So he took his father's Jag, ran her over, wrote the car reg on the kerb, drove home, waited outside for us to turn up and then walked up the drive and put on the most convincing act of innocence that I have ever seen."

Rick held his hands out, palms up. "Well, since you put it like that…"

"I'm not saying Tom Mason is absolutely, one hundred percent innocent, but it is incredibly unlikely that he had anything to do with Sharon Hall's death."

"You know he smokes marijuana, don't you?"

"I also know that you used to."

"Difficult childhood," Rick said, hiding a grin. "Peer pressure. You know how it is."

"I'm not interested in what Tom Mason smokes, and I'm not going to do anything about it. Way too much paperwork for a start."

Rick took out his notepad and thumbed back and forth through several pages.

"Tom Mason and Sharon Hall were in the same class all the way through secondary school. Musgrave went to the same school too."

"Eight years ago, give or take. I can't see how it's a factor, apart from being the means that they originally knew each other."

"No," Rick said. "Nor me."

Dan slowed down, made a left turn. "Which school did you go to?"

"Not John Blair. I went to Needle Hill with all the other illiterate thugs and dropouts."

"What year did you leave?"

"Seventy-three."

"An old man. Born in the fifties."

"Fifty-seven." Rick looked across at Dan. "But you already knew that."

Dan stopped the BMW at the kerb outside the Campbell Road police station. "How does nine o'clock tomorrow morning sound?"

"Sounds fine," Rick said. "Don't stay here too late."

Rick opened the door and the cold came into the car like an invisible, insidious wraith. He climbed out and closed the door behind him. Dan turned off the engine as Rick walked around behind the BMW, heading towards the entrance to the side street where he had parked his own car that morning.

Dan glanced in the rear-view mirror. Rick was standing behind the car. He had been looking down at the BMW's boot but he met Dan's eyes in the mirror, gestured with his hand for Dan to get out of the car.

"What is it?" Dan said as he walked around to join Rick. Then he saw what it was, and he understood the look of wary confusion in Rick's eyes.

Finger-written in the damp grime covering the BMW's boot in clear, six-inch-high capital letters were two words. VERY COLD.

***

Before he opened the thin binder that held the pathologist's report, Dan picked up the phone on his desk and dialled his home number. The CID office was empty apart from him. There were other police officers in the station, but nobody else at all on the first floor. The ceiling strip lights over Dan's desk were on, but the rest of the open plan office was in varying degrees of darkness.

The phone was picked up just before the fifth ring.

"Hello?" His wife's voice. Tired, patient, familiar with receiving calls after eight p.m. from her husband.

"It's me."

"It's late." No accusation in Rebecca Blacksmith's tone. A hint of sympathy. Knew what it was going to be like marrying a cop. One of the things he loved about her. One of the many.

"I'll be another half hour or so. New case. Bit strange. Did Mandy go to sleep okay?"

"She asked where's daddy a few times. Didn't cry."

Dan smiled. "That's good. I'll go up and tuck her in as soon as I get home."

"Just *after* you get home."

Dan smiled again, different stimulus and a different kind of smile, nodding as he held the phone close to his ear. "Maybe a few minutes after I get home."

"You getting frisky, Detective?"

Dan stared into a dark corner of the office, thought of Becky's fine, shoulder-length blonde hair and saw Sharon Hall's blank dead eyes staring up at him from the cold pavement.

"Maybe after a double whisky."

"My eternal romantic. What time do you think you'll be home?"

"Half an hour." Dan looked at his watch. "It will be before nine."

"I'll hold you to that," said Becky.

"I'll hold you."

"See you soon, honey."

"Bye."

"I love you."

"Love you too. Always."

Dan hung up, did absolutely nothing for a slow five-count to give himself the distance he always needed between his home life and his police work.

He opened the pathologist's report. It couldn't have been on his desk for more than half an hour at the most. Sharon Hall's body had been formally identified at 19:50 by Ralph Edward Hall, father of the deceased. Dan skim read all the general details. Sharon Hall was five feet six inches tall and weighed nine stone, two pounds, with no diagnosed illnesses, life-threatening or otherwise. She had been wearing a pink sweater, white vest, light blue jeans, black ankle boots and black underwear. Both her ears were pierced and she was wearing half-inch gold hoop earrings. No other piercings, and no tattoos. Pubic hair shaved in its entirety. No evidence of sexual activity within the previous 12 hours.

Dan followed the long and verbose catalogue of physical injuries with his index finger. Fractured left femur and tibia. Separated left patella. Fractured right tibia and fibula. Torn right anterior tibiofibular ligament. There was a reference to extensive abdominal injuries, but a note that no internal examination had yet been carried out. The left shoulder had sustained a glenohumeral dislocation, with damage to the teres minor muscle and tendons, and the infraspinatus tendon. Facial injuries included lacerations to the lips, tongue and soft palate. The upper right central and upper right lateral teeth were both broken.

Dan's finger stopped moving down the list.

He read the cause of death. Read it again slowly. Then one final time as he reached for the phone to make a call. The pathologist's number at the mortuary was one of the numbers stored on the phone. He pressed the speed-dial button for that number.

While he listened to the phone ringing, Dan continued to read the cause of death for the third time.

Death due to combined asphyxia, cerebral anoxia and venous congestion caused by non-ligature strangulation. Cutaneous bruising and abrasions consistent with manual strangulation are present on the front and sides of the neck. Fracture to larynx, thyroid cartilage and hyoid bone. Fractures and bruising are indicative of extreme, continual pressure that was maintained up to and after the moment of death. Patterned bruising and lesions on the neck were probably caused by the stitched seams of a pair of leather gloves.

Dan raised his left hand and touched his throat.

Strangulation.

After eight rings, the phone was answered by senior pathologist Nigel Hansom. The phone at the mortuary would have displayed the number of the incoming call, which was apparent from Nigel's response.

"I've been waiting for your call."

"Sorry, Nigel. I'm just reading the report now. The cause of death—"

"Is incontrovertibly accurate. And this hit-and-run accident was no accident."

Dan began to take notes on a fresh page of his pad.

"Go on."

"Injuries to the left femur and right ankle, most likely also the facial injuries, were caused by an initial impact where a vehicle collided with the victim, crushing her legs against the base of the lamppost. Additional upper leg and abdominal injuries were the result of subsequent trauma, where the vehicle was driven forward and then reversed over the lower half of the victim's body while she was lying prone across the kerb."

Dan exhaled hard enough to ripple the top sheaf of the pathology report on the desk in front of him. "But none of that killed her?"

"The injuries sustained from the vehicle impacts would not have killed her immediately, probably not for up to twelve hours, even without medical attention."

"Are you saying the driver of the car strangled her to death?"

"I'm not the detective, Dan. Driver, passenger, unknown third party. Take your pick, but we both know the driver is the most likely candidate."

"What else can you tell me?"

"The initial collision was probably deliberate. The subsequent crushing of the victim while she lay on the kerb was almost certainly deliberate, and the strangulation was premeditated murder. The marks on the victim's neck are very clear, very precise. There's no blurring from the kind of multiple bruises or abrasions that would occur if the assailant adjusted his grip or was fighting against a struggling victim."

"You mean she was strangled by someone who knew exactly what they were doing?"

"Yes, and with no obvious evidence of excitement or rage, although I obviously can't prove that to the level required by a court of law. They put their hands where they needed to be, and they crushed her throat until she was dead."

"How long would they have had their hands around her throat before she died?"

"Based on her state of health, unconsciousness would have occurred in no more than fifteen seconds. Given the estimated pressure and location of the assailant's hands, the victim would have died between two to three minutes later."

"Can you tell me anything about the man who killed her? I'm assuming it was a man."

"I'd say it was highly unlikely not to be a man. Measurements taken from the marks on the victim's neck give a hand length of seven and a half inches, and a width of three and two thirds. Slightly above average length and width, although not conclusive proof of a larger than average man."

In his notepad, Dan wrote *Male, average-large.*

"Can you tell if he is left or right-handed?"

"Not from the available evidence, no. From the marks on the victim's neck, it's clear that the applied pressure from both hands was extremely similar."

"You said the clarity and precision of the marks suggested that there was no excitement or rage when he was strangling her. Are you sure about that?"

"Given the available evidence, I'm almost certain of it. And that emotional detachment combined with the efficiency of the choking are clear indications of something else."

"What?" Dan said.

"Whoever killed Sharon Hall has probably killed before."

CHAPTER 11

Dan parked the unmarked BMW at the kerb in front of his house, directly under the overhead glow of a streetlight. The lights along this road were newer and taller than the streetlamps on Old Park Lane, where Sharon Hall had been killed.

Before he went into the house, Dan stood at the rear of the BMW and looked at the words that had been neatly finger-written across the boot.

"Very cold," Dan said. He thought of the writing on the kerb, the two letters and the number that had been written in blood. He thought of the unknown driver who had crushed Sharon Hall against a metal lamppost, driven his car over her, and finally throttled her to death with strong, gloved hands. "Did you write this?"

He didn't wipe the words off. He wanted to do it but he also wanted to have the boot checked by a forensic examiner, preferably Pat Davies.

He unlocked the white, wooden front door of his modest but pleasant three-bedroom detached house and stepped into the hall that was partially lit by a pale glow coming from the kitchen. He glanced up the staircase before removing his coat and shoes as quietly as he could. He didn't want to make too much noise in case Mandy was only sleeping lightly. He knew that she often tried to stay awake on the evenings when he was working past her bedtime, something she had begun to do since starting primary school just over two months earlier in the first week of September.

Dan padded softly in his socks to the half-open kitchen door, looked in and saw that it was unoccupied. The oven was turned down to a very low setting and he could smell something that was either cottage pie or possibly Becky's homemade lasagne, but either way it was certainly going to be very welcome. The house was warm, the central heating more than adequately coping in its battle against the onset of British winter.

Instead of calling out to Becky, Dan checked the room that the original architect of the house had probably labelled 'dining room' on the plans, but that had become Becky's studio. The canvas that she was currently working on was set on a three-legged A-frame easel in the centre of the room. It was eventually going to be a commissioned portrait, in oils, but it was still barely more than a first-draft charcoal sketch. It showed the head and shoulders of a man, but with no detail yet, and no features beyond the generic eyes, nose, mouth. It could have been anyone.

Dan thought it was wonderful that his wife's work had grown in popularity to the point where she was being sought out to paint portraits by customers who were willing to pay in full, in advance, and he had told her as much on several occasions. But Becky was concerned that her paintings were going to become appreciated not for their own qualities but because of the name of their creator.

"That's because Blacksmith is such a fine name," Dan had said. "If you had stuck with your maiden name I'm sure you'd still be completely unknown."

Becky had laughed at that, and told him not to upset a

famous artist. Particularly one with a loaded brush in her hand.

Dan closed the studio door and looked into the lounge, the last remaining ground-floor room that he hadn't checked. The only light in the room was coming from the TV screen in the far corner. The closing credits of a BBC sitcom were playing. Dan glanced at his watch, saw that it was a minute before nine p.m. The news would be on at nine o'clock but there would be no mention on the national news of a fatal hit-and-run in Kingston upon Hull, not until details of the strangulation were released to the press and it became more than just a nasty but mundane accidental death. When that happened, it would probably get a front page column in the Hull Daily Mail.

Dan went far enough into the room to be able to see his wife lying full-length on the wide, white faux-leather sofa.

Becky looked up and smiled. She was wearing her pink pyjamas over a white T-shirt.

Dan crouched down in front of the sofa and gave Becky a gentle kiss on the forehead.

"There's a cottage pie in the oven. Unless you've eaten already."

"I haven't. I'll get some later."

Becky looked into Dan's eyes and he blinked, forcing a wider smile. "Do you need to talk about it?" she asked.

"Car accident. A woman died."

"You don't investigate accidents."

"No, I don't."

"How did she die?"

"Somebody strangled her."

Becky frowned, reaching up to lightly touch her fingers against Dan's neck.

"I know," Dan said. "I don't like coincidences."

"Why don't you go up and kiss Mandy goodnight? I'll put a plate in the oven to warm up for you."

Dan slid his hand over the curve of Becky's hip and

kissed the tip of her nose. "Okay. I won't be long."

He went up the stairs quietly, along the landing to the second bedroom. It had been Mandy's room ever since they had moved in, a little over a year earlier, when Dan had transferred from Cheshire Constabulary to Humberside Police. Dan and Becky had chosen the house in a village called Bilstead, six miles east of the city, in the middle of a rural area that was mostly farmland. Becky had wanted the comparative quiet of the rural location, and Dan had always preferred to live at least a few miles away from his place of work. The table lamp on top of the small chest of drawers in Mandy's room was switched on, as usual, and it would remain on throughout the night. Becky and Dan had given up wondering when Mandy was going to grow out of needing a nightlight in her room, and resigned themselves to accepting that she probably just would, eventually. Dan smiled at the light. It was just one more aspect of their lives that had altered since their daughter's birth. Dan had realised very early on that it was not possible to predict or to control the phases and changes of an infant's journey through life. It was far better to join them on their journey and enjoy it with them than to constantly attempt to choreograph their personal achievements with a checklist in one hand and a stopwatch in the other. He had friends and colleagues who had kids, and many of them had regaled him with tales of perfect offspring who had slept through the night after two weeks, could talk fluently at six months, and who had probably ridden a unicycle all the way home from the maternity ward.

Dan couldn't remember when Mandy had first slept through the night. Not because he didn't care, or because he had been too busy working, but because he hadn't felt the need to mark it on the calendar and point proudly at the date whenever visitors called. It had happened, and he and Becky had been pleased. Then they had moved on with Mandy to potty training and whatever had come next and it had all been exciting and exhausting and unexpected, the way Dan's friends and colleagues wearily explained that it always would be with a first child.

Dan knelt down beside Mandy's small bed. He remembered the trepidation bordering on fear when they had replaced her safe, high-sided cot with a bed that she could actually fall out of. And, of course, she never had fallen out of it.

Dan breathed out heavily, touched the corner of his eye and brought his finger away wet.

Mandy was lying on her side, knees pulled up to her stomach under the blanket. Her shoulder-length hair was blonde, like Becky's. She was facing away from Dan but he could see the side of her face, the way her closed eyes and half-open mouth were completely relaxed as she slept. The soft toy that she always cuddled as she drifted off to sleep was behind her, half hidden underneath the pillow. It was a cheerful, chubby grey rat dressed in a striped jumper and blue cap.

Dan looked at his daughter and he thought of the name on the pathology form, where Sharon Hall's body had been identified.

Ralph Edward Hall, father of the deceased.

Father.

Dan stroked his daughter's hair while she slept. He couldn't stop himself picturing Mandy twenty years from now, walking along a narrow city street at night, hearing the rising roar of a car's engine on the road behind her. Couldn't stop himself thinking of how he would feel when he stood beside the gurney in the mortuary and the plastic sheet was pulled back.

"I'm sorry," Dan said, his voice barely more than a whisper, not even sure who the apology was for. He knelt beside Mandy's bed for a few minutes in the light of the table lamp, relishing the silence and the warmth and the presence of his sleeping daughter.

"Hey, Roland," Dan said softly, easing the stuffed toy rat from beneath the pillow. He had disliked the toy ever since a well-meaning but clearly sociopathic aunt had introduced it into Mandy's life on her fourth birthday. Mandy, of course, had instantly fallen in love with the damn thing. Dan lay Roland Rat across the top of the pillow where Mandy would be able to find him if she woke up in the night.

He leaned across and kissed the top of his daughter's head, went to the bedroom door and took one last, long look at the small sleeping form beneath the blanket before quietly going back downstairs.

"How was she?" Becky asked.

Dan gently lifted Becky's feet so that he could sit on the sofa with her. He sat back and lay her feet across his thighs. Becky rolled her shoulders and shifted position so that she was looking up at him instead of looking straight at the TV.

"Sleeping," Dan said.

Becky looked at his face. "You okay, honey?"

Dan blinked, looked at the TV. "Just tired."

Becky moved her feet in his lap. "Anything I can do about that?"

"What about the cottage pie?" Dan asked. He could feel the weariness and the fear ebbing away. A smile touched the corners of his mouth. "Won't it spoil if we leave it in the oven for too long?"

Becky moved her right foot a little higher. "Five more minutes won't hurt."

Dan looked down at her mischievous grin. "Five?"

She bit her lower lip and batted her eyelashes at him. "We can try for three if you're really worried about it."

"Come here," Dan said, pulling his wife into his arms.

CHAPTER 12

Sunday morning, quarter past nine. Sixteen hours since Sharon Hall had been killed. Detective Sergeant Dan Blacksmith was standing in front of a wall-mounted whiteboard in one of the CID briefing rooms at the Campbell Road station. In front of him, in a small semicircle of cheap, stackable, moulded-plastic chairs were three members of Humberside CID. Each of them was holding their own copy of the Sharon Hall pathology report and photocopied pages of Dan's notes.

On the whiteboard, Dan had already written Sharon Hall's name, age, approximate time of death, and the name of the street where she had been killed. He had used a non-permanent black marker pen, the same type of pen that they always used. The pen's ink never completely vanished from the whiteboard when it was erased, despite the claim of non-permanence, and so the board bore the faded, grey ghosts of dozens of previous cases scrawled all over its glossy white surface.

"Sharon Hall," Dan said. "Twenty-four years old. Waitress at *Caffe Bar Gaspari* on Hobbs Road. She was struck by a car while walking along Old Park Lane at approximately five-twenty yesterday evening, subsequently run over by the same car, and strangled to death soon after." He looked at his audience. Rick Price had his own notepad open across his left thigh, with his left ankle crossed over his right knee. In the chair to Rick's right, Detective Chief Inspector Harry West was listening to Dan, not looking down at the paperwork piled in his lap. The Detective Inspector sitting to Rick's left was Kathleen Schrader. She was listening and reading simultaneously, her eyes constantly flicking back and forth between Dan Blacksmith and the pages in her hands.

"You're assuming the driver killed her?" DI Schrader said, looking up from the pathology report.

"The driver or a passenger from the car that hit her. The marks on her neck were clear enough for a conclusive hand measurement to be taken, so we know the killer is male, average to large. Apart from that, we're waiting on the results of a forensic exam of the car that hit her."

Rick Price leaned forward. "The car was reported stolen and returned either side of the incident. It's a Jaguar XJS that belongs to William Mason."

"Triple-Eight Haulage," Schrader said.

Dan said, "DC Price and I visited the Masons yesterday evening, and SOCO Pat Davies was in attendance to examine the Jag and print the Masons."

Harry West sat back, listening.

"Is any member of the Mason household a current suspect?" Schrader asked.

Dan glanced down at his open notepad. "William Mason had taken his wife's car to a local garage and was either driving that car or at the Triple-Eight main office around the time of the incident. His wife was on their home phone reporting the stolen Jag at approximately the time of the incident. The only other member of the Mason household is their son, Thomas. He returned to the house while DC Price and I were on the drive looking at the Jag, at approximately eight o'clock last night."

"Interesting," said Schrader. "Alibi?"

"We are going to check it out, but he thinks he was in a guitar shop at around five yesterday." Dan turned back a page in his notepad. "Bailey's Guitars. Apparently someone called Chad who works at the shop will remember Tom Mason was there."

DI Schrader tapped her pen against her finger. "He *thinks* he was there? Why isn't he sure about it?"

"Tom Mason is a bit of a space cadet," Rick said.

Schrader shook her head. "I don't buy this. The car is reported stolen, then returned, but nobody saw anyone take it or bring it back. All three of the people at the address have alibis, with the son's being possibly a rather shaky one."

Dan said, "The neighbour in the house opposite witnessed the Jag leaving the Masons' property, which they described as *shooting out of the drive backwards, really fast*'.

"Did they see who was driving the car?"

"Not possible to identify or even count the occupants of the car from where they were standing, apparently."

"Reliable witness?"

"Drunk on tequila when I spoke to her at about twenty to nine."

Schrader rolled her eyes. "Marvellous. Haulage tycoons, pot smokers and alcoholics, all on the same street."

Dan continued to work through the details of every conversation and piece of information from the previous evening. When he had finished, the board behind him was a web of linked names, places, objects and times, and his throat was dry and sore despite the pint and a half of water he had sipped throughout the briefing. He encouraged questions and speculation, no restriction on how useful or ridiculous anyone might consider those comments.

DCI Harry West had remained silent throughout the briefing. When it was clear that all the information had been shared, he sat forward and cleared his throat. "Are you taking this one over, Kath?"

Schrader quickly flipped through the notes in her hands. "I'm more than happy to let Dan continue gathering information." She looked up at Dan. "You need to interview Sharon Hall's parents."

Dan nodded. "I know."

Schrader tapped her pen against the top sheet of paper. "Was the Jag actually stolen, or do we think the theft is part of a cover story?"

"Unless Mrs Mason is covering for her husband or her son, there's no obvious motive for that. Plus, there was the partial car reg written in blood at the scene. If the Masons are involved in the incident, and have gone to the trouble of concocting a phantom car theft cover story, why would they write half the Jag's registration on the kerb by the body?"

Schrader shrugged. "There's no proof that the victim didn't write it."

"Sharon Hall was left-handed. Her left hand was covered in blood but her left shoulder was dislocated and seriously injured. Also, she was killed by strangulation, not left to die from the injuries sustained from the multiple vehicle impacts. The available evidence strongly supports the theory that her killer wrote the car reg, probably after strangling her to death."

Schrader nodded, frowning as she considered what Dan was telling her. "Which turns this into some sort of conspiracy against the Masons, rather than an accident gone wrong or a deliberate attack on Sharon Hall." She looked at the board behind Dan. "And then we have the fact that Thomas Mason knew the victim, and is in a band with the victim's boyfriend."

"Yes," Dan said. "Which is why we need to check out his alibi. Also, the results of the forensic exam of the Jag will be with us today, which could give us some significant leads."

"The Coke can," Schrader said, looking at the page of notes. "Supposedly left in the car by the car thief." She shook her head. "A car thief who not only returns the car to the owner, but writes the registration at the crime scene and leaves a can of drink in the car that he stole."

"Weird, isn't it?" Rick said. "It's like there's almost too much evidence but none of it actually helps."

"Not yet," Dan said. "We should hear from Pat Davies very soon."

DI Schrader stood up. "Dan, I want you to interview the victim's parents this morning. I'll contact Pat, and I'm also going to pay a visit to the Triple-Eight office to check out William Mason's alibi for Saturday evening."

"Okay," Dan said. "I'll take Rick with me to interview the Halls." He looked at his watch. "There is one other thing, that might be related to this case."

"What's that?" Schrader asked.

"At some point yesterday, most likely when I left my car parked outside the Mason house, someone wrote two words on the boot in lettering that was a very similar style to the way the car reg was written at the crime scene."

"Really?" Schrader looked unconvinced. "Probably just kids. What did they write on there?"

"*Very cold.* Neat capital letters. I haven't wiped it off, in case it's relevant."

Schrader laughed. "I doubt it's relevant, Dan. Sounds like an unimaginative weather report to me."

***

Rick pulled the seatbelt across his chest and fastened it. "If she wasn't so gorgeous, she'd be really annoying."

Dan turned the key, started the BMW's engine. "You should tell her how you feel. Could be the start of something special."

"The start of a search for a new career."

"I almost didn't notice you staring at her through the entire briefing."

"I don't understand why she's going to the Triple-Eight office to check out Bill Mason's story. We could have done that."

"Because she's the DI and she gets to choose who interviews the grieving parents."

"Same reason we got the call last night."

"No. That was because it was called in as a hit-and-run with possible complications. Nobody would send a DI to something like that."

Rick sighed. "It's going to be shit, isn't it?"

"All around," Dan said.

Sharon Hall's parents lived on an estate not far from the golf course at Sutton Park. Dan and Rick left the unmarked BMW on the road outside the Halls' two-storey semi-detached house a few minutes before ten thirty a.m., the time they had agreed when Dan had phoned earlier and spoken to Ralph Hall. Sharon had been an only child, *their only child*. Dan was thinking about that when he pressed his thumb against the button of the doorbell, held it while he listened to the chimes from beyond the front door, and waited while he automatically counted the seven seconds until the door was opened.

"Mr Hall," Dan said. "I'm Detective Sergeant Dan Blacksmith from Humberside CID. I spoke to you earlier. This is Detective Constable Rick Price. I'm very sorry for your loss and I promise we'll make this as quick as we possibly can."

Ralph Hall nodded slowly, like he was hearing the words, but only as sounds with no meaning or context. His eyes were sunken and red-rimmed as if he had been staring at a pinpoint of light for twenty-four hours straight.

He said, "Come in," and the words sounded empty and alien, words that were so painful to say aloud that he lived only to forget them.

Dan and Rick removed their shoes and followed Ralph Hall into the lounge. It was generic suburbia, unmemorable furniture surrounded by walls of muted civility. Nothing in the room screamed of the desperate, appalling loss suffered by its two occupants.

Ralph Hall sat on the sofa next to his wife, Jane. They could have been sitting on the sofa since the previous evening, and Dan did not dismiss that notion as implausible because he had interviewed the recently bereaved on many occasions. He knew that the stock armchair psychologist explanation was that everyone dealt with grief in their own way. In Dan Blacksmith's experience, the recently bereaved did not deal with grief; they endured it minute by minute without ever understanding what they were experiencing or how they were managing to cope with it.

The room was an unassuming pastel backdrop and the two people on the sofa were monochrome in their misery, grey and still, drained of energy and devoid of hope.

"Mrs Hall," Dan said, as he and Rick took seats next to the sofa. "I'm very sorry for your loss. I fully understand that this is a difficult time for you and, as I told your husband, I promise this will not take long. From the evidence we have obtained, it is very likely that your daughter's death was not an accident."

Jane Hall rocked slightly forward, her hand tightening around her husband's.

"Are you saying…" She slowly shook her head, forcing the words out. "Sharon was murdered?"

"We are currently in the middle of the investigation. There is sufficient evidence for us to investigate it as a deliberate act." Dan glanced down at the fresh sheet in his notepad. At the top of the page he had already written the date and the words *Sharon Hall - parents interview.* "Did Sharon mention anything recently, in the last few weeks, that might have made you think that she had been threatened or had an argument with anyone?"

Jane and Ralph Hall looked at one another, both shaking their heads, both wearing expressions that confirmed their worst, unspoken fears that the circumstances of their daughter's death were even more dreadful than they already knew.

"No," Ralph Hall said, "We never heard her say anything like that."

"Have you received any phone calls here that might have seemed strange? Callers hanging up without speaking, or callers claiming they phoned the wrong number?"

Again, the Halls looked at each, shaking their heads.

Dan nodded, not wanting to force them to speak to confirm the negative response. "Have any of the people you know as your daughter's friends or acquaintances suddenly stopped calling, or otherwise apparently lost contact with her?"

They shook their heads again. Jane Hall, in addition to already looking desperately unhappy, was starting to look confused and upset by the questions.

Rick touched Dan's sleeve and pointed towards a small framed photograph on one of the shelves of a bookcase against the wall. There were at least a dozen photographs, all of Sharon Hall at various ages, but only one that included another person.

"Who is that, in the photo?" Dan asked. "The girl in the ball gown standing next to your daughter."

"Oh, what was her name, Ralph?" Jane Hall asked. "That photo is very old." She pulled a damp handkerchief from the cuff of her blouse sleeve and dabbed her eyes. "That was the day of the end-of-school ball."

"I honestly can't remember," said Ralph Hall. "Long time ago. Eight years or more. I'm sure they never kept in touch after they left school."

Dan looked at Rick. "I doubt she has anything to do with this."

"Same school," Rick said. "Tom Mason might know her name."

"Tom Mason," Ralph said. "Sharon has mentioned that name recently."

"What did she say about him?" Dan asked.

"Not much, really. She mentioned him being in Rob's band, but that was a few months ago. I think she mentioned his name because she thought we would remember him from their schooldays."

"But you didn't remember the name?"

Ralph shook his head. "I know his father's name, but then I expect everyone in Hull knows the name William Mason."

"Do you know William Mason personally?"

"No, I don't. Can't say I've ever met his son either."

Dan jotted down a brief description of the girl standing next to Sharon Hall in the photo.

"You are not aware of any recent problems between Sharon and Rob Musgrave?" Dan said. "No mention of any jealous former girlfriends, nothing at all like that?"

Ralph and Jane looked at each other, then they both looked at Dan and shook their heads. Jane Hall covered her mouth with her hand, fresh tears spilling down her cheeks. Ralph wrapped his arm around his wife's shoulders, pulling her close to him.

"No," he said. "They were very happy. Sharon was completely in love with him."

"I'm very sorry," Dan said. "Thank you very much for your time. We don't have any more questions."

He and Rick rose from their seats and made their way unaccompanied to the front door. They pulled their shoes back on in silence, not speaking until they were outside on the street with the Halls' front door closed behind them.

Rick blew out a deep sigh, his breath clouding in the cold air. "Did we get anything else from that apart from what feels like the kind of awkward guilt I'd expect to get if

I had pissed on their carpet?"

"I don't think so. And I feel exactly the same."

"You're going to tell me this never gets easier, aren't you?"

"No need."

"I thought so."

Dan approached the BMW from behind. He looked at the two words on the boot before unlocking the car. It now seemed even more unlikely to him that they were in any way related to the case. He opened the driver's side door and climbed into the car while Rick was getting into the passenger seat.

Dan started the engine and picked up the radio mic. "This is One-Six Charlie Delta. Control, is there any update for us? Over."

"One-Six Charlie Delta, please hold, over."

Dan looked out of the windscreen at the street where Sharon Hall had probably lived for most, if not all, of her twenty-four years. Just a street, like thousands of others.

The radio crackled briefly. "One-Six Charlie Delta, patching to DI Schrader. DI Schrader, please go ahead, over."

Schrader's voice came out of the radio. She sounded eager, pleased, poised for a quick victory. "Dan, it's Kath Schrader. Please confirm your location."

Dan gave Schrader the name of the road where he was parked.

"How far are you from the Mason residence?"

Dan looked at Rick. Rick held both hands up, fingers splayed.

"Ten minutes door-to-door."

"Very good. I want you to proceed directly to the Mason residence and apprehend Thomas Mason. The prints from the Coke can were a definite match, repeat a definite match."

Dan turned to look at Rick. He could see his own

surprise reflected in Rick's eyes. "Please confirm the prints match *Thomas* Mason, over."

"The prints match Thomas Mason."

Dan put the car in gear and pulled away from the kerb. "Attending Mason residence immediately. One-Six Charlie Delta out."

CHAPTER 13

Deb Mason opened the door while Dan was still hammering on it with his fist.

"Mrs Mason, I need to speak to Thomas as soon as possible."

"Oh," Deb said. "Why?" She looked past Dan at Rick Price, standing at the corner of the house where the gravel path joined the drive. "He isn't here at the moment."

"Do you know where Thomas is, Mrs Mason?"

"He said he was going to band practice." She looked at her watch. "I think they start at eleven."

Dan checked his own watch. "It's five-to now. Did he take your car?"

"Yes, he did. Can I ask what this is about?"

"We need to take a statement from him," Dan said. "At the station."

"Is this to do with the examination of the Jag?"

"We just need to take a formal statement."

"He will be at band practice until two or three." Deb Mason shook her head. "But he might not be back until much later."

"Do you know where his band practises?"

"It's a community hall in Spring Bank, near the school."

"Do you know which school?"

"I'm not sure. The primary school, I think."

Dan took a card out of his wallet and handed it to Deb Mason. "Please, if Thomas returns, contact me on this number and ask him to wait here until I arrive."

"Is he in trouble?"

"Honest answer, Mrs Mason, is that he could be. But the best thing he can do is talk to me as soon as possible."

"Tom didn't take the Jag yesterday. I know he didn't."

"Thank you, Mrs Mason. Please call me if he comes home."

Dan walked to the end of the gravel path where Rick was waiting.

"Apparently he's gone to band practice."

"Seriously?"

"Community hall near a primary school in Spring Bank. Do you know where that is."

Rick nodded slowly, thinking. "Yeah, I reckon I do." He looked at the empty drive. "Did he take the Fiesta?"

"Yes, according to his mother."

"Where's the Jag?"

"I didn't ask. I'm guessing Bill Mason drove it to work."

Rick looked at Dan as they walked down the drive towards the BMW. "You still don't think Tom Mason did it."

Dan shook his head. "So far, all we have to go on is word of mouth information and some fingerprints on a Coke can."

"Thomas Mason knew Sharon Hall. He most likely had some kind of long-term, unrequited feelings for her. The car that was used to run her over belongs to his father. His prints were on a Coke can that his father said hadn't been in the car before yesterday evening."

Dan walked around the BMW, glanced at the words on the boot, and opened the door. "How many girls did you fancy in school, and how many of them did you run over and strangle eight years later?"

"None so far."

Dan waited until they were both sitting inside the car before continuing. "I'm struggling to fit a motive to an elaborate scenario where Thomas Mason took his father's car, used it in a premeditated hit-and-run murder, left a Coke can in the car and then timed his return to the house to coincide with us being there. And don't forget how we both thought his behaviour was that of a genuinely innocent man. If he wanted to be caught so badly that he left the car reg at the scene and the Coke can in the Jag, why was he so convincingly innocent when I was questioning him?"

"Okay, I don't know," Rick said. "Maybe he's done one too many spliffs."

"Damn. Of course."

"What?"

Dan picked up the radio mic. "Control, this is One-Six Charlie Delta. Over."

"Go ahead, One-Six Charlie Delta. Over."

"Can you patch me to the Forensic Investigation Unit, SOCO Patricia Davies' extension. Over."

"Patching your call to SOCO Patricia Davies, over."

The radio crackled, the sound of empty air altering to the tone of a ringing telephone.

Dan counted the rings, got to five before the call was picked up.

"FI Unit, Pat Davies speaking."

"Pat, it's Dan. Can you confirm the prints on the Coke can in Bill Mason's Jag belong to Thomas Mason?"

"Yes, they're definitely Thomas Mason's prints. Thumb and all four fingers. Clear, no doubt whatsoever that they're a match."

"No other prints on there?"

"None. And before you ask me if that's strange, no it

isn't. Cans are almost always machine filled and packed. If the shop displays them in the original wholesale cardboard tray, then there's no need for anyone else to have ever handled the can."

"So he didn't share the drink with anyone else?"

"I would say not, unless he poured it into a separate container for them."

"Did you find anything else in the Jag, any prints that didn't match members of the Mason family?"

"Nothing at all. Just the Coke can."

"What about the blood on the side of the driver's seat?"

"It matched the victim's. Handprints and smears were made by a hand wearing a glove. No prints in the bloodstains."

"Were Thomas Mason's prints anywhere else on the inside of the Jag?"

"No, they weren't."

"I don't want to lead you, Pat, but did you smell anything obvious while you were checking the interior of the Jag?"

"Still has that new car smell, just about, but that isn't what you mean, is it?"

"No. Go on..."

On her phone line, over the radio, Pat Davies said, "If a marijuana smoker had driven the Jag for more than a few minutes on Saturday evening, it would have retained the odour of that specific class B drug for at least twenty-four hours after. The car had no trace of that type of odour."

"Thanks, Pat. A lot to ask, but could I have all of that in a written report as soon as possible."

"I'm already writing it for you."

"Thanks, that's much appreciated."

"As I said, good luck solving this one."

"Yeah. Bye, Pat."

Dan ended the call.

Rick drummed his fingers against the dashboard. "So

now he didn't do it? If he didn't, then how did the Coke can get in the Jag?"

Dan started the car and pulled away from the kerb. "The same way the car reg got on the kerb. Whoever killed Sharon Hall put it there."

Rick whistled softly. "It's a fit-up targeting Bill Mason's family. It has to be."

"Maybe. What's the quickest route to Spring Bank?"

***

Dan parked the BMW in one of the faded white rectangles painted on the cracked, uneven tarmac surface of the community hall car park. He turned off the engine and looked at the only other car that was parked there, a rusting four-door Morris Marina in a fetching shade of mustard, that somehow had all the components of a complete drum kit shoehorned inside it.

"Mrs Mason's Fiesta isn't here," Rick said.

"Wait here. I'm going to see who's inside the hall. Maybe Tom Mason went to pick someone else up on his way here. If he turns up, don't let him leave."

"Got it." Rick looked out of the window at the mustard Marina. "What if Schrader calls on the radio?"

"Tell her we're attempting to locate Thomas Mason."

"What about the new Jag evidence, the lack of weed fumes?"

"Don't mention it for now. I want to see it in writing before handing it to Schrader."

Dan got out of the car and walked around to the front entrance of the community hall. To one side of the door there was an ancient cast-iron litter bin, tilted a few inches to one side where it had probably been nudged more than a couple of times by the cars of slightly less than vigilant drivers.

Dan tried the handle and found the door was unlocked.

The door gave a long, fatigued creak as he pushed it open. The main floor space of the hall was empty. The wooden floor was marked out in white paint with the lines of a badminton court, and there were several stacks of plastic chairs against one side wall. The underside of the roof was definitely high enough to allow a fairly unhindered game of badminton to be played, although there was an exposed timber truss directly above the court running parallel to where the net would be when it was in use.

At the far end of the hall was a wooden stage raised three feet above the height of the floor. On the stage was a single microphone stand with a long lead plugged into an amplifier on top of a large speaker cabinet. Sitting on the edge of the stage were two young men who were around the same age as Tom Mason and Rob Musgrave. They stared silently at Dan as he walked across the empty hall floor towards them. Both had unkempt dark hair that looked too overtly messy to be the product of neglect. The one on the left was holding a pair of drumsticks.

Dan took out his warrant card and his notepad. "I'm Detective Sergeant Dan Blacksmith, Humberside CID. I'm trying to find Thomas Mason. Are you expecting him to turn up here today?"

The dark-haired young man holding the drumsticks looked at his companion before speaking. "Is this about Rob's girlfriend?"

"What do you know about her?"

"Nothing much. We know she's dead."

"How do you know that?" Dan asked.

"Tom phoned me this morning," said the other dark-haired man. "He said he'd tried to talk to Rob. Neither of them are coming to band practice, which is hardly surprising."

"Did Tom Mason tell you anything else?"

"He said she was killed in a hit-and-run accident. Said someone stole his old man's Jag and the police think it was the same car that ran her over. Is that true?"

"It's still an active investigation," Dan said. "I can't discuss the details of the case."

"Why are you looking for Tom?"

"We need to take a formal statement from him, that's all."

"He won't be coming here today. He said he was going to get some fresh air, clear his head, try to relax."

Dan looked around the hall. "But you two both turned up."

"Sunday," said the drummer. "What else are we going to do?"

"Can I ask you a few more questions?"

"I suppose so."

"How well do you know Rob Musgrave and Tom Mason?"

The drummer looked at his companion again. Dan guessed that the other young man was the band's singer.

"I've known Rob for about three years," the drummer said. "I've only known Tom since he joined the band, which was about six months ago."

"Same with me for how long I've known Tom," said the singer. "But I've known Rob for ages. We were in school together."

"John Blair?"

"Yeah."

"Do you know which school Tom Mason went to?"

"Same one as me and Rob. When I said I've only known him for six months, I meant as in talked to him. I never spoke to him in school, but then I never spoke to hardly anyone outside our year."

"Do you know anything at all about what he was like in school?"

"Yeah, an idiot like everyone else in school."

"What do you mean?"

"The usual stuff, but some of the kids he hung around

with were proper head-cases. Another reason I never talked to anyone outside our year."

"When you say *head-cases...?*"

"Just muppets, you know. The sort of kids who always had 'could do better' on their reports, when what the teachers really meant was 'disruptive assholes'. Like I said, idiots, just like everyone else."

"I see. And how well did you know Sharon Hall?"

"I never met her," said the drummer.

"I met her once," said the singer. "When she was out with Rob in town one night."

"Did you talk to her?"

"I think I said 'hello', but that was about it."

"How long ago was that?"

"Couple of months back."

"Did she and Rob seem happy to you?"

"Extremely."

Dan looked down at his notepad, then back up again. "Do you know which school Sharon Hall went to?"

"She went to John Blair too," said the singer. "Never spoke to her in school. Way out of my league."

"Could I take your names, purely so that I have a record of who I spoke to?"

"Duncan Pritchard," said the drummer.

"Lewis Cooper."

"Thank you for your time," Dan said.

Back at the car, Dan sat in the driver's seat and looked at the notes he had just taken.

"Nothing useful. One of them went to John Blair but he didn't know much about Tom Mason or Sharon Hall. He said she was 'out of his league', so he never talked to her, and he said Tom Mason was 'an idiot like everyone else'."

"And Mason isn't coming here today?"

"No, but I think I know where we can find him." Dan started the car, put it in gear. "How do we get to the park with the lake in it?"

"Follow this road and take the next left. Are you hoping to find Tom Mason at the park?"

"It's where he goes to relax."

"If he drove there from his house, I'd bet he parked up near the west side of the lake. Plenty of roadside parking there."

"How far away?"

"Maybe just over ten minutes from here."

"Okay," Dan said. "We'll go with your bet."

CHAPTER 14

Twelve minutes later, Rick Price spotted a red Ford Fiesta parked at the side of the road outside a corner shop, at the junction with a dead-end single-lane street that ran along the western edge of the park.

"There," he said. "Looks like you were right."

Dan drove on until he found a parking space at the side of the main road. "Did you make a note of the Fiesta's registration last night?"

"Yeah." Rick looked at his notepad. "It's Mrs Mason's car."

"I want you to wait near the shop and keep an eye on the Fiesta. If I miss him in the park, or he sees me and makes a run for the car, you can apprehend him."

"Are we arresting him?"

"I'd prefer to talk to him first, but if he runs then he's making the decision for us."

Rick crossed the road and found a lamppost to lean against outside the corner shop, a decent vantage point where he had a clear view of the red Fiesta. Dan carried on walking along the dead-end road until he reached the entrance to the park. A single path led away to the left, following the gentle curve of the lake's edge. The water was dark, no ice on the motionless surface despite the biting cold of the still morning air. A hundred yards ahead of him, Dan could see the first lakeside bench seat. A single, dark figure was sitting on it. Dan picked up his pace and strode towards the bench. The closer he came to it, the less the figure looked like Thomas Mason. It was a man, but not the scrawny young man Dan was looking for. Thirty feet away, Dan still couldn't see the man's face but he didn't need to see it to be able to tell that the man was older and thicker set than Tom Mason.

The man on the bench reached deep into a plastic bag and took out a small chunk of bread. He tore part of it away and lobbed it out onto the water where several mallards and swans were waiting.

Dan walked behind the bench to avoid interfering with the bird-feeding. He didn't say anything to the man, didn't ask if he had seen anyone in the park matching Tom Mason's description, because he had already spotted the next bench, which had an altogether far more likely looking figure reclining on it.

Dan walked directly along the path towards the bench where Tom Mason was sitting back, legs outstretched in front of him and fragrant smoke rising from the thickly packed roll-up that he was holding between the first two fingers of his right hand. He didn't move until Dan stood next to the bench and spoke to him.

"Mind if I join you?"

Tom Mason looked up at Dan, glanced at the cigarette in his own hand, and said, "Oops." He made no attempt to throw the joint away, hide it, or eat it.

Dan sat on the bench next to Tom.

"Put that out."

"This?" Tom held the cigarette up in front of his face.

"Yes. Stub it out on the ground and leave it there."

"Okay."

"Do you drink Coca-Cola?"

"Sometimes."

"Did you drink any yesterday?"

"No."

"You sound very sure about that."

"I know I didn't drink any Coke yesterday."

"Did your father tell you what the forensic investigator found in the Jag?"

"No. I didn't talk to him much at all last night."

"There was an open, empty Coke can in there."

"Really?"

"With your fingerprints all over it."

Tom Mason shook his head. "Not possible."

"And yet, there it was."

"I didn't put it there."

Dan looked out across the lake. Tom Mason made no attempt to leave, just sat there staring at the side of Dan's face.

"When did you last drink a can of Coke?" Dan asked.

"In the week. Tuesday or Wednesday."

"What did you do with the can?"

"Stamped on it and chucked it in a bin."

"Do you always do that, stamp on the empty can?"

"Not always."

"When was the most recent time you had a can and you didn't stamp on it?"

Tom exhaled, shaking his head. "I don't know. Probably band practice last weekend."

"Go on. What did you do with the can?"

"Dropped it in the bin outside the place where we practise."

"The Spring Bank community hall?"

"Yeah." Tom nodded, narrowing his eyes. "How did you know that?"

"I was there earlier, talking to Duncan Pritchard and Lewis Cooper. Your mother told me that you said you were going there."

"I changed my mind."

"How often is that bin outside the hall emptied?"

"No idea. Maybe weekly."

Dan jotted a couple of notes on his pad, flipped back and forth through several pages.

"Have you spoken to Rob Musgrave in the last twenty-four hours?"

"Phoned him this morning."

"And…?"

"He was really upset."

Dan nodded. "Hold out one of your hands."

Tom Mason's eyes went wide with fearful anticipation. "You're not going to handcuff me, are you?"

"No, just hold out your hand, palm down, fingers splayed."

Tom held his hand low down, a few inches above the surface of the bench between himself and Dan. Dan held his own hand above Tom's, noting that Tom's fingers were marginally longer than his own but also that Tom's hand was slender, narrower across the wrist and palm than Dan's.

"I need to take you to see the pathologist who attended the crime scene."

"Why?"

"I want him to measure your hands and compare them with the measurements of the hands of the man who killed Sharon Hall."

Tom swallowed hard, pushed his left hand through the heavy curtain of dark hair that had fallen across the side of his face.

"Okay," he said, but he didn't sound too sure about it.

"You want to help me, don't you? You want to help me catch whoever killed Sharon?"

"Yes."

"Come on, then. My car is parked near yours."

Walking back to the car with Tom Mason, Dan noticed

that the bench was empty where the man had been feeding the birds.

"How often do you come to this park?" Dan asked.

"Quite a lot."

"Do you always sit at the same bench?"

"Hardly ever the same one. Sometimes the park's really busy and you have to walk a long way to even find a bench. In the summer, I usually just sit on the grass in the shade."

"Do you come here with anyone else?"

"Sometimes. Usually on my own."

"Did you ever come here with Sharon Hall?"

"No." Tom looked up at the sky, then back out over the lake. "I never had that kind of relationship with her. We were in school together for five years, but she didn't fancy me and there was no way I'd ever ask her out. We both knew that, I suppose, which meant there was no pressure just being friends."

"How did you feel about her being in a relationship with Rob Musgrave?"

Tom looked at Dan as they walked. "I didn't kill her."

"Then tell me how you felt."

"Rob was always the cool kid in school, the pretty boy, you know? I didn't really know him, but I knew about him. He went out with a whole string of girls while he was at John Blair, but he didn't start seeing Sharon until about a year ago."

"Do you know how they met?"

"You mean how they started going out together? No, I don't know. The first I knew about it was when she was talking to me at the café and she said her new boyfriend was in a band."

"She was comfortable talking to you about her personal life?"

"Like I said, we were friends. I think she saw me as some sort of charity case, but at the same time she was happy taking the piss out of me because of the Triple-Eight inheritance."

Dan walked out of the park onto the street. He could see the lamppost ahead, with Rick Price leaning against it. Dan walked over to where Rick was standing, with Tom following along behind him.

"Tom has volunteered to come with us to see Nigel Hansom at the pathology lab. We're going to get his hands measured for a comparison with the assailant's."

"Did you ask him about the other evidence?"

"He said he didn't put the can in the Jag."

Rick shrugged. He looked at Tom. "Any idea how it got in there?"

"No, sorry."

Dan crossed the road and walked towards the BMW. He could see the top of the boot, and as he came closer he could see that one of the words that had been written in the grime had been partially obliterated, as if someone walking past the rear of the car had dragged one hand across the letters of the word VERY, striking it out with four finger-thick lines.

"Did you see who did this?" he asked Rick.

Rick looked at the boot. "No. I was watching the park gate and the Fiesta."

"Cold," Dan said. "No longer *very* cold."

"Probably just kids," Rick said. "Unlikely to be anything else."

"Maybe."

"You don't still think it's related to the case, do you?"

"Not unless whoever is doing it is at least one step ahead of us and knows where we're going to be leaving the car."

"Like I said, it's unlikely."

Dan unlocked the car. "Tom, could you get in the back, please?"

Tom opened the rear door on the passenger side and climbed into the car.

When he had joined them in the car, Rick said, "Did you ask Tom about the girl in the photo?"

"Not yet."

"What photo?" Tom asked.

Dan said, "Sharon's parents have a photograph of their daughter and another girl, both wearing end-of-school ball gowns. The other girl in the picture looks a little shorter than Sharon, dark hair that could be long but she has it tied back in the photo. Quite slim, very pretty."

Dan looked in the rear-view mirror and saw the clear expression of recognition on Tom Mason's face.

"Who is she, Tom? Is she likely to be involved in this?"

"I doubt it," Tom said. "But then, I haven't seen her since she left school in seventy-seven. The times I talked to Sharon about school, she never mentioned her, so I don't think they kept in touch."

"You sound as though you think that is a bit strange."

"Not really. Just, they were pretty good friends in school."

"Do you remember her name? Sharon's parents didn't."

"Yeah," Tom said. "Dee Collins."

Rick was holding his notepad open on his knee while Dan drove. He wrote the name and paused with his pen hovering over the page. "Just Dee, or is it short for something else?"

"Just Dee, that's her full name, and I don't know if she has a middle name or not."

Dan pulled away from the kerb into the light Sunday traffic. "She probably isn't involved with this at all, but we'll check her out anyway."

CHAPTER 15

Just before midday on Monday, November eighteenth, Raymond Hughes took off his black leather driving gloves and gave his hair a quick check in the rear-view mirror before getting out of his three-year-old Ford Sierra. He left the gloves shoved into the narrow door pocket, preferring to keep his hands warm in the pockets of his pinstripe suit trousers as he walked across the car park towards the shops on Prospect Street.

It only took him a few minutes to reach the shoe shop called *Bright Soles*, where he had no intention of buying any shoes. The old-fashioned jangly metallic device on the door always caused him to cringe a little as he entered. Did the shoe shop really need a jarring audible warning that a customer had entered? Raymond didn't believe that it did, but then he was in wholesale, not retail, and he was high enough up the management ladder that he never had to look at customers, let alone talk to them or try to sell them anything.

He made his way directly to the sales counter, pointedly ignoring the other customers who were browsing or trying on shoes. The young woman behind the counter watched

Raymond as he walked up to her. She didn't ask him if she could help, didn't say anything until he spoke to her.

"Is Dee Collins working today?"

She didn't smile, didn't scowl. "Yes, she is."

Raymond looked over his shoulder. There was a salesman talking to a male customer, no sign of any other staff in the shop.

"Where is she?"

"Getting some shoes from the stockroom."

Raymond nodded. He pushed his sleeve back and looked at his watch.

"She won't be long," said the young woman behind the counter. Raymond thought he caught a flash of amusement in her eyes before she glanced away.

He turned to one side, to watch the doorway that led to the stockroom but also to avoid any further conversation with the woman behind the counter. He had spoken to her before on more than one occasion, and he wasn't entirely happy that she not only recognised him but was becoming familiar enough with him to find his visits to the shop vaguely amusing.

Raymond saw Dee walk out of the stockroom carrying two shoe boxes. She took the boxes over to a middle-aged woman who was waiting on one of the rectangular vinyl customer seats, opened one of the boxes and handed the woman a pair of black high-heeled sandals. Raymond waited while the woman tried on the first pair of sandals, discussed them at length with Dee, and then repeated the whole process with the second pair of sandals.

At last, the customer seemed to have made up her mind and chosen which pair of sandals she was going to buy. Dee boxed both pairs back up, handed one box to the customer and took the other box back to the stockroom. When she returned from the stockroom, she walked over to the counter and stood in front of Raymond.

"Hello, Mr Hughes. How are you today?"

"Fine thanks, Dee. I was rather hoping that you might be able to help me out again. My wife and I will both be unavoidably working late this evening and we haven't been able to book our usual babysitter."

Dee glanced at the young woman behind the counter. "That's quite short notice. When do you need me to be there?"

"Half seven until ten."

Dee sighed, shrugged, then smiled and said, "I might have to charge you double for the inconvenience." When Raymond frowned, but before he started to speak, Dee said, "Only joking. It will be fine."

"That's great," Raymond said with considerable relief. "I really appreciate you helping us out again."

"It's only a few hours. No big deal."

"Half seven," Raymond said. "You can be there by then?"

"I might be a few minutes earlier than that, depending on the buses."

Raymond nodded eagerly. "I'll look forward to seeing you later, then."

"Sure. See you later, Mr Hughes."

The young woman behind the counter watched Raymond Hughes walk out of the shop. The old-fashioned customer alert jangled noisily as he opened the door and closed it behind him.

"Babysitting again?" she said to Dee. "Seriously?"

Dee winked at her. "Easy money."

"How many times is that this year?"

"I don't keep count. I just take the cash."

"He looks a bit old to have kids that need babysitting."

"Nine-year-old twins. A boy and a girl."

"Not really babysitting, then."

"No. I just sit and watch his TV, drink his tea, and eat his biscuits."

"How much do you get for doing that?"

Dee waggled her finger and laughed. "I can't tell you that, can I? Customer confidentiality."

"How do you know him?"

"We used to be next-door neighbours, back when I was still in school."

"Used to be?"

"He moved house."

"Where does he live now?"

"In a bigger one."

"And you're happy giving up a whole evening just sitting in his big house watching telly?"

Dee winked again. "Easy money."

***

Dee knocked on the solid walnut back door of Ray's large detached house at twenty-five minutes past seven. Four rhythmic taps with the back of her right hand, the same way she always knocked on that door. She remembered when she and Ray had been neighbours, back when she had called him Mr Hughes because that was who he was to her, not because she was faking formality in front of her co-workers at the shoe shop.

Raymond opened the door and stood to one side to let Dee into the utility room. There were several pairs of boots and shoes near the door, a washing machine and tumble dryer beneath a granite worktop on the left. The interior doorway led to the kitchen.

"Kids asleep yet?" Dee said, flashing Ray a mischievous smile. She was wearing a black trench coat and a yellow bobble hat, carrying a large tan handbag on a strap over her shoulder.

"I doubt that very much." Raymond closed the back door behind her and fastened the security chain.

Dee slipped out of her coat and hung it on a wall-hook behind the door, snagging the bobble hat over the same hook. She was wearing black jeans and a baggy white T-shirt that bore the words FRANKIE SAY RELAX in large, bold black capitals.

Raymond didn't reply. He stared at her jeans while she bent over to remove her shoes.

"Looks like I'm here just in time for Corrie," she said, straightening up after placing her shoes neatly together against the wall.

"Well, you know where everything is," Raymond said. "I have to pop out now. Help yourself to tea, coffee, whatever else you might want."

"Oh, I will."

Raymond frowned, glancing at the bag that Dee was carrying. "And if you do have to smoke…"

"I know, I know. Go outside, close the back door so the smoke doesn't come in, don't leave dog-ends all over the garden."

"Yes," Raymond said. "Thank you."

Dee winked at him. "We aim to please."

"Of course." Raymond turned and walked out of the utility room, through the kitchen and into the long hallway that led to the front door. He took a dark overcoat from one of the pegs near the door and pulled it on.

Dee had followed him into the hall. She stood in the lounge doorway while he knelt to lace up his shoes.

"I won't be too long," Raymond said. "I just need to sort a few things out."

"I know. I'll see you later."

"See you soon, Dee."

"Have a good time."

"Yes," Raymond said. He opened the front door. "Bye, Dee."

As soon as the front door had closed behind Raymond, Dee went straight back into the kitchen to fill the kettle and turn it on. She took a jar of Gold Blend coffee out of one cupboard, a pink porcelain mug from another.

"No sugar," Dee said, opening the coffee jar. She looked at her warped reflection in the gleaming chrome of the kettle's bulbous body. "I'm sweet enough already."

She made herself a mug of weak, white coffee and carried it into the lounge. She set the coffee mug down on the low table next to Ray's favourite armchair before turning on the TV and changing the channel so that she could watch *Coronation Street*.

The bookcase to the right of the TV had several framed photographs of Ray's two kids, the twins. In one picture, they were aged about three or four, dressed as pirates, probably for a birthday party. One of them was laughing, the other was crying. In another photo they were close to nine years old, the ages they had been the last time Dee had babysat for the Hughes family.

Dee looked at the most recent photo of the twins. She thought it must have been taken a couple of months earlier, because in the picture they were both wearing new University of Liverpool sweaters.

Ray's two kids were eighteen, living away at university. Before going to university, they had both been residents at a private boarding school.

Dee sat in Ray's armchair, picked up her coffee and smiled at the TV.

"Easy money," she said.

***

Raymond didn't take the Sierra. No point, really, when the *Dog and Partridge* was less than a fifteen minute walk away, and why take the risk of getting yourself pulled over and breathalysed when it wasn't raining? Very cold, but at least it was staying dry.

He pulled open the pub's front door and stepped into the welcome warmth. The *Dog* was comparatively civilised. No fruit machines, pool tables or drunken louts, but it did have a back room where poker could be played long after the taps were supposedly shut.

The tall, broad-shouldered man behind the bar looked up as Raymond walked into the pub.

"Evening, Tony," Raymond said, taking off his gloves and rubbing his palms together.

"Ray," Tony said, nodding once. "The usual?"

"Please."

Tony reached up to the wooden rafter where several pewter tankards were hanging from hooks. He took one down and filled it from the Whitbread Pale Ale beer tap.

"Gwen on the night shift again?" Tony asked.

"Indeed she is." Raymond smiled at the tankard, now more than half full, then looked up to meet Tony's eyes. "When the cat's away, right?"

"To cure what ails you," Tony said, placing the full tankard on the bar. "Give her my regards when you see her, okay?"

"Of course."

Raymond paid for his pint and carried it through the lounge bar of the pub to the closed door of the back room. He opened the door and went inside.

"Evening, Ray," said Clive, one of four men who were already sitting at the card table. According to local legend, Tony had won the table as a side bet when he had bluffed on two kings while playing against an entire family of gun-toting mobsters at a casino in Bolton. According to Tony's wife, Tony had bought the table from a bent market trader in Manchester, and had been royally ripped off because he had been drunk at the time. The table was a circular nine-seater with leather armrests, chrome cup holders and a flawless green cloth surface.

Ray nodded politely at Clive before silently taking a seat. He sat out the hand, watching the faces of the men as they played.

"Deal Ray in," said the man who had spoken first. "You

know everyone, don't you, Ray?"

"Evening, Mike," Raymond said to the slim fair-haired man to his left. "Paul," he said to the man on his right. He looked at the third man, a relative newcomer who had joined the card players at the *Dog* about six months earlier. The man had an unremarkable face, also a fairly unremarkable amount of luck at the card table. "Evening, Joe," Raymond said, pleased that he actually remembered the man's name.

"Formalities out of the way?" said Clive. "Let's play."

***

As soon as the credits began to roll at the end of *Coronation Street*, Dee grabbed her handbag and headed for the utility room through the dark kitchen. She slipped her shoes and coat on, unhooked the security chain and opened the back door. There was a switch on the wall by the door for an overhead outside light but Dee didn't turn it on, for the same reason that she left the kitchen light off. The garden wasn't overlooked by any nearby houses but Raymond insisted that she left the lights off at the back of the house, just in case someone who knew he was not at home noticed it. Dee thought that this was an extremely unlikely scenario, but she left the lights off because it was what Ray had asked her to do.

She closed the utility room door behind her and took a few steps away from it along the path at the side of the house. The garden was dark, but not absolutely devoid of light. Dee could see the outlines of bushes and trees, particularly higher up where they were silhouetted against the cloudless night sky. As her eyes grew accustomed to the darkness she could see the pale surface of the tiled path and the lines of mortar between the bricks on the wall to her right. On the far side of the lawn, right up against the high brick wall, was a wooden garden shed. Because she had seen it before, in daylight, Dee knew that the shed had dark-stained tongue-and-groove walls, two small rectangular windows and a grey weatherproof roof. In the dark, she could just about make out the shed's angular shape.

Dee reached into her bag and took out her lighter and an open pack of Silk Cut. She pulled out a cigarette without needing to see what she was doing, put it between her lips and lit it. The flare of the lighter flame near her eyes turned the whole world completely black for a while after she had put the lighter away.

While she smoked, Dee wrapped her coat tighter around herself and shifted her weight back and forth from one foot to the other. She hadn't heard a weather forecast but it definitely felt as though there would be a frost overnight.

"Too cold to be standing around out here," Dee said, drawing deeply on the cigarette to hurry it along. The tip of the cigarette glowed bright orange as she inhaled, fading in its intensity when she took it away from her lips.

The garden was quiet, with only the distant and infrequent sounds of cars passing along the road on the far side of the house to disturb the tranquillity.

Dee finished her cigarette, crouching to carefully stub it out in the short, damp grass at the edge of the lawn next to the path. When it was thoroughly extinguished, cold and rather wet, she wrapped it in a square sheet of tissue and stashed it in the side pocket of her handbag. It seemed like a lot of unnecessary fuss when she could have just dropped it in Ray's dustbin, but Ray had his list of little rules and it was easier to just follow them than get into a pointless discussion that would only end up with her doing whatever he asked her to anyway.

She walked back along the path towards the door, listening to her own footsteps in the dark, and hearing nothing else.

The cold brass door handle gave a small metallic squeak as she pulled it down, but the hinges stayed silent when she opened the door. Every noise, no matter how trivial, seemed to Dee to be amplified by the darkness.

She closed the door behind her, removed her coat and shoes, and walked through the dark kitchen towards the hall.

In the lounge there was a sitcom playing on ITV, not a show that Dee watched, so she went over to the TV and changed the channel to BBC One. She wasn't a particularly avid fan of *Starsky and Hutch* but it was the only thing worth watching right then, even if it was a repeat. She thought Hutch was fairly good-looking, had nice hair, although he wasn't exactly her type. She sat in Ray's armchair and pulled her legs up so that she was sitting on her own feet. Much warmer like that.

It didn't take long for Dee to notice the lighter tone of the TV cop show and to realise that the episode was from one of the later series where they tended to get all emotional rather than just pull out their guns and chase the bad guys in Starsky's cool red and white car.

"What you need," Dee told the TV screen, "is a good murder."

CHAPTER 16

Raymond folded on a pair of fives halfway through the third hand. Mike had won the first pot, and Paul had won the second. Clive was following his usual routine of theatrically bluffing, followed by dramatically losing. In Raymond's opinion, the seesawing emotional ride was more fun for Clive than actually winning any money would be, not that there was much chance of Clive ever winning. Joe had folded near the end of the first hand, then played to the end and lost on the second. He was as philosophical as usual, accepting both losses with a wry smile and few words. After folding, Raymond watched Joe for the remainder of the third hand but was unable to tell anything from the man's expression.

When they reached the showdown, only Clive and Joe were still in. Clive had been last to raise so he turned over his cards and spread his hands wide as he smiled at Joe.

"Full house, kings over fives."

Paul whistled.

Raymond smiled at Clive. He was so used to seeing Clive bluff and fall that the genuinely good hand was rather surprising.

Mike laughed, shaking his head. "Glad I folded when I did."

"Sorry, Joe," Clive said.

"No need," Joe said. He turned over his cards.

Paul stared at them. "Holy shit. I don't think I've ever seen that before."

Clive groaned. "Typical. Best hand I've had in weeks and he pulls that out."

"Ace high straight flush," Mike said.

"I need a drink," Clive said.

Raymond pushed his chair back and stood up. "Well, gentleman, once again I must make my apologies and also make an early exit."

"Not even going to try to win any of it back?" Mike asked.

"Afraid not. I'm on what you might call a bit of a tight schedule."

"What he means," Clive said, "is that he needs to be back in his house before his old lady gets home from work."

"Exactly," Raymond said.

"We'll see you when we see you, then," Paul said.

"You will." Raymond opened the door. "Goodnight, all. Have a good evening."

The four men replied in kind and Raymond walked out of the poker room, holding the door for Clive who was on his way to the bar.

"Take that for you?" Clive asked, pointing at the empty tankard in Raymond's hand.

"That would be most kind. Thank you."

"See you later, Ray."

"Goodnight, Clive."

Raymond left the *Dog and Partridge* a few minutes before nine p.m. He was glad that he had thought to put his driving gloves in his coat pocket because the temperature had dropped to below freezing while he had been in the pub. He pulled them on as he walked along the pavement, smiling at how well the evening was turning out.

"That's your alibi sorted out," he said to himself.

He increased his pace, eager to get back to the young woman he had left waiting for him at home.

***

Raymond reached the front door of his house a little before ten past nine. He unlocked the door and went inside, closing it and locking it behind him before taking off his gloves. He left them on the shelf in the hall next to the telephone, then he took off his coat and hung it back on its usual peg.

He found Dee in the lounge, curled up in his armchair in front of the TV. The BBC nine o'clock news was on, with the volume turned very low. The blonde news presenter had her serious face on as she described the rising death toll following the recent volcanic eruption in Colombia.

"You're in my chair," Raymond said.

Dee stretched her legs out in front of her before standing up.

"I was telling Claire in the shop," she said. "Telling her about babysitting your nine-year-old twins."

"That was how old they were when you actually did used to babysit them."

"Yeah. When I was fifteen."

"Fifteen," Raymond said. "You're making me feel very old."

"Well, I'm not fifteen now."

Raymond smiled, reading the words on her T-shirt again. "Neither am I."

"Do you know how old I am, Ray?"

"Of course."

Dee tilted her head to one side, grinning at him. "No

you don't."

"Twenty-three."

Dee laughed, shaking her head. "Close."

"Twenty-four?"

"Sorry, I can only accept your first answer."

"Turn the television off." Raymond watched her as she did a little catwalk strut across to the TV. "Second thoughts, just turn the sound off."

Dee took her time bending over in front of the TV while she adjusted the volume control on the front of the set.

"There," she said, turning to face him. "The sound is off."

"Brandy is in the cabinet."

Dee went to the drinks cabinet and poured a generous amount of Ray's favourite spirit into a short-stemmed brandy snifter. She carried it to him and he took it from her, taking a sip before placing it on the coffee table. He took out his wallet and sat in his armchair.

Dee watched him counting the notes out of his wallet. When he had finished, he placed the notes in a pile on the coffee table near his brandy glass. Mostly twenties, a couple of tens. She knew how much was there without needing to count it. A lot of money. At least ten times as much as you'd expect to get for babysitting nine-year-old twins.

The room was quiet. No music playing, and no sound from the TV apart from a low electrical hum from the screen that Dee could only hear if she concentrated on listening for it.

She stood directly in front of the armchair, a yard back from it, facing Raymond. He raised the brandy glass to his lips and nodded once for her to proceed.

Dee pulled the RELAX T-shirt up and off over her head and dropped it on the floor behind her. She took two steps forward and knelt on the thick, deep-pile carpet directly in front of the armchair.

Raymond sat back in his chair with his knees wide apart as Dee leaned forward between his legs.

Dee felt his hands move to her shoulders as she reached behind her back to unhook her bra.

Easy money.

***

Raymond Hughes stood in the shower with his face angled upwards into the gushing jet from the shower head. He felt relaxed, drained, guilty, satisfied. He felt alive. At some point earlier, when he had no longer been completely in control of his body, he had briefly glimpsed the television screen over the top of Dee's head. He had only seen the headline on the screen, had heard nothing the senior police officer had been saying because the sound was off. It had been a local news item, something about a fatal hit-and-run that had happened on Saturday. Compared to the Colombian volcano it should have seemed trivial, but the familiarity of the location almost distracted Raymond. If Dee hadn't been where she was, doing what she had been doing, he might even have been intrigued enough to turn up the volume.

He soaped himself thoroughly and took his time rinsing the suds from his body. The water was pleasurably hot, and he always enjoyed the mixture of relief and regret as he washed every incriminating trace of Dee Collins from his hair and skin.

Gwendolyn had left the house just after five for her six o'clock shift start in Accident and Emergency, and she wouldn't be home until sometime past two in the morning. But still, Raymond knew that it was always much better to be safe rather than sorry.

He turned off the shower and took a large navy towel from the radiator. He listened, but he couldn't hear any sounds from downstairs. He never watched Dee when she put her clothes back on, picked up the wad of cash, and let herself out of his house through the back door. There was no fun to be had in that, and he had already passed the point where her presence in his home was in any way entertaining or beneficial. As he stood in the bathroom, drying himself in front of the fogged mirror, he wished he had never met Dee Collins, the same as he always did, and then he started to wonder when he would next be able to have her again, the same as he always did.

Raymond paused, holding the towel at arm's length, sure that he had heard the squeak of the utility room door handle. A moment later he definitely heard the distant thud-click of the door being closed. He exhaled long and slow, relieved that she was no longer in his house.

After he had finished drying himself, Raymond went into his bedroom and put on clean pyjamas and a burgundy flannel dressing gown. As he went back downstairs he was trying to decide whether to have another small brandy or to put the kettle on and make himself a nice cup of tea.

"Tea, I think," he said as he walked along the hall towards the kitchen.

He stopped, halfway along the hall, listening.

He could hear a voice, distant and mechanical, repeating a short phrase over and over. He couldn't make out the words but he knew where the voice was coming from.

Raymond looked at the telephone on the shelf next to the black driving gloves. The handset was lying on the shelf by the phone, and the voice was coming out of it.

Raymond picked up the handset and listened.

"Mr Hughes, are you still there? Please respond, Mr Hughes."

"Hello?" Raymond said.

"Mr Hughes, please remain where you are. An ambulance is on its way."

"I'm sorry?"

The voice on the other end of the line was calm,

professional. "Mr Hughes, I need you to stay where you are and to allow the ambulance personnel immediate access to your home as soon as they arrive."

Raymond felt a strange urge to laugh, but he held it in. "I'm sorry, but I have no idea what you're talking about."

"Mr Hughes, I need you to stay on the phone. The police are also on their way to your address."

"The police?"

"Please stay on the phone."

Raymond looked down the hall. The kitchen was dark but there was light spilling into the hall from the lounge doorway on the right. He held the phone away from his ear, covered the flower petal array of holes over the speaker with his free hand, and listened.

No sound from the television, but the random pulses of light from the lounge doorway meant that it was still turned on.

Why hadn't Dee turned the volume back up while she was getting dressed?

Raymond gently placed the handset on the shelf near the black driving gloves. He could hear the crackling sound of the female voice, slightly amplified against the wooden surface of the shelf.

He took a slow, measured step away from the shelf and the phone, towards the lounge doorway. He was trying to piece together the events that must have occurred while he had been upstairs.

Two more hesitant steps along the hall and he was standing in front of the lounge doorway. Flickers of light from the television screen on the far side of the room cast an indistinct shadow against the wall behind him.

Had Dee Collins come into the hall and used the phone?

If she had, then why was the woman on the line asking if Mr Hughes was still there, and why was an ambulance on the way? He didn't even want to consider why the police were also coming.

Raymond went into the lounge.

On the television screen, Sean Connery was wearing a grey suit, white shirt, striped tie. Not a James Bond movie, some other film, but Raymond didn't know which one. Connery looked no more than forty but he was already losing his hair and making no attempt to hide it. He was talking to two other men, but in total silence on Raymond's TV.

Raymond walked further into the room, saw what was on the carpet between the armchair and the television, and stopped.

He knew why the police were coming.

He also realised why the ambulance was on its way, and he knew that it was going to arrive too late to make any difference.

CHAPTER 17

When Dan and Rick arrived in the unmarked BMW at eleven thirty p.m., the ambulance was parked on the road outside the large five-bedroom house and there were two police cars nose-to-tail on the drive. The nearest vehicle was an unmarked three litre Ford Capri and the other was a Rover V8 patrol car.

Dan pulled ahead of the ambulance and parked against the kerb.

"Think this is our guy?" Rick asked.

Dan turned off the engine and opened his door. "Let's go and find out."

The driver of the Capri was waiting at the front door of the house.

"Good of you to join us," he said as Dan and Rick walked up to the door. "Kath Schrader told me you were on your way."

"I'm DS Dan Blacksmith."

"DI Bobby Knowles." The plainclothes inspector shook Dan's hand and looked at Rick. "And I know who this reprobate is."

"DI Knowles," Rick said with a curt nod. "Good to see

you again."

"No it isn't." Knowles glanced over his shoulder into the brightly lit hall. "It's a slaughterhouse in there."

"Where's the suspect?" Dan asked.

"In the back of the ambulance."

"Injured?"

"Restrained."

"Why in the ambulance?"

"The Rover's nearside back door has got a buggered lock, and I didn't want him in my motor."

"Who's in there with him?"

"The two uniforms who came in the Rover."

Dan looked back at the ambulance. "He can wait. We'd like to see the crime scene."

Knowles smiled but it didn't reach his eyes. "If it's all the same with you, I've seen it once and that was enough. I'm more than happy to be handing this over to you two."

"Who else is in there?"

"DS Emily Clark and some kid from forensics. They came with me."

"Some kid?" asked Rick.

"They're all kids to me, Ricky. He's probably even younger than you."

Dan looked at his watch. "I'd really like Pat Davies to take a look."

"I'll get on the radio," Knowles said. "Anyone else you want to invite to the party?"

"Nigel Hansom, the pathologist."

"I was kidding. But you knew that, didn't you?"

"I'd appreciate it if you could call them both."

"Fine. Don't get too much blood on your shoes." DI Knowles turned and walked away towards his Capri.

The front door was wide open. Dan went into the brightly lit hall with Rick following him. On the wall shelf, the phone handset was lying beside the phone near a pair of black driving gloves.

Dan stopped, leaned closer to look at the gloves.

"Look at this."

"What have you found?"

"These gloves have something on them. It looks like dried blood. Not much, but you can see it in the stitches on the seams."

Rick looked at the gloves. "Dry? Not from this evening, then?"

Dan shook his head. "Come on. We'll see what Pat Davies can tell us about them later."

A tall plainclothes policewoman stepped into the hall from a room ahead of them on the right.

"Are you the ones Knowles was expecting?"

She looked too pale, drained with the kind of exhaustion that comes not from lack of sleep or excessive exertion but from seeing something that stays in your mind far beyond the point where you would have chosen to forget it forever.

"DS Dan Blacksmith. This is DC Rick Price."

"I'm DS Emily Clark."

"DI Knowles said there was an FI on the scene."

"Eddie Davenport. He's upstairs, in the bathroom. I got the distinct impression that she was his first."

Dan shook his head. "DI Knowles is radioing for Pat Davies, one of our senior SOCOs."

"I know Pat," Emily Clark said.

"Knowles didn't tell us much about the victim," Dan said. "We know it's possibly a woman called Dee Collins because of the call that was made from the phone at this address."

"There's a bag in there with various means of ID in it. There's a cheque book, even her most recent payslip from a shop called *Bright Soles*. Unless she stole the bag, her name is definitely Dee Collins."

Rick Price whistled softly. "Are you aware of the hit-and-run that occurred on Saturday night on Old Park Lane?"

"Of course I am," said DS Clark. "And it was on the local news this evening."

Rick nodded. "The victim of that hit-and-run was a twenty-four-year-old woman called Sharon Hall. She was strangled to death after being run over. We have very good reason to believe that she was a close friend of Dee Collins while they were at school together."

"Strangled?" DS Clark's eyes momentarily widened as she said the word.

Dan pointed at the shelf on the wall. "The gloves on that shelf have traces of dried blood in the seam stitches. I'm no forensic expert, but it looks like it has been on there for a lot longer than an hour or two."

"You need to see the victim," Clark said.

"Was she strangled? DI Knowles said something about blood."

"Better if you go in and take a look for yourselves. She's on the floor in front of the TV." She moved further into the hall and stood to one side to allow them into the lounge. "I'll go and check on Eddie."

"Has anyone touched anything in there?" Dan asked.

"Nothing, apart from the contents of her bag to confirm ID. The bag is where we found it, contents replaced. Eddie was going to perform an initial visual exam but he didn't even last a minute."

"Okay, thanks."

Dan waited until Emily Clark had gone upstairs. "Don't throw up on the evidence," he said to Rick. "I'm serious. If you think you're going to, get out of there as quickly as you can."

Rick swallowed. "I'll be okay."

Dan went into the lounge and stood to one side of the doorway while Rick followed him in. He could see the top of the television set on the other side of a sofa and a large armchair.

"Another big, expensive house," Dan said.

"Like the Masons'."

"Try not to jump to conclusions without any supporting evidence. But it's interesting, isn't it?"

"Do you think Hughes maybe knows Bill Mason?"

"Possibly, but it raises too many unanswerable questions at the moment." Dan looked around the room, checking the walls, the position of the furniture, the various ornaments and fixtures.

"No sign of a struggle," Rick said.

"Very good. How about no *remaining* signs of a struggle?"

"You think he tidied up before he called 999?"

"Right now, I'm keeping my mind as open as possible."

Dan walked across and stood to one side of the armchair. He sucked in a deep breath between his teeth, swallowed hard and concentrated on resisting the intensely compelling urge to look away from the body on the floor.

Rick stood next to Dan. He looked away. "Oh, Jesus."

"Deep, slow breaths. Through your mouth. Think about the photograph at the Halls' house. The girl standing next to Sharon Hall in the picture. Slim, dark hair, pretty. Now look at her, Rick."

Rick was taking in deep breaths but not slowly. He nodded once. "It's her."

"How sure are you? Look at her face."

Rick looked, but not at the face. "What *is* that?"

"It's the handle of a screwdriver. Look at her face."

"It's Dee Collins. Older than in the photo, of course, but it's her."

"What else? Start with the eyes."

"Bloodshot. The whites are almost completely red." Rick took a slower breath. "Unnatural redness on her cheeks beneath her eyes. Her mouth looks swollen. Red marks on her neck."

"Strangulation."

"Yeah."

"How do you feel?"

"Off the record, I feel like quitting this job."

Dan took a careful step to his left, moving closer to the television, closer to the corpse of Dee Collins.

"There is one very important piece of physical evidence here that tells us how she was killed."

"You're not talking about the screwdriver through the heart, are you?"

"No, but look at it and look at the blood. And start taking notes. I'm going to make a sketch of the body's position in relation to the other objects nearby."

Rick reached into his coat pocket and realised how much his hand was trembling. He took out the notepad and pen, held firmly onto the biro in case he dropped it on the body. He talked as he wrote.

"Initial visual ID of the victim, Dee Collins. Body is flat on its back between the armchair and the TV. Left knee bent and raised a couple of inches. Right leg straight. Arms flat at victim's sides. Face and neck show physical evidence of recent strangulation." Rick took another slow, deep breath. "The body is naked. The heart appears to have been punctured by a screwdriver. The handle is visible beneath the victim's left breast, probably between the fourth and fifth ribs."

"Describe the blood loss," Dan said. "Think about what you're seeing."

"Blood has pooled on the victim's abdomen and has also run onto the carpet on her right."

"Pooled is correct," Dan said. "There's the cause of death confirmation. There are no blood splatters, no sign of the blood spurting from the wound."

"He stabbed her after she was dead."

"Nigel Hansom will confirm it, but I don't think there's much doubt that was what happened." Dan looked at something on the carpet a yard away from the body. "Look at this."

Rick moved closer to Dan to see what he was pointing at. "What is it?"

"I think he got some of the blood on him. You can see a couple of spots just over there, as if it dripped off when he went that way."

"But if the blood didn't spurt out, how did he get it on him?"

"Maybe he put his hand in it, or dipped some other object into it."

Rick looked at the pile of clothes on the floor near the armchair. "Shall I make a note of the clothes?"

"Yes, go ahead. Visual check only. And see if you can count the cash on the coffee table without touching it."

"Why do you think it's there?"

Dan looked down at the naked body on the floor. "I don't think she put it there."

"Do you think Hughes put it there for her?" Rick frowned. "Do you think she was a prostitute?"

"Possible. What would his motive be for killing her like this?" Dan looked up at the ceiling, then down at the white noise of a non-transmitting channel on the screen of the silent television. "They are alone in here, she strips for him, either performs a sexual act or is preparing to, he has a sudden change of heart or maybe he can't perform, loses his temper, strangles her, then stabs her with a screwdriver. Then he calls the police, goes silent for ten minutes, picks up the phone again and claims he has no idea what's happening."

"Sounds like some kind of mental problem. Schizophrenia?"

"It was just one theory, probably incorrect. Make a note of all the visible injuries on her body. I can't see anything except the strangulation evidence and the single stab wound. There's no sign of a struggle, no other apparent injuries on the body."

"We can't see her back, or the back of her head."

"Nigel Hansom will carry out a full physical examination. Just note down what you can see."

Dan walked behind the armchair to the sofa, where a large tan handbag was standing upright on one of the cushions, the cover flap turned back to expose the contents. Without touching the bag he looked into the main compartment and saw the cheque book and folded payslip that DS Clark had mentioned.

He looked closer, peering into the narrow opening of the side pocket.

"Rick, I'm going to take something out of the side pocket of the handbag."

Rick came over to stand next to Dan while Dan reached in with his thumb and forefinger. He took out a folded square of tissue, held it flat on his palm for Rick to see.

"Looks like there's something damp in there," Rick said.

Dan carefully unfolded the tissue, turning each corner back while Rick watched.

"Nice," Rick said. "She saved a dog end."

Dan looked closely at the crushed cigarette butt. "Tiny green stains on it. My guess is it was put out in or near wet grass, and quite recently."

"Why did she wrap it up and put it in her bag?"

Dan looked at the body on the carpet, at the luxurious furniture and expensive ornaments in the room. "She didn't want to leave it behind. Maybe she was told not to leave it behind."

Rick looked up. "Do you think she smoked it outside?"

"Very likely. Not at the front of the house. No grass out there."

"Back door is probably through the kitchen."

Dan and Rick left the lounge and walked down the hall to the kitchen. The light was off. Dan found the switch and pressed it with the cap of his biro. The strip light flickered and buzzed, taking a few seconds before it was fully illuminated.

"Look at that," Dan said. There was a single drop of blood the size of a penny on one of the kitchen floor tiles.

"He came in here after he killed her," Rick said.

They walked into the kitchen, avoiding the droplet of blood.

"Over there," Dan said, pointing at the floor on the far side of the doorway into the utility room. "Another one."

Dan went into the small utility room while Rick waited in the doorway.

"I think he went outside," Dan said. "There's a tiny smear of blood on the door handle."

"This doesn't make a hell of a lot of sense."

"No, not unless he wanted us to follow the blood trail."

"Like a car reg on a kerbstone and a Coke can in a stolen car."

"But he didn't need to do any of that if he's the man they've got out there in the back of that ambulance. This is his house. This is where he phoned 999. This is where the patrol car guys found him."

"Mental problems. Schizophrenia."

"So what's outside in the back garden?"

Dan eased the door handle down with his elbow and pushed the door open with his shoulder. He looked out into the darkness, then used his biro to press the light switch on the wall next to the door. The large floodlight above the utility room door bathed the garden in light.

Dan looked out across the lawn. "Where would you keep a screwdriver?"

"In a tool box?"

"How about in a tool *shed*?"

Rick followed Dan through the utility room and out onto the paved path.

"Another spot of blood," Dan said. "He really wants us to look in the shed, doesn't he?"

"I don't think I can face finding another dead body at the moment."

The closer they came to the shed, the further they were from the light outside the utility room. Dan took a short tubular flashlight out of one of his coat's deep pockets, turned it on and aimed it at the ground ahead of them.

Dan said, "If there's any more blood on the grass, I don't think we're going to see it anyway."

"It's not on the grass," Rick said. "It's on the shed windows."

Dan and Rick stood on the wet lawn looking at the side of the shed in Raymond Hughes' garden. There was a narrow wooden sill beneath the two rectangular panes. On the sill, between the two windows, was a pink porcelain coffee mug. There was blood on the side of the mug and on the handle. The mug had probably been at least half full of blood when it had been carried to the shed.

Finger-written in neat, narrow, six-inch-high capital letters across the left window pane was the word GETTING. The word on the right pane was WARMER.

CHAPTER 18

DI Kath Schrader stood in front of Dan's desk, shook her head, and said, "He won't talk to me, not even with his lawyer sitting right next to him."

It was quarter to ten on Tuesday morning. Dan had gone home at two a.m. and been back at the Campbell Road station by nine a.m. He knew about Gwendolyn Hughes and her night shift at Accident and Emergency. He knew that she had been informed that her husband had been arrested and charged with murder, and he also knew that she had been booked into a local hotel paid for by Humberside Police because her house was currently an active crime scene.

"Did he give a reason for not wanting to talk to you?"

"His lawyer asked for a male police officer to be present. The inference was that *only* a male officer was to be present."

Dan pushed his chair back, took his notepad and two recent reports off his desk, and stood up. He had not spoken to Raymond Hughes while he had been at the man's house with Rick Price. He had read the reports that Pat Davies and Nigel Hansom had written; they were already on his desk when he had arrived at nine. Nigel Hansom's report confirmed the cause of death as non-ligature strangulation by a person with the same size hands as Sharon Hall's killer. Pat Davies had identified prints on the pink porcelain mug and matched them with prints taken posthumously from Dee Collins. The only other prints on the mug belonged to Gwendolyn Hughes, matched with those taken when Pat Davies had visited Gwen in her hotel room. Pat had also been able to determine the age of the dried blood on the gloves that had been on the shelf in Raymond Hughes' house, and to accurately match the blood type with Sharon Hall's. Evidence had been found that showed that Dee Collins had engaged in various sexual acts shortly before her death.

Dan nodded. "I need to hear the recording of the emergency call that was made from Hughes' house."

"Can you speak to Hughes first? We can get this case sewn up by lunch time if he admits to the hit-and-run."

"I don't think he will."

Schrader huffed out a gasp of exasperation. "His gloves have Sharon Hall's blood on them. His hands are a close size-match for both murders. He has already admitted to killing Dee Collins."

"How can he have admitted to the murder? He hasn't spoken to anyone since he was arrested."

"He dialled 999 last night, and he told the operator that he had just killed Dee Collins."

"Which is why I need to hear the recording of the call."

"Fine, but go and talk to Hughes now. His lawyer isn't going to hang around all day."

Dan started to walk away, stopped and turned back to Schrader. "I told Rick Price not to break his neck getting in this morning. I'm not expecting him until midday."

"You don't need him for this. If you're not around when he arrives, I'll bring him up to speed."

"Can you have the tape of the 999 call brought to the

interview room while I'm in there with Hughes and his lawyer?"

"Why?"

"It will help if you could."

"It won't change anything, Dan. Hughes killed Dee Collins and it's highly likely that he also killed Sharon Hall."

"I know. But if you could, it would be helpful."

"Fine."

Dan took the stairs to the ground floor. There were only two interview rooms at the Campbell Road station, and they were on opposite sides of the same corridor. Dan knocked on the closed door of the occupied interview room and it was opened almost immediately by a uniformed constable. The uniformed officer let Dan into the room, then left the room to wait outside.

There was a single wooden desk in the middle of the small room. On the desk was a portable cassette recorder. Raymond Hughes was sitting beside his lawyer on the far side of the desk. Dan sat in one of the two empty chairs opposite them and placed his notepad and the reports on the desk next to the tape recorder. He looked at Raymond Hughes, and he saw a red-haired man of average height who was more than a little overweight, and who wore gold-framed spectacles with thick lenses.

"I'm Detective Sergeant Dan Blacksmith. I am conducting this interview at DI Schrader's request. I shall be recording this interview, and I need to make you both aware of that before we proceed."

Raymond Hughes' solicitor held up his hand. He was a large, ruddy-faced man in a grey pinstripe suit. He had a well-worn black briefcase on the floor beside his chair.

"Before we start, could we have some drinks brought in? My client has been in this room for some time now."

Dan stood up, opened the door, and asked the officer outside to fetch a couple of cups of water.

"Two minutes," he said to Hughes and his solicitor as

he sat back down. He opened the drawer of the desk and took out a new cassette tape sealed in cellophane, picked at the seal with his fingertip, and unwrapped the cassette. He inserted the tape into the recorder and pressed the button to start recording.

"This is DS Dan Blacksmith, interview being recorded at Campbell Road police station on Tuesday, November the nineteenth, 1985. In the room with me, please state your full name…"

Hughes looked at his solicitor and the solicitor nodded.

"My name is Raymond Edgar Hughes."

"And could I have your age and your date of birth."

"I'm fifty-one years old. I was born on the ninth of April, 1934."

"Thank you, Mr Hughes." Dan looked at the lawyer. "Could I please have your full name and your official designation."

The lawyer cleared his throat. "Jeremy Gilchrist, legal representative for Raymond Hughes."

Dan picked up his notepad, turned back and forth through a couple of pages.

"Mr Hughes, could you tell me where you were between four o'clock and six o'clock on the evening of Saturday the sixteenth of November?"

Raymond blinked, started to open his mouth but said nothing.

"How is this relevant?" asked Gilchrist.

"Mr Hughes, please answer the question."

Raymond frowned, clearly unsure why he was being asked. "I was in London."

Dan turned to a clean page in his notepad. "Where exactly were you, and why were you there?"

"The Royal Garamond Hotel. I was there for my company's fortnightly executive board meeting."

"A board meeting on a Saturday?" Dan asked.

"That's when we have them, yes."

"Always on Saturdays?"

"Yes."

"Do you know the address of the hotel?"

"It's on Berkeley Street in the West End."

Dan wrote the hotel's name and location in his notepad. "When did you check in on Saturday?"

"I checked into my room at two p.m., but I arrived at the hotel at about ten because the meeting was in one of the function rooms at the hotel."

"And when did you check out?"

"After breakfast on Sunday morning."

Dan looked up from his notepad. "How did you travel to London?"

"By train. I always do."

"Do you have receipts for the hotel and train tickets, maybe ticket stubs?"

"Yes, I do."

Dan leaned back in his chair, watching the expression on Raymond Hughes' face. "Do you always keep the receipts and ticket stubs, or did you just keep them this time in case you needed to prove you were not in Hull on Saturday evening?"

Hughes frowned, shaking his head. "I always keep them. I have to, in order to make an expenses claim when I get back."

"So if I were to ask you to provide, say, the receipts for the previous three fortnightly visits to London, you would be able to show them to me?"

"Our accounts department would have the originals, but I always keep photocopies. They're filed in my study at home."

Dan made a few more notes. If Hughes was lying about the receipts, it would be a simple matter to prove it.

"Mr Hughes, while you were in London did you engage the services of a prostitute or call-girl?"

Raymond sat in open-mouthed shock, staring at Dan.

"Don't answer that," said Gilchrist. "I want that question struck from the record."

"Mr Gilchrist, your client has been charged with murder. The victim was a twenty-four-year-old woman who was found naked in Mr Hughes' lounge. Not only had she recently been sexually active, but we found two hundred pounds in cash on the nearby coffee table." Dan took a breath. "Mr Hughes, did you engage the services of a prostitute or call-girl while you were in London?"

"No," Raymond said. "No, I did not."

"Would you like to take a drink of water before we continue?" Dan asked.

Raymond picked up one of the cups and raised it to his mouth. Dan could see that the man's hands were shaking.

"Could you tell me how you knew the victim, Dee Collins?"

"We used to be neighbours, before I moved house." Raymond closed his eyes, appeared to make a decision before continuing. "She babysat for us a few times, but that was when she was still in school."

Gilchrist held up his hand. "I would advise you not to answer any questions that are not directly related to the charge."

"Mr Hughes," Dan said. "When did you start giving Dee Collins cash in exchange for sex?"

"Raymond," Gilchrist said. "I would advise you—"

"When she was sixteen."

"That was approximately eight years ago," Dan said. "How often did this happen?"

"Every two or three months."

"How many times in total would you estimate that you paid Dee Collins for sex?"

"About thirty-five times."

"To your knowledge, did Dee Collins take money from anyone else in exchange for sex?"

"No. I asked her that question once. She said she didn't.

She was actually offended that I had asked. I never mentioned it again."

"Were you in love with her?"

Raymond shook his head. "No. That makes it worse, doesn't it?"

"Raymond," Gilchrist said. "I advise you to stop speaking."

"I didn't kill her," Raymond said. "All I meant was it makes it worse that I paid her to come to my house and... when I didn't even love her."

Dan put his pen down on top of his notepad. "Did you ever meet up with Dee Collins anywhere else, or just at your house?"

"I went to the shoe shop sometimes, where she worked, but only to talk to her, to arrange her next visit."

There was a knock on the door and a uniformed WPC entered the interview room.

"I have the recording of the emergency call," she said.

"Thanks," Dan said. He took the cassette from the WPC and she left the room, closing the door behind her.

"What is that?" Gilchrist asked.

"It's the recording of the emergency call that was made from Mr Hughes' telephone last night."

"I didn't make that call," Raymond said. "The phone was out of the cradle when I came downstairs."

"It's okay, Mr Hughes," Dan said. "We'll get to that in a minute."

"You believe me, don't you?" Raymond said.

"If you could just answer the questions as accurately as possible, that's all I'm asking at the moment."

Raymond nodded. "I will."

"How did Dee Collins get to your house last night?"

"She usually comes by bus. I didn't ask, but I assume that's what she did last night."

"What time did she arrive at your house?"

"Half past seven. Maybe a couple of minutes before."

"Did she come in through the front door?"

"No, the back door. The utility room."

"Do you keep the garden gate unlocked?"

"I unlocked it earlier in the evening." Raymond sighed, shaking his head. "After my wife had left for work."

"When would you usually lock the garden gate again?"

"Later, after Dee would have left."

Dan watched Raymond Hughes' eyes. "What do you keep in the garden shed?"

Raymond shrugged. "Lawnmower, garden tools. The usual."

"What about smaller tools such as spanners, screwdrivers, hammers?"

"There's a toolbox in there with those sorts of tools in it."

"Do you keep the shed locked?"

"No."

"Did you examine Dee Collins' body when you found it in the lounge?"

Raymond swallowed, shook his head. "No. I went into the room and saw her but I didn't go any closer. I could see the blood on the carpet. It was terrible. I went back into the hall and picked up the phone again."

"Can you describe the shelf in the hall, the one with the telephone on it?"

Raymond frowned. "It's just a wooden shelf. It's white, gloss paint."

"What did you see on the shelf?"

"The phone. Sorry, I don't understand what you're asking me to say."

"Okay, what else was on the shelf near the phone?"

"On the shelf? Oh, my driving gloves."

"Are you sure?"

"Yes. I put them there when I came back from the *Dog*."

"And those gloves are definitely yours?"

"Yes."

Dan looked up from his notepad. "Sorry, did you say you put them on the shelf when you came back from the *Dog*. Is that a pub? What is the full name of it?"

"The *Dog and Partridge*. It's about half a mile up the road from my house."

"When did you go there?"

"Just after Dee arrived."

"Did she go with you?"

"No, she stayed in the house."

Dan looked at Raymond Hughes, then asked the obvious question. "Why would you go out to the local pub when Dee had just arrived at your house?"

Raymond took a breath, nodded slowly. "You have to understand, I never wanted my wife to find out about Dee. Not for the reasons that you're thinking, but because I honestly did not want my appalling infidelity to hurt her in any way. It was like a habit, an addiction. I tried to stop seeing her, I really wanted to, but it was too easy to just arrange for her to come to my house when Gwen was on the night shift. The money wasn't important to me. A few hundred pounds every two or three months. I claim more than that back on my expenses for the exec meetings every fortnight."

"Can you explain exactly why you went to the *Dog and Partridge*, please?"

"An alibi, I suppose. A cover story. So the next time Gwen and I were in the pub, Tony would make some wisecrack about how I sneaked in there whenever Gwen was working late. Also, I would have a drink, just a pint or two, to settle my nerves before I went back home."

"Who is Tony?"

"The landlord at the *Dog*."

"Did you speak to anyone else while you were at the pub?"

Raymond paused, looked at Gilchrist before continuing. "I don't want to get anyone else into trouble."

Dan straightened in his chair, stared hard at Raymond Hughes. "What do you mean, Mr Hughes?"

"There's a back room at the pub. A few of us play cards in there. It's only low stakes Texas hold 'em. I played a couple of hands before I went home last night."

Dan felt his shoulders sagging. For a moment it had seemed that Raymond Hughes was about to blow the case wide open for him.

"Don't worry about causing trouble for your friends, Mr Hughes. Can you tell me how well you know the other players, and give me their names if you could."

"I know them about as well as you might know anyone you only see every month or so. I go there more frequently than I used to see Dee. It's a way of filling the hours while Gwen is working at night."

"Could you give me their names, please?"

"They're not going to get into trouble, are they?"

"I'm not interested in a few men playing poker in a local pub, Mr Hughes. Please, just give me the names."

"I only know them by their first names, I'm afraid. Clive, Mike, Paul and Joe."

"No surnames?"

"I play cards with them in the pub. I never needed to know their surnames."

"Did one of them seem different than usual? More agitated maybe, less talkative than usual, or even more talkative, possibly excited for no apparent reason?"

"Not really. Clive always bluffs badly, which he did last night. Mike and Paul were just the same as normal. Joe didn't say much, but he never does, apart from when he won a hand. He seemed fairly pleased about that."

"Did anyone lose badly?"

"Not while I was there."

"Did anyone leave before you did?"

"No. Clive went to get a drink from the bar when I left, but the other three stayed in the back room."

Dan sighed. "Could all four of them confirm that you were there?"

Raymond frowned. "They could, but I don't think they'd like it if they thought I had told the police about the poker games in the back room."

"Mr Hughes, you're still charged with murder. Your priority is to give me as much information as possible, not to worry about the feelings of a few men you play cards with in the pub."

"Sorry. If you ask Tony, he can confirm that I was there."

Dan checked his notes. "And you said he was the landlord?"

"Yes."

"What time did you leave the pub?"

"Just before nine o'clock. I got home about ten past."

"How did you get home?"

"I walked."

"Were you wearing your gloves, the ones that were on the shelf by the phone?"

"Yes. I took them off and put them on the shelf as soon as I got home."

Dan looked down at his own hands. "Where were your gloves while you were in the pub?"

"In my coat pocket."

"Both gloves in one pocket?"

"Yes."

"Right or left pocket?"

Raymond reached to his sides and patted his hips. "Left," he said. "Yes, the left coat pocket."

"Did you take your coat off while you were in the pub?"

"Yes. I hung it on a peg on the wall in the back room where we were playing cards."

"Did anyone touch it or move it while it was there?"

"No, I don't think so."

Gilchrist leaned forward. "Why are you asking my client

about the gloves and the coat?"

Dan didn't answer the solicitor's question. He watched Raymond Hughes' face as he asked, "Who killed Sharon Hall?"

Raymond blinked, looked as though he was going to speak but merely frowned.

Gilchrist said, "Don't answer that."

"I wasn't going to," Raymond said. "I don't know anyone called Sharon Hall."

"Do you know William Mason?" Dan asked.

"I know he's a haulage tycoon. Lives in Hull."

"But you don't know him personally, or through your business?"

"My company deals in wholesale frozen foods. I'm a marketing executive, so I have no involvement with our product distribution. And, no, I don't know William Mason personally."

"Do you know any members of his family personally?"

"No."

Gilchrist shook his head. "Is any of this relevant?"

"Very," Dan said. "Sharon Hall was killed on Saturday. She was strangled to death. The gloves on Mr Hughes' shelf, which he has freely admitted are his gloves, have been examined by our forensic investigation unit. Dried blood on the gloves matches Sharon Hall's."

Raymond Hughes jolted upright in his chair. "That's impossible."

"It's actually a proven fact, Mr Hughes," Dan said. "If I had told you about the blood on the gloves earlier, would you have given the same answers when I asked you where you had left them and whether anyone else had access to them in the pub?"

"I want that question removed from the record," Gilchrist said.

"It must be a mistake," Raymond said. "Those gloves can't have had any blood on them. How could they?"

"That's what I need to find out," Dan said. He picked up the cassette that held the recording of the emergency call. "This is Detective Sergeant Dan Blacksmith. I am now ending this stage of the interview recording in order to play back the tape of the emergency call made on the telephone at Raymond Hughes' house at approximately twenty-two thirty on the night of Monday November the eighteenth, 1985."

Dan stopped the recording, ejected the interview cassette and inserted the one that held the emergency call.

"Please remain silent while this plays, Mr Hughes," Dan said. "If you wish to speak, hold up your hand and I will pause the tape."

"Just like in school," Gilchrist said.

"I would also like you to remain silent," Dan said to Gilchrist. "If we are about to hear what I suspect we are going to hear, you might want to keep your comments to yourself until you hear it too."

"What do you think we're going to hear?" Gilchrist said.

Dan looked at Raymond Hughes. "The voice of the man who killed Sharon Hall and Dee Collins."

He put his finger on the *Play* button, and pressed it.

CHAPTER 19

"What do you mean, we have to drop the charge?"

Kath Schrader stood up so quickly that her chair shot back on its rollers, crashing against the drawers of the tall filing cabinet behind her desk.

"Hughes didn't make the emergency call. There was someone else in his house. An intruder. It's almost a certainty that the intruder killed Dee Collins, and I also believe that he swapped Hughes' gloves for the gloves he was wearing when he killed Sharon Hall."

Schrader closed her eyes, exhaled heavily, and opened them again. "Hughes killed Dee Collins, Dan. He killed her, and he painted that message on his own shed windows, and he put on a fake accent or whatever you think you heard on that tape, and he also killed Sharon Hall. We lock him up, we throw away the key, and we get a sick serial killer off our streets."

"Hughes was in London on Saturday. He came home on a train on Sunday morning."

"Is that what he told you?"

"Yes. I haven't checked with his company or the London hotel yet, but—"

"Don't bother. I can tell you what they'll say. They will say that they have no idea what you are talking about."

Dan took a breath, held his rising frustration in check. "The first voice on the tape isn't his. You need to listen to it."

"Fine. I'll listen to the tape."

"Come down to the interview room. Hughes is still in there with his lawyer."

"Did you leave the tape in the room with them?"

Dan took the cassette out of his pocket. "Of course not."

"Five minutes," Schrader said. "After that, we cross my threshold for time-wasting."

In the interview room, Kath Schrader took the chair on the right while Dan put the cassette back in the tape recorder. He rewound the tape to the beginning while the three other people in the room silently waited.

"Ready?" Dan asked DI Schrader.

"Go ahead."

Dan looked at Raymond Hughes as he reached for the *Play* button. He didn't want to see the expression on Kath Schrader's face, and he didn't want her to think he was watching her to obtain any kind of personal satisfaction. Because he knew, when she listened to the tape…

He pressed *Play.*

The first voice was that of the emergency services operator asking which service was required. Before the operator had finished speaking, she was interrupted.

"I killed her."

"Sir, can you please state which emergency serv—"

"I killed Dee. Dee Collins. I killed her, do you understand?"

"Sir, do you require an ambulance?"

"She's dead. Dee Collins is dead. I killed her."

"Can you give me your name and address, sir?"

"My name is Raymond Hughes. I just killed Dee Collins. My address is Windermere, that's the name of the house, and it's on

Rowan Crescent in Kingston upon Hull. That's rowan the tree, not rowing a boat."

"Sir, I need you to stay on the line while I contact the emergency ambulance service."

"She's dead. I killed Dee Collins."

Dan stopped the tape. "He doesn't say anything else. There's a gap of approximately twelve minutes and then Mr Hughes picks up the phone, says 'Hello', and has a confusing conversation with the operator. Confusing, because he has no idea what she is talking about."

Kath Schrader had said nothing while the tape was playing. She looked at Raymond Hughes, at Hughes' solicitor, and finally she turned and looked at Dan Blacksmith. Dan could tell that Schrader was conflicted, that she really did not want to say what she was about to say, but also that she only had one possible option.

"Dan, I want you to call the hotel in London to confirm that Mr Hughes was there on the weekend. I also want you to confirm the purpose of his trip with his place of work."

She scraped the chair back, stood up, and looked down at Raymond Hughes. "I want you to do one thing for me," Schrader said to him.

Gilchrist was about to speak but Raymond held his hand up. "It's fine, Jeremy. What would you like me to do?"

"Say this for me. *My name is Raymond Hughes. I just killed Dee Collins.*"

"Don't say that," Gilchrist said.

"It's okay," Dan said. "Go ahead, Mr Hughes."

Raymond took a breath, looked straight at Kath Schrader.

"My name is Raymond Hughes. I just killed Dee Collins."

Schrader smiled briefly, but the smile was cold. "No, you didn't. But do you know who did?" She turned to Dan. "We are not dropping the charge until there's absolute proof that Mr Hughes had no involvement in either Dee

Collins' murder or the death of Sharon Hall." She walked to the door, turned once again before leaving. "Your priority now is finding whoever it was who made that emergency call."

***

Rick Price sat and listened. He had drained one mug of instant black coffee, and was more than halfway through his second, before Dan ran out of new information to share with him.

"Now you know as much as I do," Dan said.

"Which we all have to admit is precious little," Kath Schrader said. "And I'm not knocking what you have found out, or how efficiently you managed it."

Dan said, "One of the unique aspects of this case is the sheer number of potential suspects, some of whom we have already eliminated through forensic examination or physical evidence."

Kath Schrader looked at her notepad. "Thomas Mason's hand size was nothing like the size of the hands that strangled both women, and Chad Young at Bailey's Guitars confirmed that Thomas was in the shop between sixteen forty and seventeen twenty-five. I also obtained confirmation that William Mason was at the Triple-Eight office during the time period of Sharon Hall's death and the theft of his own car. Deborah Mason was at home, speaking to an officer at Marlborough Road, at approximately the same time. Sharon Hall's boyfriend was in a restaurant with at least two witnesses who can confirm he was there at the time she was killed. Raymond Hughes was in the house where Dee Collins was killed, at the time she was killed, but so far we have enough counter evidence to suggest that he was not responsible for her murder."

Rick Price had heard the recording of the emergency call. He had also listened to part of the interview tape in order to compare the voices of Raymond Hughes and whoever had made the emergency call on his phone.

"That voice on the phone didn't sound like Hughes, and it didn't sound like Bill or Tom Mason either," Rick said.

"No," Dan said. "It's someone else entirely." He looked at Kath Schrader. "The message left on the shed windows and the earlier messages on the boot of my car were written by the same person. He's goading us, playing some kind of game. *You're cold, you're getting warmer.* It's most likely just a taunt, telling us that he has been watching what we're doing. It's just bravado, and with any luck it will be the mistake that trips him up and gets him caught."

"Which it hasn't done so far," Schrader said. "Remind me when you saw the first message."

"Saturday evening, when we came back to the station after speaking to the Masons and their neighbours."

"You don't know exactly when it happened?"

"No. My guess is when the car was parked outside the Masons' house, but that is just a guess."

"And the second time?"

"On the street near the park, when I went to apprehend Thomas Mason."

"I was standing not far from the car," Rick said. "I didn't see it happen."

"So it might not have happened there," Schrader said. "That was only where you noticed it."

"I don't think we'll get anything from the messages," Dan said. "Where they might work for us is if he slips up and we catch him near my car."

"Let's leave that as an absolute outside bet," Schrader said. "I want anyone who is remotely connected to either of those two women identified and questioned."

"Better to start with anyone connected to both of them," Dan said. "Unless the killings are completely random, with no motive, we have to go with the assumption that the killer knew both women."

"And it's going to be a much shorter list," Rick said.

Dan nodded, looking down at the notepad on his knee. "Tom Mason knew Sharon Hall, and he remembered Dee Collins from the description I gave him of the girl in the photograph with Sharon. I'd like to talk to him again, find out if he can think of anyone who knew both of them and who might have had a motive for killing them."

"Long shot," Kath Schrader said. "And didn't the Halls tell you that Sharon hadn't mentioned Dee Collins since they were in school?"

"I know," Dan said. "But Thomas Mason had kept in touch with Sharon Hall for the last eight years. He might know something useful and not even realise it."

Kath Schrader looked at her watch. "Dee Collins worked in a shop in town, *Bright Soles*. I'm going to go there to speak to her co-workers, find out if any of their customers might have been interested in more than just shoes."

Dan shot a warning glance at Rick. "We'll make some calls, check Raymond Hughes' alibi and arrange a meeting with Thomas Mason."

Kath Schrader stashed her notepad in a plain black shoulder bag, picked up the bag and grabbed her coat from the stand by the door of her office. "Let me know if you turn up anything useful."

"Will do," Dan said. "See you later."

Rick watched DI Schrader as she walked across the office to the staircase. When he looked back at Dan, he was grinning.

"Don't say it."

"What?" Rick said. "That she's going to *Bright Soles* because it's a shoe shop?"

"Yeah. Don't say that."

Rick looked at the phone on Kath Schrader's desk. "What are we going to do first?"

"I'll check Raymond Hughes' alibi. Can you go to your

desk and call the Masons, see if Tom is at home, and ask if we can go over to speak to him if he is?"

"What time do you want to go there?"

Dan looked up at the clock on the wall. "In an hour or so. Two o'clock if it's convenient for them."

When Rick had left Schrader's office, Dan called Directory Enquiries and got the number for The Royal Garamond Hotel. The operator told him the number and then put his call through.

"Royal Garamond, Mia speaking. How can I help you?"

"Good afternoon, Mia. This is Detective Sergeant Dan Blacksmith from Humberside Police. I'd like to confirm the check-in and check-out times of one of the guests who stayed at the hotel on the weekend."

"I'm sorry, Dan, but I'll need confirmation that you are who you say you are before I can share that information."

"I understand. Do you have time now to call me back if I give you the name of the station and my extension number?"

"I could do that. Which police station are you calling from?"

"Campbell Road in Kingston upon Hull."

"Gosh, that really is a long-distance call. And what extension should I ask for when they put me through?"

Dan looked at the front of Schrader's phone, although he already knew her extension number. "One, double-four."

"Okay, Dan. I'll call you right back."

Dan hung up and waited. He knew that two hundred miles away there was a good chance the Royal Garamond receptionist would put the phone down, start talking to a guest who had just walked up to her desk, maybe take another call, and forget all about someone called Dan who may or may not have been a policeman from far away in the north of England…

He picked the phone up halfway through the first ring.

"Humberside CID, Dan Blacksmith speaking."

"Hi, Dan. This is Mia Palladino from the Royal Garamond Hotel."

"Hello again, Mia. Thanks for calling back so quickly. Could you check whether you had a guest called Raymond Hughes at the hotel on the weekend."

"Yes, we did." There was a brief pause. "Mr Hughes checked in on Saturday at quarter past two in the afternoon, and checked out on Sunday morning at eleven o'clock."

"Were you working on either of those days, and did you see Mr Hughes?"

"I was working on Sunday morning when he checked out. He was here with several other people for a regular fortnightly business meeting. They always use one of the function rooms at the hotel."

"Can you confirm that you definitely saw him there on Sunday morning?"

"Yes, I did."

Dan closed his eyes, pictured the foyer of an unknown hotel, a short queue of businessmen, and an Italian receptionist smiling at them from behind her desk as they checked out.

"Mia, was that the first time you had seen Raymond Hughes?"

"No, I've seen him here several times before."

"Could you describe him for me, please? Height, build, hair colour, any distinguishing features."

"Of course. Mr Hughes has reddish hair, a natural light auburn shade. I would say he was average height. Is that good enough or would you like me to guess at his actual height?"

"Average is fine, Mia. Would you say he was thin, average or overweight, if those were the only available options?"

"I wouldn't exactly call him overweight, but if that was the only available option…"

"When he checked out, was he wearing glasses?"

"Yes, he was."

"Can you remember what they looked like?"

"They had gold frames."

"Thank you, Mia. I really appreciate it."

"Is that everything I can help you with today, Dan?"

"Yes, that's everything. Thanks again."

"My pleasure, Dan. Have a great day."

"You too." Dan hung up. "Me, I'm not so sure."

Dan had one more call to make. He found the page in his notepad where he had written the name and address of the wholesale frozen goods company where Raymond Hughes worked. He called Directory Enquiries, got the number and asked to be connected.

"Osborne Wholesale. How may I direct your call?"

"Good afternoon. This is Detective Sergeant Dan Blacksmith from Humberside CID. Could I have your name, please?"

"You're speaking to Natalie Gillespie. How can I help?"

"Hello, Natalie. I've just got one very quick question. Can you confirm that an employee called Raymond Hughes attended a meeting in London on the weekend?"

"I actually can," Natalie said. She sounded pleased that she was going to be able to answer the question without transferring Dan's call elsewhere. "Give me one second."

Dan followed the second hand on his watch as it ticked around from two o'clock all the way to nine. Thirty-five seconds, not one, but he wasn't rating Natalie Gillespie on her time estimating skills.

"Hello, Dan?"

"Yes, I'm still here."

"Raymond went to the executive board meeting in London on Saturday."

"Is that a regular meeting?"

"Yes, they have one every two weeks."

"Thanks, Natalie. That's all I need to know."

"Is Raymond in any kind of trouble?"

"Mr Hughes has been helping us with our enquiries."

"Oh. That's what they say on TV when someone has been arrested."

"There was an incident at Mr Hughes' house last night. I can't discuss the details, but we are reasonably confident that Mr Hughes was not directly involved."

"Oh no. Is he alright? Is his wife okay?"

"They're both fine, Natalie. I'm sorry, but I can't say anything else as the case is still under investigation. Thanks again for your help."

"You're welcome."

Dan hung up. He jotted a few quick notes before leaving Kath Schrader's office.

Rick frowned at him as he walked over to his desk. "I took a call on your phone. It was Rob Musgrave."

"What did he want?"

"He wanted to speak to you. I said you were on another line. He asked if we had found out who killed his girlfriend. He sounded strung out, really on edge."

"What did you tell him?"

"I said the investigation was progressing, but we didn't have a confirmed suspect yet. I told him we wouldn't be able to give out any information about the case anyway."

Dan nodded. "That was fine. Did he say anything else?"

"He said he might come to the station to talk to you."

Dan sighed. "Okay. I'll deal with that when I have to."

"Did Hughes' story check out?"

Dan sat at his desk, opposite Rick. "Yes. He was definitely in London on the weekend."

"That only gets him off the hook for Sharon Hall's murder."

"You heard the emergency call recording. Even DI Schrader agreed that it wasn't Hughes' voice on that tape. How did you get on with Tom Mason?"

"He's at home, and so is his mother. We can go there at

two."

Dan glanced at his watch. "We've got some time. Let's look at what we have." He flipped back a few pages in his notepad. "Blood is very significant. Sharon Hall's blood was used to leave us a major clue at the crime scene. It was also smeared on the side of the driver's seat in the Jag, and I believe that was also deliberate. The same blood was on the gloves that were found at Raymond Hughes' house. At that crime scene, Dee Collins was stabbed after she had died and her blood was taken outside and used to write a message on the windows of the garden shed."

"The third message," Rick said. "Assuming the two messages on your car were part of a series that the killer is leaving for us."

"Okay, so let's think about this series. It could be some kind of countdown, from cold to hot, or it could be the killer's way of letting us know how close we are to catching him." Dan shook his head. "Or it could just be random misdirection, its only purpose to add a further level of confusion to the investigation."

"Where does the Coke can fit into this?"

"Its presence directly implicated Thomas Mason. I'd say it was a deliberate act of misdirection."

Rick nodded. "Thomas Mason was set up for the Sharon Hall murder, and Raymond Hughes was set up for Dee Collins."

Dan frowned. "I don't think the killer was seriously trying to frame either of them. I think he did it to confuse us, to send us on a wild goose chase, to delay us looking for anyone else."

Rick looked at a page in his notepad. "The timing of both of these murders is ridiculously precise."

Dan nodded, giving Rick a wry smile. "You noticed that?"

"Sharon Hall was apparently killed between five and ten minutes after leaving Gaspari's. But she was killed by someone who was driving a car that had been stolen no more than twenty minutes earlier. How did he know when she was going to be walking along that road?"

Dan tapped his pen on a page of his notepad. "And Hughes told me he was upstairs for about fifteen minutes, in the shower for less than ten. During that time someone came into his house, killed Dee Collins, and made the emergency call. Hughes said he heard the sound of the back door closing after he came out of the shower. That must have been when the killer left the house to write the message on the shed."

"So the killer knew when Dee Collins was going to be at Hughes' house," Rick said. "And he was either very lucky, or he knew how long Hughes would be in the shower."

"He has been watching them," Dan said. "All of them. Sharon Hall, Dee Collins, the Masons, Raymond Hughes."

"That last message, the one on the shed." Rick looked at the message he had copied into his notepad. "*Getting warmer.* That's not a final message, is it?"

"No. That's a work in progress." Dan stood up. "He hasn't finished."

CHAPTER 20

It took Kath Schrader just under twenty minutes to drive from the Campbell Road police station to the car park near Prospect Street. The car park was an outdoor lot, not much more than a big empty space with a crude tarmac surface laid by the cheapest contractors who had been available at the time, and the time had in all likelihood been more than thirty years ago.

Schrader pulled up beside the rickety wooden kiosk at the entrance to the car park. She wound down her window and held out her hand to take the ticket from the unshaven man at the kiosk window.

The man looked into the car, gave Schrader the ticket and also gave her what he probably called his winning smile.

"Nice motor," he said.

"Thank you." She started to close the window.

"What's that, Alfa Romeo GT?"

"You know your cars," Schrader said, although he obviously didn't, at least not well enough to be able to tell a GT from her model, which was a GTV6. She checked her rear-view mirror and saw that there were already two more cars queued behind her, waiting to get into the car park.

Schrader closed her window and followed the faded anti-clockwise arrows that were painted at irregular intervals on the tarmac. In addition to the rows of nose-to-tail double-parked cars, there was a line of spaces along the redbrick wall that bordered one side of the car park. Schrader spotted an empty space between a pale blue Vauxhall Cavalier and a yellow Mini Cooper. She pulled alongside the Mini, then reversed smoothly into the empty space. She preferred parking with one side of the car near the wall because it meant nobody was going to park next to her Alfa and open their door into hers, or scrape the car with their shopping bags, clumsily or otherwise.

She waited while the two cars that had followed her into the car park drove past before grabbing her bag from the passenger seat and climbing out of her car. Although it was still early afternoon, the sky mostly cloudless, there was a fresh breeze and the air was bitterly cold.

Schrader walked away past the Vauxhall towards the exit onto Prospect Street. Her dark coat was long, hanging well below her knees, but she still felt cold enough to pick up her pace, as if she might outdistance the chilling breeze that sought out the tiniest gaps between buttons and collars. She took one quick look back at her car, appreciating how arrogantly superior it looked between the Vauxhall and the Mini. The Cavalier was at least five years old and there was already rust along its door sills, and she had never liked Minis; she thought they looked like children's toys. She loved her black Alfa Romeo, in spite of the occasional comments that it wasn't really a woman's car. Comments from men, obviously, and comments that she generally chose to ignore.

She walked out of the car park onto Prospect Street, crossed the road and followed her memorised directions to *Bright Soles*. Passing a small café on her right, Schrader decided that she would stop off for a cup of tea when she was on her way back from the shoe shop. It was already close to two p.m. and she felt as though she had been on her feet all day.

When she reached *Bright Soles*, Kath Schrader stood outside in the cold for a few moments longer than necessary, looking at the window displays much like any casual weekday afternoon shopper might do.

The door had one of those useless-but-noisy security devices fitted to it that clanged and jangled when the door was opened, no matter whether someone was entering or leaving the shop. Schrader reached up and stopped it jangling as she closed the door behind her. She saw the girl behind the counter stare at her, the instinctively reproachful look in the shop assistant's eyes morphing awkwardly into a welcoming smile as Schrader stared back at her.

Schrader walked straight up to the counter, pulling off her tight burgundy leather gloves and slipping them into her shoulder bag.

"How can I help?" asked the girl behind the counter.

Schrader took her hand out of her bag, holding her warrant card between her thumb and forefinger. She held it out for the girl to look at.

"I'm DI Schrader from Humberside CID. I would like to speak to the manager."

"Oh," said the girl. "Shall I go and get him?"

"If you could, please."

The assistant hurried away through a door at the rear of the shop. Schrader had picked up on the flash of genuine concern, almost anxiety, in the girl's eyes when she had asked to speak to the manager.

While she waited, Kath Schrader unbuttoned her coat. The shop was more than pleasantly warm. The girl who had been behind the counter was wearing a cap-sleeved blouse, thin white material, not November clothing unless you happened to be in Egypt. Schrader had been to Egypt in November when she had been twenty-two, when her husband was still just her boyfriend, and when the police force was still just an ambition, not a career and a full-time lifestyle.

The assistant came back through the door. A man was following her. He looked anxious, borderline worried, and he looked like he was trying hard to hide the anxiety. He walked up to Kath Schrader, looked at his right hand as if not entirely sure of the correct etiquette when faced with a female police officer, and offered it anyway.

"Hello," he said, as Schrader firmly returned his tentative handshake. "I'm Derek Simmons, retail sales manager. Claire was telling me that you wanted to speak to me about something."

Schrader released his hand. "DI Schrader, Humberside CID. Could we speak in private?"

"Of course, yes," Simmons said. He gestured towards the door at the rear of the shop. "My office is through there."

Schrader nodded. "After you."

***

Dan tilted his head slightly, reading the titles on the spines of the VHS cases that were packed in a row along one of the wall shelves in Tom Mason's first-floor bedroom. Technically, it was no longer a single room. Two of the house's original five bedrooms had been converted into a single space by the partial removal of the dividing wall. Two ends of the wall remained, three feet on each side. One half of the resulting room looked very much like a bedroom, the other half was a jumbled maze of electrical equipment. There were guitar amplifiers, speaker cabinets, two televisions, an Atari personal computer on a desk with its own monitor, several guitars hanging on the walls, and multi-coloured cables coiled and snaking everywhere.

Rick Price was looking at one of the guitars, a cherry red electric six-string with a monkey sticker on the body.

"Is this real?" Rick asked.

Dan didn't look round. He knew Rick wasn't talking to him. He read some more film titles, wondering if there was possibly an entire career to be made from the charges he had no intention of bringing against Tom Mason. So far, there was possession and public use of a class B narcotic. The videos were making things a little more interesting.

"Yeah," Tom Mason said to Rick. "It's one of Iommi's from the *Never Say Die* tour."

"Seventy-eight," Rick said. "I saw them in Manchester."

"No way. I was there too. The Apollo. Amazing gig."

"How did you get the guitar?"

"Money," Tom said. "You can buy most things with money."

Dan was mentally adding a variety of infringements of the Obscene Publications Act to Tom Mason's catalogue of crimes and misdemeanours. Some of the banned film titles were notoriously familiar, others he had never heard of. *The Driller Killer*, *Cannibal Ferox*, *Cannibal Holocaust*, *I Spit on Your Grave*, *The Evil Dead*, *2000 Maniacs*. In amongst the video nasties there were several other VHS films that were not on any banned or obscene list, but the majority were horror films.

"*Christine*," Dan said. "My wife read the book."

"Then tell her not to watch the film," Tom said. "Nowhere near as good."

"Do you actually watch these banned films?" Dan asked.

"Do I go to prison for longer if I say I do?"

Dan walked away from the shelf, shaking his head. "Rick, can we get back to why we came here?"

"Okay," Rick said. "But some of this gear is very impressive."

"Tom, we need you to tell us the names of anyone who knew both Sharon Hall and Dee Collins."

"That's just going to be kids who were in school with us. I haven't seen Dee since the end of the fifth form, and I'm pretty sure Sharon didn't keep in touch with her. She never mentioned her to me, anyway."

"Has anyone else from your school kept in touch with Sharon, that you know of?"

Tom looked up at the ceiling, slowly shaking his head from side to side. Instead of one of his own band's black T-shirts, he was wearing one bearing a large monochrome image from a very old vampire movie. Above the movie frame, which showed a large bat-shaped shadow against a white wall, was the word 'bauhaus', printed lowercase in a simple, bold geometric typeface. Beneath the image, in a handwritten signature style, were the words *Bela Lugosi's dead.*

"Maybe," Tom said. "I didn't see her at all while I was in the sixth form. I started hanging out in Gaspari's when they had a tabletop *Asteroids* in there, which was in 1981. Sharon started working there in 1982."

Dan jotted a quick note on his pad. "You started going to the café before Sharon worked there?"

"Yeah. Don't ask me to prove it, because how could I? It's not as if anyone who works there is going to remember when I started going there."

"Hey," Dan said. "You're not under suspicion. I just want to make sure I've got every detail correct."

"Were you any good at *Asteroids*?" Rick asked.

"You ever play it?"

"A little."

"Ever clock it?" Tom asked.

"Once or twice."

"What are you talking about?" Dan asked.

"Arcade games," Rick said. "Come on, you're not *that* old."

"Never saw the attraction," Dan said.

Tom sighed. "Sounds like my old man." He looked at Rick. "So you like Sabbath and you played *Asteroids*. Not bad for a policeman. No offence."

"Tell me about *Asteroids*," Dan said. "Keep it quick. Just make me understand the attraction."

Tom looked at Rick. "Okay. The first time you play it, it's just chaos. Screen full of spinning rocks, five buttons, ship won't stop flying off the side of the screen, you last about ten seconds. Then you get out of the way and someone who knows what they're doing gets on the machine, and it's like they're playing a totally different game. It still looks like chaos but the ship they're flying is fluid and controlled, and it's like they're invincible. Rocks exploding all over the place, UFOs fly on and get wasted immediately, and the game goes on and on because they're pretty much untouchable. And you watch them, and you think, yeah, I can do that. And a few weeks later, you can. If you're actually any good at it."

Dan shrugged. "I'm still not convinced."

"Well," Tom said, "one of the guys who showed me most of the high-scoring techniques wasn't much younger than you. He was also actually pretty cool. He even gave me the name for the band, *Never There*. He said that was what you had to be to master the chaos. I know, totally pretentious, but he made it sound like something cool."

"See," Rick said. "Old men can play arcade games."

"How could he have given you the name of the band?" Dan asked. "You only joined it recently."

"Rob and the others didn't like the name they had. I think the guitarist who left had come up with it."

Dan said, "I see." He didn't bother writing down any of what Tom had said.

Tom Mason was looking at the notepad in Dan's hands, reading the upside-down writing. The smile that had appeared during the Black Sabbath and *Asteroids* fuelled nostalgia was no longer there.

"Has something happened to Dee Collins?"

***

"How well did you know Dee?"

Kath Schrader was sitting opposite Derek Simmons, coat folded over her crossed knees, shoulder bag hanging on the back of the chair. Her back was straight, eyes fixed on Simmons, notepad flat on top of her folded coat. Her biro was poised an inch above the notepad while she waited to add more words to the page.

On the other side of the desk Simmons frowned, adjusted his position on his chair as if it was unfamiliar or uncomfortable.

"Fairly well, as an employee. I didn't know her outside work, if that's what you mean."

Schrader took a few seconds before she wrote anything. She was used to dealing with men. It was all part of the daily routine. They talked to your chest, pretended they hadn't been doing it, and you pretended you hadn't noticed. Or you did what Kath Schrader did in Simmons' office, which was to casually touch the lapel of her blouse and gently pull it half an inch to the left, closing the tiny gap at her throat.

Simmons had been shocked by the news that one of his employees was dead, shocked to the point of speechlessness. Schrader had noted the response, and carried on. She had only told Simmons that Dee Collins was dead. No details, no mention of foul play or cause of death.

"Was she involved in a relationship with anyone who works here?"

"No, not that I know of."

"Have any of your customers asked for Dee Collins specifically, or ignored the other assistants in order to be served by her when she became available?"

"I don't think so." Derek Simmons held up a finger. "Wait, there was a man in here yesterday asking for her. I know because Claire mentioned it. Claire Thomas, the assistant you spoke to."

"Do you know who he was?"

"No, but Claire said he had been here before a few times. He didn't buy anything, just asked to speak to Dee."

"Can you give me a description of this man?"

"I didn't see him. I could ask Claire."

Schrader waited before she replied. She knew why Simmons was uncomfortable. It was the way he had said the assistant's name. She touched the nib of her pen against the notepad.

"Claire with an I, or without?"

Simmons swallowed before answering. "With."

"Middle name?"

"Beverly."

Schrader looked over her shoulder at the closed office door. There was a narrow chrome barrel bolt near the top of the door. Small, but solid enough to prevent the door being accidentally opened from outside. Effective enough to remove the risk of being interrupted while balancing some complicated figures, or while balancing a junior sales assistant on one's lap. The bolt looked new, looked as though it probably hadn't been there for more than a few months.

"Is it the excitement?" Schrader asked, turning back to face Derek Simmons. "Or is it that you just can't help yourself?"

"I'm sorry, what?"

"Claire Beverly Thomas. With an I."

Simmons squirmed on his chair. He touched his tie, shook his head. "I don't know what you're talk—"

"Dee Collins was murdered last night."

"Murdered?"

"Are you able to account for your movements and whereabouts between six o'clock and midnight, Mr Simmons?"

"What? Yes, I was at home. With my wife and two sons."

"From six o'clock?"

Simmons looked at his desk, shook his head. "I was working until seven last night."

"Working?" Schrader said. She wrote something on her pad.

"In this office. Doing some stock control."

"Alone?"

Simmons swallowed hard, moistened his lips with his tongue. "No."

"How many employees were here with you?"

"Just one."

"And could I ask her to confirm that you were here until seven?"

"Do you really have to?"

Schrader moved her chair backwards a few inches, looked at her watch and smiled at Derek Simmons. "I'll call the station. They can have a patrol car here in ten minutes. Uniformed officers, probably handcuffs. Will the shop have to close early if you are not on the premises?"

"It was only Claire. I never even bothered trying with Dee. I swear. I have no idea what happened to her. I didn't know anything had, not until you just told me. I'll stop, I promise. I won't see Claire any more. If my wife ever found out…"

"Why didn't you try with Dee, Mr Simmons? Did someone warn you off? Did Dee know someone who scared you? A boyfriend, maybe?"

Simmons sat back in his chair, shaking his head. "No," he said. "She didn't have a boyfriend."

"Are you sure about that?"

"Yes."

"How can you be sure? Perhaps she didn't want to talk about him."

"No, it wasn't that."

"What, then? How do you know she didn't have a boyfriend?"

Simmons shook his head. "Dee wasn't interested in

men. She liked other women."

***

"That's why we had to talk to you," Dan said. "We really need any help you can give us."

Tom Mason was sitting on the edge of his bed, his hands resting on his thighs, his fingers moving with an unconscious nervous energy.

"It can't be a coincidence." He looked from Rick to Dan. "I gave you her name. Please don't tell me that you think I had anything to do with any of this."

"We don't," Dan said.

"Why didn't you tell me straight away? All that about music and arcade games, what was that about?"

"Just seeing if you were feeling relaxed, conversational."

"Seeing if I looked guilty."

Rick crouched down beside the bed. "We just want some help, Tom. That's all. We're not going to drag you down the station, we just want to talk to you."

"I haven't seen Dee Collins since the end of the fifth form."

Dan checked something in his notepad. "Seventy-seven."

"Yeah. Last time I saw her was the day of the English lit O-level exam."

"You actually remember that?" Dan asked.

Tom nodded. "I liked English lit. The books we had to read weren't great, but all you had to do was read them and have an opinion."

"Was Dee Collins in your English lit group?"

"Yeah. And Sharon Hall. And about twenty-five other kids."

"How many other subjects did you do with both of them?"

Tom tilted his head back and exhaled. "Biology and

History."

"Just those three subjects?"

"There were two fifth form classes at John Blair. Each O-level subject had a mix of kids from both classes. Sharon was in my class, Five-G. Dee was in the other one, Five-L."

"Okay," Dan said. "But Sharon and Dee were friends despite being in different classes."

"Yeah. They were friends all the way through secondary school."

"Were you friends with them in school?"

"Not really, not until the fifth form. Sharon had cadged fags off me for ages and Dee got into doing it too in the fifth form. Eventually they started talking to me when we were all smoking behind the maths hut. I knew I didn't have a chance with either of them, so I was happy just talking bollocks."

"Who else was in this smoking group?"

"It wasn't really a group. Lots of kids from the third form up used to smoke there. Weird, really, because half the older kids who smoked there were total psychos but they never did anything to anyone else while we were all smoking. Like it was a bullying cease-fire or something."

"Did you get bullied in school?" Dan asked.

"You're kidding, right? Who didn't get bullied in school?"

Dan glanced at Rick, then looked back at Tom. "When you said some of the kids were total psychos, do you think any of them would be capable of carrying a schoolyard grudge into later life and then acting on it?"

"It was school," Tom said. "Nobody gives a shit about what happened back then. I'm only talking about it because you asked me. I doubt half those kids remember each other, let alone spend time thinking about who said what, or who hit who in the playground."

Dan looked through the gap where the dividing wall used to be. "If it is only a coincidence that two murder victims were friends in school, then we have to look for another link." He turned back to face Tom. "You said you didn't think they had been in touch since school. Do you know why that happened, if they had been friends all that time?"

Tom looked down at his hands. He took a deep breath, let it out slowly. "It's probably not what I think."

Dan took a step closer to where Tom was sitting. "What, Tom? However trivial it might seem, it could be the clue we need."

"I doubt it. It's a bit personal."

"Personal?"

"They just did it for a laugh a couple of times, just to wind one of the teachers up. But I always thought Dee was a lot more into it than she was pretending to be. She was definitely more into it than Sharon."

"What do you mean, Tom? What did they do?"

Tom exhaled, looked like he was still thinking about not telling them.

"Tom, it could be important. What did they do?"

"Kissed each other. In class."

CHAPTER 21

"And the… other thing," Derek Simmons said as Kath Schrader pulled her coat over her shoulders. "That isn't going to go any further, is it?"

"I can't arrest you for screwing one of your employees, Mr Simmons, no matter how sleazy and pathetic I personally think it is."

Simmons nodded nervously, like he was still apprehensive about the patrol car and the handcuffs.

"I want you to stay here," Schrader said, standing in the frame of the open office door. "I'd prefer to speak to Claire Thomas without you hovering around out there."

Simmons stood behind his desk, hands hanging limp at his sides. "If that's what you want."

"Thank you for your time." Schrader smiled briefly, devoid of empathy, as if Simmons were one of those beggars she always saw around town. No food, no money, but some fags and a dog. "I'll be in touch if I need any more of it."

She turned and walked away from Derek Simmons and his seedy little office before he could say anything else. The office was at the back of a stockroom lined with row after row of shelf units that reached the ceiling, all completely packed with shoeboxes. Schrader walked out of the stockroom and went straight over to the counter. There were no customers being served. Claire Thomas was standing behind the counter in her flimsy white blouse. She gave Schrader a cautious smile.

"Hello, Claire," Schrader said. "I would like to ask you a few very quick questions."

"Okay, sure," Claire said.

"You seem nervous. There's no need for you to be nervous."

"Oh, good. But I'm not. Really, I'm not."

"Tell me about the man who came into the shop to see Dee Collins yesterday."

Claire appeared to relax when she heard the question.

"Do you mean Mr Hughes?"

"Was he the man who came in to talk to Dee?"

Claire nodded. "He came in just after twelve o'clock."

"What does Mr Hughes look like?"

"Sort of a bit overweight."

"What about his hair? What colour is it?"

"Kind of reddish. A bit like Ralph Malph, you know, from *Happy Days*, but he's about twice as old."

"Anything else?"

"He wears glasses."

"Do you know what they talked about?"

"He asked her to do some baby-sitting for him last night."

Schrader briefly glanced away, considering what Claire had just said. "Had Dee done that before?"

"A few times, I think."

Schrader nodded, but didn't write anything else in her notepad. The baby-sitting was a cover story, obviously. She didn't need to find out anything more about Mr Hughes. He was safely locked up at the Campbell Road station.

"Has anyone else ever come into the shop to talk to

Dee, apart from people buying shoes?"

"No, not that I've ever seen anyway."

Kath Schrader put her notepad and pen back in her shoulder bag. "Thank you, Claire. You've been very helpful."

Claire looked across the counter at Kath Schrader. "Has something happened to Dee?"

"I've given Mr Simmons all the information I am currently able to share." Schrader took a business card out of her bag. "Take this. If you need to call me, about anything at all, you can reach me on this number."

Claire took the card and looked at it. "Call you about what?"

Schrader looked back at the doorway of the stockroom. "Anything at all."

"Okay."

Outside, the breeze was stronger and the air felt even colder than it had before Kath Schrader had gone into *Bright Soles*. She strode briskly along the pavement until she reached the café that she had passed earlier.

She bought tea that came in a small, stubby white teapot from a short-haired woman with a permanent smile. Schrader pondered the relative merits and shortcomings of a job which involved a constant level of either natural or forced joviality. By the time she had carried the tray with the teapot, cup and saucer to an empty table, she had concluded that such a career would not suit her.

While she sipped her tea, Schrader read the notes that she had taken in *Bright Soles*.

"Hughes visited Dee Collins yesterday," she said softly, confirming her thoughts as she worked through her notes. "Probably arranging last night's visit."

She looked across the café at the partly curtained windows, the dark shapes of midweek shoppers hurrying past on the far side of the fogged glass, mostly head-down against the cold. As she watched, one of the shapes paused at the window and looked in. Schrader couldn't make out any distinct facial features during the few brief seconds when the backlit man was looking in, and whoever it had been did not seem to have been looking at her. She was sure it hadn't been Derek Simmons. He was a tall, insubstantial collection of sticks in a loose suit. The person who had paused at the window had been a far more solidly built man.

Schrader went back to her tea and her notepad.

"Derek Simmons," she said, quickly taking a sip of tea as if the name had put a sour taste on her tongue. "Perhaps I should have called the patrol car after all." She frowned at the words on her pad. "What does she see in you? Probably an early promotion."

Kath Schrader knew a lot of men, and she was confident that she knew a lot about men. Her own husband, Gerard, was a roaming freelance journalist who specialised in reviews and personal experience articles for motorcycle magazines. Their careers dramatically reduced the amount of time that they spent together, but Kath Schrader was a pragmatist when it came to relationships; the periods of absence gave their time together a purity and a focus that she was sure would have waned long ago if they saw each other every day.

She packed her notepad back in her shoulder bag, finishing her tea while she mulled over the information she had for the two murders.

Rick Price had been on the right track, she had to admit, when he had said that there was too much evidence but none of it helped. She took one last sip of tea and smiled to herself. Price had some kind of awkward crush on her, awkward but not disturbing. She had worked with a lot of men. She knew how they generally reacted to her, and Price's crush wasn't unique.

Schrader put the cup and saucer back on the tray with the teapot. She carried the tray across to the counter and handed it to the smiling short-haired woman.

"Thanks very much," said the woman.

"You're welcome. That was a nice cup of tea."

The woman's smile widened. "Back out into the cold, now?"

"Afraid so. No rest for the wicked."

"None at all," said the woman, laughing heartily at the tired cliché.

Schrader buttoned her coat to her throat and slipped her gloves on before opening the café door and stepping out into the cold. She looked back along the pavement in the direction of *Bright Soles*. No loitering, suspicious looking dark figures, nobody ducking out of sight into a shop doorway. Not that she had expected to see anything like that, but it was always worth checking your immediate vicinity. One of the first things they taught you.

She walked along the street towards the car park, wondering whether Dan Blacksmith had turned up any new leads when he talked to Thomas Mason. She appreciated the positive way that Dan was dealing with his demotion and recent transfer, and also how well he was coping with the additional challenge of coaching Rick Price. Dan's transfer to Humberside Police, specifically his appointment at Campbell Road CID, had been a topic that she and Harry West had spent a good deal of time discussing, both before and after Dan's arrival.

Schrader had met Dan Blacksmith's wife just once, when the department had organised a meal-and-drinks night out for officers and their partners. She remembered that Dan and Rebecca had left early, around ten p.m., because they had to collect their daughter from a child-minder. She also remembered that Dan's wife was an artist who was making a considerable name for herself with her portrait work.

Schrader strode into the car park through the main entrance. She kept her eyes straight ahead because the stubble-chinned automobile aficionado had looked as though he was fully prepared to strike up another conversation. Most likely with her chest. She took a shortcut on the crumbling, pitted tarmac between two rows of cars, heading towards the wall on the far left of the car park.

Schrader reached the line of cars parked along the car park wall. The cars were all parked nose-to-tail, all facing away from her. She walked closer to the parked cars when she heard the sound of a vehicle approaching behind her. She looked back, checking that there was plenty of room for the car to pass her. The car was a white Escort RS2000 with wide tyres, blue racing stripes, and a row of four spotlights across the radiator grille. In the handful of seconds it took to draw level and pass her, Schrader saw the young male driver glance at her, and the young female passenger scowl at him and then glare briefly at her. She gave the girl a version of the empty smile she had used on Derek Simmons. The Escort carried on until it reached the right turn about twenty yards away, where it disappeared from her view.

Kath Schrader could see her Alfa four cars ahead of her, with the rusting Vauxhall still parked behind it. The Mini had gone, and there was now a red Peugeot 205 in its place. She looked down at the bag that was slung on a strap over her left shoulder, reached into the front pocket and took out her keys. It felt slightly less precise, a little more of a fumble than usual, because she was wearing gloves.

Kath Schrader was thinking about several things, about baby-sitters and gloves and messages left at crime scenes. She drew level with the Vauxhall, keen to climb into her own car, get the engine running and turn up the heater. She was looking forward to exchanging information with Dan Blacksmith when she got back to Campbell Road, where it would be warm. She had honestly had enough of walking around in the cold.

The driver's side door of the Vauxhall swung wide open and Kath Schrader walked straight into it. No warning, no chance to dodge it, or to stop walking, or to even slow down.

Her left knee collided with the edge of the door, low down where the metal was heavy and solid, mostly free of rust, and where the edge was a tapered, welded seam not that much different from a curved, blunted blade. The impact was jarring and cruel, and it sent a wave of dizzying nausea roiling through her body.

The sharp corner at the top of the doorframe jabbed into her chest, high up, only an inch or two below her throat. Her coat saved her from what could have been a worse injury; as it was, the skin was still painfully gouged.

Kath Schrader would have cried out, would have rounded on the idiot who had opened the door without checking that it was safe to do so, but she couldn't.

The man who had opened the door came out of the car in a hurry, and he led with his fists. Schrader had seen a TV documentary about oceanic predators that had included a sequence where an octopus had attacked a shark from its hiding place in a tight fissure of rock. The footage had played in real-time, and been subsequently slowed down by a factor of ten to capture the incredible speed and aggression of the octopus.

The memory barely registered, hardly more than an instant of associated shock between moments of extreme pain.

The man was dressed all in black. Coat, trousers, boots, gloves. Balaclava. He hit Schrader three times in less than a second. Hard, short-travel punches to her stomach, throat and solar plexus.

He caught her before she fell, nudging the Vauxhall's door closed at the same time as he grabbed the keys that fell from her gloved hand.

Schrader's vision was unfocussed, her balance gone,

consciousness phasing like a poorly tuned channel on an ancient TV. The blow to her throat had robbed her of the ability to cry out, or to utter anything more than feeble, hoarse gasps.

The man was half dragging her, half walking her across the tarmac towards her black Alfa Romeo. He turned her right wrist back on itself, twisting her arm behind her back as he unlocked the Alfa and partially opened the driver's door. She was facing him, her back to the car, knowing she should be fighting back but overwhelmed by multiple sources of pain and a numbing shock that she had only ever heard described before, by victims of road accidents and rapes.

She felt her left arm being lifted and forced across her chest, as if her attacker was trying to crush her with her own arm. He was holding her wrist, pressing her hand against hard, cold metal. Kath Schrader didn't realise what was happening until the man rammed his shoulder against her body, slamming the car door shut on her left hand.

Her weak, pitiful shriek was muffled behind the palm of his gloved left hand. His right hand twisted hard against her right wrist, forcing it further beyond its natural range of motion. He rammed her backwards again and she knew that her right wrist had broken.

The man opened the Alfa's door wide, spun Schrader around like an untutored dance partner and shoved her inside, where she sprawled in a limp heap across the front seats. He followed her in, crushing her shins beneath his knees as he pulled the door closed behind him.

Schrader was on her back, legs trapped beneath her assailant, left hand crushed and bleeding, right wrist broken. She was barely able to breathe, let alone cry out for help. The Alfa's handbrake was pressing into her lower back and the leather bucket seats that she had always considered to be sporty and elegant were now cruelly unanticipated sources of discomfort.

She looked up at the featureless silhouette of the balaclava mask. Her vision was blurred with tears and agony but she could still see his eyes. She saw no anger in them, no sign of drug use. She saw something in his eyes that in that moment was infinitely worse. His eyes looked distant and calm. He looked bored.

Schrader knew right then that all her training had been useless. The unarmed combat sessions, the lectures on how to avoid having a victim mentality, threat assessment, controlling a situation with voice commands, tactical negotiation… None of that would help her, and nothing that she had learned could have stopped what was happening, and what was about to happen. It was a fantasy, a textbook charade of rehearsals and practices played out in comfortably heated rooms with safety procedures and noisy, testosterone-rich instructors. They had ice-breakers and audience participation and they asked for volunteers and the rest of the group had a good laugh when you got tripped and fell on a padded crash mat. It was just a daydream, a game, a reassuring lie.

Reality was being attacked in a busy car park in daylight, incapacitated and crippled, overpowered in a matter of seconds. Schrader thought of Gerard, of how he was somewhere in Europe at that very second, riding a powerful German motorcycle along a motorway or a meandering mountain road. When would he hear about what had happened to his wife, and who would tell him?

The man leaned forward, held her chin with one hand and punched her in the face with the other. Not hard enough to render her unconscious, just hard enough to split her lips and break her nose.

And then he started speaking to her.

Schrader heard the sounds but couldn't understand what was being said. Three syllables, which she first thought were three words, but they were being repeated and they were not words that she recognised. He wasn't ranting incoherently, just saying whatever it was that he was saying. Over and over. Three syllables.

Schrader didn't want to listen. She wanted to go away, to be anywhere but trapped on the front seats of her own car, powerless and terrified.

The man kept repeating the three syllables. Slowly. Clearly.

He didn't stop speaking while he tore open Schrader's coat, sending several of the large black buttons bouncing onto the clean carpet of the passenger footwell.

Schrader tried to plead, but all that came out was a sob of hopeless despair.

The man in black used both hands to pull the front of her blouse apart.

Three syllables. Over and over. Calm. Bored.

Schrader couldn't stop herself listening to his voice, even through her own strangled gasps of horror. Not even when he opened the penknife that had been in his pocket and pressed the sharp point of the blade against the lacy right cup of her bra.

CHAPTER 22

Dan looked across the top of the BMW at Rick Price. Rick was half smiling, half frowning.

"I know," Rick said. "If I had seen a couple of pretty fifth-formers kissing each other when I was in school, that's the one image that I would have carried with me for the next couple of hundred years too."

Dan nodded. "I'll add it to the list of things to check out when we've exhausted all the potentially useful leads that actually relate to the case."

They both climbed into the car at the same time, pulling the doors closed with relief as they shut out the cold.

"It's still interesting, though," Rick said.

"I'll be sure to mention your inappropriate fascination with schoolgirls to DI Schrader."

Rick grinned appreciatively. "I wonder if she got anything nice from *Bright Soles*. Maybe some stiletto heels."

Dan said nothing. There were times when you had to just stop encouraging Rick Price, for his own good.

"Better check in," Dan said. He started the car, put a call through to the station as he drove away from the Masons' house. "Control, this is One-Six Charlie Delta. Do you have anything for us on the Hall or Collins cases, over?"

"One-Six Charlie Delta, please hold, over."

Dan drove down the gentle slope that led back towards the city centre.

The radio crackled. "Dan? It's Harry. Get to the General. I'm already on my way."

"The hospital?"

"Kath was attacked, Dan. She was admitted less than fifteen minutes ago."

Dan glanced sideways at Rick Price. Rick's eyes were wide with surprise and concern.

"Attacked?" Dan said. "How bad is she?"

"She's alive."

"Who attacked her?"

"We don't know."

"Did it happen at the shoe shop?"

"No. Public car park near Prospect Street."

"Witnesses?"

"Not that we know of. She radioed it in herself."

Dan let out a sigh of relief. "So she was well enough to radio it in?"

"Not exactly."

"What do you mean?"

"We don't know the precise details, but it seems that her attacker radioed the station and held the mic for Kath to talk to them."

"What? From Kath's car?"

"I don't know exactly what happened, Dan. Just get to the hospital."

"On our way. Over and out." Dan's hands tightened on the rim of the steering wheel. "It's him. It has to be."

***

The doctor kept them waiting for an hour outside a private treatment room in a corridor that smelled strongly of the type of disinfectant that only hospitals use. Dan was sitting against the wall in one of the cheap plastic chairs that he and Rick had carried from a mostly empty waiting room. Harry West was pacing back and forth in front of the treatment room door, constantly looking at his wristwatch and shaking his head.

"Shall I get some more coffees?" Rick asked.

"Not for me," Dan said. "They're not going to be much longer."

Harry West stopped pacing for a few seconds and stood in front of Dan and Rick. "I just can't understand how he got the jump on her in a car park in broad daylight."

Dan looked up. "He watches, and he plans."

"You think it's the same person, the one who killed both those young women?"

"At the moment, that seems extremely likely."

Rick sighed, shaking his head. "Tom Mason and Raymond Hughes are totally off the hook, then."

"We had already pretty much discounted them as viable suspects."

"I honestly wasn't sure about Hughes," Rick said. "His alibi for the Hall murder was just a bit too watertight."

"Sometimes genuine alibis are."

Harry West said, "If it was the same man, then Kath will be able to tell us about him, give us some kind of a description."

"Maybe," Dan said. "Do you know if he tried to strangle Kath?"

"Not sure," Harry said. "We'll find out when we get a chance to talk to her."

The door of the treatment room opened. The doctor who had briefly spoken to them earlier stepped out into the corridor, closing the door behind him. He was Greek, late thirties, with close-cropped black hair, dark eyes, and a prominent aquiline nose.

"I would like to request that you gentleman give Mrs

Schrader some uninterrupted privacy, but she has chosen to overrule my qualified medical opinion."

Dan stood up. "Can we go in?"

The doctor held up his hand. "However, I insisted on a compromise. I told her that I would only allow one immediate visitor who was not a spouse or family member." He looked at the three police officers. "Which one of you is Detective Sergeant Dan Blacksmith?"

"I am."

The doctor nodded. "She chose you." He looked at Harry and Rick. "If you two could wait out here while Sergeant Blacksmith goes into the room for a few minutes." He turned to Dan. "Only a few minutes, please. No more than that."

"Okay," Dan said. "Is she awake?"

"Yes, but if she isn't then do not attempt to wake her up."

"I won't."

Dan opened the door just wide enough to enter the room. He went in, closing the door before crossing the small room to stand beside the bed. He looked down at the woman who was lying on it. He saw bruises and bandages. A lot of bandages. She was lying back against the raised head of the bed, canted at an angle of about thirty degrees. The flexible transparent pipe from a saline drip hanging from a stand attached to the bed frame disappeared under the bandages around her left wrist.

"I know, I look like shit."

Her voice was barely more than a whisper, hoarse and reedy as if she had been yelling over the din of an all-night disco while smoking unfiltered Capstans for six hours straight.

"You look okay."

"Don't bullshit me, Dan." She winced in pain when she turned her head less than half an inch to the side to look at him.

Dan sat in the chair that was next to the bed. "Do you need anything?"

Schrader took a breath. It caught in her throat as if she were on the verge of bursting into tears. "Stop him."

"We will." He looked at her face, thinking of Rick Price and how Rick had reacted when he had seen Dee Collins' body on Raymond Hughes' carpet. Easy enough to mask your reactions when they're dead, but this was nothing like that. Kath's right eye was completely closed, the left one not much more than a narrow slit. Her nose was covered with a thick white dressing, which Dan knew was a sure sign that it had been broken. Her lips were cut, but he didn't think she had lost any teeth.

"Try not to talk," Dan said. "Do you want me to stay?"

Schrader moved her head slightly, just a tiny forward inclination.

"Can I ask you some questions about what happened?"

"Yes."

"You don't have to talk if it hurts."

"Hurts more to nod."

"Sorry." Dan took out his notepad. "Did you see his face?"

"Mask."

"How about eye colour?"

"Brown."

"Light brown or dark brown?"

"Dark."

"Could you see his skin?"

"White."

"Absolutely sure?"

"Yes."

Dan had been writing as Schrader answered his questions. He looked at what he had noted so far.

"Hair colour?"

"Don't know."

"Could you see his eyebrows?"

Schrader didn't answer immediately. After a few seconds, she said, "I can't remember if I did."

"That's okay. You're doing great."

"I'm not." She gingerly ran her tongue over her bottom lip, groaning at the pain. "I was useless."

"No," Dan said. "He took you by surprise. There was nothing you could do."

Schrader said no more for a while. She stared straight ahead with her half-open left eye. Dan didn't push her for more answers. He sat next to the bed in silence, waiting for her to be ready to continue.

"In the drawer," Schrader said.

Dan turned to look at the cabinet beside the bed. Schrader's shoulder bag was on top of it.

"In here?"

"Yes."

Dan pulled the drawer open. The wooden cabinet was cheap, the drawer a tight, uneven fit between its runners. He had to pull it quite hard and it squeaked when it opened. There was a single Polaroid photograph face down in the drawer. Dan didn't touch it.

"What is it?"

"I made them take it after they cleaned me up, before they put the dressing on." As she was speaking, Schrader's bandaged right hand moved towards her chest. "Go on, look at it."

Dan took the photograph out of the drawer and turned it over.

Schrader didn't look at him. "Don't show it to Rick. I think it would spoil his crush."

Dan felt his throat tightening. "Jesus."

"Doctor Michaelides assured me the permanent scarring would be minimal."

Dan pinched the bridge of his nose, blinking hard to keep himself focussed. Schrader's voice had come close to breaking completely when she had said the word 'permanent'.

"You don't have to tell me anything else, Kath."

"He did it with a red Swiss Army penknife."

"Kath…"

"He left the knife in my car."

Dan looked up from the Polaroid photo. He wanted to tear it up and hurl the shredded strips into a toilet, flush them away forever. He knew he couldn't do it. It was evidence.

"Are you sure?"

"He put it in the glove box."

"In your car? Is it still there?"

"I made them lock the car before they put me in the ambulance. The keys are in my bag."

"Did you tell anyone else about the knife?"

"No."

"He wants us to find it," Dan said. "Wants us to examine it. It's going to have someone's prints on it, but not his."

"How do you know?"

"It's what he does. He leaves messages." Dan looked at the Polaroid, read the message that had been carved in three-inch capitals across DI Kath Schrader's chest. The letters were not as precise and consistent as in the previous messages, probably because Schrader had been writhing in horrified agony while her attacker was doing it. "I think he was writing W-A-R-M but he only got as far as W-A-R."

"No." Schrader fought to suppress a sob. "He had time. He wasn't interrupted."

Dan nodded slowly. "War." He looked down at the photograph in his hand. "He's declaring war on us, on the police."

Schrader sniffed, instantly gasping at the pain from her broken nose. "There's something else. He wasn't angry at all. He was completely calm the whole time, almost indifferent."

"Emotional detachment," Dan said. "No excitement or rage. That's what Nigel Hansom told me after he had examined Sharon Hall's body."

Schrader took a long breath. "Why didn't he…?"

"Don't, Kath."

"Why didn't he kill me?"

Dan looked at the photograph again. The wounds were shallow, the blood loss wouldn't have been life-threatening even if Schrader hadn't been found for hours. And she hadn't been strangled.

"Harry told us the attacker called the station on your radio."

"Yes, he did."

"Did he tell you why he was doing it?"

"No."

"He wanted to make sure you were taken to hospital as soon as possible."

"I don't understand."

"He watches, Kath. He knows what we're doing. He left you alive because he wanted you to tell us something."

"I didn't see anything except his eyes."

"What did he say to you? Did he say anything at all?"

"Yes, but it didn't mean anything."

Dan put the photograph on the top of the cabinet next to Schrader's bag. He held his pen over a fresh line in his notepad.

"Tell me anyway. It might be useful."

"It was just one word. At first it sounded like three words, but they didn't make any sense. He kept repeating it, over and over, and eventually I realised what it was."

"He repeated it because he wanted to make sure you remembered it." Dan nodded, his pen poised over the page. "Go on, what was he saying?"

Kath Schrader said the word.

Dan didn't write it down. The biro froze above the page. There was a throb of tension in his throat and a memory of hard, calloused hands that had trembled as they closed around it.

Kath had said, "*At first it sounded like three words, but they didn't make any sense.*"

But when you knew where the guy had been, when you remembered what had happened, the syllables came together differently and you could never hear them any other way.

CHAPTER 23

The BMW slewed sideways, tyres screeching and losing traction as it hurtled out of the hospital car park.

"Christ, Dan, slow down!"

"What's the quickest way to the *Golden Hart*?"

"Keep going this way." Rick fumbled with the seatbelt, jamming it into the anchor point as he stared out of the windscreen. "You need to slow down, seriously."

"He said *Exocet.* Kath was positive that was what he was saying."

"So you already said. I still don't—"

"Last Friday, in the pub, the big guy who was strangling me, that was what he kept saying."

"Are you sure?"

"He was on the HMS Sheffield when it was hit by an Exocet missile."

"How do you know that?"

"The barman in the *Golden Hart* told me."

"Did he? You didn't say anything at the time."

"My throat was hurting and I just wanted a quiet drink."

"And you're absolutely sure about all this?"

"I know what I heard him saying, and Kath said her

attacker was saying the same thing."

"Next left," Rick said. "And then there's the whole strangling M.O."

"It can't be a coincidence." Dan slowed to take the left turn, immediately accelerating afterwards. "But it still feels too much like one."

"I don't know. Psychotic war vet strangling people and leaving messages written in blood because all he really wants is to be caught and locked away makes some kind of sense."

"Maybe."

"You never said anything about how badly Kath was hurt."

"She'll be okay."

"You gave Harry her car keys. I didn't catch what you said to him."

"Kath thought the guy might have left something in her car that could have had his prints on it."

"Really? What?"

"She wasn't sure."

"Go straight across this roundabout, second exit." Rick checked the time on his watch. "It's way past three o'clock. You know the pub will be shut by now."

"I'm betting on the barman still being there. They'll be opening up again at half six."

Rick swayed left and right as Dan took the mini roundabout without noticeably slowing down. "Did the guy *do anything* to her?"

"Do you mean did he sexually assault her?"

"Yeah."

"No, he didn't."

Rick gave a relieved sigh.

"He did hurt her quite badly," Dan said. "Broken wrist, a couple of nasty cuts and bruises on her face."

"Her face? Shit."

"She'll be okay, Rick. She's old school, tough as they

come."

"At the end of this road, there's a T-junction. Turn right and you should recognise where we are."

Five minutes later, Dan parked the BMW against the kerb on a side street just around the corner from the *Golden Hart.*

Outside the pub, Dan tried the handle on the closed front door. "Yeah, it's locked," he said to Rick.

"Wait here."

Rick stood close to the nearest window and rapped on the glass with his knuckles. After a few seconds, Dan saw him take out his warrant card and press it flat against the window pane.

Rick pointed towards the front door of the pub. Dan couldn't see through the window from where he was standing but he heard a sturdy metal bolt being drawn back, followed by the sound of a large key turning in an ancient lock.

The barman looked out at Dan and Rick, smiling affably. "Afternoon, gentlemen. How can I help you?"

"Could we come inside? I'd like to ask you a few questions and it's not exactly warm out here."

"Of course you can, but I have to advise you that I can't sell you anything alcoholic until after six thirty."

Dan and Rick went inside while the barman held the door open.

"Now," he said, after he had closed and locked the door. "What would you like to know?"

The light from the small ground-floor windows was the only source of illumination inside the bar. The large room felt stale and abandoned without the clamour and the heat of jostling customers. The furniture, curtains, and even the walls held the lingering, pervasive stench of tobacco smoke.

"Friday night," Dan said. "We were in here when the lights went off."

"That you were," the barman said, nodding.

"You told me about the big man, the one who had been on the Sheffield."

"Aye."

"Do you know his name?"

The barman stared at Dan but didn't reply.

Dan looked at the row of spirit bottles clamped upside down on the wall behind the bar. In the low natural light they looked dusty and unappealing. "At the moment, all I want to do is talk to him, but I don't know who he is. That's why I'm here, talking to you. Can I have your name, just so I know who I'm talking to?"

"Dave Brown."

"Thank you. Now, Dave, can you tell me the big guy's name, please?"

"He didn't do anything wrong."

"In that case, you've got no reason to withhold information."

The barman shook his head. "Wait a minute, I'm not withholding anything."

Rick walked across to the bar and leaned against it.

"Do you know his name?" Dan asked the barman.

"Most people hereabouts know his name."

"Then it's already in the public domain. I could have heard it while I was walking down the street."

The barman glanced at Rick, then turned back to Dan. "You didn't hear this from me." He took a breath, looked Dan straight in the eye as he said the name. "Peter Jones."

Dan wrote the name in his notepad. "Do you know where he lives?"

"That, I don't know."

"Do you know what rank he held in the Navy?"

"No. Just his name."

"What about the other man who was with him on Friday?"

"No idea."

"You don't know his name?"

"No, I don't."

"Had you seen him before Friday night?"

"He might have been in here once or twice."

"With Peter Jones?"

"Aye, possibly."

"You don't sound sure."

"Can't say I actually remembered his face. Just got the feeling I'd seen him in here before."

"Okay. Thanks for your time."

"Always a pleasure to help the police."

"Not that you did," Dan said.

The barman started to look as though he was going to get righteously indignant until he realised what Dan meant. "Oh, yeah. I didn't help you at all, did I?"

"Not in the slightest." Dan took the barman's hand and pressed one of his contact cards into it. "And if you feel like not helping us again, you can reach me on the number on this card."

The barman glanced at the card before slipping it into his pocket.

Dan said, "Call me if you ever see either of them in the pub again."

"Aye. I might just do that."

"Come on," Dan said to Rick. "Time to go. Let's leave Dave to get the pub ready for opening time."

Rick pushed himself away from the bar. He frowned at the heavy stench of stale beer in the air. "Shame. I was hoping we could stick around for a pint."

Back on the pavement outside the *Golden Hart*, Dan heard the key turn and the bolt slide into place on the other side of the door. He and Rick started to walk back to where they had left the BMW.

"Peter Jones," Rick said. "Not exactly an uncommon name."

"The fact that he was in the Navy should narrow it down."

Rick looked up at the sky. It was starting to cloud over. "What are the chances, really, of you getting strangled in a pub by some guy, the day before he strangles a young woman to death and we end up investigating it?"

Dan could see the BMW at the edge of the kerb, ten car lengths away. "Before this week, I would have said that was about as unlikely as it could get."

"I would have got him off you if that other guy hadn't shown up. You know that, don't you?"

"Has that been bothering you?"

"Been bothering me that maybe you didn't think I would have done it."

"You were flat on your back in the dark. Don't worry about it."

"Do you think that other guy is involved?" Rick asked.

Dan shrugged. "He was talking to Jones as though he knew him. He was calming him down, telling him it was *over now.* He must have understood why Jones had lost it and grabbed me. That's the impression I got, but my head wasn't really with it at the time."

When they reached the car, Dan looked at the writing on the boot. He hadn't wiped it off, also hadn't bothered asking Pat Davies to look at it. Dan knew she wouldn't find anything more than a couple of words written in the grime by a finger inside a glove.

"What are you thinking?" Rick asked. "Were you expecting the message to have changed again?"

Dan thought of the message he had seen in the Polaroid photo. "Not really." He looked back in the direction of the *Golden Hart.* "He can't be everywhere."

Dan started the engine as soon as they were back in the BMW. The heater immediately began to warm the car up because the engine hadn't fully cooled down after the drive from the hospital. Dan called the Campbell Road station and asked them to look up an address for Peter Jones, who was either ex-Navy or, rather less likely in Dan's opinion, still enlisted. He told them to limit the search to addresses within a twenty mile radius of Kingston upon Hull.

"What do you think?" Rick said. "It could take them a while to get back to us. Shall we head back to Campbell Road?"

"All we can do, really."

***

Harry West stood in front of the whiteboard, jabbing the air with his finger. Dan Blacksmith was standing alone in front of him.

Harry said, "Well, we can forget the Vauxhall where Kath's attacker was waiting. The owner is a pensioner called Glynis Woodcock. She was shopping, came back to the car park and started creating merry hell for the bloke in the ticket shed because someone had broken into her pride and joy."

"You're absolutely sure she isn't connected?"

"Husband is dead, one daughter called Jean who lives in London."

"How old is the daughter?"

"Thirty-six."

"Okay. He broke into the car closest to Schrader's. Dead-end. I'm getting tired of waiting for this search warrant."

"Two more hours, Dan. It's not ideal, but that's the way it is."

"We've got Jones' address and we've got his fingerprints on the knife that was used in an assault on an officer from this station. We don't need a warrant to enter his home to arrest him."

"I don't want us to blow this case on a technicality."

"You mean you don't want *me* to blow it."

Harry sighed, shaking his head. "Well, that didn't take as long to come up as Kath and I were hoping."

"I'm not going to screw this case up, Harry. I know you read the official report of what happened in Runcorn. Woman and two kids hostage in their own home, stepfather out of his tree on acid and vodka. He had a sawn-off shotgun in one hand and a machete in the other."

"Yes," Harry said, his voice low and steady. "And you forced the back door, walked inside like Charles Bronson and shot him twice in the chest in front of his wife and step-kids."

"He was going to kill them."

Harry West nodded but didn't reply, effectively drawing a line under that particular conversation. He looked at the writing on the whiteboard. There was more of it now, the board covered with names, locations, descriptions of injuries and positions of dead bodies. "You heard the name Peter Jones just over an hour ago. Do you think he's responsible for all that?"

"I know he is involved with it," Dan said.

"The person who attacked Kath Schrader radioed this station and deliberately left his penknife in the glove box of her car. I honestly do not know what to make of that."

"Rick thinks he wants us to catch him."

"That's possible. What do you think?"

"Whoever is doing this has left misleading evidence at each crime scene. The knife has the fingerprints of a man who tried to strangle me on Friday night."

Harry West pointed at a single six-letter word that had been hurriedly written in capital letters and outlined with a large black oval. "*Exocet.* That word was all over the news in eighty-two. You said the barman at the *Golden Hart* told you Peter Jones was on HMS Sheffield when it was hit by one."

"He kept saying the word while he was trying to strangle me. And the guy who attacked Kath said it while he was assaulting her."

Harry shook his head. "I don't like any of this, Dan."

"I didn't tell Rick about the knife, or about how it was

used."

"Well, someone is going to have to tell him. Do you want to leave it to me?"

Dan said, "No. I'll tell him when he gets back from the magistrate with the search warrant."

Dan and Harry both looked round as a uniformed WPC walked up to them, the same young woman who had brought the recording of the emergency call to Dan in the interview room. She was carrying a single sheet of A4 paper.

"I have a fax from Northwood Naval HQ, sir," she said to Harry West. "Personal details about Peter Jones, and an ID photo."

She handed the sheet of fax paper to Harry.

"Thank you, Jeanette," Harry said.

The WPC gave Harry a quick smile before turning to walk away across the office.

"Here," Harry said, handing the paper to Dan. "See if any of this is useful."

"We already have his address." Dan skim-read the information. He saw that Jones had been a petty officer in the Royal Navy, and that his blood type was A-positive. "I don't know what else this is going to tell us that we don't…" He paused, swallowed hard. "Peter Jones was born on July twenty-fifth, 1961. He's twenty-four years old." Dan held the fax so that Harry could see it, pointing at a line beneath Jones' date of birth. "He went to John Blair Comprehensive."

Harry West looked at the whiteboard. "The same school as the Hall girl and Dee Collins."

"And Thomas Mason. At the same time, too. Jones is twenty-four, which means he was in the same year as them, and even in the same class as one of the girls."

"This can't be a coincidence, Dan."

Dan went to his desk and picked up the phone. He found the Masons' number in his notepad and dialled it.

He counted four rings before Deb Mason answered the phone.

"Mrs Mason, it's Dan Blacksmith. Is Tom there?"

"He's upstairs. Shall I fetch him?"

"If you could, please."

Dan waited. He could hear the sound of a radio, probably coming from the kitchen, voices followed by laughter that sounded spontaneous rather than pre-recorded. The talking and the laughter carried on over the intro of the next record. Dan recognised the song; it was by an American band that he wasn't particularly keen on. Just as they were about to announce that they were on a road to nowhere, Tom Mason picked up the phone.

"Hello?"

"Tom, it's Dan Blacksmith. I just want to ask you a couple of quick questions."

"Okay."

"Was Peter Jones in your class at John Blair?"

"Yeah. Same class as me and Sharon."

Dan started writing on a clean page of his notepad. "How well do you remember him?"

"He left at the end of the fifth form. I think he joined the Navy."

"What was he like in school?"

"Big, but not a bully. I saw him get in a few fights but only when he couldn't get out of it."

"What do you mean?"

"He got picked on sometimes because he was big. Sounds stupid, doesn't it? He was big but he was quiet."

"Was he ever in any kind of a relationship with either Sharon or Dee?"

"No."

"Are you sure about that? Was it something that maybe he wanted but they turned him down?"

"No, he didn't ask either of them out that I know of. I don't remember him saying he fancied either of them, but he probably did. I expect most of the kids in our year did."

"In the fifth form, was Peter in any of the same subject classes as Sharon or Dee?"

"He was in the same history class I was in with Dee and Sharon. Apart from that, I don't know. I can't remember which kids were in lessons I wasn't in."

"History," Dan said. He listened to the silence on the line. "Tom? What is it?"

"We were all in the same career choices class in the fifth form. Those weren't proper lessons, just a dozen kids being told to study hard or we'd end up cleaning toilets."

Dan thought about what Thomas Mason was saying. He knew Tom was going to inherit his father's haulage company.

"You didn't find those career classes useful, did you?"

"Not really, no."

"What about Peter Jones?"

"He had already decided he was going to join the Navy."

"So he wasn't interested in the career class either?"

"No. We both thought it was a waste of time. Actually, most of the kids did."

"What about Sharon and Dee?"

"They weren't interested either." Tom paused. When he spoke again, his voice was low, in an attempt to avoid being overheard by his mother. "What I told you earlier, about them kissing in class to wind a teacher up, they did it a couple of times in the career class."

Dan didn't write that down.

"Thanks, Tom. I don't have any further questions at the moment. Thanks again for your time."

"Is Peter Jones involved in this?"

"I can't discuss the case with you, I'm afraid."

"Okay."

"Bye, Tom."

Dan hung up, thinking he had just wasted another five minutes of his life talking to Tom Mason. He looked up as he saw Rick Price walking into the office. Rick was carrying an envelope.

"Got it," Rick said, waving the envelope in the air. "Half an hour early. Not bad."

"Right," Dan said, standing up and shoving his chair under his desk. "Let's go."

CHAPTER 24

The housing estate on the northern fringe of the city was called Paddock Park. The first buildings to be built on the estate were narrow three-bedroom terraced houses that went up in the early sixties. The single, central tower block where Peter Jones lived in a two-bedroom flat on the fifth floor was called the Berrystone Tower.

"This is it," Dan said. He pointed at the number on the dirty white door.

The corridor floor was tiled with the kind of shiny brown rectangles that wouldn't have looked out of place on the floor of a public toilet. After taking the internal stairs up to the fifth floor, Dan thought the choice of tiles was rather apt as the first two floors had the overpowering stench of an infrequently maintained urinal. It was close to quarter past five, already getting dark, and the corridor was lit with an unhealthy yellow glow from its recessed ceiling lights.

At the far end of the corridor, three teenage boys were productively filling their time smoking and swearing at each other. Dan noticed that one of them kept glancing furtively in his direction.

Dan knocked three times on the door of Peter Jones'

flat. The kid who kept looking at Dan and Rick stared a little longer that time. He was pale and skinny, with short-cropped fair hair.

Dan waited for a few seconds, then knocked again. The skinny blonde kid said something to his two friends and they all stared at Dan and Rick.

"I can't hear anyone in there," Dan said.

"How long do we give it before we force entry?"

Dan knocked on the door again.

The blonde kid took a few steps along the corridor towards them. His two friends hung back, watching.

When he was close enough, the blonde kid called out, "Are you Plod?"

Rick looked at Dan and rolled his eyes. "Better than pigs, I suppose."

"Do you know the occupant of this flat?" Dan said.

The kid came a few steps closer and stopped. "Are you the Old Bill?"

Dan took out his warrant card. "Humberside CID. Do you know Peter Jones?"

"He's not in."

"Does he live alone?"

"He does now."

"What do you mean?"

"Didn't you know? His girlfriend moved out because he kept trying to kill her."

Dan looked at Rick. "There's nothing on file or it would have come up when they ran the search for his details." He turned back to the blonde kid. "How do you know about it?"

"I heard about it."

"What's your name?" Dan asked.

The blonde kid glanced back at his two friends. "Do I have to tell you?"

"Not if you don't want to." Dan raised his voice. "I'll just call you Daisy."

"Vic Nelson."

"Thank you, Vic. Why don't you come a bit closer so we don't have to shout?"

Vic Nelson walked up to the door of Peter Jones' flat.

"I thought that's why you were here, because of his girlfriend."

"I don't think she ever reported it," Dan said.

"What you here for, then?"

"We need to talk to Peter Jones. Do you know when he will be back?"

"No idea. He hasn't been here since Saturday."

"Here we go," Rick said. "Saturday. What do you think?"

"The coincidences just keep on coming, don't they?" Dan said.

Vic Nelson looked at the dirty white door. "D'you think he's got any bodies in there?"

"Let's hope not," Dan said. He took his notepad out of his coat pocket. "Vic, do you know the girlfriend's name?"

"Laura Potter."

"How do you know her name?"

"I know her brother, Steve."

"Is he one of those two over there?"

"Nah. He doesn't live in Paddock."

Rick said, "How old is Laura Potter?"

"Twenty-two."

"Not twenty-four, then," Rick said to Dan.

"Did you hear about the alleged assault from Laura's brother?" Dan asked Vic.

"Yeah."

"Do you know what Laura claimed Peter Jones did to her?"

"Yeah, he tried to strangle her while she was sleeping."

"Do you know how she managed to stop him?"

"Steve said Laura told him Pete stopped strangling her when she turned the light on. But it happened more than once and she got really scared. That's when she moved out."

"How long ago was this?"

"Couple of months."

Dan frowned. "But you thought that was why we were here, even though she moved out two months ago."

"Plod's always too busy to come straight away," Vic said. He shrugged. "Well, you are, when it's some problem on an estate."

Dan looked at his watch. "Vic, do you know how to get into a locked flat without damaging the door?"

Vic gave a brief, nervous laugh. "No."

"In that case, can I ask you to rejoin your friends over there while I open this one, because I don't want to teach you how to do it."

"Don't you want to know where Laura Potter is living now?"

"I would appreciate the information if you have it."

"She's back with her folks."

"Do you know the address?"

Vic told Dan the address and he wrote it in his notepad.

"Thanks, Vic. Now, if you don't mind…"

Vic turned away without another word. Dan watched him walk to the end of the corridor where his friends were waiting.

"Stand there," Dan said to Rick. "Make sure the three stooges don't see what I do."

When Rick was standing between him and the three kids at the end of the corridor, Dan took out his wallet and opened it. He showed Rick a worn, faded plastic credit card.

"Don't try it with one that you actually use. This is an old cancelled card I keep on me for exactly this sort of situation."

Dan tried the door handle. It was spherical, dull silver metal, with a central cylinder lock. It rattled with an encouraging combination of low cost component parts and many years of use, so he turned it as far as it would go and leaned his weight against the door. He forced the edge of the flexible plastic card into the gap between the door and the frame, just above the height of the handle. He began to work the card further into the gap, tilting it and bending it as he braced his shoulder hard against the door and pushed.

Rick said, "Is that really going to work?"

Dan stumbled forward into the flat as the latch popped and the door swung open. The flat was in relative darkness compared to the corridor.

"I think it might," he said.

Once Rick was in the flat with him, Dan checked that he could lock and unlock the door from the inside before closing and locking it behind them.

Dan found a light switch on the wall. He pressed it with the edge of his old credit card.

"Better," he said. "Now we can see what we're doing."

"Are we sure there's nobody here?"

"Let's take it slowly, one room at a time." Dan raised his voice. "Humberside CID. Please make yourself known and step forward."

They waited, listening, but nothing happened.

Dan looked around before moving. "Looks like the kitchen is through there, and that one ahead is a living room. Those doors must be the two bedrooms."

"Kitchen first?"

"Okay. Visual exam only. Let's not touch anything yet."

Rick used his elbow to gently open the kitchen door wide enough to allow them to enter.

"Can you do the thing with the light switch in here?"

"You should really get yourself one of these," Dan said as he pressed his credit card against the switch.

Rick stood in the middle of the cramped kitchen and looked around. "Well," he sighed. "It's a kitchen."

"What were you expecting, a big notice board on the wall covered with photos of Sharon Hall and Dee Collins?"

"It all looks normal. It's tidy, but not obsessively tidy."

"Doesn't look like he left in a rush. No unwashed crockery or cutlery in the sink."

"There's nothing useful here in the kitchen, is there?" Rick said.

"Are you asking me or telling me?"

"Okay, I'll say there is nothing useful here. We know it's his flat, so everything is going to have his prints all over it. There's nothing that looks like it could be remotely useful as evidence for the two murders."

"I noticed one thing, as soon as we came in the flat. I think it's interesting."

"The stale smell?"

"No. That's what the entire tower block probably smells like. Try another of your five senses."

"It's quiet?"

"No. The lights were all off in here."

Rick shrugged, shaking his head. "Because he isn't here."

"What happened in the pub when the lights went out?"

"He totally flipped. Oh, I see what you mean."

Dan looked at his watch. "The corridor lights must come on automatically in the evening. It's possible that he doesn't need to leave the lights on in the flat because he can turn the first light on while he is standing in the light from the corridor. Or maybe an absence of light isn't the issue, maybe he reacts like he did when the lights suddenly go off and it's completely dark."

"That kid, Vic, said Laura's brother told him Jones stopped strangling Laura when she turned the light on."

"Third-hand hearsay, Rick. I want to talk to Laura Potter before making any assumptions about the accuracy of what Vic Nelson told us."

"Okay."

"Let's try the living room."

It was just a room, the way the kitchen was just a

kitchen. Unremarkable, with a cheap two-seater sofa and an even cheaper pair of folding wooden chairs under a yellow Formica table. In one corner was a small television on a low coffee table that appeared barely capable of supporting its weight.

Dan stood by the Formica table, scratching his chin. "No old school photos, no to-do list of murders. Just a normal guy going out in the evening, killing on a whim."

"Do you believe that?"

"Just thinking out loud. If someone really did fit Peter Jones up for the two murders and the attack on Kath Schrader, I think they would have left something here to incriminate him. Something obvious. There's not even a pair of black leather gloves on the table."

"We still haven't checked the bedrooms."

Dan stood outside the first of the two bedrooms and pushed the door open with the toe of his shoe. He leaned inside and switched the light on the same way that he had operated the other light switches.

"Look at that," Dan said. "Two lamps side by side on that bedside cabinet."

Rick went into the room and stood near Dan. "Two lamps." He snapped his finger and thumb together. "Belt and braces. It's in case one of the bulbs blows. He doesn't want to wake up in the dark."

"Looks that way, doesn't it."

"Maybe Laura Potter made him put the second lamp there."

The cabinet with the two lamps was on the left side of the double bed. A second cabinet on the right side of the bed only had a single lamp on it, but there was a framed photograph next to the lamp.

Rick looked closer. "That's him, isn't it?"

Dan studied the photograph. "Yes. Not a whole lot younger than he looks now. The girl is probably Laura."

"He isn't smiling."

"She looks happy enough." Dan wrote a few quick notes describing the young woman in the photograph. "Everything else in the room looks as normal as the rest of the flat."

"Shall I have a look in the wardrobe?"

"Okay, but don't touch the handle with your hands."

Rick stretched the sleeve of his sweater far enough to allow him to use it to cover his fingers like a makeshift glove. He pulled the wardrobe door open.

"Should have brought my gloves," he said.

Dan moved closer to look inside the wardrobe. He saw two pairs of shoes on the floor, a jacket and a coat on hangers. Some other clothes, but nothing that seemed remotely like incriminating evidence. "Vic will be disappointed."

"No bodies."

"No anything. And we're running out of rooms."

"Last chance, then," Rick said. "What's inside bedroom number two?"

The first thing they noticed about the second bedroom was that it wasn't being used as a bedroom. Against the back wall there was a yellow Formica table which looked like the twin of the one in the living room. Papers and unopened envelopes were scattered across its shiny surface. Also on the table was a pint glass that was being used to hold several pens and pencils. But the papers and envelopes weren't the cause of Rick Price's excitement when he nudged the light switch with his sleeve-covered knuckles and saw what else was on the table. There were a dozen Polaroid photographs arranged in a rudimentary three-by-four rectangle. Each photo was of a young woman.

"Bingo," Rick said as he and Dan rushed to the table.

"Almost," Dan said.

"Damn. They're all pictures of Laura Potter."

"And she looks happy in all of them."

Rick pointed at one of the pictures. "Is that underwear

or a black bikini?"

"I think it's underwear." Dan shook his head. "None of this is evidence of a criminal mentality. He's possibly regretful because she moved out, maybe even depressed, but none of the pictures are torn or defaced. He does his paperwork in here, that's all, and he probably sits here looking at these pictures because he misses her."

"Okay," Rick said. "The kid told us Laura Potter moved out because she was scared of being strangled in her sleep…"

"Which we're still not certain is true, but go on."

"The two lamps on that bedroom cabinet suggest that either Jones or his girlfriend were trying to make sure he didn't wake up in the dark. She apparently moved out about two months ago, so Jones kept both those lights there even though he was sleeping alone as far as we know."

"Good," Dan said. "And the conclusion is that Peter Jones is afraid of being in the dark when he is on his own."

"Do you think so? He was in the pub on Friday night at half ten. He would have had to leave the pub and go home in the dark."

"We're just guessing. Maybe he can cope with the dark if he is with someone he trusts and the darkness is gradual or expected. It was the sudden way the lights went out that set him off in the pub."

"I don't know." Rick looked around the bedroom. "And we can't figure it out from the contents of this flat."

Dan looked at the calendar that was hanging on the wall to the right of the table. There were scribbled notes on several of the dates. He couldn't read them from where he was so he went closer to the calendar.

"What is it?" Rick asked.

"Weekly appointments."

"For what?"

"I don't know. It's the only thing written on here. Every Thursday. All they say is *Bob Laing* and a time."

"Is there one for this Thursday?"

"Yes, at fourteen thirty."

"Bob Laing," Rick said. He looked down at the papers and envelopes on the table. After only a few seconds, he looked up with a wide smile. "Definitely bingo this time."

"Really?"

"There's a recent invoice here from Robert Laing. Header on the invoice says Robert K. Laing - Consultant Psychiatrist, then a load of letters after his name. MB, MRCPsych, MMedSc."

Dan stood at the table, looking down at the folded invoice.

"Looks like Peter is getting professional help for whatever is wrong with him."

Rick looked at Dan. "Based on what happened on Friday, I don't think it's working."

"But we do know one thing." Dan started to write in his notepad. "We know where Peter Jones is going to be on Thursday at half past two."

CHAPTER 25

Dan was arranging the paperwork on his desk with one hand while he held the phone handset to his ear with the other. The clock on the office wall said it was quarter past six. Rick had left the station a few minutes earlier. Harry West was still around, but he wasn't in the open plan office.

"I'll be out of here in five minutes," Dan said.

"That's early for you," Becky said. "Has something happened?"

"Quite a few things, but I'm not going to do any more today. I just want to come home and see my family."

"Mandy's going to be really pleased. She's also probably going to want to stay up past her bedtime to spend time with you."

"That'll be fine. Has she had her bath yet?"

"I was just about to run it. Do you want to bath her when you get home?"

"Yeah. If you start running it in fifteen minutes, I'll take her straight up when I get in."

"Deal," Becky said. Dan heard the pause. He could see her bright, appraising eyes as clearly as if she had been right in front of him, instead of eight miles away in the hallway of their home. "Is everything okay, honey?"

"Mostly," Dan said.

"You sound tired."

"Tired, baffled, grumpy and old."

"Is that an alternative comedy version of the seven dwarves?"

Dan laughed softly, wishing he could just be home right at that moment without the walk to the car and the fifteen minute drive.

"Only four of them. Who are the other three?"

"Sexy, handsome and all mine."

"Did I mention I have you on speakerphone?"

"He uses his handcuffs when we role-play."

Behind Becky's laughter, Dan could hear his daughter's voice calling for Daddy.

"Put Mandy on," Dan said.

There was a fumbling sound and then, "Hello, Daddy."

"Hello, sweetie. Are you being a good girl for Mummy?"

"We did painting. I painted you."

"In school?"

"I painted you with your car."

"That sounds great, Mandy. Can I see the painting when I get home?"

"It's in school. Dawn painted her cat."

Dan felt the irresistible smile tugging his face into an expression that didn't belong behind a desk in Campbell Road police station. He looked up at the ceiling to avoid seeing the paperwork on his desk or the case notes scrawled all over the whiteboard.

"Mandy, do you want Daddy to bath you?"

"Are you at home?"

"No, sweetie, I'm at work. I'll be home very soon."

"Mummy is laughing. Why is Mummy laughing?"

"Can you give the phone back to Mummy, please?"

"Bye."

There was a slight pause, then Becky said, "She's

walking around the house in her pyjamas carrying that rat you like so much."

"She told me she did some painting in school today."

"I think she got most of it on her uniform."

"I'm glad she likes school. Who's Dawn?"

"A girl in her class."

Dan looked at the clock on the wall. "How's your portrait going?"

"I'll show you later. Are you coming home now?"

"I'm leaving the station as soon as I hang up."

"On three, Detective. One…"

"Two."

"I love you."

"I love you, Becky Blacksmith."

"Leave as soon as you hang up."

"I promise."

"Three."

Dan dropped the handset into the cradle. He closed his eyes, did the slow five-count before opening them again.

The Peter Jones fax was on top of a pile of papers at the edge of the desk. Dan looked at the unsmiling face of the former petty officer in the black and white ID photo. Jones had been honourably discharged from the Royal Navy six months after the Sheffield had sunk in the South Atlantic. Dan didn't know what Peter Jones had been doing for the two years since then, and he had very little confidence that he really knew what Jones had been doing since the previous weekend. The available evidence supported the theory that Peter Jones was responsible for two murders and an assault on a police officer, but Dan knew the evidence was not trustworthy.

"I'm leaving now," Dan said under his breath. He opened the top drawer and dumped all the case paperwork inside before closing and locking it.

On his way to the stairs, Dan stuck his head into Harry West's office. Harry was holding the phone to his ear but he took it away and covered the mouthpiece with his hand when he saw Dan.

"See you tomorrow, Harry."

"I'm trying to get on the local news again tonight. They've put me on hold, as usual."

"You're not going to mention Peter Jones, are you?"

"No. Just the usual plea for witnesses."

"Are you including the attack on Kath?"

"Yes. I can't believe nobody saw anything in that car park."

Harry put the phone back against his ear. "Yes, I'm still here. Good, yes, that will be perfect. No, I'll come to the studio. Yes, I know where it is. Half eight, yes, that will be fine."

While he was talking to the local TV studio, Harry gave Dan a thumbs-up. Dan replied with a quick wave before heading for the stairs.

Outside, the air was cold and damp. The chill of the strong wind stung Dan's face with its intensity. Dan pulled his coat collar up and hurried along the pavement to the corner of the street. Campbell Road was well-lit by streetlamps but the adjacent street where Dan had left the BMW was much darker. The cars that parked there were safe despite the lack of lighting, because who would be stupid enough to try to break into a car parked close to a large police station? *Pretty much nobody*, Dan thought.

Despite his confidence regarding the safety of his car, Dan walked all around it before he got in, looking for fresh messages written in the film of wintery grime. He found nothing new.

The drive home was uneventful, the traffic much lighter than it would have been an hour earlier. Dan arrived home just after half past six. It felt good to be walking into his own house early in the evening rather than halfway into the night. He closed the front door without needing to worry about waking Mandy. He could see the landing light on upstairs but there was no sound of the bathtub being filled ready for him to wash his daughter.

Dan took off his coat and shoes.

He thought about watching Mandy play with her big plastic duck in the bath, splashing the wall tiles, the floor, and probably splashing him too.

Thinking about it made Dan smile.

He checked the lounge, but his wife and daughter weren't on the sofa. The television was tuned to BBC1 with the volume barely audible. The six o'clock news was on, Reagan and Gorbachev having a polite chat in Geneva about ensuring peace through superior firepower. The whole world was waiting to hear whether an orbiting shield of lasers really was the solution to the threat of nuclear war. Harry West's brief, formal plea for witnesses to two murders and an assault would not be shown for another three hours, in the regional slot following the nine o'clock news.

Dan didn't want to listen to the various theories and scaremongering about a possible apocalypse. It was all media speculation until Thursday anyway, due to the summit's news blackout.

Dan thought of the collection of photographs on the desk in Peter Jones' flat, and the face-down Polaroid in the drawer of the treatment room at the hospital. He wanted to do what Kath Schrader had asked him to do.

Stop him.

Dan walked out of the lounge and opened the door of Becky's studio. The room was dark, nobody in there. In the darkness, the portrait was just a rectangular silhouette on the A-frame easel. Dan left the light off. He would wait for Becky to show him the painting later, if she wanted to. He closed the door.

Dan didn't want to think about murders and strangulation, penknife mutilation and saline drips, dead women and messages written in blood.

But he did think about it. He thought about it all.

Stop him.

Dan didn't want to think about the man in Runcorn with the shotgun and the machete, but he did. He had stopped that man, stopped him in the most fundamental of ways.

Dan shook his head, clearing the images of death and blood, telling himself it wouldn't happen again. It couldn't happen again.

He thought of the gloves on the shelf in Raymond Hughes' house. He thought of two possibilities. The first was that the killer had swapped the gloves when he had made the emergency call. The second was that he had swapped them earlier.

"It's me," he called up the stairs. "I'm home."

No answer.

He saw Sharon Hall's face staring up at him from the cold, wet pavement. Dee Collins, naked, strangled to death, lying on the carpet in front of the television. The screwdriver buried in her chest.

The message on the shed windows. On his car. On Schrader's body.

COLD

GETTING WARMER

WAR

He watches, Dan had told Kath Schrader while she lay in her hospital bed. Kath had said her attacker had been indifferent while he cut into her with a penknife.

Dan paused on the third step of the staircase, listening. He thought he had heard a single stealthy sound, someone taking a soft step on the carpeted floor of one of the bedrooms.

"Becky?"

There was no reply, but then Dan heard a muffled gasp from somewhere above him.

He took the stairs two at a time, all the way to the

landing. He was already breathing hard, his skin bristling with terrified energy. The bathroom light was on. It was the door nearest the stairs. Dan looked in, saw the bath with four inches of water in it, the surface covered with white foam bubbles. The bathroom window was closed, damp with condensation. There was a large question mark finger-written in the moisture on one of the panes.

"Becky!"

Standing in the bathroom doorway, Dan felt the promises falling apart. The promises he had made to himself, to his wife, to the senior officers at the internal hearing to determine appropriate use of force. There was nothing he wouldn't do…

"Daddy!"

Mandy ran out of the dark doorway of the second bedroom. She was smiling, little legs pumping as she ran along the landing towards him. She was carrying Roland by his arm. The toy rat was swinging back and forth, pirouetting as it bumped against her leg.

Dan dropped to one knee, pulling his daughter into his arms. The rush of relief hurt more than the awful dread he had felt when he had seen the message on the bathroom window. He let out the breath he had been holding since he had called out his wife's name.

"I was hiding," Mandy said.

Dan didn't say anything. He knew that if he spoke, he wouldn't be able to keep the tears back.

Becky came out of the same bedroom doorway as Mandy. She stopped smiling as soon as she saw Dan's face.

"Honey," she said. She sank to her knees on the carpet, looking over Mandy's shoulders at Dan. "What is it?"

Dan shook his head, tried to force a smile.

"We were hiding," Mandy said.

"Give Daddy a big cuddle," Becky said.

"I am."

Dan drew in a deep breath. He had it under control.

"Shall I bath you now, sweetie?"

"I've got bubbles."

"I know. I saw them."

"Maybe Daddy is a bit tired." Becky raised her eyebrows at Dan. Mandy still had her face nuzzled into her father's neck. "Mummy could bath you."

"No. Daddy."

"It's okay," Dan said to Becky. "I want to."

"If you're sure," Becky said.

"I'm fine, honestly."

"Shall I go and put the kettle on?"

"Great idea."

Becky stood up but she kept looking at Dan. She narrowed her eyes, mouthed the words *What's wrong?*

Dan shook his head, no longer needing to force a smile as he enjoyed the closeness and the unconditional love of his daughter.

***

Harry West read the announcement from a sheet of paper attached to a clipboard. The location was outdoors, most likely the car park of the television studio. Harry was standing in front of a rough stucco wall, lit from the front and sides. There was nobody else in the shot.

Dan was on the sofa in the lounge, his arm lightly around Becky's shoulders. He would have preferred not to have watched the local news but Becky had insisted. She would never press Dan to discuss the cases he was working on, but she said that if it was going to be on TV then she had as much right as everyone else to hear what the police had to say.

On the screen, Harry West was nearing the end of his five-minute slot. "*Can anyone who has information relating to any of these incidents please contact Humberside police on…*"

"Who is the officer who was attacked?" Becky asked

Dan. Harry West had not given the name, just the date, time and location of the assault.

"Kath Schrader."

"Your boss. I met her at that police dinner, didn't I?"

"Yes." Dan stroked a few strands of hair back behind Becky's ear. "She's not exactly my boss."

"What rank is she?"

"Detective Inspector."

Becky said nothing. Before the demotion that had followed the Runcorn incident, Dan had held the same rank.

Dan said, "Did you see Mandy's painting when you picked her up from school?"

"No. I didn't go into the classroom today."

The weather forecast immediately followed the news programme. The map of Britain and Europe was mostly covered by a large, single series of concentric ovals. The word LOW was right over the middle of England. The north of England had several black cloud outlines on and around it, most with a pair of white snowflakes beneath them. The local temperatures forecast for the rest of the week went as low as minus eight centigrade.

"Great," Dan said.

"They'll probably close the school."

"Will you be okay looking after Mandy?"

"Of course." Becky smiled. "She's my little princess."

When the Met Office weatherman had finished announcing the equivalent of the next ice age, albeit one that was only likely to last until the following Monday, the next programme started.

Dan groaned, shaking his head.

"Don't you like *Cagney and Lacey*?" Becky asked, but she gave him a lazy wink as she said it. She knew her husband wasn't a fan of any television cop show, not just that one.

"Would you like me to change the channel or shall I just turn the TV off altogether?"

Becky snuggled in closer. "Why do you want to turn it off? Are you thinking of having an early night?"

"I am now."

Becky absently smoothed a crease out of her pyjama trouser leg. "I think we might be able to arrange an early night."

"Would you like to show me the portrait first? We didn't get around to it earlier."

"You're such a tease, Detective." Becky untangled herself from Dan's arm. "Come on," she said, standing up. "But let's make it quick."

Dan followed his wife to the door of her studio. She opened the door and turned on the light.

"It's still not quite finished," Becky said. She sounded apologetic. "If it really does start snowing, it could take me at least another week if he can't make it here through the herds of woolly mammoths."

Dan stood in front of the easel, looking at the portrait.

"Is he smiling, or just going for straight up enigmatic?"

"Hard to tell, isn't it? A bit like the *Mona Lisa*, except I'm not going to be able to retire on the money this one makes me."

"I forgot what you said his name is."

"Mark Sykes."

"What's he like?"

Becky wrinkled her nose. "Normal, I suppose. He obviously has enough money to afford to waste eight hundred pounds on a painting."

"It's not a waste," Dan said. "You're an amazing artist."

"You're biased."

"Maybe you should paint me."

"You have a daughter who does that."

Dan kept looking at the portrait. "You said the other day that he didn't want you to work from a photo. Why was that?"

"I told you. He enjoys sitting for me. He doesn't think

he ever looks right in photographs."

"How long does he have to sit still?"

"Today, we did two sessions of about one hour each with a break when he went out to get some lunch."

"You comfortable having him in the house?"

"Of course I am. It's not like I have much choice, really. He's fine, Dan. Very polite, not at all weird or creepy, and he's long gone by the time I fetch Mandy from school."

"And you always keep the safeguards I gave you close by, don't you?"

Becky rolled her eyes. "Yes. Not that I'm likely to use pepper spray on one of my subjects, or whack them over the head with a truncheon."

"He doesn't look particularly distinctive. That's not a criticism of your work, by the way."

"Well, the portrait isn't finished." Becky slid her arms around Dan's waist. "And not everyone can have chiselled good looks and piercing blue eyes."

"My eyes aren't blue."

"Yours? Oh, were we talking about you? I wasn't."

Dan touched the tip of his finger against his tongue. He pressed his finger lightly against the lapel of Becky's pyjama top. "We'd better get you out of these wet clothes, miss," he said. "And then I think I need to take you to the station for a thorough interrogation."

Becky kissed the side of Dan's neck. "I might resist arrest, Detective."

"That's not appropriate behaviour for a famous artist."

Becky giggled, squirming against him. "The fun stuff never is."

Dan backed towards the door with Becky in his arms. He was still looking at the portrait of the unremarkable man when Becky touched the wall switch and turned off the light. In the dark, the painting was just a rectangular silhouette on a skeletal A-frame easel.

CHAPTER 26

"Change of plan," Dan said, as Rick walked to his desk.

It was Wednesday the twentieth of November. The clock on the wall showed it was five minutes before nine o'clock in the morning. Rick's coat was buttoned all the way to his neck. The shoulders were dusted with a fine covering of melting snow.

Rick pulled his chair from under his desk and sat down without removing his coat or his gloves. "What's happened?"

"Harry has brought DI Knowles in on the case. I don't know how many people Knowles has with him, but this case is becoming a priority."

Rick talked as he took off his gloves. "Where does that leave us?"

"It's actually good news. We're still on the case, but we get to choose who does what because we've been on it since the start. I asked Harry to send Knowles over to talk to Laura Potter. All we really need from her is a first-hand account of Peter Jones' behaviour, and whether or not he did actually try to strangle her."

"Okay, that sounds good. What are we going to do?"

"Drink lots of coffee and figure out where Peter Jones has gone."

Rick smiled at that, nodding as he started to unbutton his coat. "You already have the day planned out, don't you?"

"Not exactly. The weather might throw a small spanner in there, but what I want us to do is go visit Robert Laing and find out what treatment he's been giving Peter Jones."

"Can we do that?"

"Of course we can."

"What if Laing refuses to discuss Peter Jones because of patient confidentiality?"

Dan looked at the wall clock before picking up the phone. "Don't worry about that."

He looked at a number he had copied into his notepad from the invoice on Peter Jones' desk, then he dialled it. When the call was answered, he tapped the speakerphone button so that Rick could hear both sides of the conversation.

"Laing Counselling Clinic, Tanya speaking. How may I help?"

"Good morning, Tanya," Dan said. "Is Robert Laing available?"

"Doctor Laing is currently with a patient. Can I ask who is calling?"

"This is Detective Sergeant Dan Blacksmith from Humberside CID. I'd like to make an appointment to speak to Doctor Laing as soon as possible."

"Hi, Dan. Can I call you Dan?"

"Of course."

Rick grinned across the desk at Dan.

"Dan, is this a request for a personal appointment or is it regarding a patient of Doctor Laing's?"

Rick stopped grinning.

"I'd prefer to discuss the details with Doctor Laing."

There was a pause of several seconds, and then Tanya

said, "Doctor Laing has a cancellation at eleven. Would that be convenient for you?"

"That would be perfect."

"Do you know how to find us, Dan?"

"I've got the address. I just have to get a sledge and half a dozen huskies and it should be no problem at all."

On the phone, Tanya laughed politely. "Very good, then. We will expect you at eleven."

"Thanks, Tanya."

"Goodbye, Dan."

Dan hung up. "That was almost too easy."

"Lovely voice," Rick said. "What are we going to do until eleven?"

"Drink lots of coffee."

Fifteen minutes later, the phone on Dan's desk started ringing.

"Humberside CID, DS Blacksmith speaking."

"This is Rob Musgrave. I need to talk to you."

Dan swapped the handset to his left hand, flipped his notepad to a fresh page with his right hand and picked up a biro. "What do you want to tell me, Rob?"

Musgrave sounded tired, right on the edge of frustrated anger. "Have you found him yet, the bastard who killed Sharon?"

"We have a team working full-time on the case. We're making progress but we have no confirmed suspects yet."

"I saw that cop on the news last night. He said another girl had been killed. Is it the same person who killed Sharon?" His voice hitched on the name of his dead girlfriend. "Is the bastard a serial killer? How haven't you found out who it is yet?"

"I'm sorry, Rob. We're doing everything we can. If you have any additional information that you could—"

"I haven't slept since Friday. All I can think about is…" He choked back a sob. Dan could hear the sound of the handset being pressed against fabric for several seconds while Musgrave fought to control his grief. "I just want to know that you've caught him and that he's going down forever."

"I understand. But, Rob, I won't be able to give you any names, not of suspects, and not of anyone we take into custody."

"Just tell me when you catch the bastard."

"We're doing everything we can. Are you sure there's nothing else that you can tell me?"

"Yeah." He sounded defeated, his voice trailing off. He hung up before Dan could say anything else.

***

Dan asked Rick to drive from Campbell Road station to the street where Robert Laing had his psychiatry practice because he had already had enough fun keeping the back end of the BMW on the road when he had driven to the station from his house. Rick's car was a silver Sierra XR4x4, and he had been waiting for the chance to show Dan that its all-wheel drive wasn't a pointless gimmick, so he was more than happy to drive them across the city through the falling snow.

"Park it anywhere on this street," Dan said.

Rick looked out of the windscreen at the featureless white surface of the road. "How do you know it's not double yellows?"

"It doesn't matter. Traffic wardens are going to be tucked up at home or building snowmen with their kids, and this is a police vehicle anyway."

"It isn't, though," Rick said. The Sierra was his own car, not like Dan's BMW which was owned by Humberside Police.

"We're on police business, so it's a police vehicle."

"You're the boss."

"This will do, here. That's the building we want, right

over there."

Rick parked next to what he thought was the kerb, although it was almost impossible to see where the road stopped and the pavement started.

"I cannot wait for the summer," Rick said as he turned off the engine.

The Laing Counselling Clinic occupied the first floor of a Victorian town house that had been largely rebuilt after sustaining serious damage during the Blitz. The ground-floor entrance led directly to a flight of stairs to the first floor.

Dan walked into the small reception area and held the door open for Rick. The walls were panelled floor to ceiling with maple. There was a large framed print on the wall opposite the window, a reproduction oil painting of two sailboats on calm water against a background of a predominantly orange sunset.

The woman at the reception desk looked up and smiled. "Can I help you?"

"Dan Blacksmith, Humberside CID. We spoke earlier."

"Ah, yes. Please take a seat, Dan. Doctor Laing will see you very shortly." The receptionist looked at Rick. "And you are…?"

Rick stared at the woman behind the desk. She was slim, elegant, probably mid-thirties, wearing a grey suit over a black silk blouse. Long auburn hair with a side braid, hazel eyes behind black-framed glasses. The glasses looked expensive.

"Rick Price. I'm with Dan. I mean I'm a Detective Constable. We're here on the same business. Are you Tanya?"

The receptionist casually tapped her right index finger against the platinum wedding band on her ring finger.

"Yes, Tanya Redmond."

"Pleased to meet you."

"Please take a seat, Rick. They're just there."

Rick sat next to Dan, pretending not to notice when Dan slowly shook his head.

After five long, quiet minutes, the door to the right of the reception desk opened. A middle-aged woman walked in, followed by the man who had been holding the door for her.

"Tanya will book your next session, Mrs Harding. Take care in the snow, and I'll see you in three weeks."

The woman smiled. "Thank you, Robert. I look forward to it."

Dan and Rick stood up as Robert Laing walked over to them.

"Good morning," Laing said, offering his hand to Dan. "Robert Laing."

"Dan Blacksmith." Laing's grip was solid but not forceful. The man was close to Dan's height, a shade over six foot, with broad shoulders and a head of carelessly brushed blonde curls. Dan thought he looked more like a prop forward than a doctor. He was wearing a formal shirt, powder blue, open collar with no tie, and grey trousers.

Laing greeted Rick in a similar manner. He seemed unperturbed by the unexpected presence of a second police officer.

"If you would like to step this way," Laing said, leading them to the door he had just come through. He took Dan and Rick into a consultation room. There was a desk in there, but no chair behind it. Instead, there were two deep, comfortable looking leather armchairs and a similarly upholstered three-seat sofa against the wall. On the wall above the sofa, Dan saw another framed print. This one showed a rowing boat on a large stretch of water, with a cathedral on a hill in the background.

"Henry Dawson," Laing said.

"He was from Hull," Rick said to Dan. "My folks had a couple of his pictures at home."

Laing sank into one of the armchairs. "I understand that

you requested an appointment but that no specifics were given."

Dan took a seat at one end of the sofa. Rick sat in the second armchair.

"We're here because we need to ask you some questions about Peter Jones," Dan said. "It is in connection with several serious crimes that have recently been committed in the city."

Laing didn't change his position in the chair. His hands lay flat along the arms of the chair, and his legs remained uncrossed.

"How did you know Peter was receiving treatment here?"

Dan took out his notepad and biro. "We found a recent invoice at his flat during an authorised search of the premises. He also had the appointments marked on his calendar."

Laing nodded. "Peter missed his appointment last week."

"When did you last see him?"

"At his appointment the week before that."

"When you say he missed the appointment last week, do you mean he called to cancel it or he just didn't turn up?"

"He didn't cancel the appointment in advance."

Dan looked at his notepad before asking the next question. "What treatment is Peter Jones receiving?"

"I'm sorry, but I can't discuss that."

"Of course you can, Doctor Laing. Patient confidentiality only covers information that a patient gives you, but even that can be disclosed under a court order."

"Do you have a court order?"

"I could have one by three o'clock."

Laing glanced at the Dawson print on the wall behind Dan. "Patient confidentiality is very important to me. I'm sure you are aware of what happened to Peter Jones during the Falklands conflict."

"Is that why he was receiving treatment here, because of what happened on the Sheffield?"

Laing didn't answer.

"Let's do this a different way," Dan said. "Let's talk in general terms about how a person might be affected by an event like that."

"It's widely documented," Laing said. "Most modern theories and treatments have been developed relatively recently, since the Vietnam war."

"You're talking about post traumatic stress disorder, aren't you?"

"Yes, I am. PTSD isn't limited to combat veterans, but the majority of documented cases do involve military personnel."

"Was Peter Jones receiving treatment for PTSD?"

"I can't discuss my patient's treatment, Dan."

Dan put his notepad down on the arm of the sofa. He thumbed the biro, retracting the nib, and placed it across the open page of the notepad.

"Peter Jones is a suspect in two concurrent murder investigations and a serious assault on a member of Humberside CID. We will arrest him, he will be charged, and he will go to court. At that point, you will be called to provide expert psychiatric witness testimony. Jones is out there somewhere, and it is likely he will kill again. If you help us now, you could save someone's life. I'll be honest with you, Doctor Laing, Peter Jones' right to privacy is very low on my list of priorities."

Laing looked at Dan for a while, his expression neutral. Finally, he took a slow breath before speaking.

"Peter first came here in August. He wasn't referred, he told me he found us in the Yellow Pages."

"Three months ago," Dan said to Rick. "If Vic's information was correct, that was before Laura Potter moved out."

"Have you spoken to Laura Potter?" Laing asked.

"One of our colleagues is going to see her today."

"I never met her, but Peter came to me because he was scared that he was going to harm her."

"Jones came here voluntarily?" Dan said. "You are absolutely sure about that?"

"Yes."

"How many times did you see him?"

"He had weekly appointments every Thursday, starting on the fifteenth of August. He cancelled a handful of them, with no notice and no reason subsequently given. Tanya can give you the exact dates of the cancellations if you need them."

"You said he also missed last week's appointment."

"Yes. Again, we received no notification of the cancellation and he has not been in touch since then."

"What can you tell us about him? In your opinion, is he capable of premeditated murder?"

Laing took another long breath before answering. "When Peter first came here, all he wanted was to talk. He talked about Laura Potter, and he talked about darkness. As a child, many of us are instinctively afraid of the dark. This can be the case for children who have suffered trauma such as being left alone in a dark room, but it can also affect children who have no history of trauma related directly to darkness. For some, the fear of darkness is linked to death anxiety."

"Was Jones' fear of the dark caused by what happened on the Sheffield?"

"What you have to understand, is that Peter is not simply scared of the dark. Imagine a child, alone in a dark room. They will cry, their heart rate will rise, they may shiver, experience nausea, and wet themselves. Turn on the light and they will immediately experience relief. They may continue to cry, but the fear is reduced."

"My daughter won't sleep without a light on in her room," Dan said.

"And so you leave the light on," Laing said.

"Is that wrong?"

"Not at all. Your daughter is comforted by the light, and she sleeps through the night. How old is she?"

"Five."

"I have had parents of teenagers ask me when their child will stop sleeping with the light on. I tell them they will stop when, and if, they are ready. The need for a nightlight is not a negative condition, despite what you might have been told."

"What about Jones? You said it wasn't a simple fear of the dark for him."

"No," Laing said. "For Peter, the darkness is a trigger. His memories of the missile strike and the aftermath are linked to an extreme reaction to being plunged into total darkness. Details of that day on the Sheffield are mostly repressed, hidden from him by his own mind. It is a defence mechanism we call psychogenic amnesia, but for Peter the memories can return temporarily if he wakes in darkness, or if a room he is in suddenly becomes dark."

"Have you actually seen this happen to him?" Dan asked.

Laing frowned, shaking his head. "No. Peter's own accounts of his experiences were more than adequate for me to make a conclusive diagnosis."

"I've seen it happen," Dan said.

Laing sat forward in his chair. "I don't understand."

"Last Friday, Rick and I were in a pub, the *Golden Hart*. Peter Jones was sitting alone at a nearby table. There was a power cut for about ten seconds, and all the lights went out."

"What happened?"

"He tried to strangle me. The lights came back on and someone pulled him away from me."

"You were incredibly lucky that the lights came back on."

"I know."

"But you didn't arrest him?"

"We were off duty, and the barman told me about what had happened to Jones. I suppose I felt sorry for him."

"Was this before he became a suspect for the murders?"

"The first murder occurred the next day, Saturday."

Laing paused for a few seconds, then his eyes widened with realisation. "The murders that were on the local news last night. Is Peter the suspect for those?"

"Yes, he is."

"It's very unlikely that he was responsible."

"Why?"

"The policeman on the news said that one of the murders happened at around ten o'clock at night, at a detached property. I can't believe Peter would risk going to someone else's house at night with his condition."

"He knew both victims," Dan said. "He was in school with them."

"Remind me of their names, please. I can't remember them from the police report."

"Sharon Hall and Dee Collins."

"Peter never mentioned those names to me."

"Did he ever mention the names of anyone he was in school with?"

"Sometimes he would talk about people he used to know. They could have been Naval colleagues, old friends, maybe people he remembered from school. I don't recall every name he ever told me, but I'm sure he didn't mention either of those women."

"What about Thomas Mason? Did he ever say that name?"

"I'm fairly sure he didn't."

"Only fairly sure?"

"The majority of names he mentioned were male. He might have told me about a Tom or a Thomas, but it's likely to have been someone from the Navy."

Dan picked up his notepad. "What was Peter Jones like at his most recent appointment, two weeks ago? Was his behaviour any different from previous appointments?"

"Two months ago, Peter was upset when Laura Potter moved out of his flat, which was understandable, but there was also a certain sense of relief because he knew that she was in danger in his flat at night. After that, his mood seemed to fluctuate from one appointment to the next. I know that a friend had been trying to help him, but I'm not sure they were actually making a positive contribution."

"Wait," Dan said. "A friend? What friend?"

"Peter didn't tell me much about him. I had the feeling it was possibly someone he had served with on the Sheffield."

Dan looked at Rick. "The other guy in the *Golden Hart*."

"Do you think so?"

"Did Jones tell you the name of this friend?" Dan asked Laing.

"No, he didn't."

Dan tapped his pen against his notepad. "Did Jones ever say the word Exocet to you?"

Laing nodded slowly. "Only once, at his last appointment."

"He had never said it before?"

"The word Exocet was a key memory that had been suppressed by Peter's psychogenic amnesia. Something brought the word back. I don't know what it was."

"Is that what he's afraid of, the word Exocet?" Rick asked. "It makes sense, doesn't it?"

Laing shook his head. "It's not as simple as that. As far as I can determine, and this is solely based on what he said at the last appointment, there has been an element of traumatic threat reversal."

"What do you mean?" Dan asked.

"Peter isn't scared of a memory of the Exocet missile. He is scared because he believes he has become one."

CHAPTER 27

Rick's four-wheel drive Sierra was the perfect car for negotiating snow-covered inner city streets, but there was one major drawback to using his personal car instead of Dan's police BMW.

Dan sat in the passenger seat and looked at the Sierra's civilian dashboard. "We can't radio in to see if Knowles has got any useful information from Laura Potter."

"Shall we go back inside and ask Laing if we can use his phone?"

"Not worth it. It's only going to take us a quarter of an hour to get back to Campbell Road. I was expecting this snow to be a lot worse."

Rick leaned forward, looking up at the sky through the windscreen. "At least it's stopped for now."

"Still really bloody cold."

Rick started the engine. "I'll get us back as quick as I can."

Dan fastened his seatbelt. "I'll settle for safe over quick."

Rick pulled away onto the empty white road. "What did you make of what Laing said at the end?"

"The bit about Jones thinking he's a missile?"

"That was just psych-speak, though, wasn't it? If Jones actually did say that, it's likely he was inventing some kind of cover story for his attacks on his girlfriend."

"Maybe. Or it was the only explanation he could come up with, trying to rationalise his fear of what he was capable of doing."

"You sound like you still feel sorry for him."

"You have to, really, knowing what happened to him. Don't get me wrong, we're going to catch him and we're going to put him away for a long, long time. I don't care if he goes to Belle Vue or Rampton, as long as we get him off our streets."

"Belle Vue?"

"Sorry. Old joke. Not that funny now."

"I'm sure I've heard of Belle Vue. It was a prison, wasn't it?"

"Closed last century. Apparently it wasn't exactly a Stakis hotel."

Rick stopped at a T-junction. There were no other cars driving along the road in either direction, no fresh tyre tracks in the snow. He turned right, heading back towards Campbell Road.

"How are we going to find him?"

"He'll turn up," Dan said. "I'm going to ask Harry to put the tower block under surveillance. Should have done it last night, really."

"You think he'll go back there?"

"It didn't look like he had packed up and moved out, so we can assume he intends to go back there."

Rick turned the car's heater up to its maximum setting. "Laing seemed convinced that Jones wouldn't have gone out in the dark to Raymond Hughes' house. Do you believe that?"

"I don't know. I had almost completely convinced myself that Jones was being set up, but I'm really not sure any more."

Rick got them back to Campbell Road station a few minutes before midday. The sky was thick with pale grey cloud, the air bitter against their faces as soon as they opened the Sierra's doors.

"I suppose we should be grateful the wind has dropped," Rick said.

Dan clapped his hands and rubbed them together. "Come on, let's get inside."

Harry West came straight out of his office when Dan and Rick walked out of the stairwell onto the first floor. Harry looked anxious, not at all happy about something.

"What's happened?" Dan said. "Is it Laura Potter?"

"It's Thomas Mason," Harry said. He exhaled heavily. "He's killed himself."

"What?" Dan looked at Rick, saw an expression of dazed shock that exactly matched how he was feeling. "When?"

"Not long ago. Maybe within the last hour. I just took a call from Marlborough Road. One of their cars responded to a complaint about a loud noise at the community hall in Spring Bank. When they went inside they found Thomas Mason's body."

Dan started to refasten the coat buttons he had undone after they had entered the station. "We're going there now."

Rick stared at Harry West. "How did he do it?"

"They found him hanging from a rope tied to a ceiling beam."

"Rick," Dan said. "We need to go now."

"I don't get it," Rick said. "Why would he kill himself?"

***

Rick stopped the Sierra a few yards behind the patrol car that was parked at the side of the road outside the community hall. There was only one car in the small car park, a red Ford Fiesta.

Dan and Rick walked up to the entrance to the hall. There was a uniformed constable waiting at the closed door. He looked cold and miserable. A second officer was sitting in the patrol car. Dan figured the uniform in the car had won the coin-toss.

Dan recognised the one waiting at the door. He had been part of the impromptu road block at the junction with Old Park Lane on Saturday evening.

"Who made the call?" Dan asked.

"Local resident," said the uniform. "Guitar had been feeding back on full volume through a bloody big speaker for half an hour or so."

"What happened to the noise?"

"We turned the amplifier off at the mains."

"Did you touch anything else?"

"No, Sarge. We had a look at what was in there and called it straight in."

Dan looked at the splintered wood next to the door handle. "What happened to the door?"

"It was locked. We had to force it."

"Locked with a key or bolted from inside?"

"Just locked. It wasn't bolted."

"Did you find the key?"

"There's a key inside, on the floor near the body. It looks like the sort of key that would fit that lock."

"Do you want to go and wait in the patrol car?"

The uniformed constable nodded gratefully. When he was back inside the car, Dan turned to Rick. "You're going to be okay with this." A statement, not a question.

"If you say so."

"Open mind, remember. No conclusions without evidence."

Rick blew out a long, steady breath. "Okay. Got it."

Dan pushed the door open and went inside. Behind him, he heard Rick say, "Oh, shit."

Dan saw the wooden floor with the badminton court markings that he had seen before, the stacks of plastic chairs, the high ceiling. He saw the exposed timber truss above the centre of the marked-out court.

One end of a length of thick, braided hemp rope was tied to the middle of the truss. The other end was looped around Thomas Mason's neck. The hanging body's feet were about six inches above the wooden floor. The body was fully clothed in faded jeans, black boots, green and black striped sweater and black leather jacket. A yard away, one of the stackable plastic chairs was lying on its side.

Near the stage, a cream coloured guitar was leaning against the front of a large black speaker cabinet. On top of the cabinet was a separate amplifier. On top of the amplifier was an open pack of cigarettes and an unopened can of Coca Cola. On the floor, about five feet from the speaker, there was a smudged damp stain. It looked recent.

Dan stood in front of the hanging body. "Come here."

"Poor bastard. Why did he do it?"

"Tell me what you can see. Don't worry about writing anything down, just look and tell me what you see."

"He's dead. Looks like he tied the rope up there, climbed on that chair…" Rick swallowed hard. "Then jumped off."

"What else can you see. Look at him, and look around."

"Face is swollen, red and purple patches. No other signs of injury. Looks like he pissed himself. I don't know what else—"

"Okay, stop."

"What have I missed?"

"Everything, but it's okay."

Rick took a step back, confusion all over his face. "What do you mean?"

"Start with the urine stain."

"It's just a damp patch on the front of his jeans."

"Has it run down his legs?"

"No." Rick looked at Dan. "It should have."

"Yes. Now look at his hands."

"I can't see anything odd. They're pale, just hanging there."

"I've seen two hanging suicides before. In both cases, the victims instinctively grabbed at the noose. One of them had both hands stuck inside it after death. The other tore three nails off while they were clawing at the rope. It doesn't matter how much you might think you want to kill yourself, those last moments are never easy, never calm."

"But he doesn't look like he did that."

"No, he doesn't. And he didn't piss himself while he was hanging there."

"What about the chair?"

"Whoever killed him put it there. Misdirection."

"You think someone else hanged him?"

"No. Someone strangled him over there near his guitar and speaker. There's a damp patch on the floor, which is probably where he lost control of his bladder. They hanged him afterwards, and they left the guitar feeding back to make sure the body was found quickly."

"You saw all that straight away?"

"There's more. Look at the Coke can. It's not even open. Who takes a canned drink to their own suicide but doesn't drink any of it? I doubt any of those cigarettes have been smoked in here today either."

Rick looked at all the things Dan was talking about. He looked down at the key on the floor. "What about the locked door?"

"They must have had another key. I'm guessing they left that key right there, where it would immediately be seen, to make the fake suicide look more convincing."

Rick walked behind the hanging body and looked up. "I can see the knot. It's a figure-eight loop."

"You sure?"

"One of the first they taught me in Sea Scouts."

Dan looked at his watch. "Now you can start writing all this down. I'm going to radio in from the patrol car, tell Harry what we found."

"One thing I don't understand. Why would Tom come all the way here in this weather to play his guitar?"

Dan sighed. "Maybe we'll find out when we talk to his parents."

"Yeah. We have to do that, don't we?"

"Afraid so."

Dan went outside, walked through the two-inch-deep snow to the patrol car and tapped on the passenger side window.

"What's up, Sarge?"

"Can I use your radio?"

"Problem with yours?"

"We came in DC Price's personal vehicle. Four-wheel drive but no radio."

"Nice motor, though."

"Not bad."

"Hold on a sec. I'll sit in the back while you use the radio."

"Thanks. You really don't want to be standing out here in this if you don't have to."

The uniformed constable climbed out of the front of the Granada and got into the back seat.

Dan sat in the passenger seat and picked up the radio mic. "This is DS Blacksmith requesting contact with DCI Harry West, over."

"Control here, Dan. Patching to DCI West, over."

"Dan, it's Harry. Bob Knowles has made it back. He spoke to the Potter girl, but tell me what you found first."

Dan said, "It's not a suicide. Someone killed Thomas Mason and had a go at making it look like a suicide."

"Are you absolutely sure about that?" Harry asked.

"Rick and I both came to the same conclusion. Too much evidence for it to be anything but a hastily covered-up murder."

"Damn. And now you're going to tell me you think it's the same suspect as the Hall and Collins murders."

"And the assault on DI Schrader."

"Three murders in less than a week. We've definitely got a serial killer on our hands."

"What did DI Knowles find out from Laura Potter?"

"The story you had about her was only half right. She didn't walk out on Peter Jones. He kicked her out of his flat and told her to never go back."

Dan frowned. "Did she say why he did that?"

"She said he told her he was scared he was going to hurt her, that even though he loved her he would rather live without her than risk hurting her, or worse."

"That's exactly what she told Knowles?"

"Pretty much word for word," Harry said.

Dan looked out of the windscreen at a world of white and grey. "Three murders, and a missing man who knew all three victims. The missing man broke up with someone he loved because he was scared of hurting them. The same man has been receiving psychiatric treatment for post traumatic stress."

"We have to find him, Dan."

"First, we have to find everyone else who was in that career choices class eight years ago at John Blair Comprehensive, and we have to warn them."

Harry said, "It's more than a coincidence now, isn't it? It's a definite link between all four of them."

Dan didn't speak. He was thinking about kids in school, and why something that happened eight years ago would cause one of them to start killing the others who had been there.

"Dan," Harry said. "Why was Thomas Mason's death called in as a suicide?"

Dan didn't look at the uniformed constable in the driving seat. He could feel the man staring at him as he replied to Harry. "Because the killer made it look like one."

"I'll get forensics and a pathologist over to the scene as soon as I can, which might not be for a while with the weather the way it is."

"Understood," Dan said. "Can you get someone to drop a couple of coffees off for the lads in the patrol car here? Maybe some hot food if possible. They're likely to be here for a while."

"I'll see what I can do. Are you coming back to the station?"

"Not yet. I'm going to John Blair. It's probably closed because of the snow but someone might be there."

"Dan, someone is going to have to notify the Masons about their son."

"I was planning to, but I'm not going to have time."

"DI Knowles is here. I'll ask him to go."

"I'd go if I could, Harry."

"I know. Give me a full report when you get back from the school."

***

The roads close to John Blair Comprehensive had been gritted the previous day. The surface of the road outside the school was covered with dirty orange slush instead of crisp white snow. Rick parked near the open school gates as a blue transit van drove past in the opposite lane.

Rick watched the shallow wake of sludge washing back from the van's tyres. "If they keep this gritting up, the whole city might get back to normal by March."

"There are kids in that classroom," Dan said.

"Not many. Do you think the school is actually open?"

"Must be. Come on."

Dan and Rick walked across the schoolyard towards the main building, a two-storey redbrick with sombre arched windows and a huge granite slab for a doorstep. The door was open.

Dan walked into the high-ceilinged hall, listening to his own footsteps on the worn, tiled floor. To his left, the door of the school secretary's office was wide open. As Dan was about to look inside, a tall man in an old brown suit came out of the office. He looked early forties, stocky but running to fat, with receding hair. He peered at Dan over a pair of half-moon spectacles that were halfway down the bridge of his nose.

"Can I help you?"

Dan already had his warrant card in his hand. "Sergeant Dan Blacksmith, Humberside CID. This is DC Price."

"Oh, good afternoon. I'm Oswald Graves, the headmaster." Graves offered his hand to Dan and Rick in turn. "You will have to bear with me, I'm afraid. The school is supposed to be closed but at least a quarter of the children turned up and we either can't contact their parents or they have told us their parents will not be at home until later, so we can't send them home."

"I understand," Dan said. "I wanted to ask—"

"The school secretary is snowed in at home, can't make it in. I'm having to answer the phone and it has been ringing all day."

"I see. I promise to keep this as short as possible."

"What are the roads like now? I assume you managed to drive here."

"Passable, but we are in a four-wheel drive."

The phone in the office started to ring.

"If you could excuse me just for a moment, I need to answer that." Graves spread his hands apologetically before hurrying into the office.

Rick shook his head. "Useless."

"We all have our own problems to deal with."

"He hasn't got three dead bodies and a nutter on the loose." Rick sniffed the air. "And I hate the smell of school."

Graves reappeared two minutes later.

"Awfully sorry about that. Parents phoning to ask if the school will be open tomorrow. I honestly have no idea. Hard to know what to tell them."

Dan held up his hand. "Mr Graves, could I just ask you a couple of very quick questions?"

"Of course, yes. What would you like to know?"

"Do you have records of pupils who attended particular classes, specifically from the fifth form that would have left in 1977?"

"Good lord, no."

"You're that certain?"

"It's more than five years ago. Do you know how much storage space that kind of paperwork takes up? If we kept more than five years' worth of records we wouldn't have any room left in school for the pupils."

"What about on microfiche?"

"Microfiche? Maybe if we were a library or a record office, but we're a secondary school."

"What about a list of the pupils from that year, kids who would have left in 1977?"

"Yes," Graves said slowly. "We would have that list."

"Could I see it, please?"

Graves stood where he was. "Can I ask what this is about?"

Dan looked along the empty corridor that led further into the large, quiet building. He pictured Sharon Hall and Dee Collins walking along the corridor together, giggling at something trivial, unaware that they had eight years until their lives would end within a couple of days of each other, and that the person responsible for their brutal deaths was likely to be someone who had walked this same corridor.

"Three former pupils of John Blair Comprehensive were killed within the last five days. All three were in the fifth form in 1977, and they all attended the same two classes, history and a career choices class."

Graves gasped, shaking his head. "That's terrible, truly awful." He glanced at the ceiling. "That would make them, what, twenty-four or twenty-five?"

"They were all twenty-four years old."

Graves' eyes widened above his glasses. "I saw it on the news last night. I didn't realise they were our former pupils."

"You didn't recognise the names?"

"I took over the headship in eighty-one." Graves blinked. "The police only mentioned two deaths on the news."

"The third death happened earlier today."

"Today? I can't believe this. It's terrible."

"Mr Graves, we really need your help. We need to contact the other pupils who were in the same career choices class as the ones who have been killed."

"Wait," Graves said. "The career choices class?"

"Yes. I believe that's the group that is being targeted."

"I can find the name of the teacher who ran that class in 1977. That will still be on record."

"Will they remember which kids were in that class?"

"They are quite likely to, and I can give you the full list of pupils from that year to cross-reference with what they remember, or to help prompt their memory if it isn't perfect."

Dan nodded, exchanging a quick, encouraging smile with Rick. "That sounds good, Mr Graves. How soon can you find this information?"

"Give me five minutes. The class lists going back to 1950 are all filed in the office. I can get the one for seventy-seven straight away. The teacher's name might take me a little longer, but it's definitely going to be there."

"Can we help with this?" Dan asked.

"You won't know where to start looking, I promise you."

Graves turned and disappeared back into the secretary's

office.

"Okay, maybe I was wrong," Rick said.

"Let's wait and see what he finds."

CHAPTER 28

Dan ran his finger down the faded, photocopied list of twenty-eight alphabetically ordered names. He saw Sharon Hall's name not far from the top of the list, and Tom Mason near the middle. The fifth-form class was called 5G. Dee Collins' name was second from the top of the list on the second sheet that showed the names of twenty-seven pupils in the class called 5L.

"Fifty-five kids," Dan said. "And we don't know which ones were the others in that careers choice class."

Oswald Graves looked at a third sheet of paper that he was holding. "The teacher who ran those classes was definitely Jacob Sorrell. His name is right here, but I never met him. According to the records, he resigned on the twenty-seventh of May, 1977."

Dan looked up from the lists of names. "Does it say why he resigned?"

"No, and this was all several years before my time."

Rick looked down at the lists that Dan was holding. "If we could speak to this Jacob Sorrell, and show him these lists, that would be our best chance of finding out who else was in that class."

Dan checked his watch. It was a couple of minutes after one o'clock. "Do you have a phone number or address for Jacob Sorrell?"

"Both, but this information is over eight years old. He may have moved house by now."

"It's all we've got, Mr Graves." Dan held out his hand. "Could I have that, please, and could I use the phone in the office?"

Graves hesitated for a second before giving Dan the sheet of paper. "Of course. I'm still trying to come to terms with the news about three former pupils being killed this week."

Dan and Rick went into the school office. Dan sat at the desk, arranged the lists of names in front of him, and dialled Jacob Sorrell's eight-year-old phone number. It rang six times before it was answered.

A woman's voice said, "Hello?"

"Good afternoon. This is Sergeant Dan Blacksmith from Humberside Police. Is that Mrs Sorrell?"

"I'm sorry, who did you want to speak to?"

"Does Jacob Sorrell live at that address?"

"Jacob Sorrell? No, no he doesn't. I think you have the wrong number."

"This was Jacob Sorrell's number in 1977. Have you moved into the house since then?"

"Oh, I see. Yes, we moved in back in 1980."

"Did you buy the house from Jacob Sorrell?"

"No, I've never heard that name before."

"Who did you buy the house from?"

"Well, it was through an estate agent, of course, but I believe the seller's name was Smith."

"Just Smith, you don't know their first name?"

"Honestly, that's all I remember. You're lucky I remember that much."

"Could I take your name, please, just so that I have a record of who I spoke to?"

"Mary Winters."

"Thank you, Mary. Thanks for your time."

Dan hung up. "Nothing. She's been in the house since 1980, never heard of Jacob Sorrell."

"Yeah, I gathered that much." Rick snapped his fingers. "The previous headmaster. We should call him. Maybe Sorrell resigned here because he was moving away to a new job. The head might know where he went."

Dan nodded. "That's not a bad idea at all. Call Graves in here."

It took Oswald Graves a few minutes of scrabbling through dusty folders of yellowing papers but he found the contact information for the previous headmaster, a man called Charles Wilson, which included a phone number with a Hull area code.

Dan dialled the number, fully prepared to speak to another baffled woman who had probably bought her house from someone called Jones, or Davies, or Brown, or…

"Good afternoon, Charles Wilson speaking."

Dan sighed with relief. "Good afternoon, Mr Wilson. This is Detective Sergeant Dan Blacksmith from Humberside Police. I would very much like to ask you a few questions if you have two minutes."

The phone line was quiet for several seconds, just the distant sound of an elderly man taking a slow, deep breath.

"Are you calling about the two dead girls?"

Dan's hand tightened on the phone as he pressed it harder against his ear. "What do you know about them, Mr Wilson?"

"Just what I saw on the news last night. If you're not calling about them, it must be a terrible coincidence."

"Do you know anything about the two deaths?"

"No more than I heard on the news. It's very sad."

Dan looked at the lists of names on the desk in front of him. "Mr Wilson, I need to get in touch with Jacob Sorrell, a former teacher from John Blair."

Dan heard Charles Wilson take another breath. He could tell that the man on the other end of the line had been surprised to hear Sorrell's name.

"Jacob Sorrell," Wilson said. "He died. He died a month after he resigned from John Blair."

Dan covered the mouthpiece of the phone. "Sorrell is dead," he said to Rick. He saw the expression on Rick's face and shook his head. "No, he died in 1977." He put the phone back to his ear. "Mr Wilson, do you know how Jacob Sorrell died?"

"I'm afraid I do. He took his own life."

Dan looked at the sparse notes he had taken, the lists of names, and he considered his options. "Mr Wilson, how far do you live from the school?"

"Not far at all. A mile and a half by road."

"I know this is an imposition, but I would very much like to speak to you in person as soon as possible."

"Were you hoping to come today? The roads are treacherous here."

"Could we come right now, please?"

"Well, of course, if you need to talk to me face to face."

"Thank you. Could you just confirm your address, as the information we have here at the school is rather old."

"Are you at the school now?"

"Yes. We will be coming straight from here to see you."

"In that case, I'll ask my wife to put the kettle on."

***

Charles Wilson lived with his wife in a three-bedroom bungalow on one of Hull's more upmarket estates. Most of the houses were detached, set back from the road with long driveways and tall, well-established hedges. He had been correct about the condition of the roads nearby, but Rick had no trouble reaching the address in his Sierra. He reversed the car onto the bungalow's drive and parked it facing the road.

Dan counted four seconds between pressing the bell button and seeing Charles Wilson open the door. The ex-headmaster was a shade under six feet tall, round-shouldered and already wearing the comfort of retirement as a fresh layer of fat around his midriff.

He led Dan and Rick into the lounge, waiting for them to sit on a firm, paisley-patterned sofa before sinking into what was obviously his favourite armchair.

"Thank you for agreeing to speak to us at such short notice," Dan said.

Wilson spread his hands apart. "I didn't have any other plans, not with the weather the way it is."

"I wanted to ask you about Jacob Sorrell, and the fifth form pupils who were in the career choices class in 1977."

Wilson sat back in his chair, his expression distant. "Oswald didn't know anything about what happened, did he?"

"No. He just had a file that said Sorrell had resigned at the end of May in 1977." Dan glanced at Rick before continuing. "What did happen, Mr Wilson?"

"To put it into context, you need to understand that Jacob was what some people would call a sensitive man. He was deeply religious, and he never married. I was never personally aware of him having any kind of relationship at all, but some of the staff, and many of the pupils, nurtured various rumours and gossip regarding his preference for other men."

Dan hadn't written anything down as he listened to what Wilson said. "Okay, I can see how that might have been awkward for him as a teacher."

"Awkward?" Wilson said. "Awkward doesn't come close. The fifth form that year was unusually packed with creatively vicious pupils. They preyed on each other, on younger children, and on some of the more susceptible members of staff."

"Are you talking about bullying?"

"Bullying is just a word. Some of the things that these children did went beyond the boundaries of common decency."

"Was the career choices class particularly bad?"

"It was bad every week, and every week they managed to exceed whatever they had done the week before."

"Did this somehow lead to Jacob Sorrell's resignation?"

"I would say it was a significant contributing factor. There were so many things that happened. For example, Jacob was an asthmatic and he used a prescription inhaler which he carried at all times in school. His asthma attacks could be triggered by a variety of conditions. Dust from a chalk board, or high levels of stress would do it. On more than one occasion, the pupils in the career choices class took the inhaler from his jacket pocket without his knowledge. They hid the inhaler and then one of them would quite unnecessarily write and erase a great deal of words on the blackboard, followed by pounding the board rubber against the blackboard to create a cloud of dust near Jacob."

Dan shook his head. "Didn't Sorrell do anything to stop them?"

"Of course he did. We're talking about children who thrived on acts of mental and physical cruelty, who treated after-school detention as a reward, and who saw canings as a badge of honour."

Rick tapped Dan on the shoulder. "We had plenty of kids like that at Needle Hill. The stuff they did, if an adult did it to someone in the street they'd go down for ten years."

Wilson cleared his throat. "While Jacob tried to find the inhaler, staggering and wheezing up and down between the rows of desks, the pupils would call out things like 'cold' and 'warmer', as if it were some kind of birthday treasure hunt."

Dan's hand jerked as he caught the biro before it fell from his fingers. He could feel gooseflesh bristling the backs of his arms.

"Shit," Rick said.

"Mr Wilson," Dan said. "How do you know that happened?"

"Jacob told me. He told me everything, on a weekly basis. He didn't want to give up on the children. He said he wanted to encourage them, not punish them."

"But were they punished?"

"To the extent that they could be at school. Detentions, corporal punishment. It didn't stop them."

Dan said, "The two young women who were killed, Sharon Hall and Dee Collins, were they involved with any of this?"

Wilson looked up as his wife came into the lounge carrying a tray. She handed her husband a large blue mug before holding the tray near Dan and Rick so that they could take their coffees.

"Thank you, Mrs Wilson," Dan said.

"No trouble at all. I hope Charles isn't boring you to death with all his old school stories."

Wilson waited until his wife had left the room and closed the door behind her.

"Sharon and Dee were very much involved, I'm afraid. When I heard their names on the news last night, I recognised them immediately. I'm sorry to say it was because I will always remember what they did to Jacob, and how terribly badly it affected him. I believe it was the final straw, the thing that caused him to resign, and although I hate to say it, I believe it was probably the reason he took his own life."

Dan leaned forward and placed the coffee mug on a coaster on top of the small table next to the sofa. The coaster had a sketched picture on it of a kitten playing with a ball of wool.

"What did they do?" Dan asked. "They were just school kids."

"As I told you, Jacob was a very religious man, and there were constant rumours and tales circulating regarding his sexual preferences. He told me that Sharon and Dee would leave their desks during the career choices class, walk to the front of the classroom where he was standing, and proceed to touch and kiss each other while the other pupils in the class applauded."

Dan stared, slowly shaking his head. "That's what Thomas Mason told us, and I just ignored him. I thought it was irrelevant."

"We couldn't have known," Rick said. "It's the same as those messages on your car and the shed. How could we have known it all went back to that class eight years ago?"

"There's more," Wilson said. "I think you need to hear it. When I found out what the girls had been doing, they were summoned to my office. I spoke to them with the deputy head, who was female, and they told us that Jacob had been making crude advances to them during class, had in fact been putting his hands on their breasts and under their skirts. Of course, we accused them of lying, of making the whole thing up to avoid punishment for what they had been doing, but when we spoke to each member of that class individually they all backed the girls up. They all told us exactly the same story about Jacob molesting Dee and Sharon. And when I say *exactly the same*, I mean it sounded rehearsed, as if they had planned it."

Rick sighed heavily. "That's pretty bad. That would be bad even for Needle Hill."

"And is that the reason Jacob Sorrell resigned?" Dan asked.

"I believe that was the main reason. We didn't involve the police because I had no doubt that the pupils were all lying. I knew Jacob, and I knew he wouldn't do the things that they had said he had done. Although I felt sorry for him, and I have no pride in this at all, it made it simpler for me when he handed in his notice of resignation."

"The kids never reported it outside school? They didn't tell their parents?"

"Not to my knowledge. No parent ever came to me with any kind of complaint about Jacob."

Dan rubbed his forehead. "Did Peter Jones ever do anything to Jacob Sorrell?"

"Peter? Nothing specific that I can remember apart from going along with the other pupils, backing up the story that Jacob had been touching Dee and Sharon."

Dan made a couple of quick notes. "The more we find out, the less sense it makes."

Rick said, "I think it's guilt. I think Jones is doing it because he's guilty about what happened to Jacob Sorrell. It must be the PTSD. Maybe it messed his real memories up."

Dan looked at the notes he had taken. Rick's theory was based largely on conjecture, an attempt to shoehorn a motive onto a current suspect without considering all the alternative possibilities. He asked Charles Wilson how Jacob Sorrell had killed himself.

Wilson held his hot mug of coffee with both hands, staring into the wisps of rising steam. "They found him in his back garden, hanging from the branch of an Oak growing in the field behind his house."

"He hanged himself," Dan said. "Was there any doubt at all about it being suicide?"

"Not that I'am aware of. Jacob left what was reported as a suicide note, but it was more than just a note. He also left a diary that contained detailed information about his time at John Blair."

"How do you know all this?"

"The police talked to me about it. They were not looking to blame any of the pupils, they were just going through the motions of checking the veracity of Jacob's last written words."

Dan turned to Rick. "Do you remember any of this?"

"No. I'd never heard of Jacob Sorrell before today. When that happened, the summer of seventy-seven, I would have been finishing my final year at college in Manchester."

Wilson took a sip of his coffee. "It barely got a mention in the papers, and I kept the news under wraps at school. I didn't want the pupils to find out what had happened. It would have started all manner of rumours and unrest."

"So the kids who left school that year might not have known that Sorrell killed himself?"

"The fifth form classes would have already left by then."

Dan asked, "What about someone who came back to the sixth form in September?"

"After two months out of school, they wouldn't have been thinking about a teacher who resigned the previous term. I don't remember anyone ever talking about Jacob Sorrell again, let alone mentioning his suicide."

Rick leaned forward on the sofa. "Peter Jones might not even have known that Sorrell killed himself."

"That's exactly what I was thinking," Dan said. "So who did know about it?"

Wilson took a breath, nodding slowly, considering what he was about to say. "There was only his brother."

"Sorrell had a brother?"

"Younger, by two or three years."

"Did he see the suicide note and the diary?"

Wilson shook his head. "I don't know. I can only assume that he did."

"Did you ever meet him?"

"I shook his hand at the funeral. He didn't speak to me, apart from to thank me for attending, but he did stand up in church and deliver a short eulogy."

Dan jotted some brief notes before asking the next question. "Do you remember what he said in his eulogy?"

"It was mostly about forgiveness. He read two lines from *Ephesians*, the part about getting rid of bitterness, rage and anger, and forgiving each other."

"Was Jacob's brother also a religious man?"

"He may have been, but I didn't get that impression. I know I only saw him for a short period, and at a time when he would have been grieving, but he seemed very different from Jacob."

Dan wrote some more notes. "Do you know his name?"

"Oliver."

"Oliver Sorrell," Dan said, writing the name in his notepad. "Any middle name?"

"That was how he introduced himself. I don't know if he has a middle name."

"Does he live locally?"

"I don't think so."

Dan looked up from his notes. "You don't know where he lives?"

"I believe he travelled here for the funeral, but he didn't say where from." Wilson paused, his eyes widening. "I probably should have told you this first…"

"What?" Dan asked.

"I know he had to travel a long way to get here for the funeral. He was serving abroad at the time."

"Serving? You mean he was with one of the armed forces?"

"Yes, although I never heard anyone say which one."

Dan finished what he was writing. "Now, I really want to talk to Oliver Sorrell. Thank you, Mr Wilson, for remembering so much about Jacob. I have one last thing to ask you, if you could look at these lists of fifth-form pupils and circle the names of the ones who were in Jacob Sorrell's career choices class."

"Do you really think Oliver Sorrell will be able to help you?" Wilson asked.

"I think he will," Dan said. "All we have to do is figure

out how to get in touch with him."

CHAPTER 29

Dan waited near the fax machine for twenty minutes before it flickered to life. He jabbed the button to receive the incoming transmission, watching as the shiny sheet of paper began to inch its way out of the bottom of the machine into the plastic tray.

It was a single sheet of paper bearing the same official Northwood Naval HQ header as the earlier fax that had contained Peter Jones' details. Beneath the header, the word CONFIDENTIAL was printed in a bold military typeface.

Dan read the sparse details and wondered exactly which of them were classified as confidential information. He already knew Oliver Sorrell's name, and the fax didn't show that the man had a middle name or initial. It also didn't show his rank, which Dan immediately thought was strange. There was no home address, no personal phone number, no marital status, no next of kin. There was a date of birth, 25 October 1946, which made Oliver Sorrell thirty-nine years old. There was an eight-digit number that Dan assumed was Sorrell's military service number. Beneath the service number it said: *Prince of Wales Regiment of Yorkshire (Infantry) 1964-1973*. There was a rough rectangular space between the regiment details and the final piece of information on the fax. To Dan, it looked as though the original document had been photocopied with something the size of a playing card that had been folded lengthwise to obscure some of the information.

At the bottom of the page was the name of a military base - RAF Hereford, Credenhill - followed by a single telephone number.

Dan took the fax to the CID office where Rick Price was sitting at his desk.

Rick looked up, his expression eager but not overly confident. "What did you get? Does it say where he is?"

"There's just the name of an RAF base, and a phone number. I don't even know if it's where he serves."

"RAF? What is he, a pilot?"

Dan showed Rick the fax.

"Shit, Dan. Credenhill. You know what that place is, don't you?"

"I thought the name looked familiar, but I can't think why."

"1980, the Iranian embassy siege. The special forces team that went in and rescued the hostages, you know, the SAS. That's where most of them are based." Rick pointed at the rectangular gap on the fax. "I bet that's why this part has been cut out. Sorrell must be in the SAS. Look, it doesn't show his rank, or pretty much anything else."

Dan sat at his desk opposite Rick. "This isn't good."

"Do you think Sorrell killed the two girls and Tom Mason?"

"You heard what Wilson said. Jacob Sorrell hanged himself, and we have two deaths by strangulation and a faked suicide by hanging. And then there was that story about the inhaler, and the treasure hunt mockery while Jacob was trying to find it, which matches the messages left on my car and at one of the crime scenes. There's one other thing, that you may not have picked up."

Rick shook his head. "Go on."

"Kath Schrader described her attacker as calm, almost indifferent, and Nigel Hansom said the marks on Sharon Hall's neck showed no signs of rage from her attacker. Did you make a note of the words Oliver Sorrell used in the eulogy?" Dan turned his notepad so that Rick could read it. "The part about getting rid of bitterness, rage and anger. That's exactly what he did. He killed without rage or anger."

"But he didn't exactly forgive them, did he?" Rick said.

"It's all way too much to be a coincidence."

"We wouldn't have found any of this without talking to Wilson, would we?"

"Probably not. I wish I'd given Tom Mason's information more credence. Might have saved his life."

Rick said nothing. He looked at the writing in his own notepad, but the answers weren't there.

Dan looked at the clock on the wall. "We should start getting some contact details through soon for the ex-pupils Wilson identified as being in that careers class."

"I suppose we're lucky there were only eleven kids in that class."

"And only eight of them left alive. Jones is one, so we have seven others to warn."

"Yeah." Rick raised his chin. "Hey, it isn't your fault. We were both running around chasing leads, trying to find Peter Jones. And where does he fit into this now?"

"I'm really not sure. He grabbed me around the throat in the pub, and his ex-girlfriend confirmed to DI Knowles that he had tried to strangle her. I wish I could remember what that other guy in the pub looked like. I think he might have been Oliver Sorrell."

"I saw him too," Rick said. "But I couldn't pick him out of a line-up."

Dan looked at the hastily typed report Knowles had left for him. It was peppered with misspellings and other typos but it was an otherwise clear and concise record of the interview with Laura Potter.

"Knowles must still be with the Masons," Dan said.

"Or stuck in the snow somewhere between there and here."

"I don't like it that he got lumbered with that job. I should have gone to talk to Bill and Deb Mason."

"You can't do everything, Dan. It was important that we went to the school, and look what turned up when we spoke to the ex-head. Do you want me to go check how Jeanette is getting on with finding contact details for the kids from Jacob Sorrell's class?"

"No, leave that for now. I'm going to call the army first, find out if Oliver Sorrell is even in this country at the moment. I'll put the call on speaker so you can hear what they say."

Dan dialled the Hereford phone number. It only rang twice before it was picked up.

"RAF Credenhill, Staff Sergeant Blake."

"Hello, Sergeant. This is Detective Sergeant Dan Blacksmith from Humberside CID in Kingston upon Hull. I would like to find out if a former Yorkshire regiment infantryman called Oliver Sorrell is based there."

There was a considerable pause before Blake replied. The line was not entirely silent. Dan heard distant, unidentifiable sounds, as if the room with the telephone had a large open door with a parade ground or airfield beyond it. "If you give me your phone number, sir, I'll ask the duty officer to call you back."

"Thanks, but do you know whether Oliver Sorrell is based there?"

"I'm not able to confirm or deny that, sir."

"Fair enough." Dan gave Sergeant Blake the main number for Campbell Road police station, plus his own extension number and also the full address of the station in case the duty officer decided to check whether Dan's claim to be a member of Humberside Police was legitimate.

He hung up after Blake told him that he couldn't give an estimate for when the duty officer would call back.

Dan frowned at the silent telephone on his desk. "I'll give them an hour, but I don't think they're going to call back at all."

Ten minutes later, the phone rang.

Dan tapped the speaker button and Rick leaned across the desk to listen.

"Humberside CID, DS Dan Blacksmith speaking."

"Good afternoon. This is Captain James Farrow from RAF Credenhill."

The phone line sounded different from earlier, when Dan had been talking to Staff Sergeant Blake, as if this phone was in another part of the base, somewhere more secluded.

"Captain Farrow, thank you for returning my call."

"What can I do for you?"

"I need to speak to a former infantryman, Oliver Sorrell. I received some basic information about him from Northwood HQ on a fax. There wasn't much detail on it, but it included the name of your base, and the number I called earlier."

"I see. What was the purpose of the request for information about Oliver Sorrell?"

"I need to speak to him with regard to a case that several members of Humberside CID are currently investigating."

"What is the nature of the case?"

Dan looked across the desk at Rick. Rick shrugged, because it was a direct question, no way to avoid answering it if they wanted any kind of assistance from Captain Farrow.

"We are investigating three deaths that occurred within the last week, all under suspicious circumstances. The deaths appear to be linked to something that happened approximately eight years ago."

"Why do you want to speak to Oliver Sorrell about this?"

"He is currently a suspect."

"I see."

"Captain Farrow, is Oliver Sorrell based at RAF Credenhill?"

"I'm unable to confirm or deny that."

"That's what Sergeant Blake said. But you know the name Oliver Sorrell, don't you?"

"Detective Blacksmith, I'm going to pass the information that you have given me to the commanding officer here. If we require anything further from you, we will be in touch."

"Wait, can't you even confirm that you know the name Oliver Sorrell?" Dan didn't give Farrow time to answer. "What's the commanding officer's name?"

"He will contact you if he needs more information."

Dan stared at Rick. Rick was nodding urgently, jabbing his finger at the phone. "It's him," Rick mouthed soundlessly. "Their CO is Sorrell."

"Please, Captain," Dan said. "If you can just give me the name and rank of the commanding officer there."

"He won't accept incoming calls from civilians."

"I honestly don't care about that. Please just tell me his name and rank."

There was a long silence, at least twenty seconds, before Farrow spoke again.

"The commanding officer here is Major Michael Bradshaw."

***

Harry West looked down at the numerous sheets of paper lined up along the edge of his desk. There were two that appeared to be school registers, a handful of names circled on each page, the fax of Peter Jones' military details and a similar sheet with less information on it, for a man of unspecified rank called Oliver Sorrell. There were other sheets of paper, mostly photocopied pages of Dan Blacksmith's notes relating to the interviews of a sixty-eight-year-old former headmaster and a local psychiatrist.

"What I think," Harry said, "is that the investigation has lost its focus in the wake of Thomas Mason's most unfortunate death."

"Harry," Dan said. "Charles Wilson provided unprompted corroborating evidence that tied several elements of the three murders to an event that occurred eight years ago. An event that was directly linked to the three victims."

Harry West shook his head. "Do you know what William Mason told DI Knowles? He said that his son left the house in a state of extreme agitation this morning. Although he hasn't issued a formal complaint, it's likely that Mr Mason blames his only son's unhealthy state of mind on the constant harassment he received from officers of Humberside CID."

"Harassment?" Dan held up his hands in disbelief. "We didn't harass him. The last time we went to their house, he was chatting to Rick about music and video games. When I phoned him to ask about Peter Jones, you were right there. Did that sound like harassment to you?"

"All I'm doing is telling you how this is going to look if they raise an official complaint. You went to their house numerous times, apprehended their son without charging him while he was sitting on a bench in the park, subjected him to various physical examinations, again, all without charging him with anything."

"Damn, Harry. I had the size of his hands checked. I did it to prove he wasn't the man who killed Sharon Hall, and that's what it did prove. Tom Mason knew he wasn't a suspect after that. He wanted to help us catch Sharon Hall's killer. He didn't kill himself, he was murdered by someone who did a fairly poor job of making it look like suicide."

"I just read DI Knowles' report," Rick said. "Mrs Mason told him that her husband couldn't drive to work because of the snow, so he was making work phone calls from home. Tom had been playing his guitar upstairs and Bill Mason went up and pulled the plug because the noise was annoying him. I reckon that was the reason Tom left the house in a strop. He went to the hall to play his guitar in peace, not to kill himself. Would have been luckier for him if he'd pranged the car in the snow on the way there."

"Some of that is pure conjecture," Harry said.

"But it's probably also correct," Dan said.

Harry gathered the paperwork into a neat stack, picked it up and held it out across his desk to Dan. "Do not phone the army again. There's a reason they don't want to talk to you about one of their soldiers, and it's the same reason I wouldn't talk to someone who phoned me out of the blue to accuse one of my officers of three murders on the other side of the country."

Dan swallowed hard, keeping his temper in check. "Charles Wilson gave us the name, the motive, and a number of very specific details that connect Oliver Sorrell with the three murders."

Harry sighed. "And Wilson is almost seventy years old, giving you vague, half-remembered details of events that occurred eight years ago."

"The events left a strong, lasting impression on him. I didn't sense any doubt or confusion when he was telling us what had happened."

"So, where's Peter Jones?" Harry asked. "He appears to have vanished at precisely the same time the murders began."

"We're still working on that."

"You should be working on that *as a priority*."

Dan glanced sideways at Rick. "Okay. That's what we'll do."

Back at their own desks, Rick started to thumb through the pages of notes. "It isn't Jones, is it? We agreed that."

"He's involved, but so is Sorrell. I'm certain of it. Harry is right about one thing, the army won't talk to us because they have no reason to suspect one of their own without solid, compelling evidence. Captain Farrow definitely recognised the name, and I reckon the sergeant did too. That line about being unable to confirm or deny, that's just official bullshit. If Sorrell wasn't based there, they would have just said that and hung up."

Dan watched the uniformed WPC walk out of the stairwell and head towards his desk. She was holding a single sheet of A4. She didn't smile as she stood at the side of Dan's desk and handed the sheet to him. The notes on the paper were in WPC Jeanette Powell's elegantly precise handwriting. Somehow that made it even worse.

"Five so far," Jeanette said. "We're still working on locating the remaining two, Gareth Pugh and Caroline Stanton."

Dan read it all, couldn't stop himself until he had finished the last line of graceful blue-biro notes.

"Dan?" Rick said. "What is it?"

Dan slowly tracked his finger down the page, summarising aloud and hearing his own voice, unfamiliar and defeated.

"Michael Scott, Manchester address. Died in a car accident twelve months ago. Terry Richards, still lived locally. Died after drinking heavily and falling from his hotel balcony while on holiday in Cyprus in 1983. Donna Bradley, now Donna Thorpe, Gainsborough address. Reported missing six months ago. Steven Dale, Withernsea. Fell in the sea while fishing last August. RNLI recovered the body. His neck was broken."

Rick was shaking his head, his mouth hanging open. "This can't be happening."

"It is. Listen to the last one. Cindy Rogers, emigrated to

Canada in 1982. Found hanging from a tree in a park half a mile from her home, on March the fifth this year."

"I'm really sorry," Jeanette said. "Are these all..."

"Yes," Dan said. "And we were wrong about Oliver Sorrell."

"What?" Rick said. "What were we wrong about?"

"We thought Sharon Hall was the first one."

"He's been killing them since eighty-three. Dan, we have to tell Harry."

Dan held up his finger, his eyes brightening despite the fresh, appalling revelation. "Jeanette, can you get the number of the last call that came through to my extension?"

"I should be able to."

"Can you try, and can you do it right now, please?"

"Of course, Sarge."

Dan didn't watch Jeanette walk away. He was staring at the page of handwritten notes. With just that one piece of paper, the death toll had gone from three to eight.

"What are we going to do?" Rick asked.

"We're going to catch him. And we're going to put him away forever."

"He's killed eight people that we know of. He might have already killed the last two."

"Three," Dan said.

"Yeah, Jones." Rick stared at the sheet of paper on the desk in front of Dan. "Why did you send Jeanette to get that phone number?"

"I think Captain Farrow called back on a different phone, somewhere else on the base. I don't want to speak to Sergeant Blake again. I suspect he will have been given orders to stonewall us."

Rick whistled softly, running his hand over his forehead. "Harry said not to call the army again."

"I'd say the situation has changed. It's my assumption that DCI West would reverse that order, given the recent information we've received."

"But you're not going to ask him, are you?"

"He's very busy," Dan said, without turning to look in the direction of Harry West's open office door. "I don't want to disturb him."

Five minutes later, WPC Jeanette Powell came out of the stairwell and walked straight to Dan's desk.

"I've got it," she said. She handed Dan a small square of yellow paper with a phone number written on it.

"Thanks, Jeanette." Dan looked at the number. "Last two digits are different from the number on the fax."

"Do you need anything else, Sarge?"

"That's all for now. Thanks for your help, it's much appreciated."

Dan dialled the number as Jeanette walked away towards the stairwell. Rick's eyes kept flicking back and forth between Dan and the open door to Harry's office.

The phone rang three times before it was answered.

"Twenty-two SAS. This is Farrow."

"Captain Farrow, this is Dan Blacksmith." Dan didn't stop talking, didn't want to give Farrow the opportunity to interrupt. "Oliver Sorrell was in Cyprus in 1983, and he was in Canada in March this year. He has already killed eight British citizens that we know of, former pupils at a school where his brother taught. He has faked suicides and left conflicting evidence at several crime scenes."

For a while, Dan thought Farrow was going to hang up. He held his finger against his lips when Rick Price looked as though he might break the silence.

The speaker on Dan's phone rustled and crackled. A muffled voice could be heard, but the words were undecipherable. There was more muffled discussion with a second voice, and then the rustling and crackling ceased before a new voice came out of the speaker.

"This is Major Michael Bradshaw. State your name, rank and location."

Rick didn't smile but he raised the thumb of his right

hand and nodded with satisfaction.

"Good afternoon, Major. My name is Dan Blacksmith, Detective Sergeant with Humberside CID. I'm calling from Campbell Road police station in Kingston upon Hull."

"Who is the senior officer there?"

"The senior officer on this case is in hospital. Oliver Sorrell attacked her in a car park and mutilated her body with a penknife."

"Have you seen Sorrell?"

Rick stared at Dan. He had expected shocked outrage from Major Bradshaw, or blustering denial at the very least.

"Last Friday night, I saw a man who was probably Oliver Sorrell."

"Did he make himself known to you?"

"No, he did not."

"Where did you see him?"

"In a pub called the *Golden Hart*." Dan paused, made a decision. "He was with a man called Peter Jones, a former petty officer in the Royal Navy. He was serving on HMS Sheffield when it was attacked by the Argentine air force."

"Why did you phone this number?"

"I want to know who Sorrell is, and I want to know where he is."

"I can't discuss it any further on the phone."

Dan looked down at the five names on the piece of paper. If the final three former-pupils were still alive, he knew he had to do everything he could to stop Oliver Sorrell.

"Where *can* you discuss it, Major?"

The phone rustled and Dan could picture Major Bradshaw covering the mouthpiece with his hand. He heard something spoken, a short command, then the sound of a door closing as Bradshaw took his hand away from the phone.

"We are not having this conversation, Detective Blacksmith."

"Understood."

"Do you have a map of England there, one that shows roads and motorways?"

Dan looked at the wall behind Rick's desk. "Yes."

"Are you looking at it now?"

Dan jabbed his finger in the direction of the map. Rick jumped out of his chair and tore the map away from the drawing pins that were securing it to the wall. He spread the large sheet of paper across the top of his desk.

"Yes, I'm looking at it now," Dan said.

"Find the M1."

Dan traced a line west and south from Hull, all the way to Rotherham. "Got it."

"Follow the M1 south as far as Nottingham."

"Okay."

"Directly west of Nottingham, near the M1, can you see a village called Trowell?"

"Got it," Dan said.

"There's a motorway service station about a mile north of there. It's roughly halfway between Hereford and Hull."

Dan drew a small biro circle around the word Trowell on the map. "When?" he said.

"I'll be there tomorrow at eleven hundred. I will leave at thirteen hundred."

"Where are we going to meet?"

"I'm not meeting anyone, Detective. A friend recommended the place for lunch, and tomorrow is a convenient day for me to go there."

"I understand."

"Goodbye, Detective."

The line went dead.

Rick looked at the map. "That service station is about ninety miles from here."

Dan sat back in his chair. "The CO of that SAS base just agreed to meet me to discuss Oliver Sorrell."

"Yeah. Didn't take much convincing, did he?"

Dan looked at the circle he had drawn on the map. "No, and that's not entirely encouraging."

"Weather looks like it might be even worse tomorrow."

"That's okay. I know someone who's going to lend me his Sierra four-by-four."

Rick looked disappointed. "Aren't we both going?"

"Sorry, but I want you to stay in Hull. There are a few things that we need to do, which won't get done if we're both ninety miles away. Plus, I don't know for sure if Bradshaw is going to show, or if he will still talk to me if I'm not alone."

"Okay. I hope you know what you're doing."

CHAPTER 30

Technically, by a margin of six minutes, it was still Thursday morning when Dan parked Rick Price's Sierra XR4x4 in three inches of soft, even snow in the car park of the Trowell motorway service station. He and Rick had estimated the ninety-two-mile journey would have taken an hour and a half in decent weather, so he had allowed three hours and it had taken just under four.

The M1 hadn't been the problem. Two of its three lanes had been virtually clear of lying snow, and Dan had been able to keep the Sierra's speed between forty and sixty miles per hour in the light to moderate traffic. That was where he had clawed back much of the time he had lost earlier in stationary, backed-up traffic waiting for an accident to be cleared. Without a police radio onboard, Dan had no warning that the accident had occurred, and also no means of finding out exactly what had happened. By the time he passed the site of the accident, three of the vehicles that had been involved were lined up along the hard shoulder. One abandoned car had been straddling the central reservation, partially impaled on the metal crash barrier.

In the car park, Dan turned off the Sierra's engine and

looked out of the windscreen at the large service station building. Light snow was still falling but it was already starting to lose its battle against the midday sun. The sky was bluer, and far brighter, than it had been when Dan had driven away from the Campbell Road station. It had only been four hours ago, but it felt considerably longer. As Dan climbed out of the car and closed the door, he hoped his trip wasn't going to be a complete waste of those four hours.

Beneath his feet the snow was soft and wet, not frozen. It lacked the wintry crispness he had expected, and he cautiously looked forward to a swifter and less eventful return journey.

As Dan crossed the car park, he saw that although there weren't rows and rows of parked cars, the place was not entirely deserted. He looked at the cars he walked past, wondering what type of car a major in the SAS would be driving. He didn't spot one that stood out as a military vehicle, but then he hadn't driven all the way from Hull in a police car.

Inside the main entrance of the service station, Dan stamped the slush off his boots on the soaking floor and looked around until he spotted a sign that pointed to the restaurant. It took him a few seconds to make the connection between the quaintly named *Sheriff's Restaurant* and the service station's close proximity to Nottingham.

He followed a small family group along a brightly-lit corridor, listening to the two children as they pointed and giggled at the life-size, wall-mounted models of two garishly decorated jousting knights.

The staff in the restaurant were dressed in cheap but commendably cheerful Robin Hood outfits. One of them bowed theatrically as the family group walked in ahead of Dan.

"Please find a table, we have plenty of room. The queue for hot meals starts right over there."

Dan walked past the merry man and his forced, professional smile of greeting. On any other day, he might have sympathised with the guy for having such a tough job. He went to the closest empty table and stood behind one of the chairs, taking his time unbuttoning his coat as he casually scanned the restaurant.

He didn't pick out the SAS major the first time he saw him, despite the fact that the man was alone at a table for two. He was wearing a dark blue sweater and jeans, with a black overcoat hanging on the back of his chair. There were other tables with single occupants, who Dan guessed were most likely to be lorry drivers or travelling salesmen. As he was assessing each lone customer for their probability of being a senior ranking officer in the SAS, the man in the blue sweater briefly caught his eye and nodded almost imperceptibly.

Dan walked towards the table for two, studying the man's face. He didn't expect the face to trigger a visual memory of the man who had walked Peter Jones out of the door of the *Golden Hart* on Friday night, but he was also not about to calmly sit down at a table with someone who could potentially be Oliver Sorrell.

The man in the blue sweater looked up, but didn't stand up. There was a cleared dinner plate and a half-empty mug of coffee on the table in front of him. On the floor next to his chair was a small blue rucksack.

"Take a seat, Detective Blacksmith."

"Tell me your name first."

"Bradshaw."

Dan pulled the second chair out and hung his coat on it before sitting down.

Major Bradshaw placed both hands flat on the table, palms down. "No recording devices, no note-taking. I'm on a day's leave, and I'm having lunch. I'm not meeting you here, and we are not having this conversation."

Dan looked at the SAS major's face. If he had to guess,

he would put the man's age at around forty-five. His face was lightly tanned, recently in Dan's opinion, with clearly defined cheekbones and a half-inch line of old white scar tissue on one side of his chin. There was an air of calmness about him, but not of relaxation, as if he were entirely comfortable being where he was, with no intention to take any particular course of action but with the knowledge that he was eminently capable of doing so if the need arose.

Dan left his notepad and pen in his pocket.

"What can you tell me about Oliver Sorrell?"

"Nothing at all." Bradshaw looked away from Dan, his gaze drifting over the customers at nearby tables. None were close enough to overhear what he said. "But I can talk to myself as I sit here, considering whether to follow my lunch with dessert."

"Are you his commanding officer?"

"I was."

"Is he still serving in the SAS?"

"He wasn't discharged, honourably or otherwise."

"Do you know where he is?"

"From what you told me yesterday, I think you already know that."

Dan thought about the replies he had received so far. "Sorrell has gone AWOL."

"I prefer the term absence at self-discretion."

"When did he go?"

"It was more a case of when did he not return."

Dan thought of the names on the list, the earliest death that had occurred.

"1983."

"Close enough."

"Did Sorrell serve in the Falklands war?"

"He was there."

"In what capacity?"

"What do you know about the Special Air Service?"

"Not much. The Iranian embassy siege, but only

because it was on TV."

"Small teams. Usually just four men, occasionally two. A team of four can be more effective than an army of ten thousand in certain circumstances. What we found with Oliver Sorrell, was that a soldier with very particular skills could function optimally when working alone."

"Is Sorrell a trained killer?"

Bradshaw smiled, as if he had just tossed a bloody steak to a Rottweiler, and the dog had made a clean mid-air catch. "In our line of work, that would hardly be a unique qualification."

"I believe he has killed eight people who were former pupils at the secondary school where his brother, Jacob, taught."

"Is that the link, that they were taught by his brother?"

"They tormented his brother, particularly in a career choices class. Jacob resigned, and within a month had taken his own life."

Bradshaw nodded. "I've heard that story."

"From Oliver Sorrell?"

"He took two days' leave to attend the funeral and deal with the paperwork."

"Did he ever mention how his brother's suicide made him feel? Did he say anything about taking revenge?"

"No."

Dan tried to piece together the snippets he was getting from Bradshaw. While not entirely inscrutable, the major was not exactly a gushing torrent of helpful information.

"Was Sorrell some kind of war hero?"

Bradshaw's expression remained neutral. It was a civilian question, drawn from civilian preconceptions.

"We don't have heroes, Detective. We have men who finish the job."

"Can you tell me anything about the jobs Sorrell finished?"

"No places, no dates, no names."

Dan paused, thinking about all the possible topics that Bradshaw had not just excluded.

"What specialisations did he have?"

"A great deal. He spent two years in Mountain Troop, exhibiting an above-average ability to survive and fight in extreme weather conditions."

"In the cold?"

"Mostly, yes."

"Without mentioning places, names or dates, can you tell me the type of missions he would have been sent on?"

"At first, mostly the type you might expect. Our squads are rotated through roles. Sorrell's team excelled at contingency work, the type of emergency deployment similar to the hostage rescue that you mentioned, but he was also involved with foreign soil counter-terrorism."

Dan realised he was grinding his teeth, his frustration building as he resisted the instinctive urge to take out his notepad and pen.

"You said that was what he did *at first*. What else did he do?"

"A great deal that I can't talk about. If I said Revolutionary Warfare Wing, or The Increment, would either of those mean anything to you?"

"No."

"What about SIS, the Secret Intelligence Service?"

"No, but I can make a fairly good guess."

"A very small number of hand-picked, elite members of the SAS carry out special operations directed by the Secret Intelligence Service."

"And Sorrell was one of them?"

"All I know, and I was his CO at the time, is that I signed several documents that I was not even allowed to read. However, his absences always seemed to coincide with sudden bulletins of good news from regions that were, shall we say, undergoing political shifts."

"Did you ever hear about anything that he had done?"

"One word kept being used to describe both the means and the outcome, without focussing on specifics. That word was chaos."

"Chaos." Dan thought of the three recent deaths in Hull, of the crime scenes with their conflicting evidence, a faked suicide, messages written in blood and winter grime, a pair of black gloves, and a left-handed woman who had apparently written half a car registration on the kerb after she had died. "That's a good word for it," he said.

"It covers a multitude of possibilities. I can't confirm or deny any of them, of course."

"Assassination?"

"Possible."

"Kidnapping?"

"Possible."

"Is there anything else that might be possible, that you obviously can't confirm or deny?"

"Initiating unrest. Causing and assisting uprisings and coups. Sabotage. All possible." Bradshaw smiled again, the smile of the attack-dog handler. "They had a name for him that I always thought was very apt, and I suspect he appreciated it himself. I forget which specific region gave him this name, of course, but in Arabic it's pronounced *abadaan hnak*."

"What does it mean?"

"The literal translation is quite simple. *Never there*."

Dan rocked back in his chair, shaking his head. "No," he said. "That can't be right."

Bradshaw was staring at Dan's face, watching his expression change. "You've heard it before."

"The last man who was killed, Tom Mason. He was in a band called *Never There*. He told me a story about someone he met in a café, an older man who played video games. That man gave him the name of his band, and there was something else that he said, something about mastering chaos."

"Did he say when he met this man?"

Dan hissed out a sigh of frustration. He hadn't made any notes the last time he had talked to Tom Mason. "Yes, but I can't remember the year he said, and I didn't write it down. It definitely wasn't recent."

"He has been in their lives for a long time, possibly many years. They might even have seen him, but they wouldn't know, wouldn't realise who or what he was."

"We figured out that he must have been watching us, always keeping one step ahead. But he made mistakes. He tried to confuse us with phony evidence and other misdirection, but by doing it he accidentally left useful clues."

Bradshaw was smiling again, nodding as if he were waiting for the punch-line to a joke he had heard a dozen times before. "Whatever you found, or think you found, it wasn't because he made a mistake. I can guarantee that."

"I'm here, talking to you. I know his name. Are you telling me he wanted the police to get this far, to identify him and be this close to catching him?"

"Chaos, Detective. It's what he does, it's how he operates. Don't presume that knowing his name means you will be able to catch him."

Dan shook his head again. "He killed eight civilians who were innocent as far as we know, apart from playing a few cruel pranks in school. Where is he going to stop? Will he kill the next person who short-changes him in a corner shop, or looks twice at him in the street? I have to catch him. I have to stop him."

"He won't let you."

"Are you saying he will kill police officers to avoid being arrested?"

Bradshaw looked around the restaurant again. Nobody was looking their way. "Keep it down."

Dan leaned towards the table and lowered his voice. "Is he likely to be armed?"

"You mean with a firearm?"

Dan nodded. "Is he?"

"It's possible, but he would still be unstoppable without one."

"Are you really that proud of what you have created?"

"We didn't create Oliver Sorrell. That's not how it works." Bradshaw very deliberately turned back his sweater sleeve and looked at his watch. "Several of the SIS missions he was sent on were rated Foxtrot-Zero. It means zero friendly, nobody in the mission zone to call on for assistance, or to trust, or to run to when it all went wrong. He completed the missions and he came home, every time."

"Zero friendly," Dan said. "He still thinks that's how it is. He is acting as though he's on one of those missions."

"I've told you everything I can."

Dan looked at the time on his own watch. "Could you stop him?"

Bradshaw considered the question. He wasn't smiling. "One-on-one, with a weapons advantage and the element of surprise… I might get lucky."

"He's that good?"

"Being good has nothing to do with it."

Dan looked over his shoulder towards the only way in or out of the restaurant. "You have to give me more than this. I need to find him."

"You need to understand something. He wins because he is unpredictable. He doesn't have a routine, or a preferred method of operating. He could be living in a barn, or an empty house, or the best room in the most expensive hotel. Chaos, Sergeant. He mastered it years ago."

"He is never going back to Hereford, is he? You don't expect to ever see him again."

"I can't confirm or deny that."

"Shit. I'm on my own and you don't think I have a chance."

"Accurate sitrep."

Bradshaw reached down to the side of his chair and hoisted his rucksack onto his lap. He unzipped one of the side pockets and pulled out a small rectangle of stiff card, a passport size black and white photograph. He placed the photograph face down and slid it across to the middle of the table.

"I didn't give you that."

Dan looked at the plain white back of the photograph.

"Is it him? How recent?"

"Less than three years ago." Bradshaw was smiling again. "He has the most unremarkable face, and he can look like a completely different person just by subtly altering his expression. Call it part of the genetic advantage, if you like. As I said, *we* don't create these men."

Dan took a breath and held it. He reached out, picked up the photo and turned it in his hand.

Oliver Sorrell was looking back at him. Not really a smile, not really any discernible expression at all.

A flashbulb memory of strangulation in the bar of the *Golden Hart*, and one man leading another away towards the bar.

Another memory, static and dark, yet horrifyingly familiar.

A portrait on an easel, the hint of a smile.

Enigmatic.

Unremarkable.

CHAPTER 31

The phone kept ringing. Nobody was picking up.

Dan had counted fifteen rings while he stared along the corridor past the wall-mounted mural of merry men and archers, all the way to a tall window and the world of grey beyond it. He was holding a coin over the payphone's slot, waiting to thumb it in when the call was answered, knowing that it wasn't going to happen. There was nowhere in the house where a person capable of walking, or even crawling, would not be able to get to the phone within fifteen rings.

"I've got to warn my wife," he had told Bradshaw, just before he had straightened, stood up too quickly, and toppled his chair over backwards onto the tiled floor. That was when people had started to turn and stare.

The SAS major had said nothing, watching Dan as he righted the fallen chair. He hadn't needed to ask. It was all too clear what was happening.

Dan counted another five rings.

Even if Becky hadn't heard the first few rings, she would have answered by then.

Dan pressed the handset into the cradle, swallowing hard, thinking of the distance between his current location and his home, the four-hour drive to get to where he was, and the portrait of an elite, unstoppable killer on an easel in his wife's studio.

He picked up the handset and dialled a different number.

Two rings before it was answered.

"Humberside CID, DC Price speaking."

"It's Dan. Sorrell has been in my house several times. I just phoned, no answer. Take a car, any car, and go there now." Dan took a breath that sounded like a gasp. "Rick, he's extremely dangerous."

"Okay, I'm on my way. But how do you know he's been to your house?"

"Bradshaw gave me a photo of Sorrell. The portrait Becky is working on, it's him."

"Are you sure? Why would he—"

"Rick, Bradshaw has been telling me all about him. This is how he operates. Chaos, misdirection, infiltration. It's probably one of the ways he's been keeping ahead of us, but it could be more than that. You have to go to my house now. I'm useless here."

"Dan, it'll be okay. I'm going to go there right now. The snow stopped hours ago, so the roads shouldn't be too bad."

"Thank you, Rick, but be careful. Don't confront Sorrell unless there's no other option."

"Are you coming back now?"

"Yeah, but it took me four hours to get here."

"Shit. Okay, I'm going. Call the station later and they can patch you through to whichever car I take."

After he had hung up, Dan took another coin out of his pocket before dialling his home phone again. He gave up on the fifteenth ring. Mandy's primary school was closed because of the weather. It was possible Becky had taken her for a walk in the snow. Lots of things were possible.

Dan went back to the restaurant. He had been working

on a mental list of questions for Major Bradshaw while he listened to the ringing phone, in between wishing he had stayed in Hull that morning, or never pulled the trigger that ultimately sent him to Hull. Maybe he should have never filled in the application form to join Cheshire Constabulary, taken a dull but safe career in wholesale frozen food marketing. Lots of things he could have done differently.

Dan walked into the restaurant, looked across to the table where Bradshaw had been sitting, and saw that the table was unoccupied. He went over to the table to check, but Bradshaw had definitely gone. No coat on the back of the chair, no rucksack on the floor. The plate, mug and cutlery were also gone.

Two unanswered phone calls and a short conversation with Rick. More than enough time for a special forces major to stroll out of a restaurant. Dan went back to the service station's main entrance, looked in the small newsagent's shop and also checked the toilet, but he didn't see Bradshaw. 12:40 by the clock on the wall in the service station foyer. The major had left twenty minutes earlier than he said he would.

In the newsagent's, Dan found an OS map of England. He followed his return journey with his finger, decided that he would leave the M18 at Doncaster to call Rick on a payphone. Doncaster was roughly halfway to Hull from the Trowell service station. Forty-five minutes in good weather, but it was likely to be double that in the current conditions. Dan tried not to think about how long it might take him if there was another accident on the motorway. He bought the map, just in case, buttoned up his coat and walked out of the service station into the car park. No snow was falling from the flat grey sky, the breeze was light and the temperature had flatlined two degrees above freezing. It was quarter to one when Dan closed the Sierra's door and started the engine.

***

He reached the junction nearest to Doncaster an hour later. No more snow had fallen, and the temperature had managed to stay above freezing, which helped contribute to an uneventful journey. Five minutes after leaving the motorway, Dan reached the scattered outskirts of an urban district. He passed a sign pointing towards Doncaster Rovers' ground, Belle Vue Stadium, a mile and a half away, and it reminded him of the conversation he had been having with Rick, when they still had Peter Jones down as their most likely suspect.

Ahead, on the left, Dan saw a public phone box. It was red, but hardly any of that colour was showing. There was a solid four-inch white cap of snow on top of it, and the horizontal edges of every window frame were rimed with frost.

With the weather keeping most sane people off the roads, there was plenty of space to park nearby. The phone box door must have frozen to the frame during the night, and it withstood several of Dan's increasingly frantic attempts before finally opening with a creak of protest and a spray of loose snow and shards of ice.

The first number Dan dialled was his home phone. He tried not to count the rings, but it was impossible. He reached four, and was already anticipating the fifth with a dreadful sense of hopelessness, when the phone was answered.

He jammed the coin hard into the slot.

A man's voice said, "Who is that?"

For a moment, barely a second before he realised that he recognised the voice, Dan felt his hand tightening around the handset as he fought to hold his fear and rising anger in check.

"Rick?"

"Yeah, it's me. Where are—"

"Are they there? Is Becky okay? Is Mandy there?"

"They're fine, Dan. Here…"

Vague sounds of the phone being passed from one person to another.

"Dan?"

"Becky, is everything okay? Are the doors locked?"

"We're fine, Dan. Rick won't tell me what's going on."

"Is Mandy there?"

"She's playing in the lounge. Dan, what's happening, and where are you?"

"Doncaster. I'm on my way back from a service station on the M1, but that isn't important. Becky, the man in the painting, the portrait you're working on, you can't let him in the house if he comes round."

"I don't understand. Is he dangerous? When did you find this out?"

"About an hour ago. I met someone who gave me a photograph of the suspect in the recent murders, the ones that have been on the local news. The man in the photo looks like the man in the portrait."

"That's crazy."

"I know, but you have to lock the doors and you cannot let him in the house."

"He won't be coming back here, Dan."

"Why not?"

"He was here this morning, he turned up while I was outside building a snowman for Mandy."

Dan stared through the fogged glass of the phone box windows at the Sierra. He took a breath. "What did he do?"

"Well, he asked for the portrait and he took it away."

"I didn't think it was finished."

"That's what I told him, but he said he was happy with it as it was. He had already paid in full, in advance, so the picture was his."

"Did he go in the house?"

"Of course he did. I couldn't leave him outside in the

cold while I packed the portrait for him."

"What did he do in the house?"

"Nothing, just stood in the studio waiting for the portrait."

"Was he out of your sight at any time while he was in the house?"

"No."

Dan took the photo of Oliver Sorrell out of his pocket and looked at it. Sorrell's enigmatic, unremarkable face looked back at him.

"Beck, did you see his car?"

"It was parked on the road."

"What kind of car was it?"

"I didn't go out onto the road, I only saw the top of the car. It was dark blue."

"Was there any snow on it?"

"No, I don't think there was."

"I'm going to come straight home. Stay inside and keep all the doors locked until I get there."

"Dan, are you sure about this? I've been alone in the house with this man, Mark Sykes, half a dozen times. I've never felt threatened or uncomfortable while he has been here. He has never said or done anything inappropriate or strange. Could you possibly have got it wrong?"

Dan turned the photo around in his hand. Passport size. Not extremely detailed. His memory of the portrait was not perfect, but when he had first seen the photo he had reacted the way that he had because he had recognised the face. *He had known.*

Chaos.

Misdirection.

"Possibly," Dan said. "But keep the doors locked anyway, just in case."

"Do you want to say hello to Mandy?"

Dan looked at his watch. "I should be home by half three. I really need to get back on the road."

"Okay, honey. See you soon."

"Bye, Becky."

"I love you." No hint of embarrassment in her voice, and Dan knew that Rick must have been waiting close enough to hear what she had said.

"Love you too. Always."

"Shall I put Rick back on?"

"Thanks."

Dan heard the phone change hands again.

"I only got some of that," Rick said. "What do you want me to do?"

"Could you stay there until I get back? I'll take whatever flak Harry throws at us."

"No problem. It'll be fine. I'll radio in, let Harry know what's going on."

"We don't really know what's going on."

"We're following leads, making progress."

"I think we already wore that one out. Oh, Rick, Becky said the car he was in was dark blue, with no snow on it. It could have been in a garage or under some other kind of cover last night and earlier today."

"Does that help us?"

"Maybe. Just keep an eye out for any dark blue cars driving past or parking nearby. I won't call again. I'll come straight back, should be there by half three if the weather stays like this."

"Okay. I'll see you when you get here."

***

The snow started to fall again when Dan was still more than half an hour from his destination, travelling along a single carriageway A-road through the bleak, white countryside, eight miles west of Hull.

The Sierra's radio was tuned to BBC Humberside, giving frequent weather bulletins with their ominous promises of sub-zero temperatures, freezing rain, more snow, and severe disruption to public transport, schools, and life in general.

Dan drove past the scenes of two serious road accidents, but they were both several hours old, the abandoned carcasses of damaged vehicles lying still and silent at the roadside as fresh snow began to cover them.

Although he was going to pass within a mile of the Campbell Road station, Dan had no intention of calling in on his way to his house. During the journey from Doncaster he had tried to convince himself that he had been wrong about the similarity between Oliver Sorrell's ID photo and the portrait his wife had painted, but he hadn't been successful.

The gritted A road that led from Hull to Bilstead became a narrower, non-gritted B road at a roundabout just under three miles from Dan's house. Patches of the road's surface were covered with dark slush where mud and melted snow had been churned together beneath tractor tyres, but most of the time the road was white, scrawled with multi-layered, criss-crossing tyre tracks.

The Sierra was holding the road well, but Dan fought the temptation to accelerate above forty along the straight, empty stretches because there was always the risk of hitting a sheet of ice hidden beneath the snow, where even a surefooted four-wheel drive would be likely to go into an unrecoverable skid and end up in a ditch or wrapped around a tree.

With the combination of the minor Doncaster detour, the worsening weather, and Dan's reluctance to fully stress-test the road-holding abilities of Rick's car, it was close to four o'clock when he made the final turn onto the road where he lived.

When Dan saw the old brown Triumph Dolomite parked at the side of the road in front of his house, an ugly dark shape in the gathering dusk, he finally allowed himself a long, heartfelt sigh of relief. He recognised the car as soon as he saw it, before he had pulled up behind it and was close enough to read the registration plate through its light covering of fresh snow. The Dolomite was the shunned runt of Campbell Road's small fleet of unmarked cars, the one that nobody chose if they actually had a choice. Harry West called it the Pile-o-shite.

Dan smiled at the car as he walked past it towards the front door of his house. He saw the snowman that Becky had made for their daughter on the small front lawn. It was a perfect example of his artistically talented wife's work, a chubby snow sculpture approximately Mandy's height. Dan imagined Mandy dancing around it in the falling snow, giggling and skipping as Becky stood back to watch. He could see that some of the ground-floor lights were on, in the hall and the lounge, but he didn't see anyone moving around inside. Rick and Becky were probably in the kitchen, drinking coffee, bored out of their minds waiting for him to get back. He hoped Rick wasn't going to catch any grief from Harry for spending the afternoon hanging around at his house.

Remembering he had told both of them to keep the doors locked until he got home, Dan stood on the doorstep and rapped three times on the door knocker.

He started counting, because that was what he always did.

At five seconds he wondered what was keeping them.

At eight, he knocked again and unconsciously reset his count.

When five more seconds had passed he took his own keys out of his coat pocket and slid the front door key into the lock. It didn't turn all the way, because the door was already unlocked.

Dan wrenched the handle down and shouldered the door open.

He was already screaming his wife's name before the

wildly swinging door had slammed against the wall.

CHAPTER 32

Nobody in the hall, just lights turned on and open doors. And a small, soft object on the floor by the doorway into the lounge, where the television was playing a *Godzilla* cartoon to the empty room.

Dan called Becky's name again before he leaned down and picked up the Roland Rat toy. It was undamaged, but it shouldn't have been lying abandoned on the floor. Mandy wouldn't drop Roland and leave him like that. She loved the toy with a small child's relentlessly loyal devotion to an inanimate cuddly object, and she always made sure he was comfortable on her bed or on the sofa in the lounge if she had to be parted from him for even a minute.

Unless she wasn't given the chance to do that, Dan thought.

He held the toy in both hands and yelled Becky's name. His voice was shrill with desperation, the word tearing from his throat to fill the bright, empty hall.

Dan went into the lounge and turned off the TV. He listened to the quiet house, heard no sounds of stealthy movement or whispered threats.

"Rick!"

His voice was starting to sound hoarse and helpless. The

rasping soreness made him think of big, calloused hands around his throat, a memory of the unnatural buzzing in his head when Peter Jones had choked him.

Dan looked at the furniture in the lounge. Undisturbed, nothing out of place. He forced himself to examine the lounge carpet for fresh scuff marks or bloodstains, found none, then repeated the process in the hallway. He was carrying Mandy's soft toy, barely aware that it was still clutched in his hand.

The lights in the kitchen and Becky's studio were both turned off. Dan checked the kitchen first, taking a breath and holding it as he pressed the wall switch. He didn't want to find anyone lying cold and silent on the tiled kitchen floor, sightless eyes staring up at him…

The light came on.

The kitchen was empty. No bodies, no blood. No signs of a struggle. Nothing. The kitchen knives were all in place in their wooden block. All the cupboard doors and drawers were closed.

He went to the half-open studio door and pushed it wide open while he stood in the hall, trembling with anxious tension. He could see the dark silhouette of the A-frame easel in the middle of the room. The portrait had gone, taken and paid for by the man who called himself Mark Sykes. Dan had convinced himself that the portrait subject was Oliver Sorrell, the Sykes name just an alias, another piece of misdirection. But now, standing alone in his quiet, empty house, Dan wanted more than anything to be wrong.

He took a step inside the room before reaching to one side to find the light switch. Again, he took a breath and held it.

The light came on.

Dan was still breathing out, clinging to the brief sense of relief at finding another empty room, when he saw the triangle of roughly torn paper that had been pinned with a thumb tack to the top of the easel, right where it wouldn't be missed by someone who came into the room and turned on the main light.

He could see the words that were written on it from where he was standing. There were two words, written in clear, consistent capital letters. He recognised the writing because he had seen it before. The words were new, but they were part of a sequence, part of a classroom taunt from the past.

RED HOT

The toy rat fell from his hand and lay face-down on the studio floor.

"No," Dan said, shaking his head as the tears came.

Two words on the torn triangle of white paper. Written in biro, not blood, but there was no comfort in that detail, no reassurance at all.

His house was empty, his wife and daughter gone. No sign of them, or of Rick Price.

Sykes was Sorrell, and Sorrell was an unstoppable killer.

Dan checked the rooms upstairs in a state of detached bewilderment. He stood in Mandy's bedroom, shaking with guilt and fear, and a complete lack of comprehension. Neither he nor Becky had gone to school in Hull, yet Sorrell had found a way into their lives by creating the fake Sykes persona, a man who wanted his portrait painted by Rebecca Blacksmith.

It made no sense to Dan because it appeared to serve no logical purpose, and that very lack of logic filled him with an appalling uncertainty.

He went back downstairs, out into the constant cold, closing and locking the front door behind him. When he saw the snowman again his chest heaved and he clutched at his throat, blinking the tears from his eyes.

He tried the Dolomite's doors but they were locked. The Sierra had a hand-crank scissor jack in the boot recess with the spare wheel. Dan carried the crank handle back to the Dolomite, held it in both hands and jabbed one end of it against the quarterlight window on the driver's side, smashing the glass. He used the metal crank to clear the remaining pieces of glass from the edges of the window, reached inside and unlocked the door.

The police radio in the Dolomite worked without needing the engine to be running. Dan turned the radio on and picked up the mic.

"This is One-Six Charlie Delta. Control, patch me to Harry West."

"One-Six Charlie Delta, patching to DCI West. Please wait, over."

Dan stared through the glaze of snow on the car's windscreen. The road ahead was dark and empty. The words on the note had said RED HOT. Was it a taunt or a threat, or was Sorrell signing off, preparing to disappear forever?

"Dan, it's Harry. Where the bloody hell—"

"Shut up, Harry. Oliver Sorrell has taken my wife and daughter."

"Now wait a… What? Say that again."

Dan heard his own voice as he spoke. He sounded too calm, as if he were reporting a failed break-in at a post office. "Sorrell came to my house. He left one of his notes for me to find. My wife and daughter have gone. There's no sign of Rick Price either."

"Rick took that heap of junk Triumph. He's probably stuck in a snow drift."

"No, the car is here. I'm sitting in it."

"He must be around there somewhere, Dan. They all must be outside together."

Dan let his breath out slowly. "You're not listening. Sorrell was here. He left a note. He has taken my wife and daughter."

"How do you know who left the note, Dan? Maybe your wife left it. More to the point, where have you been all day?"

For several seconds, Dan kept his thumb off the transmit button, holding his exasperation in check before he leaned closer to the microphone. "I met the commanding officer from the SAS base in Hereford. He told me Sorrell is currently AWOL, and that he is a specialist in chaos and misdirection."

"Dan, I explicitly ordered you not to contact the army again. If you—"

"Listen to me, Harry. Sorrell must have had the same list of John Blair pupils that we've got. His brother probably left all the details in his diary. There are only two names unaccounted for, and I'm betting they're already dead. The SAS major I spoke to told me that Sorrell worked alone on top secret infiltration missions, that he is a specialist at operating and fighting in extreme weather conditions, and that he has effectively been AWOL for two years."

"Dan…" Harry paused. "I want you to come back to the station. I don't know what's been happening and I need you to file a full report."

"Did you hear what I said about my wife and daughter?"

"I did, and we need to discuss that too. Also DC Price's absence."

"They're in danger, Harry. Right now. I can't waste time writing reports, I need to find them."

"Do you have any idea where they are?"

Dan blew out a sigh of desperate frustration. "No, I don't."

"Then come back to the station. We'll go over all the evidence together."

Outside the Dolomite, snow was still falling from the darkening sky. There would be no tyre tracks to follow, no clues to find. Ironically, the only glimmer of hope was the note that had been left pinned to the easel. It suggested that Sorrell had still not finished, and it also suggested that he wanted Dan to know that.

Dan slammed the Dolomite's door and trudged back through the snow to Rick Price's Sierra. He started the engine, turned on the headlights and executed an angry three-point turn on the slippery road. As he headed back towards the city he took one last look at his empty home, dwindling to nothing in the rear-view mirror.

***

Dan walked into Harry West's office and placed the requisition form on the desk in front of him. Harry looked down at the form, shook his head and pushed the form away.

"I am not signing that. Not today, not ever."

"I haven't got a chance without it."

Harry spread his hands wide apart. "Listen to yourself. You've lost it, Dan. Seriously. If we weren't so shorthanded, I'd take you off the case completely."

Dan leaned forward, his hands gripping the edge of the desk. "Sorrell is most likely armed. Bradshaw told me he would be unstoppable even if he doesn't have a firearm. I need it, Harry."

Harry took a breath, lowering his voice. "We don't know where he is. We don't even know if he's doing all this on his own. If I send you out there with a gun, it's going to turn into a complete disaster."

"It already is. He's taken my wife and daughter. That note he left, he wanted me to see it, wanted me to know what he's done."

"Where's Rick Price?"

"I don't know."

Harry sat back in his chair. "I'll get control to try him on the radio every fifteen minutes. He'll show up, Dan, and he will probably have your wife and daughter with him."

Dan held his reply in check, realising that its futility would be matched only by its potential to turn Harry West completely against him. He straightened up, taking his hands away from the edge of the desk. As if it were an afterthought, he picked up the requisition form.

"I'll check in with DI Knowles, exchange current information and go over what we have on Peter Jones."

"Good," Harry said. "Jones is still the most likely suspect. I honestly think this Sorrell story is a red herring."

Dan nodded. "Yeah. I'll give you a progress report in an hour."

"Thank you."

Dan left Harry's office and went to sit at his own desk. He picked up the phone, found a number that he had written in his notepad, and dialled it.

"Hull General. How can I help?"

Dan held the phone close to his mouth, keeping his voice low. "Can you find out whether a patient called Kath Schrader is still there, please. She was admitted on Tuesday."

"One moment, please."

While Dan waited, he read the fine print beneath the box where the authorising officer would write their name in block capitals next to their signature and thumb print. The required rank of the authoriser was Detective Inspector or higher, and the authoriser always had to be at least one rank higher than the officer named on the form as the requester.

"Mrs Schrader is still with us," said the voice on the phone. "She was moved into Amy Johnson ward this morning."

"Thanks," Dan said.

"Would you like me to try the ward for you?"

"No, thanks. What time are visiting hours?"

"Four until half five on the wards."

"Thank you."

Dan looked at his watch. It was a few minutes before five. He hung up the phone, folded the requisition form in half and slipped it into his coat pocket next to the Sierra's keys.

***

There were eight beds in the ward, four along each of the two long walls. The nurse at the entrance to the ward had told Dan that there were no empty beds in any of the wards because of the high number of recent slip and fall injuries due to the weather.

Kath Schrader's bed was the third on the left. The privacy curtain was drawn back and she had the head of her bed raised about thirty degrees from horizontal. When she saw Dan Blacksmith walking through the ward towards her bed, Schrader clumsily closed the paperback she was reading and dropped the book face down on the small bedside cabinet.

Dan stood at the side of the bed and looked at her. The bruising on her face had spread and darkened but her right eye was no longer completely closed. Her nose was still bandaged, as were her hands. Dan found himself wondering how difficult it must be for her to turn the pages of a book.

"How are you feeling?"

Schrader glanced around the ward. "I'd rather be at home."

"Have they told you when you can leave?"

"Take a seat, Dan. No, they haven't. Doctor Michaelides doesn't want me to go home to an empty house while my hands are…" She sighed, shaking her head. "Like this."

Dan sat on the cheap plastic chair beside the bed. "Haven't they been able to contact your husband?"

"No, not yet. He's somewhere in the Black Forest but the magazine isn't expecting him to call in until the weekend." Schrader looked at Dan's eyes. "This isn't a social visit, is it?"

"Officially, I'm not here at all."

"Tell me."

Dan pulled the chair closer to the bed so that he could keep his voice as low as possible. "The man who attacked you is a special forces soldier from the SAS base in Hereford. His name is Oliver Sorrell. He has killed at least eight of eleven former pupils from John Blair, kids who tormented his brother while he was a teacher there. His brother committed suicide shortly after resigning from the school."

Schrader lay very still, saying nothing while she thought about what Dan had just told her. When she spoke, her voice was lowered, like his, her eyes narrowed and wary.

"You're absolutely sure of this? He's killing complete strangers because of something that happened in school… how long ago was it?"

"Eight years ago."

"Eight years. That's a long time, Dan, a long time to wait for this kind of revenge."

"I know. Harry thinks it's still more likely to be Peter Jones, but I talked to Oliver Sorrell's former commanding officer, an SAS major called Bradshaw; he told me about Sorrell's specialisation in misdirection, and it ties with the type of faked evidence we found at the crime scenes. I also talked to the former head of John Blair, and he told me about the things the pupils did to Sorrell's brother. There are clear links between what happened eight years ago and elements of the murders and your assault." Dan showed Schrader the photograph of Oliver Sorrell. "This is the man who attacked you, Kath." He let her take a good look at the picture, then he slid it between the cover and the first page of her paperback. "I can't do anything with it now."

Schrader nodded slowly, processing the information. She looked down at her bandaged hands.

"So why did you come here to tell me about this?"

Dan glanced over his shoulder, checking that the conversation wasn't being overheard.

"My wife and daughter are missing, and so is Rick Price.

There was a note left at my house, similar to the other messages Sorrell has been leaving for us. It said red hot."

Above the white strip of nasal tape, Schrader's eyes went wide with shock and concern. "How long have they been missing?"

"At least one hour, probably longer. I spoke to them on the phone at about two o'clock, didn't get home until close to four."

Schrader's left hand moved to her chest. "I knew something was wrong as soon as I saw you walk in here. What are you going to do?"

"You wanted to know why I came here to tell you about it." Dan took the requisition form out of his pocket, unfolded it, and held it where Schrader could read it. "I need you to sign this."

Schrader looked at the sheet of paper. "That form is out of date."

"What do you mean?"

"New guidelines came out in eighty-three. The authoriser has to be at least assistant chief constable. Where did you get that form?"

"The stationery cupboard." Dan screwed the form into a ball and shoved it back in his pocket. "Stupid."

"I'm sorry," Schrader said.

"No. I'm sorry I came here to take advantage. I shouldn't have done that. I'm not thinking straight, Kath. He's got my wife and daughter."

"Did you ask Harry?"

Dan took a slow breath before answering. "Yes."

"Did he tell you the form was obsolete?"

"No, he just refused to sign it."

Schrader nodded, fixing him with a cool, appraising gaze. "Why did you think my response would be any different?"

Dan didn't reply. He had thought Schrader would sign the form because she was a helpless victim lying in a hospital bed, that she would want revenge on the man who had put her there, and that she would gladly put a gun in Dan Blacksmith's hand if she thought it would bring that revenge along a little sooner and more effectively.

"It's okay, Dan." Schrader said. "I would have signed it."

"Even though it would have probably been the end of your career?"

"Look at me. Do you think I've still got one?"

"I'm sorry."

"Stop saying that." Schrader closed her eyes, opened them after a few seconds had passed. "Tell me that you will arrest him if possible, and only use deadly force if there is no other viable course of action, and that you will not endanger the lives of yourself, another police officer, or any member of the public."

"What?"

"I'm paraphrasing the content of the form."

"But why—"

"Just tell me you will."

"Okay, I will. I still don't understand why—"

Schrader held up a bandaged hand to silence him. When she spoke, her voice was so low that Dan could barely hear the words.

"I've got a gun."

CHAPTER 33

Kath Schrader's house was three miles away from the hospital in Hull's western suburb of Anlaby. She had assured Dan that the house was going to be easy to find, even without Rick Price to navigate Hull's streets for him.

Dan hadn't needed to write down the directions because they were extremely simple. *Turn right at the crossroads outside the hospital. Take the second exit at the first roundabout, the first exit at the second.*

As he drove away from the second roundabout, Dan recited the remainder of Schrader's instructions. "The *White Lion* will be on your right after about a mile. Take the first left turn after you pass it."

A couple of minutes later he saw the illuminated pub sign ahead, a promise of welcome and warmth shining through the falling snow for anyone brave enough or desperate enough to be on the road in that weather. Dan drove past, looking for the next junction on the left.

He slowed the Sierra almost to a standstill as he made the left turn. Schrader's road hadn't been ploughed or gritted and it didn't appear that anyone else had driven down it since the most recent snowfall had started several hours earlier.

"Third house on the right," Dan said, peering through the windshield at the entrances to driveways on the far side of the road. He indicated, despite the total absence of traffic, and drove the Sierra between a pair of wooden gateposts onto the snow-covered space in front of Kath Schrader's house. He guessed there was a tarmac drive under the snow, but there was no way to know where the drive ended and the lawn began, or even whether there was a lawn there at all.

Dan locked the Sierra and walked through ankle-deep snow to the front door of the house. Hearing the sound of a car turning into the road behind him, he turned around to watch the slow-moving headlights travel past Schrader's drive. The car was a dark shape behind its lights, briefly visible in the gap between the gateposts and then gone as it travelled further along the road. Dan hadn't been able to see the driver, or whether the car was carrying any passengers.

He fished Schrader's house key out of his pocket and slid it into the lock on the front door. He had taken the key from her key-fob while she whispered the location of her gun to him. Kath Schrader had a full, current firearm certificate that allowed her to own multiple handguns and rifles. The events that had led to the tightening of controls relating to police firearms had not yet had a similar effect on the private ownership of guns.

Dan felt some resistance as he pushed the front door open. Two days' worth of unopened mail on the hall floor of Schrader's empty house. He closed the door after scooping up the handful of envelopes. There was a narrow ledge beneath the window at the side of the front door. Dan dumped the mail on it, then crouched to remove his shoes.

He straightened up, found the wall switch and turned on

the hall light. It felt strange to be alone in someone else's house when he wasn't on official police business. Plenty of times he had been in a similar situation with a search warrant in his pocket, but this was different and it made him feel awkward. He concentrated on the single purpose of his visit, barely noticing the shade of matt paint on the walls or the pattern of the carpet.

"Go up the stairs," Schrader had told him, her voice husky and nasal from the combination of covert whispering and a recently broken nose. Dan went straight up the stairs and turned on the landing light. Schrader had told him to head for the first doorway on the left, the main bedroom.

"You're not embarrassed by underwear, are you?" she had asked him.

"Not normally, no."

"Chest of drawers, middle drawer. Jewellery box at the back on the right. Key for the gun safe is in there."

Dan turned the bedroom light on, found the chest of drawers and paused with his fingers on the handle of the middle drawer. He had a fairly good idea about what he was going to see when he pulled it open.

Jumbled lingerie, bras and thongs, silk knickers and suspender belts, stockings and hold-ups in balled-up pairs. Reds and blacks and whites, ivories and skin tones.

Dan pulled the drawer out as far as it would go without falling to the floor. As he moved a semi-transparent peach-coloured bra away from the jewellery box at the back of the drawer he had a jarring memory of the Polaroid photo of Schrader's mutilated breasts. There was no embarrassment as he rummaged through her underwear drawer, just a painfully raw sadness and a growing desire for revenge.

The jewellery box wasn't locked. Inside were a few pairs of earrings, a silver necklace and a small chrome split ring with a single key attached to it. Dan took the key, left the jewellery box and the drawer both open. The gun safe was inside Schrader's wardrobe, at the back on the right-hand side, bolted to the floor and wall.

Dan took everything out of the safe and placed it on the carpet in front of the wardrobe. According to the handbook that had been underneath it inside the safe, Schrader's gun was a Smith and Wesson six-shot revolver, a .357 calibre 686 model with a four-inch barrel. There were two boxes of ammunition, one already opened and the other still sealed. Both boxes were dark blue, bearing a white shield emblem and the manufacturer's name. Dan read the technical information on the front of the opened box. It was half empty but had originally contained fifty jacketed, hollow-point Magnum rounds. The box bore a single, simple warning: *Keep out of reach of children.* The warning was repeated in French.

The final item on the floor in front of him was a cleaning and maintenance kit in a polished wooden box that was fastened with a couple of gold clips. He opened the box, saw a small tin of oil and several tools, closed it and put it back in the safe.

Dan flipped through the handbook to the section on loading and unloading the gun. He had experience with semi-automatic pistols, mostly the Browning Hi-Power which had been the firearm he had been using during the incident at Runcorn, but he had never loaded or fired a revolver. He picked up Schrader's stainless steel handgun, letting the weight sit in his palm for a while as he inhaled the subtle oily fumes and read the instructions.

It was a very simple weapon to use. Pressing a small thumb-piece on the left of the gun released the cylinder. Dan held the gun the way the handbook told him to, with his finger off the trigger and outside the trigger guard. He pressed the thumb-piece and pushed the cylinder to the left with his free hand. He felt like a beginner. Schrader probably flipped the cylinder out with a casual flick of her wrist.

Dan looked at the six identical, empty holes in the

cylinder. Something precise and perfect about them, like part of a performance car engine or a sculpture celebrating the stark beauty of functional form. He reached into the open box and took out one of the cartridges. The brass case was about an inch in length. The hollow-point lead bullet was jacketed in copper. The handbook told him to never load a gun until you were ready to use it. He slid the cartridge into one of the empty holes in the cylinder, then he filled the remaining five holes with five more cartridges.

Dan checked the handbook but found no mention of a safety mechanism. The revolver could be fired using either a double or a single action. The first method was to simply pull the trigger, rotating the cylinder and cycling the hammer back before releasing it. The second method involved manually cocking the hammer and then pulling the trigger to release it. Dan decided to stick with the simplest method.

There was no holster in the gun safe. Schrader hadn't mentioned a holster and Dan didn't even think about searching for one. He put the loaded revolver in the outside left pocket of his coat, the opened box of bullets in the right pocket.

After placing the unopened box of bullets and the handbook back in the safe, Dan locked the safe and put the key back in the jewellery box before sliding the underwear drawer shut. He turned off the lights in Schrader's house, locked the front door behind him, and went back outside into the cold.

***

"Have you got it?"

Schrader looked up at him from her hospital bed. Visiting time was over but Dan's warrant card had got him past the nurses, together with a promise that he needed no more than two minutes with their patient.

He patted his coat pocket. "Right here."

"How's my house?"

"It's fine. I locked everything up, left it how I found it." He took Schrader's house key out of his pocket and put it on top of the bedside cabinet.

"What are you going to do?"

"Go back to the station. I don't know what else I can do."

Schrader looked down at her bandaged hands. "I wish I could help."

"You already have. And I know I shouldn't have asked you to."

Schrader closed her eyes, shook her head, dismissing his apology. "Do you have any idea at all why he would have taken your wife and daughter?"

Dan sighed heavily. "It's all I've been thinking about, but it doesn't make any sense. Neither of us lived anywhere near Hull before we moved here a year ago."

"What about Runcorn?"

"What do you mean?"

"The man you shot, the reason you moved here. Is it possible that he was related to Sorrell, or maybe a friend of his?"

"No, I don't…" Dan slowly shook his head as he considered the possibilities. "That would be too much of a coincidence. Targeting my family must be part of his plan, but I can't figure out how or why."

"Keep an open mind."

"I know. That's what I kept telling Rick."

"You should go. The station might have heard something."

"Do you need anything? I could ask them before I go."

"Don't worry about me, Dan. Just go, and please be careful."

"Yeah." Dan nodded, but couldn't force any kind of a smile.

Schrader's eyes flicked briefly to the left pocket of his coat. "And don't hesitate."

"Wasn't planning on it."

Schrader nodded silently. She said nothing more as Dan turned and walked away towards the exit.

***

Dan left Rick Price's Sierra on the side street adjacent to the Campbell Road station, a few yards away from the junction with the main road. The terms road and street were relatively meaningless given the impartial covering of snow and the gathering darkness of the winter evening.

When Dan shouldered his way through the main doors of the police station, the first thing he saw was the man who was sitting on one of the wooden benches on the left hand side of the small foyer.

Rob Musgrave stood up immediately. He looked angry, exhausted, desperately in need of an outlet for his frustration. He didn't offer Dan his hand. "Do you know who did it?"

Dan stepped to one side but Musgrave moved with him. "I'm sorry. I really don't have time for this."

"Tom Mason is dead now. What are you doing about any of this?"

"I'm sorry, Rob. I'm going to have to ask you to go home. I can't discuss the case with you."

"Then why is it all over the news, asking for people to come forward with information?"

Dan took a breath, let it out as slowly as he could. "If there was anything I could tell you, anything at all, then I would."

"I've hardly slept since last Friday. All I want to know is that you're closer to catching the bastard."

Dan looked at the desk sergeant sitting on the other side of the toughened glass partition window. He held up his palm, gave a quick shake of his head, tried to force a smile but knew it wasn't going to convince anyone.

"We're closer," he said quietly to Rob. "I honestly cannot tell you anything more than that."

For a moment, there was a brief flare of hope in Rob Musgrave's tired, sunken blue eyes. "You know who it is."

"Not yet. Look, I really need to go inside and check for updates. Keeping me out here talking isn't going to help solve this case."

Rob shrugged, the light of anticipation gone from his eyes as his shoulders sagged under his heavy jacket. "I just need to know."

Dan could feel the weights in his coat pockets, the revolver and the box of ammunition. They caused the coat to swing unnaturally when he walked, bumping rhythmically against him. He could feel the gun against his hip as he stood in front of Rob Musgrave. What would happen if he gave Musgrave the name Oliver Sorrell? Did the two men know each other? Dan thought not, but he couldn't be completely sure. What if Rob Musgrave had information that would help? It was unlikely. What was likely, was that by telling Rob about Oliver Sorrell Dan would create an irredeemably dire escalation of the current situation. It could jeopardise the case and it would potentially put his wife and daughter at even greater risk.

"I'll call you tomorrow," Dan said. "I promise."

"Okay." There was no hope in Rob Musgrave's eyes now, just a distant look of defeated acceptance accompanied by a resigned sigh of loss.

"Go home. Try to get some sleep."

"Yeah. Will you call me tomorrow?"

"I will."

On his way to the stairwell, Dan stopped at the door of the communication room. Jeanette was in there with Paula, one of the station radio operators.

"Have I had any calls while I was out?" Dan asked.

"Two," Jeanette said. She picked up a notepad and looked at it. "I took both of them. The first was Rob Musgrave, again." She gave a sad shrug before continuing. "He said he was going to come to the station."

"He did. He was waiting for me in the foyer when I came in."

"Sorry, sarge. There was no way to get in touch with you to warn you."

"It's fine, Jeanette. I had a chat with him, and he's gone home. Who was the other call from?"

Jeanette checked what she had written in her notepad. "Someone trying to get in touch with your wife, or so he said."

Dan could feel a coldness that went far beyond the chill of November snow. "What was his name?"

"Mark Sykes. He said he thought he might have left something at your house, and he was calling to ask if you had seen it. Didn't tell me what it was, though."

Dan's hand moved to cover the solid weight of the revolver in his coat pocket. He fought to keep the tremor out of his voice. "When did he call?"

"Not long ago, maybe fifteen minutes."

"Did he say anything else?"

"He said he was calling from a phone box near a pub, and that he would try to call you again later."

"Did he say which pub?"

"No, sorry. I didn't ask."

"That's okay. I think I know which one it is."

Dan took the stairs to the first floor, went to his desk and picked up the phone. He found the number for the *Golden Hart* and dialled it. The clock on the wall showed that it was just after six-thirty, so the pub would have only been open for a few minutes. While he listened to the ringing phone, Dan looked across at the half-open door of Harry West's office. He had promised Harry a progress report but he had nothing to tell him that wouldn't end in an argument and probably a suspension.

The phone rang five times before it was picked up.

"*Golden Hart*, Dave speaking."

"Dave, it's DS Blacksmith. Is the pub open?"

"More or less."

"What do you mean?"

"This weather, not too many people out and about."

"How many customers do you have at the moment?"

"Half a dozen, give or take."

"Is Peter Jones there, or the man who was with him last Friday night?"

There was a brief pause, as if the barman was giving his customers a quick once-over. "Nope. Haven't seen either of them since we had our little chat a couple of days ago."

"You're absolutely sure about that?"

"Sure as I can be, yes."

Sorrell had told Jeanette he was near a pub, and he must have planned on that piece of information reaching Dan. Whether it was true or yet another attempt at misdirection was unimportant, because it was the only lead that Dan had. He knew how to get to the *Golden Hart* from Campbell Road and he had a car that was more than able to make the journey in under fifteen minutes, even in heavy snow.

Dan didn't check in with Harry West after he hung up. In another half hour he might be giving Harry a final report rather than what was more likely to be a weak cover story if he spoke to him now. He fastened his coat as he went down the stairs, feeling the deadweight of the revolver bumping against his hip every other step. The rhythmic thuds of the gun were comforting, the knowledge that he was carrying it giving him the feeling that he had an edge now. Not much of one, given everything that Bradshaw had told him about Oliver Sorrell, but it meant that he could take the man on with a definite tactical advantage and an element of surprise.

Dan knew that walking into the bar of the *Golden Hart*

wasn't going to be the best plan. It was unlikely that Sorrell would be waiting inside, more probable that he would be watching from concealment somewhere on the street, using his ability to function and fight in extreme weather conditions. If Dan kept the gun out of sight, played along by taking the bait Sorrell had placed when he mentioned being near a pub, and just got close enough to force Sorrell into making a move…

Dan didn't speak to the desk sergeant as he walked through to the foyer. He was thinking about Mandy and Becky, about a hand-written note pinned to an A-frame easel, a man with an unremarkable face, and the loaded revolver in his own pocket. He opened the main door and walked out into the cold. The world was nothing more than several dark shades of grey, the falling snow only visible in the cones of light beneath the streetlamps.

Dan looked down the road to his left, saw no-one on the street. He remembered a warning from the Smith and Wesson handbook, a single line that told the reader to always keep the muzzle pointed in a safe direction. *Until I see Oliver Sorrell*, Dan thought.

He turned to the right and walked to the corner of the street, the junction where he had left the Sierra, close enough to pick up some peripheral illumination from the nearest streetlight. There was fresh snow all over the car, but no cryptic messages written in it. If he hurried, which he knew would be an additional risk in this weather, he could get to the *Golden Hart* in fifteen minutes.

Dan stood at the driver's side door of the Sierra, unlocked the car and reached down to the handle. Something moved at the very edge of his vision, a dark shape more than a hundred yards away from the junction with Campbell Road. Someone had stepped into the light of a streetlamp for a couple of seconds, or Dan wouldn't have noticed them. He stared down the street, feeling the snowflakes as they hit the side of his face, stuck briefly, and melted. Dan could see the man standing just outside the illuminated area beneath the streetlight, near a public phone box, a silhouette against a background of dimly lit greys. From the stance and the hair, Dan was almost certain it was Rob Musgrave, hanging around in the cold and the dark, waiting in vain with nowhere to go, no girlfriend to meet. Musgrave didn't move, and Dan had no intention of walking all the way over there to find out why he was just standing around in the snow.

Dan opened the Sierra's door, climbed in and closed it. He pulled at his coat, adjusted the uncomfortable weight of the revolver so that it wasn't digging into his thigh. He pulled the seatbelt across his chest and plugged it into the anchor point.

He thought about the phone call that Jeanette had taken. The man calling himself Mark Sykes had told her he was near a pub. He had offered the information unprompted.

Dan inserted the key and turned it.

As the engine started, the overhead courtesy light faded out.

Dan had assumed Sorrell had given away his location because he wanted Dan to make the connection and drive to the *Golden Hart*. But what if Sorrell hadn't made the call from a phone box near the pub?

Chaos. Misdirection.

When the passenger door opened, less than a second later, the courtesy light winked back on.

Oliver Sorrell sat in the passenger seat and pulled the door closed behind him. He was holding a pair of blued-steel police handcuffs in his left hand. He was dressed in black, wearing gloves, but his face was not covered. His expression was one of jaded indifference. He hit Dan in the throat with the edge of his right hand, a short strike but a hard one, followed up with a clubbing backhanded fist that pounded Dan's head against the driver's side window.

As the glow from the courtesy light faded, Dan's vision

swam, his ears ringing with the impact. He choked on a shocked gasp that drew no air into his lungs. He felt Sorrell hit him again, and then there was nothing but a brief, terrifying sensation of falling helplessly into blackness.

CHAPTER 34

Dan didn't completely lose consciousness. There was just a time when he wasn't really there. It could have been a minute, could have been ten, but his memories were fractured and vague, drawn from a fuzzy temporal awareness and a bone-deep dread that drowned out the pain and the absence of light.

He thought he was blind until he managed to focus on the indistinct red glow that was right in front of his face. He could hear a constant droning noise that at first sounded like water being forced over a weir by an intensely strong current but eventually resolved itself in his mind as tyres travelling fast along a snow-covered road.

The rising panic as he struggled beneath what felt like an immovable weight was an instinctive reaction to the fear of being buried alive. When he managed to focus enough rational thought to put the red glow together with the road noise, he was able to figure out where he was. At the same time, with far less deduction required, he realised that the reason he couldn't move his hands was because his wrists were cuffed behind his back.

The Sierra slowed before making a left turn. The red

glow near Dan's face intensified briefly as the brakes were applied. The coarse carpeting inside the hatchback boot space was rough against his cheek, and his ability to move was severely hampered by the limited amount of room and the parcel shelf pressing down on him.

After several more minutes the car slowed again and he heard the road noise change, despite the layer of snow between the car's tyres and the road surface. The steady rushing noise, like fast-moving water, was replaced by a low frequency rumble. Tarmac to gravel, maybe, as if the car had turned off the road onto a farm track or a long driveway that led to a secluded house.

Dan felt two jolts in quick succession as the car's left front and rear wheels hit the same pothole or roadside drain cover. After that there was no further break in the constant rumbling until the car stopped moving and the engine was turned off. There was a soft click as the driver's door opened, followed by a harder thud that Dan felt rather than heard when the door was closed. He listened, straining to hear the crunching footsteps of boots on snow.

The click of the hatch release was amplified inside the confined space. The interior lamp blinked on, a pale yellow glow near Dan's feet. Dan turned his head as the parcel shelf tilted up and away. Snow was still falling, the flakes illuminated by the light of the interior lamp.

Oliver Sorrell leaned into the boot, grabbed Dan under both arms and hauled him backwards out of the car. Dan didn't feel the revolver or the box of ammunition bump against the edge of the boot as he came out of it. He hadn't been able to reach his pockets while he had been in the back of the car, didn't know whether the gun and the ammo had fallen out while he was in there but he suspected that they hadn't. It was far more likely that Sorrell had found them and taken them.

Dan stood in the snow, blinking as he tried to assess the surrounding area. He saw nothing but varying levels of darkness, no lights from any nearby buildings or streetlamps.

Sorrell kicked the back of Dan's right knee, shoving him forward onto the hard, snow-covered ground. He closed the Sierra's hatchback and crouched next to Dan.

"Burning up," Sorrell said. His voice was calm, disinterested. It was the voice from the emergency call that had been made from Raymond Hughes' phone. He pulled Dan's shoulder, rolling him onto his back.

Dan looked up at Sorrell's impassive face. His throat was sore from the first vicious blow he had received, tight and dry with fear and anxiety. Immobilised behind his back, his bare hands were pressed into the freezing snow.

"I'm a police officer." There was no authority in his voice, nothing but the desperate plea of a man who knows he has already lost.

"Yes. That's why you're here."

"What have you done to my wife… and my daughter?"

Sorrell rolled Dan over so that he was face-down in the snow. He grabbed him beneath the arms again, effortlessly pulling him to his feet as he stood up behind him.

"I'll show you," Sorrell said. He pushed Dan forward towards a looming expanse of darkness that blotted out the paler grey of the sky.

Dan stopped trudging through the ankle-deep snow when he was a yard from the wall of the structure. It was a barn, or some other kind of massive agricultural outbuilding. The wall was featureless, no windows or openings. There was a door that looked just like part of the wall. An old but sturdy looking broom was leaning against the wall next to the door. Sorrell moved past Dan, ten feet to his right, took hold of a metal handle and pulled on it. The door was metal, solid and heavy. It slid sideways on stubborn, frozen rollers until Sorrell had it open just wide enough to give them room to enter the building.

"Go inside," Sorrell said.

Dan stepped over the raised metal runner at the base of the door frame. The interior of the building was completely black, no sign of any light at all. Dan could hear sounds deep in the darkness, low grunts and muted scuffling noises. He thought of livestock, maybe pigs or cattle, but there was something about the sounds that caused him to pause, the daunting notion that those sounds were not being made by any kind of farm animal.

Sorrell pushed Dan in the lower back, urging him forward. "Keep moving."

Dan took two more steps, heard the door being slid shut behind him, and stopped. He could still see nothing, but he could hear the sounds more clearly, rising in intensity as if whatever or whoever was responsible for them was reacting to his presence.

From behind him, Dan heard a solid metallic click as a large switch was thrown. Far overhead, above him in the darkness, a pair of tired fluorescent tube lights flickered on and off for several seconds before stabilising. The light wasn't powerful, the domestic lamps not designed to illuminate a large interior area such as the one Dan was now looking at. They had probably been fitted years earlier, chosen by a farmer for their low initial cost rather than a practical assessment of their functionality.

The light was low, but it was enough to show Dan everything that was in the barn.

The rusted, skeletal tiller, abandoned in a far corner in the shadow of the crudely constructed wooden loft which extended above approximately a quarter of the barn's floor area. Half a dozen large hay bales, originally cylindrical but sagging and deformed with age and moisture, clumps of new grass somehow managing to have sprung to life on top of them. There was a single barrel, very large, five feet high, its curved wooden staves wrapped with seven copper hoops. The floor around it was soaked with water, and a length of rope hung from the ceiling beam above it. There were tools scattered on the floor, some rusted and ancient, and others so new that the metal gleamed under the strip lights. More than one of the tools was streaked with blood.

There was a deep service trench cut into the concrete floor, the kind of inspection pit used for carrying out maintenance work on farm vehicles or coaches, where jacking the vehicle up was not an option. Above the service trench, six ropes hung from the huge central ceiling joist. The ropes were evenly spaced, five feet apart. The end of each rope was tied around the neck of one of the six people who were standing in a line on wooden planks placed across the service trench. The six people were standing still, their arms tied behind their backs and their ankles duct-taped together. They all had black hoods over their heads. Five of the people were adults. One was a small child.

Dan cried out in horror, lurching forward towards them. He sprawled awkwardly to the floor when Oliver Sorrell kicked him in the back.

"Calm down," Sorrell said. He took hold of Dan's handcuffed wrists and pulled him to his feet. "I've got your spot marked out over here."

Dan stared at the hooded child as he felt himself being dragged backwards by Sorrell. He recognised the pyjamas the child was wearing. They belonged to his daughter.

"Mandy," Dan said. The child's head moved under the hood, blindly seeking the source of the voice.

"Yes," Sorrell said. "That is Mandy. The woman on her right is the moderately talented artist, Rebecca Blacksmith."

"If you—"

"Not if, Dan. When."

Sorrell pushed Dan towards the wall of the barn, backing him up against a massive vertical wooden beam. A few inches above Dan's head, a large steel ring had been screwed into the beam. Without warning, Sorrell jabbed a short punch into Dan's gut, just below his rib cage. As Dan gasped, doubling over in pain, Sorrell unlocked the cuff around Dan's right wrist, raised his cuffed left arm and locked the free end of the handcuffs to the metal ring.

"Now we're ready," Sorrell said. "This won't take long."

Dan patted his coat pockets with his right hand. They were empty, as he had suspected.

Sorrell reached into his own coat pocket and pulled out Schrader's revolver. His expression briefly altered, not exactly a smile, and for a moment he looked very different, as if the change of expression had also changed his facial features. Dan remembered what Bradshaw had told him about Sorrell having a genetic advantage, and he realised that it hadn't been an exaggeration.

Sorrell walked to the first hooded person in the line. Mandy was at the other end of the line, thirty feet away from where Sorrell was standing. Sorrell took the hood off the man and Dan saw Rick Price's wide, terrified eyes staring at him, his mouth covered by a tightly wound gag of duct tape. One of Rick's eyes was bruised, partially shut, his hair and shirt were soaking wet, and his left ear was missing.

Sorrell tapped the bloody remains of Rick's ear with the butt of Schrader's revolver. "Had to ask him more than once. Thought the ear would do it, or the thumbs, but in the end it was the water barrel that got him really chatty."

Rick's eyes were pleading, sorrowful, absent of hope. Dan pulled against the handcuff but there was no way he was going to be able to free his left hand from it.

"Guess what he told me," Sorrell said to Dan. "He said you talked to a major from the SAS base in Hereford. A tired old dog called Bradshaw. That right, Dan?"

"You don't have to do this," Dan said.

"What about this?" Sorrell asked. He kicked the plank that Rick was standing on. The plank slid backwards on the concrete floor, tilted, and clattered into the service trench.

Rick Price dropped a couple of inches before the rope around his neck tightened and held him. With his arms tied behind him, his ankles bound together, his body began to thrash and wriggle at the end of the rope. For a few seconds he seemed to be trying to reach the edge of the service trench with his feet, and Dan was screaming at him to do it, to save himself, but there was no real chance that he was going to be able to manage it before panic robbed him of the last vestiges of reason, shortly before unconsciousness took him completely.

"Cut the rope!" Dan yelled at Sorrell. Over and over he repeated it, shouting, screaming, then finally sobbing the words through his own tears as Rick's body stopped moving and just hung there, slowly swaying back and forth at the end of the rope.

Dan slumped forward, his cuffed left hand the only thing preventing him from collapsing to the floor.

"Buck up," Sorrell said. "Another two minutes and it will all be over."

Dan rubbed his eyes with the heel of his right hand. He watched as Sorrell moved to the next figure in the line. It was a man, tall and thickset. Dan had guessed who it was a moment before Sorrell pulled the black hood from his head.

Peter Jones had his eyes squeezed tightly shut. His mouth was covered with silver duct tape. Dan stared at him. There was no noose around Jones' neck. Instead, the rope was looped under his arms.

"Remember Pete?" Sorrell asked Dan. "Of course you do. Love at first choke. If you were wondering who killed the power that night, well, modesty forbids, but you're more than welcome."

Dan remained silent. He couldn't bring himself to respond, knowing that his wife and daughter were standing at the end of that line, nooses around their necks, minutes away from death at the hands of Oliver Sorrell.

Sorrell didn't do anything to Peter Jones. Instead, he moved to the next person in the line and removed their hood. It was a dark-haired man, quite young, probably no more than twenty-four years old, the first of the two remaining kids from the career class at John Blair.

"Gareth Pugh," Dan said.

"Good work, Detective," Sorrell said, stepping away from Gareth Pugh to stand beside the fourth person in the line. "Bonus point if you can tell me this young lady's name."

Dan tried to remember the name that had been on the list. He had read it, only heard it once or maybe twice, but he couldn't focus his mind on recalling the name. He was thinking about his wife and daughter, the ropes around their necks. He was thinking about a soft toy rat in a striped jumper and blue cap, lying alone on the floor of Becky's studio. Mandy would never hold that toy again, never blow out the five candles on her next birthday cake.

Sorrell pulled the hood off the young woman's head. "It's Caroline Stanton, Dan. Come on, at least try."

Dan straightened up, leaning back against the wall with his left hand resting on top of his head.

"They were kids in school. You don't need to kill anyone else."

"Kids in school?" Sorrell coughed out a humourless laugh. "I've been shot at with assault rifles by kids of twelve, Dan. I've seen younger kids than that hack chunks off prisoners and feed the meat to their pet dogs." He reached behind Caroline Stanton's head and grabbed a handful of her hair. Above the duct tape strip, her nostrils flared and her eyes went wide with terror. "Caroline and her friends killed my brother. No remorse, no regrets. They don't even remember doing it. Act of war, Dan. And that's what I know, that's what I deal with."

"Just stop," Dan said. He knew it was no use, because he could see the inevitability of victory in Sorrell's eyes. It wasn't the wild-eyed anticipation of a psychopath, just the same calm indifference of the man who always won. He was going to kill everyone in the barn and he was going to get away with it. He knew it, and he knew it was all going to be over in a couple of minutes.

Sorrell stood next to Becky, pulled the black hood off her head and dropped it on the floor. Becky blinked, glanced down at Mandy, then looked up and saw Dan.

Sorrell crouched down, put his hands against the plank that Becky was standing on.

"No!" Dan screamed, straining against the handcuff.

Sorrell stood up, shrugged, and put his arm around Becky's shoulders. Her eyes were bright with tears, her head shaking from side to side.

"I'm not cruel," Sorrell said. "I'll do you first, Dan. So you don't have to watch your wife and daughter thrashing about at the end of a rope. That's fair, isn't it?" He looked at Becky. She was choking, fighting to breathe through her nose while she sobbed behind the duct tape gag.

Sorrell tore at one side of the tape, ripping enough of it away to free half of Becky's mouth. She sucked air in, shuddering feverishly as she balanced on her tightly bound ankles.

"I'm sorry," Dan said.

Becky gasped, coughed, shook her head again. She tried to speak but only one side of her mouth was functioning.

Sorrell walked away from Becky and stood halfway between Dan and Peter Jones. He raised the hand that was holding the stainless steel six-shot revolver.

"You came into the barn," Sorrell said to Dan. "You saw what Peter had done to your wife and daughter, so you took Kath Schrader's gun out of your pocket, and…"

He extended his arm, aimed the gun and fired.

The report was a deafeningly brutal blast of sudden thunder that filled the barn and left Dan's ears ringing.

The bullet hit Peter Jones high up on the right side of his chest. The impact spun him around, and a splatter of blood decorated the side of Gareth Pugh's face like wet confetti.

"Good shot, Dan. Just like Runcorn. But you needed to be sure he wasn't coming back, wasn't going to dodge justice on a technicality."

Sorrell aimed and fired again. Another ear-deadening thunderclap, another chest shot. Jones sagged, his knees buckling under him as the rope around his chest took all of his weight.

"Case closed," Sorrell said. He picked up the bloody knife that had been lying on the floor near Rick Price. It was a hunting knife with a fixed, seven-inch blade. "I'll cut Peter down from there, arrange the body in a convincing pose just here. You did a good job, Detective." He walked towards Dan. "But before you got that first shot off, Peter surprised you, like this."

Sorrell's hand snaked forward, fast and without hesitation. The knife went through Dan's coat, through skin and flesh and muscle, further in, too deep to be shrugged off as a graze. Deep enough to feel more like a heavy blow from a sledgehammer than a quick stab from a knife with a seven-inch blade. Deep enough to be fatal without medical attention.

Through the shock of the awful, blazing spear of pain, Dan heard Becky scream. He pressed his right hand over the hole in his coat, low down beneath his ribs, staggering backwards against the immovable wooden pillar with his breath coming in ragged gasps. His right hand was warm and wet. He didn't look, didn't want to see.

"We're nearly done here," Sorrell said. "You certainly are. I've got four more quick things to do." He studied Dan for a few seconds. "Got something you want to say?"

Dan was leaning against the wall, his right leg bent at the knee, threatening to betray him and topple him forwards. He wasn't looking at Sorrell, he was looking at Becky. Becky wasn't looking at Dan, she was looking across the barn towards the door. Dan didn't look at the door.

"Here you go," Sorrell said. "Do what you have to."

He took hold of Dan's right wrist, pulled his hand away from the bloody hole in his coat. He pressed Schrader's revolver into the palm of Dan's hand. Four-inch barrel, .357 calibre rounds. Double-action. *Always keep the muzzle pointed in a safe direction.*

Sorrell took a step backwards away from Dan.

Dan raised his arm, grimacing at the searing pain in his belly. He pointed the gun at Sorrell. His arm was shaking, but at that range it would make no difference.

Dan pulled the trigger all the way back until the hammer fell.

CHAPTER 35

There was just a click, a hollow echo as the hammer fell on an empty chamber.

Dan bellowed with rage, pulling the trigger again and again while Sorrell stood four feet in front of him, regarding him with that familiarly indifferent, slightly bored expression.

"How do you get a policeman to put his prints all over the murder weapon?" Sorrell asked.

Dan lowered the gun. He almost cocked his arm back and hurled it in Sorrell's face but he stopped himself before he did it.

Sorrell nodded slowly. The knife he had used on Dan was still in his right hand. "You hang onto that, then. Either way, they'll find it in your hand when they get here." He backed away towards the four figures standing over the service trench, watching Dan until he was far enough away from him for a hit with a thrown gun to be both extremely unlikely and no threat at all. He stood in front of the first person in the line who was still alive.

"Time to piss your pants, Gareth. I know you've been holding it in for at least a day."

Sorrell took a short step back, preparing to kick the plank out from beneath Gareth Pugh's feet.

With a shriek of rusty protest, the door at the side of the barn slid wide open. Dan looked around at the same time as Sorrell. He saw Michael Bradshaw step inside the barn. Bradshaw was holding the handle of the broom that had been leaning against the outside wall.

"Stand down," Bradshaw said to Oliver Sorrell. "Or I will put you down."

Dan looked from Bradshaw to Sorrell. Seven-inch knife versus four-foot broom handle. The outcome should have been inevitable, but Dan remembered Bradshaw's words and he knew there was not going to be anything inevitable about it.

One-on-one, with a weapons advantage and the element of surprise… I might get lucky.

Becky was staring urgently at Dan. She didn't know who Bradshaw was. All she knew was that her husband had been stabbed, and her daughter was standing next to her with a noose around her neck.

"Walk away," Sorrell said to Bradshaw. Even as he spoke, he was circling away, putting more distance between himself and his former commanding officer. "This isn't your mission."

"It's nobody's mission," Bradshaw said. "Lay down the knife. I'll take you in."

Dan felt an agonising bolt of pain searing through his gut. He looked at the useless gun in his hand.

"No," he said. "Not useless."

Dan turned to face the wooden beam. He raised his right hand, grinding his teeth against the crashing waves of pain. He jammed the four-inch stainless steel barrel through the metal ring. There was no way that he would have been able to unscrew the ring with his bare hands, but Sorrell had handed him the perfect crank-handle to get the job done. He knew it was going to hurt, more than any pain he had ever known, so he thought about Becky and Mandy, about how wide Mandy was going to smile when she picked up Roland Rat and hugged him to her chest. He tried not to think about how he wouldn't be there to see it. He pulled down on the butt of the revolver and he screamed. And the ring started to turn.

Sorrell was moving towards the back of the barn, closer to Mandy and Becky, facing Bradshaw but taking in everything that was happening. Bradshaw strode forward, closing the distance between himself and Sorrell.

Dan pulled the revolver all the way down, one anticlockwise half turn of the metal ring. It was an eighth of an inch out of the wood, still solidly held, still a long way to go. Dan butted his head against the wooden beam, finding a way through the pain as he reversed his grip on the handle of the revolver and pushed it up, completing the first full turn.

Bradshaw sidestepped to his left, putting himself closer to the four people with ropes around their necks. Sorrell stood his ground, watching as Bradshaw drew closer. His posture was relaxed, the knife held loosely in his right hand.

"They're civilians," Bradshaw said. "British civilians."

"Should have had that inscribed on Jacob's headstone."

Bradshaw stopped moving when he was ten feet from Sorrell. He was holding the broom handle in a reverse grip, diagonally across his chest, ready to strike or defend. "Drop the knife. This is only going to end one way."

Dan sucked in a laboured gasp of air as he took the barrel of the revolver out of the metal ring, untwisted the short handcuff chain and pushed the barrel back through the ring. He rotated it through another half turn and it was already starting to feel easier, but the shaft screwed into the wood was probably two or three inches long. He was facing at least another seven turns of the metal ring before he would be free.

Sorrell took a single step towards Bradshaw. Eight feet

separated them.

"You know how it will end," Sorrell said. "A public lie and a private cover-up."

"I'm not going to let you kill anyone else."

"You're not going to stop me."

Sorrell lunged at the instant when Bradshaw started to reply. Bradshaw whipped the broom handle horizontally at waist height, too low for it to be ducked and too hard to be blocked or parried. Sorrell didn't stop. He raised his arm, leaned forward and took the blow's full force against the side of his chest.

Bradshaw had started to turn his body at the start of the swing of the broom handle. He kept the momentum going, yanking the stick back just as Sorrell brought his arm down in an attempt to trap it between his arm and the side of his body.

Sorrell let the stick go, following it as Bradshaw spun around to deliver another strike. He was pirouetting rather than drawing the stick back in preparation for the next attack. Sorrell had seen the move coming before it had even started. He sidestepped in the direction that the stick was travelling, bringing himself in range for a strike of his own.

Bradshaw blocked Sorrell's knife arm with his free hand as he came out of the pirouette, but Sorrell had been prepared for that too, and he countered with a short left jab to the centre of Bradshaw's chest. Bradshaw took the punch and dodged backwards to avoid the knife strike that followed.

Sorrell backed up too, edging to his right, taking a step closer to the service trench.

Dan had turned the ring through another two whole rotations. There was more than an inch of exposed thread showing, and the metal ring was no longer feeling so solidly attached to the beam. He didn't need to pause the next rotation at the half turn, just palmed the handle of the revolver all the way around. The relief he felt was overpowering, but he also felt weaker, unsteady on his feet, and he knew that he didn't have much time left.

Bradshaw went straight back on the offensive. He held the broom handle in both hands, one over, one under, jabbing it at Sorrell as he forced him further back. Sorrell appeared to be waiting for an opportunity to block a jab and grab the end of the stick, but it was a devious ruse. He backhanded the broom handle, twisting his arm over the top of it as he lunged forward with his knife hand.

Bradshaw swayed to his right, kicked hard at the side of Sorrell's leading knee at the same time as he swapped his grip on the broom handle and slashed upwards. The tip of the rapidly rising stick caught the underside of Sorrell's knife hand, cracking hard against Sorrell's ring and middle fingers where they were wrapped around the handle of the knife. Sorrell grunted with pain as the knife was knocked out of his hand.

The knife arced away through the air, turning end over end.

Sorrell ignored the lost knife, his free hand snapping forward to grab the broom handle. Bradshaw went for a short punch to Sorrell's throat but he wasn't quick enough. Sorrell twisted the broom handle, forcing Bradshaw's wrist backwards as he drove his knee hard into Bradshaw's thigh.

Dan saw the knife fly from Sorrell's hand, momentarily feeling a glimmer of elation as Bradshaw gained an advantage. He watched the knife tumble through the air, saw it rise and then fall, its trajectory taking it straight towards Becky. She saw it coming too, but she couldn't move out of its path. She tilted her head hard to one side, leaning as far as she could, closing her eyes against the inevitable impact.

"No!" Dan cried in dismay, but the blade hadn't hit Becky. The handle clipped her hard against the temple and the knife bounced away to land on the concrete a foot from the edge of the trench.

Becky lurched from the shock of the blow. Her bound feet jerked as her body twisted away from the pain. She slipped, caught off balance, unable to prevent her feet skidding out from under her. The plank she was standing on slid forward with her feet. It only moved a few inches, but that was enough.

Dan stared in horrified disbelief as the plank tilted under Becky's feet before sliding backwards into the trench. When she had slipped, the rope around her neck had already gone taut, the slack taken up by her falling body, so there was no sudden drop. But the noose was still around her neck and she was hanging from it, her bound legs kicking helplessly over the void of the trench as she started to strangle.

Dan screamed in desperation. The pain in his belly was a raging fire but it no longer mattered. Switches were being thrown in his head; anything that wasn't hooked up to the most primitive survival instincts was shutting down.

Unconsciousness in fifteen seconds, Hansom had told him. *Death in two to three minutes.*

Dan grabbed the revolver and turned it. He could hear his own voice, but nothing coherent, just a constant roar of fury. Two more turns. The metal ring was wobbling now. Becky was writhing at the end of the rope, still conscious but her struggles were growing weaker with every passing second.

Sorrell had seen what had happened. He was grappling with Bradshaw for control of the broom handle. Both men had one hand on the stick while they punched and blocked with their free hands, risking kicks when they saw an opportunity.

Dan gave the ring one more half turn and then took hold of Schrader's revolver with both hands, pressed the sole of his right foot against the wall and heaved the remaining three quarters of an inch of threaded steel clear of the wooden beam. The metal ring tore free and Dan felt something else tear as he staggered backwards. He ignored the pain, the fresh heat of wetness under his shirt. When he turned around to face the trench, Bradshaw and Sorrell were far away to his right, near the rotting bales and the rusted tiller at the rear of the barn, both still holding the broom handle, fists and feet blurring as they hammered blows into each other.

Becky was no longer moving.

Dan lurched towards the trench. His body was trying to quit, starting with his legs, but he forced himself to keep going.

Sorrell had Bradshaw backed up against one of the mouldy hay bales, his body twisted at the waist as he leaned all his weight on the broom handle, jabbing his fist at Bradshaw's face and throat. To his right, Sorrell could see the rusted tines of the ancient tiller, curved blades two feet long attached to four central hubs. He feinted right, stepped left and tried to trip Bradshaw as he shoved him towards the tiller.

Dan reached the edge of the trench, his whole body shivering with a spasm of nauseating agony as he reached for the rope around Becky's neck. He dropped to one knee, slapping himself across the face to clear his head. The hunting knife was there on the dusty concrete floor, close enough to touch. He pulled his hand away from his stomach, staring with detached disbelief at the amount of blood covering his fingers. His hand moved towards the knife, fingers dripping blood as they first touched the handle, then curled around it with a surge of frantic strength.

Bradshaw had anticipated Sorrell's attempt to push him onto the blades of the tiller. He dropped his free arm from its defensive position across his face, grabbed the broom handle with both hands and jerked it viciously up under Sorrell's chin as Sorrell pushed him sideways. Taking advantage of Sorrell's momentary loss of balance, Bradshaw grabbed both of Sorrell's arms and swung him around in a fast half-circle into the tiller's blades.

Dan rose to his feet, the knife in his hand. He took hold of the rope above Becky's head and rammed the blade of the knife against it. His legs shuddered violently as he sawed the keenly honed edge of the blade back and forth against the rope. He watched the fibres splitting, the blade slicing further and further through. Before he had completely cut the rope, his legs finally gave way, pitching him forward towards Becky. He reached for the rope with both hands, desperately grasping one last chance to save his wife. The extra weight was too much for the damaged rope. It snapped above Dan's hands, dropping him straight down into the five-foot deep trench. He slammed into the wet, oil-slick floor of the trench on his back, and Becky fell on top of him.

Sorrell had been pierced through the right thigh by one of the tines, with a second blade grazing his ribs. When Bradshaw had grabbed his arms, Sorrell had taken the broom handle away from him. Even as the metal blade gouged into his leg, he had swung the heavy wooden handle and it had caught Bradshaw across the side of the head, spinning him around and dropping him to the floor.

Dan was drifting in and out of consciousness. He worked his fingers under the noose around Becky's neck, found the knot and fumbled at it, loosening the rope until it was no longer constricting his wife's throat. He pressed his fingertips against the side of her neck, just below her jaw. He could feel a weak, throbbing pulse but he could also feel the same sensation all over his own body.

This is what it feels like, Dan thought. *To die.*

Sorrell let out a howl of victorious agony as he hurled himself forward, tearing his leg away from the curved, rusted blade. He looked at the trench, saw Pugh and Stanton and the kid still standing there with the ropes around their necks, an empty gap between Stanton and the Blacksmith girl. When he took a step forward, his injured leg buckled and he fell awkwardly to the floor. Bradshaw was lying motionless, his eyes open but staring sightlessly at the overhanging wooden loft. Sorrell ignored him, dragging himself towards the trench on his hands and knees.

Dan was stroking Becky's hair, waiting for the darkness as he lay on his back beneath her. Above him, the beams and rafters of the barn roof were a distant mystery. The edge of the trench was close, but out of reach. He knew he could look out of the trench if he stood up, but standing up was such an impossible concept that it almost made him smile.

Not long now.

Something moved up there, at the side of the trench. Not just a shadow, there was someone there now, looking down at him.

"Tactical error," Sorrell said. "Giving up the high ground."

Dan could feel a wooden plank under his heels, the one Becky had been standing on before she fell. Five feet above him, and a similar distance along the trench, Mandy was standing on her plank, staying quiet, not moving. Dan said nothing, knowing that it was likely he couldn't have spoken even if he had tried.

"You're not doing so well," Sorrell said. "Lost a lot of blood. Probably starting to feel cold, am I right?"

Dan moved his fingers against Becky's neck. He could still feel a pulse. This time he knew it must be hers, because he was sure his own heart had already stopped beating.

"She still alive?" Sorrell asked.

Dan wrapped his limp arms around Becky, knowing that he had to protect her, to keep Sorrell away from her.

"Better make sure," Sorrell said. He swung his legs over the edge of the trench. In his right hand, he was holding the hunting knife. "I would have loaded the revolver, but it's all the way over there." He looked at the knife. "I prefer blades anyway."

Dan stared up at Sorrell, too weak to move his legs, let alone try to squirm out from underneath Becky. He heard Sorrell say something else. It sounded like, "Then you're going to love this," but Sorrell's mouth hadn't moved when he spoke.

Sorrell heard the voice, turned his head, and saw two things. Bradshaw was rising shakily to his feet near the tiller at the back of the barn, and a tall, terminally-exhausted looking blonde-haired guy with dead blue eyes was standing less than a foot away from the edge of the trench to Sorrell's left. Sorrell knew who it was; just a boyfriend, a carpenter, not part of the mission. The carpenter boyfriend was holding a tool, a nine-inch paring chisel with a one-inch-wide blade. Sorrell knew that cabinet makers used paring chisels to shave thin slivers of wood. It would make an effective stabbing weapon, particularly against a wounded opponent who was sitting on the ground, already at a distinct disadvantage.

Sorrell was still trying to figure out how he had been caught off-guard when the carpenter boyfriend thrust the blade of the chisel through the side of his neck.

Some of the blood fell on Dan's face. He blinked, hearing wild laughter that he thought was just in his head. He saw Sorrell's torso topple backwards out of sight, saw an arm holding a long, narrow blade rising and falling while Sorrell's legs twitched and jerked over the edge of the trench. After a while, the legs stopped moving.

Rob Musgrave looked into the trench.

Bradshaw stood next to him, patting him on the back. "Good work. Let's get them out of that hole."

"We should have jumped him earlier."

"I had to wait until the gun was no longer a factor. Now hop down there and lift the woman up first."

Rob climbed down into the trench, standing with his feet either side of Dan and Becky. He gently moved Dan's arms out of the way, then bent down, took hold of Becky beneath her arms and lifted her upright. He held her like that, with the top of her head a couple of inches above the edge of trench, while Bradshaw crouched down and hauled Becky up and out of the trench.

Dan saw Rob Musgrave floating above him, a vague shape surrounded by gathering darkness. He heard Musgrave's voice asking if she was still alive. He didn't hear the reply.

Bradshaw had to climb down into the trench to help Rob lift Dan out of it. It was awkward work in the narrow space, on a smooth surface slippery with old oil and fresh blood. They lifted him together, wary of worsening the wound in his abdomen, but they eventually managed to get him back to ground level where they lay him on his back next to his wife.

Rob removed the noose from the little girl's neck, took the hood off her head and carefully peeled the strip of tape away from her mouth.

The first thing Mandy said was, "Daddy."

Dan's eyes blinked open. He looked in the direction of his daughter's voice.

"Hello, Daddy. It was dark. I heard noises. Is Mummy sleeping?"

Dan heard the words, saw only a gathering of blackness that echoed the dark that his daughter had endured. But she hadn't cried, hadn't panicked. Dan closed his eyes, feeling a smile that never quite formed. He thought of the nightlight in her room, the one they left on while she slept. At the end, when it had mattered, Mandy hadn't been afraid of the dark.

Bradshaw looked at Rob Musgrave and held his finger to his lips. "Come get the first aid kit from my car. I'll radio for an ambulance. Do that before we cut the other two free."

"Do you think they'll get here in time?"

Bradshaw looked down at Dan and Becky. "It's all we

can do."

CHAPTER 36

They couldn't save him.

Not from the nightmares or the gnawing regret that he had made a series of mistakes that had ended in disaster, the unshakeable knowledge that he had failed and that Rick Price had died because of his failure.

Visiting time had ended twenty minutes earlier. Becky had taken Mandy home after Mandy had spent half an hour making Roland Rat dance on Daddy's hospital bed. Becky had only spent a few hours in the hospital as a patient, and that had been five days ago, when she and Dan had both been rushed into Casualty.

Dan's left foot and most of his lower leg were covered with a plaster cast. Breaking his ankle when he fell into the trench was only one of the things that he couldn't remember from that night. The stab wound had required major surgery to repair his small intestine. A nurse who sounded very much like someone who knew exactly what she was talking about had told Dan that another half hour without medical attention would have definitely killed him. The tube from a saline drip was attached to a small valve that was half covered by a dressing across the back of his left hand. Another tube hung down from beneath the bandages around his abdomen. He tried not think about that tube, or the dark, viscous liquid that occasionally dripped from it into the large flask under the bed.

Kath Schrader sat in the cheap plastic chair beside Dan's bed. Her hands were bandaged, but not as heavily as they had been, and her face was still bruised, mostly around the eyes, but the bruises were fading and she had started wearing makeup again. She had been discharged on the weekend, as soon as her husband had returned home from Germany. Leaving hospital and spending time with Gerard in her own house had done more for her healing than any medicinal remedies the hospital could have offered her.

"Feels different when you're sitting here, not lying there."

Dan could see the difference in her eyes. She looked stronger, no longer a helpless victim in a hospital bed. He asked her, "How are you feeling?"

"I should be asking you that, although I think I know what the answer would be."

"I'm alive. They told me I was lucky, but they don't know the half of it."

Schrader opened the handbag that she was holding on her knees, looked inside but didn't take anything out. "I came to see you the day before yesterday but you were out cold."

"Unconscious?"

"Just sleeping, but they wouldn't let me in."

"Dr Michaelides," Dan said. "He's my doctor now."

"He's good. I didn't have any complaints."

"How's your husband?"

"Do you mean what does my husband think of my scars?"

Dan looked away, saying nothing.

"I showed him, and he hid his reaction rather well."

"Kath…"

"I can't pretend it didn't happen, Dan. Any of it. I told Gerard I'd get a tattoo to hide the scars if they still looked bad twelve months from now."

Dan shook his head. "What did he say?"

"He said it would be my choice."

"Are you serious?"

"About the tattoo? Yes, if that's what it takes."

Dan glanced at Schrader's coat where it covered her chest. "Harry came to see me yesterday."

"He already gave me the official report."

Cautiously, Dan asked, "Did he tell you anything else?"

"Enough. The case is closed. Peter Jones killed Sharon Hall, Dee Collins…" She swallowed, wiped at the corner of her mouth with a bandaged hand. "And DC Rick Price. A member of Humberside Police tracked Jones to an abandoned barn where he was hiding out alone. The officer was wounded during the arrest and Jones was fatally shot in a justified use of deadly force. They're keeping your name out of it completely."

Dan let out a long, slow breath. "Bradshaw. Harry refused to talk about him yesterday, which made me suspect that Bradshaw had got to him."

"It wasn't just Bradshaw. Harry wouldn't give me a name, but someone representing a government department with an interest in national security was also involved. It went higher, several rungs above Harry, and it came back as a highly classified order."

"It's what Sorrell said would happen. A public lie and a private cover-up."

"The other two who were there," Schrader said, "Gareth Pugh and Caroline Stanton. They were given some kind of debriefing by the government agent. Let's just say they won't be talking to reporters any time soon."

"Were they threatened?"

"Officially, no, but I suspect there was a combination of financial compensation and a very clear warning that anything other than complete silence on the matter would not be in their best interests. You already know they had a similar chat with your wife."

Dan looked up at the ceiling before he spoke again. "What about Rob Musgrave?"

Schrader laughed softly, little more than a polite sniff. "He was never there."

"He killed Oliver Sorrell."

"Who was also never there."

Dan felt gooseflesh chilling the backs of his arms. "*Never there.*"

"Dan?"

"It was a name they gave Sorrell, something in Arabic that translated as *never there*. Tom Mason knew the name. It was what he called his band."

"How did Tom Mason know the name?"

"Sorrell made contact with him a few years ago. He had been watching everyone, planning everything. He knew about Runcorn, and he knew that you had a gun. I think one of the reasons he attacked you was to provoke you into giving it to me."

Schrader slowly shook her head. "But the amount of risk involved, with no guarantee it would play out the way he wanted it to…"

"He would have had a backup plan, probably several. From our perspective, it all worked out the way that it did because that was all we saw."

Schrader touched her hair with a bandaged hand. "I talked to Rob Musgrave, unofficially again."

"I don't even know how he managed to be at the barn."

"He told me, eventually, after I convinced him that I wasn't going to lock him up and throw away the key."

"He saved us, probably saved six lives that night. More than I did."

Schrader frowned. "You did everything that you could. If you hadn't contacted Bradshaw, hadn't forced his hand with the information about Sorrell, you wouldn't be here and I doubt anyone else who was in that barn would be alive."

Dan nodded, but it was reluctant acceptance rather than agreement. "So how did Musgrave get to the barn?"

"He told me he went to Campbell Road to speak to you. You apparently fobbed him off, in his words, and went inside. He went to a phone box down the street, not to make a call, just to get out of the snow for a while. I didn't ask why he did that, I suspect he wasn't exactly thinking rationally at the time."

"He was totally exhausted, pretty much running on fumes and adrenaline."

Schrader nodded. "He said he had noticed a car parked near the phone box, further away from the police station. He could see there was someone sitting in the car so he stayed where he was and watched them. While he was waiting by the phone box, he saw you come out of the station and walk to your car."

"Rick's Sierra," Dan said.

"Musgrave saw you get into the car, then someone appeared right next to it on the passenger side. He didn't know where they had come from, said they were just suddenly there and then they opened the door and got in the car."

"It was Sorrell. That's how he caught me out. He had phoned the station and told them he was calling from a pub. He hit me so hard I started blacking out. When I came to, I was in the boot, handcuffed."

"When Sorrell put you in the boot, the car near the phone box started up and began to pull away towards where the Sierra was parked. Musgrave jumped in front of it and forced it to stop. He thought he had seen a fight in the car before the light inside went out, and he saw Sorrell dumping you in the boot. He was going to tell the driver to follow your car, but that was already the driver's intention."

"The car was Bradshaw's," Dan said. "I told him I was based at Campbell Road. He must have driven from Trowell, parked up and waited to watch what happened."

"Musgrave claims he talked Bradshaw into taking him along, but I suspect the major chose to take him because he thought another person on his side would give him more of a chance against Sorrell. Also, from what Rob Musgrave told me, I think Bradshaw had already followed you to the hospital and to my house."

Dan nodded. "A car drove past your house before I went in. That could have been Bradshaw."

"Probably was. Anyway, Musgrave said they stayed a long way back and followed the Sierra with their lights off. There were hardly any other vehicles on the road so it wasn't difficult to keep the Sierra in sight."

"Bradshaw did well. They both did. I'll have to thank them one day."

"Apart from the fact that neither of them was ever there." Schrader opened her purse and took out the passport size photograph that Dan had left inside her paperback novel. "I showed this to Raymond Hughes. He said it looked like a man he knows, called Joe. He didn't know the surname."

"One of the card players from his local." Dan moved his right leg beneath the heavy sheets of the hospital bed. "When did you see Hughes?"

"Gerard drove me to his house yesterday morning. The snow is almost all gone."

"How is he doing?"

"Better than he expected. His wife already knew about his sordid little trysts with Dee Collins, so his marriage isn't in any immediate danger. He said he thought she was more annoyed about the bloodstains on the carpet."

Dan shook his head. "I keep thinking about Rick."

"It wasn't your fault. It was all part of Sorrell's plan, wasn't it? There was nothing you could have done to stop it happening."

"I phoned him. I told him to go to my house. I might as well have put the noose around his neck myself."

Schrader leaned forward, her elbows resting on her knees. "You need to stop thinking that way. I'm telling you that as a friend, and as an order from a senior police officer."

Dan looked at Schrader's beautiful, deadly serious eyes. "I thought you were going to quit."

"Who'd keep you in line if I did?"

"I thought I was quitting too. Didn't think I was going to be given the choice not to."

"The official report doesn't mention your name."

Dan looked at his left hand, the valve and the tube, saline solution and painkillers. "Because I was never there."

"Dr Michaelides told me you'd be fit to return to work in two and a half months. I asked him to sign you off for three. Take a winter break in the sun somewhere. Relax on the beach, build sandcastles with your daughter."

Dan could feel the beginnings of a smile. It seemed alien and inappropriate, but it also felt good. "I might just do that."

"You should. Becky would like it."

"Have you talked to her?"

"Unofficially, of course." Schrader checked the time on her watch. "You saved her life, Dan. She told me what you did."

"She didn't see what I did. She was unconscious."

"She saw some of it, and Bradshaw told her the rest. He brought her round before the ambulance arrived. She said your daughter was sitting next to you, talking to you, but you weren't moving, just lying on the floor. Becky thought you were dead."

Dan blinked the tears away, unable to find the words to express how he felt.

"Don't doubt yourself, Dan, and don't blame yourself

for any of it. Even without their officially skewed version of events, you didn't do anything wrong." Schrader gave him a wry smile. "I even got my gun back, although you did make quite a mess of the barrel."

"Sorry about that."

Schrader closed her handbag and stood up. She leaned over the bed and kissed Dan on the forehead. "Time to go."

"I'll see you in a few months."

"We'll catch up before then."

"Okay. That sounds good."

Schrader stood by the door. "Send me a postcard from the beach." She gave him a wave with one of her bandaged hands before she walked out of the room, leaving Dan on his own.

Dan listened to the faint hospital sounds outside his room. He thought about Schrader, and how he shouldn't have been surprised by her decision to stay with the police force. He thought about Becky and Mandy, wishing he didn't have to wait almost twenty-four hours until he would see them again. And then there was Oliver Sorrell, an unstoppable killer driven by vengeance, defeated by an unexpected opponent while he was weakened by blood-loss and already embracing the thrill of victory. Sorrell's plan had been formed over many years, but in the end it was as volatile as any plan, once the first shot has been fired.

Before he closed his eyes and slipped into an undisturbed sleep, Dan thought about the horrors of the barn, the appalling helplessness that he had felt, and how he was officially never there. But he had been there, and even with the passing of time and the end of winter, he knew that part of him always would be.

AUTHOR'S NOTE

Thank you for reading Cold Inside.

Please can you take a few minutes to leave a review of this book on Amazon. As an independent author I really appreciate reader feedback, and I also rely on it to provide invaluable assistance spreading the word about my books.

To discover more of my books, a great place to start is my author page on Amazon.

If you would like to find out some more about me, my writing, and my other interests, I have a blog and details of current and forthcoming books on my website: http://jwtapper.co.uk

The Truth About Kate Hayes

Currently a trilogy, with the fourth instalment 'done when it's done', this is a bloke-lit contemporary romance series following the risqué escapades of Dave Fletcher and the seductive, mysterious, and frequently downright filthy Kate Hayes.

Books in this series are 'Kissing The Scorpion', 'Playing The Ace', and 'Painting The Dragon'.

Blood:Lust

This series of neo-noir vampire novels currently includes 'Midnight Cocktail' and 'Cheating Sunrise'.

Samples of all my books are available via Amazon's 'Look Inside' feature for both paperback and Kindle versions.

J.W. Tapper - October 2017

25660138R00199

Printed in Great Britain
by Amazon